PRAISE FOR JANIS REAMS HUDSON'S NOVELS

HAWK'S WOMAN

"Hawk-on-the-Moon and Abby's love story makes you long for life and love to be that true and steadfast in your own life. A wonderful story of human courage and love that triumphs against all odds. This is a KEEPER for all time. Breathtaking!! Six Bells!!!!"

—Bell, Book and Candle

WARRIOR'S SONG

"Ms. Hudson knows how to play on readers' heartstrings and strum an emotionally powerful tune. Exquisitely rendered and imbued with a deep sense of family love, *Warrior's Song* is another masterpiece from this consummate storyteller."

—Kathe Robin, *Romantic Times*

APACHE FLAME

"Entertaining in the extreme. Janis Reams Hudson's Apache books make me proud to be a Chiricahua Apache."

—Ann Wassal, "Ann's World," South Bay Cable
(San Francisco Bay Area)

Books by Janis Reams Hudson

WILD TEXAS FLAME
APACHE MAGIC
APACHE PROMISE
APACHE TEMPTATION
APACHE LEGACY
APACHE HEARTSONG
APACHE FLAME
WARRIOR'S SONG
HAWK'S WOMAN

Published by Zebra Books

WINTER'S TOUCH

JANIS REAMS HUDSON

Zebra Books
Kensington Publishing Corp.
http://www.zebrabooks.com

ZEBRA BOOKS are published by

Kensington Publishing Corp.
850 Third Avenue
New York, NY 10022

First Printing: March, 1999
10 9 8 7 6 5 4 3 2 1

Printed in the United States of America

To Dean Sterling. The nugget was there, right where you said it was. Bright and shiny and gold. Thank you. Every day, in every way . . .

And to Ron, my hero, without whom I would have starved long before this book was finished. I love you.

ACKNOWLEDGMENTS

Special thanks to Susan Tichy of Hungry Gulch Books in Westcliffe, Colorado, for all her help on location research, and for walking me through the graveyard. Any errors are strictly mine.

And to the wonderful people at the Colorado Visitors Center in Trinidad, who are always waiting with smiles and maps and helpful information whenever I visit.

PROLOG

The prophecy was old. So old that some said it was told to the First Pipe Keeper by Man-Above, Himself, and that the First Pipe Keeper entrusted it to the first man and woman.

Others argued that it was first told by the wind to an ancient holy man generation upon generation ago, long before the ones who call themselves Our People ever learned of the wide, treeless plains they would one day roam. Long before Our People ever saw a horse, ever encountered a white man.

The prophecy warned of a Plague of White Locusts. That one day Our People would become divided. Again and again they would divide, until their numbers paled in comparison to what they once had been. Game would grow scarce, and war would fill the land. Our People would be threatened with extinction.

There will come a Woman Whose Touch Can Heal, and the Man Who Walks By Her Side.

When Our People face great strife, the Woman shall heal a wound, and Man Who Walks By Her Side will show Our People the way to survive the Plague of White.

Take heed, the prophecy cautioned. The way will not be easy.

* * *

And now, the Plague of White Locusts is upon the land, and Our People, known to the whites as Arapaho, are few in number. Game is scarce, and war is upon the land. Our People are faced with extinction, if only they will realize it before it is too late.

As promised, there is a Woman Whose Touch Can Heal, but her touch is as yet a secret, and she walks alone. There is no Man Who Walks By Her Side.

Unless . . .

CHAPTER 1

The smell of burning cedar leaves, to keep the spirits of the dead at bay, wafted on the afternoon breeze. Wails of mourning echoed hauntingly through the small, protected valley in the Sierra Mojada. Winter Fawn's throat tightened at the sound. One of the dead, now resting on a scaffold braced in the branches of a cottonwood along the creek, was her cousin's friend, Long Nose.

Long Nose and two others had ridden out of camp three days ago to bring down a deer. They would all be leaving the valley soon to spend the coming summer with the rest of the tribe hunting the buffalo and camping along the banks of the Arkansas River. The deer was to have been roasted for a feast the night before they left their winter encampment.

Even as recently as two winters ago, Our People would not have needed to leave their winter valley to bring down a large buck for the feast. The animals would have watered at the stream at dawn and sunset, there for the taking, yet taken only as needed. But every day more white people came to these foothills at the edge of the plains, crowding in, tearing up the land with their plows, dumping their waste in the streams. Every day the game became more scarce as the animals retreated higher up into the mountains, or were slaughtered dozens at a time by the greedy white man. To find a large buck for this year's feast, it had been necessary for the hunters to leave the valley.

Now there would be no feast, no deer. No Long Nose or Spotted Beaver or Walks with Limp.

If only the Cheyenne had not killed those soldiers so nearby. If only the bluecoats could tell the difference between a Cheyenne and an Arapaho. If only the bluecoats cared that there was a difference, that Our People, whom whites called Arapaho, had been staying away from whites, had been at peace with them for two summers now, soon three.

But they did not. Winter Fawn, as well as the rest of Our People, knew that to most white men, the bluecoat army in particular, an Indian was an Indian, and they should all be killed. For the deeds of the Cheyenne, the bluecoats had yesterday killed three of Our People.

Now, while the elders of the Stoic Lodge urged caution and patience, the young warriors of the Staff Lodge, and the older Dogmen, the fiercest warriors of all, cried out for blood. A half-dozen men from both groups had spoken all morning of riding out to punish the whites for killing three of Our People.

"Why do you frown so, granddaughter? Does the work displease you?"

"Of course not." The work in hand was a new buckskin shirt for Winter Fawn's brother, Hunter. When finished, the shirt would be given to Grandmother, who would give it to Grandfather, who would present it to Hunter. Since young men and young women, even brothers and sisters, were not permitted to speak to each other, or even be in each other's company, this was the only practical way for him to receive the shirt.

Hunter would be told it was from his grandmother, but he would know the truth. He would understand that the shirt was a gift in honor of the anniversary of his birth. Their father had taught them the white man's custom of what he called birthdays. Keeping to the custom was Winter Fawn's way of feeling closer to her father. For he had also taught them another white man custom—sometimes fathers went away. Sometimes they left their children to be raised by grandparents so they could roam the mountains season upon season, alone.

Oh, their father came back to Our People now and then. He usually visited each spring and traveled with the band to meet with the rest of the tribe for the annual buffalo hunt and summer gathering.

But a visit once a year had never been enough for Winter Fawn's heart. She loved her father deeply. After her mother's death, during Winter Fawn's twelfth winter, she had clung to her father as the only certainty in her world. He had been everything to her. Yet he had left.

Grandmother's sister said that Red Beard had left to wander the mountains alone because he could not face life without Smiling Woman.

Winter Fawn knew in her mind that such was the truth, or at least part of it. Her father had seemed so lost after the storm took her mother's life. Yet in her heart, Winter Fawn blamed herself for her father's leaving. If only she had not—

"If the work does not displease you," Grandmother said, drawing Winter Fawn from her painful thoughts, "then why do you look so troubled?"

Winter Fawn finished attaching the bead in the center of the flower on the shoulder of the shirt, then let the garment fall to her lap. "I am troubled about Crooked Oak and the others."

A sly look came over Grandmother's face. "Are you worried that Crooked Oak might be killed if they ride out to attack the whites?"

Winter Fawn's frown deepened. "Not like you mean. Of course I am concerned that no more of Our People be killed."

"And Crooked Oak in particular?"

"No, Grandmother. I have told you—"

"Yes, you have told me that you have no fond feelings for Crooked Oak. If your father had not left such foolish instructions—that we were not to accept a marriage offer for you without his permission—Crooked Oak would long since be your husband."

Winter Fawn breathed a silent prayer of thanks that her father *had* left such instructions. The thought of being wife to Crooked Oak was not a pleasant one.

"It does not matter what you think, you know that." Grandmother paused and looked at her. "Your uncle thinks highly of Crooked Oak. He is a strong and brave Dogman. A fierce warrior. A man to make his wife proud. You will marry the man chosen for you."

"Yes, Grandmother. If it is my father's wish."

Grandmother made a sound of disgust. "And what kind of father is it who leaves his children?"

"Grandmother—"

"I know you do not like to hear bad talk about him, but a father who abandons his children is no father."

"He is my father," Winter Fawn said hotly. "I will hear no ill spoken of him."

"Do not take that tone with me. I am your grandmother."

"Yes, and I love you and honor you and respect you. But I am not a child to be scolded. I have passed my twentieth winter. I will hear no more ill talk of my father. When I spoke of my concern for Crooked Oak and the others, it was not their safety I meant. I am concerned about what will happen if they ride out and succeed in exacting their revenge against the whites."

"Why should such a thing trouble you?"

"Our leaders have tried so hard to keep us out of the fighting. I fear that Crooked Oak will bring the army down on us and we will all be slaughtered."

"You are thinking of Sand Creek."

"Yes."

Grandmother lowered her gaze and turned back to the deer hide stretched on the frame beside her. Neither woman liked to think of the hundreds of Cheyenne, and a few Arapaho, who were killed by the bluecoats at Sand Creek two summers past. Most were women, babies, and old men. Crooked Oak's father had been among those slain at Sand Creek. Since then he and others had urged all-out war against all whites, while the leaders of Our People had pled for caution.

No matter which side a person took, what had happened at Sand Creek was too terrible to remember, too horrifying to forget.

"The council will consider tonight," Grandmother reminded her, "whether or not to send warriors out."

"There is talk," Winter Fawn said quietly, "that Crooked Oak and a few others may ride the path to revenge regardless of what the elders decide."

Grandmother made a low sound in her throat, but did not otherwise comment. She knew as well as Winter Fawn that the Dogmen wanted to fight, lived to fight. It was not unlikely that they would go their own way and seek revenge on their own. Not unlikely at all.

As the two women worked side by side in the late afternoon sun, the sounds of camp life penetrated the tension between them, dissipated it, pushed away the sad reminder of Sand Creek.

Nearby, children laughed, splashed in the stream beyond the last row of tepees, shrieked at the shock of icy water. Dogs barked and chased the children. Women called quietly to each other as they worked. Men laughed, talked. The smell of roasting rabbit drifted from nearby.

And faintly, on the breeze, lingered the wails of mourning, the smell of cedar smoke.

The sounds and smells of life, the sounds and scents of death. Weaving in and out among each other. Intermingled.

A low rumble sounded, tightening the muscles in Winter Fawn's shoulders as if in fear of a blow. A moment later she identified the sound as hoofbeats and relaxed. Now that the council had broken up for a time, several of the men were racing their horses beyond the stream with the older boys. The pounding hooves, for an instant, had sounded like thunder. Thunder meant storms. Winter Fawn did not like storms.

Grandmother noticed Winter Fawn's reaction, but made no comment. She, too, remembered that day during Winter Fawn's twelfth summer when the bolt of lightning from the eye of the thunderbird struck the hilltop near their camp and killed Smiling Woman. Winter Fawn had lost her mother; Grandmother, her youngest daughter.

Red Beard, thought Grandmother, had never been the same. Smiling Woman had been his wife for nearly fifteen summers. She had given him two fine children, and he had loved her deeply. Within a week of her death he had left Our People to roam the mountains, seeking respite from his grief. Leaving his children for her to raise.

He, too, had left during a storm.

Hunter had been so young, only five when his mother died and his father left. He still missed his parents, but not to the extent Winter Fawn did. Being six years older than her brother, she had suffered more from their loss. In her mind, Grandmother knew, storms were to be dreaded. Storms took loved ones away.

Someday, thought Grandmother, Winter Fawn would perhaps come to understand that storms were not evil. They were simply Man-Above's way of cleansing the land and reminding Our People that nothing lasts forever. Sometimes they took, sometimes they gave. Rain was necessary to grow the grass that fed the buffalo that fed Our People. When brought on the wings of a storm, rain carved out new paths for rivers, tore down old trees that had lived too long, uprooted young trees that were too weak.

Storms, to Grandmother's way of thinking, were merely a part of life. As was death.

"Look, Grandmother." Winter Fawn touched Grandmother's arm, excitement lifting her voice. "Hunter is going to race."

"Is it him you look at, Granddaughter, or the one he races against?"

Winter Fawn made a sound of disgust. Until her grandmother had spoken, she had paid no mind to the other rider. "I assure you, Grandmother, I am not interested in Crooked Oak. It is Hunter I watch and none other."

"You speak with such pride." Grandmother smiled, for she did not intend her words to sting.

"I am proud."

"One would think you were his mother rather than his sister."

Winter Fawn smiled and stood to get a better view of her brother. "I suppose I have felt a little like his mother since he was born and I held him in my arms."

"A child yourself at that time."

Winter Fawn's smile turned poignant, almost sad. "For a

time. I was a child for a time.'' There was no need for her to say more. Grandmother knew Winter Fawn's sadness.

But Winter Fawn was never sad when thinking about her brother. ''Look at him,'' she said in awe. ''All he has to do is lean down and whisper in his horse's ear, and the horse will run his heart out for him. Look! He's telling him to run like the wind.''

''He has a gift,'' Grandmother acknowledged without looking up from the hide she was scraping. ''And he uses it wisely for one so young. I trust that you are being as wise with yours.''

Startled, Winter Fawn gaped at her grandmother. Heat rushed to her face, and her heart leapt to her throat. ''Wha—'' Her voice croaked. She had to swallow and start again. ''What do you mean? I have no gift.''

Dragging the scraper toward her across the hide, Grandmother arched a brow. ''Has the warmth of your hand not taken the pain from my shoulder? Did you think I would not notice such a thing?''

Winter Fawn looked away quickly. ''I don't know what you're talking about.'' She felt her grandmother's stare, as if the old woman could see into her very soul.

''Very well,'' Grandmother finally said. ''Perhaps you are right. Perhaps your gift is better kept to yourself for now.''

A deep shudder tore through Winter Fawn. ''I have no gift.''

CHAPTER 2

When the Barlow, Sanderson and Company afternoon stage rolled to a stop at the depot in Pueblo, Carson Dulaney was the first passenger off. Despite the cloud of dust that had yet to settle around the coach, he took a long breath and smiled. It was good to be back. Better than he'd expected. Not that he was so fond of Pueblo—he'd only been there twice. No, it was simply good to be back in Colorado. He hadn't realized how much he had already come to think of it as home.

The West was for starting over.

That's what his father had done. That's what Carson was doing. Starting over. Building a new life for himself and what was left of his family.

Turning back to the coach, he helped his thirteen-year-old sister, Bess, alight, then Megan, his six-year-old daughter.

"Ladies," he said with a flourish, "welcome to Colorado Territory."

"You said that two days ago." Frowning, Bess studied the dust coating her skirt, then tried her best to shake it off. "I do believe I'm wearing a sizeable portion of this territory of yours on my skirt."

Not for the first time since deciding to move what was left

of his family to Colorado, Carson felt his gut tighten. Was he doing the right thing, uprooting two young girls from everything familiar and bringing them out here to this wild, unsettled land?

It had to be the right thing, he told himself for the hundredth time. The war had taken everything and left the girls and Aunt Augusta living off the kindness of friends, with barely enough food to eat. He couldn't make things better for them in Atlanta. The plantation that had once supported more than a hundred people was gone. Atlanta, indeed most of the South, lay in ruins.

Carson's father had been killed in the fighting. Megan's mother was dead. Augusta's husband.

So many. So many dead. The four of them, Carson, Bess, Megan, and Augusta, were all that was left of the once sprawling Dulaney clan.

All they had left was each other, and the ranch that Carson's father had started just before the war.

Edmond Dulaney had lost interest in life when his wife died back in '54. He turned the running of the plantation over to Carson, and in '58, when rumors of a gold strike in Colorado made their way to the Eastern newspapers, Edmond had headed west.

Carson remembered the letters his father had sent home describing the bitter cold, the back-breaking work, the thefts, the murders, the claim jumping. The exorbitant cost of goods, so high that it took nearly every ounce of gold dust a man managed to find just to buy enough food to eat. Bad food, at that.

It hadn't taken Edmond long to realize that a man could make more money supplying good beef to the miners than he could mining for gold. Carson was grateful for his father's intuition on that matter. Edmond Dulaney had scrounged up enough cattle to make a modest start at a cattle ranch in the southern part of the territory. He'd been making a pretty good go of things until he'd headed east to fight for the Confederacy.

Carson had thanked God at the time that his father had arrived too late to join the 12th Georgia Regiment until after McDowell in May of '62. Cocky sons of the Confederacy they'd been, those Georgia boys, Carson among them. They'd been assigned to the Army of Northern Virginia, commanded by General Lee himself. They'd fought at Rich Mountain that first summer, then Cheat Mount that fall. In the spring of '62, when Edmond had been on his way east to join up, the 12th Georgia had joined General Jackson, ol' Stonewall, on his triumphant campaign through the Shenandoah.

We were good, Carson thought of the 12th Georgia. Too damn good, and too damn cocky, as it turned out. At McDowell they were the only out-of-state unit with the Army of Northern Virginia, yet were given the most vulnerable part of the line to hold. The onslaught of Yankee fire had been terrible. When ordered to pull back to a more defensible position, the 12th Georgia's reply, to a man, had been, "We did not come all this way to Virginia to run before Yankees."

They should have run, Carson had admitted later, but they'd held steady in the face of wave after wave of Union blue.

Yes, they should have run. Of all the Confederate casualties that day, a full third had been from the 12th Georgia. There hadn't been much left of those cocky boys by the end of that day.

Jesus, but Carson had been glad his father had not been there. Surely, he'd thought, nothing could ever be that bad again.

How naive he'd been. It was incredible how naive a twenty-three-year-old man could be, even after that month back in '62.

More men—including Edmond Dulaney—had poured in to fill the ranks decimated at McDowell. Side by side, father and son, along with neighbors, friends, and strangers who had come to rebuild the ranks of the 12th Georgia, followed General Jackson to hell and back. Trouble was, far too many hadn't made it back.

In the rare quiet times between the bloody battles at Sharpsburg, Chancellorville, and the Wilderness, Edmond had talked of his ranch. Colorado was a splendid place, he'd said. Wild and free, with land for the taking. A huge land, with room for a man to spread out without worrying about neighbors. Air so crisp and clean you almost expect it to snap in the breeze.

He wanted Carson to join him. Wanted him to bring the rest of the family after the war. Wanted to build the ranch into a real showplace.

"Hey, Son!"

Standing shoulder to shoulder with his father, Carson barely heard the shout. Day after day of unrelenting, continual cannon and rifle fire had nearly deafened them all. "Yeah, Dad?"

"Did I tell you it was quiet in Colorado?"

Despite the hip-deep blood and gore and the threat of imminent death—or perhaps because of them—Carson chuckled. "What's that? I can't hear you! It's too noisy!"

"I said—" Edmond Dulaney turned his head just enough to see his son's grin, and laughed.

A volley of fire from the advancing Yankees had them ducking down into their trench.

"So," Edmond called out, "you comin' back to Colorado with me or not?"

Carson, using the time to reload, glanced at the overcast sky, then at his father. "I suspect I'll give it a try."

"Good. That's good, son."

Reloaded, they stood and fired.

A minute later Edmond Dulaney had slumped against Carson's shoulder, one more dead Reb out of the ten thousand who had died that May of '64 at that godforsaken crossroads before the courthouse at Spotsylvania.

As soon as possible after Lee's surrender, Carson had kept his promise and come west to see this ranch of his father's. He'd found it abandoned, the house in desperate need of repairs, cattle scattered to hell and back.

But the possibilities . . . the possibilities, along with his father's dreams, had infected him. After the devastation of so much of the South, this land was like heaven.

And it was quiet.

Not so much here, in Pueblo, but the valley where the ranch lay. A healing quiet he had desperately needed. Still needed.

Carson had spent the better part of a year fixing the place, rounding up stray cattle. He'd brought Frank Johansen and Beau Rivers with him to help. Like him, they had lost everything in the war.

At least I still have some family, he thought, looking down at Bess and Megan, thinking of Aunt Gussie.

Frank and Beau were there now, at the ranch, waiting for

him. He was going to pick up where his father left off. He was going to build his father's dream, a new home for the Dulaneys.

He wished Aunt Gussie had come with them. What the hell did he know about raising girls? Not a damn thing, he feared. Gussie, his father's sister, had not been able to bring herself to leave her lifelong friend Lucille, who was dying in Atlanta, but had promised to join them later.

So here they were, Carson and Bess and Megan. It didn't matter if he didn't know how to raise girls. He loved them both, would do anything for them, so he guessed he'd be learning.

The problem with Bess, he knew, was that she hadn't wanted to come. It was evident in the quarrelsome tone in her voice. Plus, he figured she was still in a tiff because he had limited her and Megan to one single trunk each for their belongings. Carson touched a finger to her chin until she looked up at him. "You promised to give it a chance, Bess."

She opened her mouth, then closed it. Her shoulders heaved on a dramatic sigh. "You're right. I promised. I'm sorry. I'm just tired, I think."

"I'm thirsty," Megan whined.

There was another one who was tired, Carson thought with sympathy. Traveling by stage, particularly for two young girls, was an exhausting experience.

"I think what we all need it a good meal, and something to drink," he added, touching the tip of his finger to Megan's tiny nose. "And a good night's sleep in a hotel."

"On a real bed?" Bess's eyes lit. "Not a cot?"

"On a real bed. Not a cot." Pueblo was a thriving community. Finding a decent hotel would be no problem.

The clerk at the stage depot pointed out three hotels down the street, any one of which, he assured, would serve their needs. Hoping the man was right, Carson arranged with him to have their luggage sent over to the nearest one. After taking the girls there and checking in, he escorted them to the restaurant three doors down for the promised meal. By the time they finished eating, both girls were barely able to keep their eyes open.

Truth to tell, he was ready for a good night's sleep himself. He'd learned during the war to sleep whenever and wherever the opportunity arose. Even afterward, when the nightmares started, he'd at least slept some. But on this trip, knowing the safety and comfort of the girls was his sole responsibility, his sleep at the various stage stops had been in fits and starts, and very, very brief. He didn't like the girls sleeping on cots in the same room with a bunch of strange men. He didn't much care for sleeping in a roomful of strange men himself, for that matter.

Tonight would be different. A bath, a private room, a real bed, and a change of clothes would improve the girls' moods better than anything else.

Not that he would be much more at ease about their safety, but at least they would be more comfortable than they'd been since they'd left the train in Kansas and had taken the stage the rest of the way.

If the talk he'd heard before he'd headed east to get the girls could be credited, there would soon be a railroad in Colorado. Someone up in Denver had supposedly formed the Denver Pacific Railway, with plans to lay track more than a hundred miles between Denver and Cheyenne, where it would connect with the Union Pacific. From there, a person could go anywhere in the world.

Of course, Carson thought wryly, even a railroad clear to Denver wouldn't negate what lay ahead of them between Pueblo and the ranch. He dearly hoped the girls enjoyed their night or two in a hotel.

"How long will it take us to get to the ranch from here?" Bess asked.

It was uncanny the way his baby sister could sometimes seem to read his mind. He wasn't used to this. The last time he'd spent much time around her had been before the war. She'd been about Megan's age. Now she was thirteen, a young lady.

Once again his mind mocked him. *What do you know about raising girls?* And once again, the answer was, nothing.

Watching him, Bess tilted her head in the way their mother used to do. She must have inherited the gesture. She'd been less than a day old when their mother had died.

"Carson?"

"Sorry." He smiled at her. "I was just wondering when you grew up on me."

"I grew up," she said softly, "while you and Daddy were off fighting Yankees."

Carson forced his smile to stay in place, although God knew there was nothing about that cursed war to smile about. *May I never live long enough to take the life of another man,* he thought fervently.

He still carried a rifle. The trusty Maynard that had seen him through the war was in his hotel room with the rest of his belongings. In this wild, unsettled territory, a man never knew when, or from whom or what, he would have to protect his own. But Carson would be damned if he would do like so many men in Colorado did and wear a sidearm. Rifles were for hunting, or killing wild animals in defense, and sometimes, when your country called, they were for war.

Pistols, on the other hand, existed for one thing and one thing only—killing men. There was no other purpose for them. His was wrapped in leather and tucked away in the bottom drawer of his bureau at the ranch, and that was where it would stay. Carson Dulaney had killed his last man. He wanted no more dead or dying eyes following him into his sleep. He had enough, more than enough, already.

Which was why the talk he was overhearing from the other tables concerned him. Indian trouble, people were saying. Three people had been found dead a half-day's ride south of Pueblo. Cheyenne had done it, they said.

Carson's father had told him that the Kiowa and Comanche were gone from the territory, and the Southern Arapaho pretty much kept quiet in the area, but the Cheyenne still liked to cause trouble. But as a rule, none of the tribes roamed up the river to his ranch.

But getting home from Pueblo might prove to be a challenge if the talk Carson was hearing now was to be believed.

Damn. What was he supposed to do? He couldn't put the girls in danger by exposing them to possible attack.

"You said we would have to go by wagon from here."

"That's right," he answered Bess, pulling his mind into the present. At least she seemed unaware of the potential danger.

He didn't intend to enlighten her. "I'll see about that in the morning. A wagon and team. We'll need supplies, too. It might take a day or two before we're ready to leave."

"And then?"

"And then we head home. It'll take us a couple of days to get there."

"A couple of days of sleeping out in the open."

He didn't much care for the disapproval in Bess's voice. "Probably one night." He started to remind her again that she had promised to give Colorado a chance. To give *them* a chance, him and Megan and herself, to be a family. But Bess was tired, and so was he, and poor Megan was about to fall asleep in her plate—and then there was the threat of Indians along the way—so he let it go.

"Come on, let's go back to the hotel," he said. There had to be a way to get them safely to the ranch. All he needed to do was find it. "I bet we could arrange for you to have a bath."

Bess's eyes lit. "A real bath? In a tub?"

"I don't see why not."

"Megan, wake up," Bess said swiftly. "We're going now."

A decent meal, a bath, and a good night's sleep did the trick. The next morning both girls were their old cheerful selves again, much to Carson's relief.

His relief was short-lived, however, when, after breakfast, he took the girls with him to the livery to see about buying a wagon.

The livery was several blocks from the hotel. Carson escorted the girls down the street, walking between them and the wagons and horses that raised dust on their way by. He passed several saloons, a barber shop, a boardinghouse, two small churches, and a general mercantile along the way.

Bess was not impressed. "This is the whole town?"

"It's young still, but it's growing. Don't worry, we probably won't have occasion to come back here in the near future."

Bess looked over her shoulder and gave a delicate sniff. It was such a perfect imitation of Aunt Gussie's method of showing disapproval that Carson nearly smiled.

"Thank goodness," Bess muttered.

Carson followed her gaze to see what she found so particularly disparaging. All he saw of note was a big bear of a man in fringed buckskins a few yards behind them. What people would have called a mountain man in the old days, from the look of him. With this man, Carson wasn't sure if the appellation referred to the man's assumed preference for living in the mountains, or to the size of him. His shoulders were massive, and even without the big floppy-brimmed hat that left the upper half of his face in shadows, he topped Carson's own six-foot height by several inches.

"But you'll remember," Carson said, facing forward again, "I told you before we left that we won't be living anywhere near a decent-sized town."

Bess heaved an exaggerated sigh. "Yes, you told me."

"Bess," he warned.

"I know." She sighed again. "I promised to give this a chance. I just don't see why we had to come all the way to Colorado, that's all. Why couldn't we have been a family in Atlanta?"

"You liked living on charity?"

Bess's face flushed. She lowered her head and studied the boards of the sidewalk.

Carson knew she had hated losing their home, not having any place to call their own. It had stung her young pride to have to live off of friends. The once proud Dulaneys reduced to accepting handouts. It damn sure would have stung his pride, too.

"Come on," he said, hoping to cheer her. "After we see about a wagon and team, we'll go to the mercantile and you can help me select our supplies."

As he'd hoped, the prospect of shopping, or perhaps of having her advice sought, seemed to brighten Bess's mood. Her gaze lingered on the window of the mercantile as they passed it.

Then she stiffened and abruptly stared straight ahead. "Is that man following us?"

"What man?" Carson glanced over his shoulder to see that the man in buckskins was still a few yards behind them. "He's probably just minding his own business. There are a dozen people headed the same direction we are."

The livery was located a block away from what appeared to be the edge of town. The girls stood to one side while Carson approached the man who was cleaning out a stall. "Are you in charge here?"

"I am." The man propped his pitchfork against the side of the stall and stuck out his hand. He was of average height, maybe thirty years old, with a balding head. His face was long, his teeth big, giving him a look amazingly similar to the horses around him. But his handshake was firm and friendly. "Lester Bacon's the name. What can I do for you?"

"I'm in need of a wagon to haul people and supplies."

"Well, now." Lester beamed. "Believe I can help ye."

Taking Megan by the hand, and with Bess beside him, Carson followed the man back outside to the alley beside the stables.

"Sturdy as the day is long." Bacon slapped a hand against the blue-painted side of the platform spring Studebaker.

"Looks like an army wagon," Carson noted. If nothing else, that Yankee blue paint was a dead giveaway.

"Yes, sir. U.S. Army surplus. Took it in on trade last week from the man who bought it from the army. Greased the axles myself, I did."

"What do you want for it?"

"Well, now, I think fifty dollars would be fair."

Carson snorted. "Only if you're throwing in the team and harness with it."

Lester Bacon's eyes sharpened with the glee of a man who loves to haggle. "Well, now, you want a team, too, do you? Well, now, then, we're talking a sight more money."

Carson was just settling down to do some serious negotiating when he happened to glance around to make sure Bess and Megan were still nearby. They were, but so was the buckskin man standing at the corner across the alley from the girls, watching them.

"We'll talk," Carson told Bacon. "I'll be right back."

Carson strode across the alley and stopped before the man in buckskins. He had a broad face, a crooked nose, and piercing gray eyes, but what a person noticed most, aside from his sheer size, was his thick, flaming red hair hanging past his shoulders, and an equally thick, equally red beard that bushed out and tangled with the hair until it looked as though he was peering out from behind a busy red wreath.

With narrowed eyes, Carson met the man's flinty stare. "Something I can do for you, mister?"

"What makes ye ask?" The Scottish brogue was slight but unmistakable.

"You've been following us. Why?"

The man eyed him keenly. "I hear yer name be Dulaney."

"Depends on who wants to know."

"I knew a man named Dulaney, I did," the man said, ignoring Carson's statement. "Had himself a ranch upstream along the Huerfano."

Sharp interest, mixed with a healthy dose of caution, stirred in Carson. "What about him?"

"His name was Edmond Dulaney. He was a good friend of mine. I hear he got himself killed. I hear his son, by name of Carson Dulaney, be takin' over the ranch. I come lookin' for him."

"Mind telling me your name?" Carson asked.

"I be Innes MacDougall."

A slow, wide smile spread across Carson's face. This was the man his father had spoken so eloquently about so many times in his letters home, and then in person when he came home to fight.

The two men, according to Carson's father, had saved each other's life several times throughout their friendship. They'd stumbled into each other shortly after Edmond had arrived in the Colorado Territory. Both sloppy drunk, mourning the loss of their wives, shamed by having walked out on their children. Two lonely men trying to learn to face life by running from it.

They were so drunk, that first night they met in a saloon in one of those disreputable tent towns that sprang up around gold strikes, that despite both being big men, they'd been easy prey for the gang of thugs that roamed the rutted, muddy streets in search of easy money.

Edmond had written in one of his letters of the two of them

waking the next morning, in the icy mud of a back alley, their heads pounding, pockets empty. They had helped each other out of the mud and decided that perhaps providence was trying to tell them something. Perhaps this road to destruction they were on was not what they really wanted after all.

The last time Edmond had spoken of MacDougall had been during the rushed march to Spotsylvania in the middle of a thick, foggy night. "Wish Innes was with us," Edmond had said. "I love that man like a brother, son. I would trust him with my life. He's a crack shot, too. We could sure use him."

So this, then was the famous Innes MacDougall. "Well I'll be damned. My father spoke of you often. He set a great store by your friendship."

MacDougall nodded soberly. "And I by his. You have the look of him when you smile. Is it true, then? He was killed in that damned war?"

Carson, too, sobered. "Yes. At Spotsylvania."

The big man looked away and blinked. "Damn shame, that. He was a good man, was Edmond Dulaney."

"I agree. He was the best."

"So you're taking over his ranch?"

"I am. I—Wait. You said you had come looking for me?"

"Aye. I went by to visit a spell with Edmond, at his ranch. Man by the name of Rivers told me you'd been there, that you'd gone back East to bring your family out."

"He told you right. We just got in on the stage yesterday. Girls?" Carson turned toward them and motioned them over. "Girls, meet a friend of dad's. This is Mr. MacDougall. Mr. MacDougall, I'd like you to meet my sister, Elizabeth. Bess, we call her. And this is my daughter, Megan."

"Ladies." MacDougall swept off his floppy-brimmed hat and executed an elaborate bow. " 'Tis a right great pleasure to make yer acquaintance, to be sure, lassies. Yer father," he said to Bess, "and yer grandfather," he added to Megan, "was the best friend a man could hope to have. I place myself at your service."

Megan giggled. "You talk funny."

MacDougall let out a booming laugh that threatened the

windows in the building across the street. "So I'm told, lassie, so I be told."

"It's a pleasure to meet you, Mr. MacDougall." Bess held out her hand like the grand Southern Belle she hoped to become.

MacDougall took her fingertips gently in his giant paw of a hand and bowed to her. "The pleasure be all mine, Mistress Dulaney. All mine, indeed."

When Lester Bacon realized the man wanting the wagon was a friend of MacDougall's, he kissed his profit goodbye. It was a fact up and down the front range of the Rockies, and, from what Lester had heard, deep into the heart of the mountains themselves, that Red Beard MacDougall was just about the toughest son of a bitch walking. Not mean, not greedy, but tough, and fair. The big Scot expected everyone else to be as fair and honest as he was, and woe be unto the man who wasn't.

In a matter of minutes the sale of the wagon, team, and harnessing was complete.

As the Scot, the Southerner, and the two young girls walked away, Lester Bacon let out a sigh. There was always another greenhorn coming along. He would make a profit yet, before this day was done.

"You're a handy man to have around," Carson said to MacDougall as they walked away from the livery. "I doubt I would have gotten the wagon and team so cheaply if it weren't for you. You have my thanks."

MacDougall chuckled through his bushy red beard. "Ye be welcome, lad. Bacon and me, we go back a ways. Yon wagon'll get ye and yer lassies home in fine shape. Would ye be mindin' a wee bit o' company on the trip, I be wondering."

"If you have a mind to ride with us, Mr. MacDougall, we'd be honored."

"Innes, lad. Call me Innes. I may not go all the way to the ranch with you, mind. I've family—a son and daughter—south of here. The place where their band winters would be on my way."

"Their band?"

"Aye." Innes feigned indifference, but watched this young Dulaney carefully. The lad might not be as open-minded as his father had been. "My wife—their mother, God rest her soul—was Arapaho. Winter Fawn and Hunter live with their Arapaho grandmother."

"My father told me you'd lost your wife. That was one of the things the two of you had in common, he said."

That, and that we both ran off and left our bairns for others to raise, thought Innes, his gut tightening as it did every time he thought of the way he'd left them.

But that was old news. More importantly just now was that this Carson Dulaney hadn't batted an eye at hearing that Innes's children were half Arapaho. Maybe Edmond had told him, but that was all right with Innes. He wasn't one to put up with any nonsense about his wife and bairns from anybody. The last man who had sneered and called him a squaw man had swallowed his own teeth for his supper. After Innes had obligingly knocked them out for him.

"To tell you the truth," Carson said, slowing his pace to let the girls walk on ahead toward the trading post, "I've been wondering how safe it is to travel the direction we're headed, after the talk I heard yesterday when we got in."

"Ach, 'tis the Cheyenne you be meanin'."

"I hear they killed some people south of here a few days ago."

"Aye. And the army, in all their wisdom, went out and found themselves three Indians to kill in retaliation."

"I heard that, too."

"The trouble is," Innes said with disgust, "the army didna notice, or more rightly, didna care, that the Indians they killed were Arapaho, not Cheyenne."

"Which means what? That the Arapaho will want revenge?"

Innes scratched his beard. "If it was anybody else but the Arapaho, I'd say aye. But the ones who winter in this area have made a deliberate attempt to stay clear of whites. They want peace. Still, they have their young hotheads, just like all people do. Which is why you need me, lad. These are people who know me. I lived with them for many years."

"We could wait," Carson said reluctantly. "Not that I don't want you to ride with us. I do. But if waiting a few days would be safer . . . I have to think of the girls."

"Aye, and right bonny lassies they be, too. But unless you've got a mind to lock them in their hotel room for the next day or two, you'd be better off heading out. The Cheyenne are long gone from the area. Like to hit and run, they do. Our People won't cause any trouble."

"Our People?"

"The Arapaho. That's what they call themselves in their own language. *Inuna-ina.* Our People."

Carson filed that bit of information away, and frowned. "Why would I need to keep the girls in their room if we stay?"

" 'Tis Saturday, lad. Come this evening, ever farmer and rancher within thirty miles will be coming to town to let off steam. So will a goodly number of soldiers from Fort Reynolds just east of here. There'll be whoopin' and hollerin' and fightin' in the streets from sundown tonight until sundown tomorrow. It gets fair wild here of a Saturday night. No a fit place for yon wee lassies at all."

Carson gnawed on the inside of his jaw as he weighed staying in Pueblo for a few more days versus leaving right away. According to his father, no one knew the Indians in the area better than did Innes MacDougall. If Innes thought it was better to leave now, then that's what they would do.

"All right." He gave a sharp nod. "How soon can you be ready to leave?"

Innes grinned. "If you started hitching up your new team right this minute, I'd be ready afore ye."

By noon that same day they were out of Pueblo and headed south along the Santa Fe Trail. When they neared Colorado City—a rather grandiose name for the small town twenty-five miles south of Pueblo—they would take the Taos cutoff, which would angle them southwest toward the ranch.

The wagon was loaded with basic supplies: flour, sugar, coffee, bacon, beans, corn, oats, two ground sheets, three blankets, a skillet, coffeepot, tin plates, and eating utensils. Carson's, Megan's, and Bess's luggage rode easily in with all the rest.

They could have waited and bought most of the supplies from Hernandez in Badito down near the ranch, but prices were better in Pueblo, and he'd needed the wagon and team in any case.

The girls rode on the seat with Carson, while the Scotsman trailed along beside them on his big sorrel gelding. It took a big horse to easily carry a man the size of Innes MacDougall. His pack mule followed along untethered.

When they had started out, Carson had suggested Innes tie the mule to the back of the wagon.

"No need," he'd responded with a booming laugh. "Hail Mary would follow this horse off the edge of the earth, she would, and that's a fact."

"Hail Mary?" Carson's lips had twitched. "Sounds Catholic. I thought all you Scotsmen were dyed-in-the-wool Protestants."

"Oh, Aye. Presbyterian and proud of it. Got Hail Mary off an old papist up in the gold digs. Seein' as how she took a great affection for me gelding, I decided to leave her name alone."

Carson had laughed. "Should I ask the horse's name?"

White teeth gleamed through the bushy red beard. "Auld Kirk is his name. Scottish for Old Church, meanin' the Church of Scotland."

"Hedging your bets?"

"Couldna hurt, lad, couldna hurt."

The road they traveled rose toward the south. He'd ridden it before, last year when he'd first come to see about the ranch. About ten or so miles south of Pueblo it crossed the St. Charles River, with its scattering of cottonwoods and willows. Off to the west, looking closer than they actually were, sat the Sierra Mojada, the Wet Mountains, with a gathering of gray clouds trapped by their peaks.

He'd been there, too, the Wet Mountains, just about this same time of year. He'd gone there looking for something. Peace, maybe, or maybe he'd just been trying to find some small piece of himself. The tall pines had been startlingly green against the oak and scrub oak just starting to bud. Higher up the oaks thinned, and aspen, slower to leaf out than the oaks, replaced them, spruce overtook pines, and patches of snow hid in the shade.

Valleys and meadows, from tiny spots to acres and acres wide, dotted the mountain slopes, as did the occasional outcropping of bare rock. There were huge flat slabs of granite, along with giant chunks worn smooth by time, and others still jagged from where they'd broken off from the mountain above or been thrust up from the earth beneath.

The soil in the mountains ranged from rich loam to barren sand to red clay.

And there were streams. The Spaniards weren't joking when they'd named them the Wets. Clear, rushing streams in every depression of land, icy cold from snowmelt.

One day, he remembered, he'd been lost up there in the clouds. Another he'd been surprised to run across a deserted cabin. He'd wondered about the type of man who would choose to live in so isolated a place. According to his father, Innes MacDougall was just such a man.

Someday, when he had the ranch in order, Carson would go back there.

East of the trail they now traveled, the plains stretched clear to tomorrow's sunrise and flat as milk on a saucer. Overhead the sky was a pale spring blue.

The trail dipped into gullies and washes, crested small rises that didn't deserve the word "hills," and skirted outcroppings of rocks. By the time the sun had started its descent, both girls were nodding drowsily. Ahead the track disappeared around yet another outcropping of tall, tumbled rocks. The team rounded the bend, and for a moment Innes and his packhorse were out of sight behind them.

That's when it happened. One minute the only sounds were the creak and rattle of the wagon, the soft clomp of hooves on dusty ground, the jingle of the harness. The next, the air was rent with the shrill cries of attack from a half-dozen mounted Indians with tattoos on their chests and paint on their faces.

There was no time to think or plan. With rifles pointed at him and one warrior moving to grab the harness and halt the team, Carson shouted a hoarse, "Get down!" at the girls and cracked the reins sharply against the horses' backs. "Giddup!"

The wagon team bolted.

The Indians fired. Carson felt a sting along the outside of his left shoulder as one shot came too close.

Behind the wagon and coming on fast, Innes bellowed in outrage.

The wagon hit a rock, jolting it severely. Bess lost her grip on the seat and, with a high scream of terror, sailed over the side.

Carson's heart stopped. *Bess!* Bracing his foot against the brake with all his weight, he pulled back as hard as he could on the traces to halt the team. Down on the floorboard, next to his leg where she'd fallen when he had first shouted at the girls to get down, Megan screamed and screamed and screamed. There was no time to comfort her, no words with which to do the job if there had been time.

Damn his hide. What the hell had he been thinking to bring two innocent young girls into this wild land? They would die now, because of him, because of his need to get away from the South and all its reminders of war.

Damn his hide to hell.

The team stopped so suddenly that the wagon slewed sideways. Before it stopped skidding Carson had his rifle out from beneath the seat and was standing, turning, taking aim at the Indian who had Bess by the hair. He fired and swore. He'd hit the Indian in the shoulder. It was enough to make the bastard release Bess, but not enough to take him out of the fight.

Megan had hold of his leg now, hampering him as he tried to turn back and face the others. Pain exploded across the back of his head.

He never heard his daughter scream again for her daddy, never saw the look of horror on his sister's face. Never felt himself fall to the ground.

He never heard the wild shrill cry of victory as Crooked Oak raised his rifle into the air in triumph.

CHAPTER 3

The sun was down, the sky turning a deep, dark blue and the air beginning to cool rapidly when the first shrill cries of victory echoed across the small valley camp. Winter Fawn was on her way back from the stream with a jug of water when she heard the commotion.

The warriors had returned!

Alarm skittered down her arms in the form of gooseflesh. Victory? Over whom? Had they fought? Was the army even now riding to destroy them? Would the children and old people be slaughtered, as they were at Sand Creek?

Heart pounding, Winter Fawn dropped her water jug near the hide her grandmother was tanning and rushed toward the commotion at the center of camp.

She was nearly the last to arrive. Yet even before she reached the returning warriors, she knew something was wrong. Most of the shouting was from the warriors themselves. Those who had come to meet them had fallen into an uneasy silence.

"A captive?" someone said in a shocked voice.

"What have they done?" said another. "Is he dead?"

"Why have they brought him here?"

Murmurs and mutters rose around her, growing and building until they sounded like a hive of upset bees.

Finally Winter Fawn broke through the crowd.

The warriors had returned, making as much noise as if they had just come victorious from some huge battle. Winter Fawn's uncle, Two Feathers, rode in the lead. Then came Talks Loud, Long Chin, Red Bull, and Spotted Calf, who sported a bloody hole in his shouder.

Crooked Oak trailed behind the others, worrying his horse to make it prance. With jaw set and eyes blazing, he held his rifle above his head and shouted victory. He led another horse which bore the body of a white man slung belly-down over its back. The white man did not move, except to sway with the horse's movements. His hands and feet were tightly bound, and the back of his head was bloody.

Had they done it, then? Had they gone out and found themselves a white man to kill?

Why would they tie his hands and feet if he was dead? Why bring a dead man back to camp?

But the answer to the latter was simple. To prove they had avenged the deaths of their friends.

But really, Winter Fawn thought with irritation, a simple scalp would have sufficed.

Then another shout rang out that took Winter Fawn's attention completely away from the warriors.

"Red Beard!"

Winter Fawn whirled. He rode easily on his big sorrel horse. The wide brim of his hat hid half his face, and he carried a small white girl before him, with an older white girl riding the cantle at his back, but Winter Fawn would have known him if he'd had a buffalo robe over his head and a bear cub before and behind him instead of a girl. She knew those shoulders, that beard, the way he sat a horse. Oh, how she knew them! Shoving her way through the crowd, she rushed to his side. "Father!"

Hunter echoed her cry as he ran to join her.

Before dismounting, her father lifted the small girl from before him and handed her to Winter Fawn.

"This be Megan, and her aunt," he added, helping the older

girl slide down, "Bess. They be me guests. Keep them safe, lass. Don't let your uncle or any o' his bloody friends get their hands on 'em."

"What's happened?" Winter Fawn asked. "What's going on?"

He swung down from the saddle and handed his reins to Hunter. There was anger in his eyes. "That's what I be after findin' oot." With a roar of outrage, he shouldered his way through the throng of people who had gathered around the white man.

Winter Fawn was adult enough to understand that these were extraordinary circumstances. She knew the look of rage in her father's eyes was not directed at her, and that he had serious business on his mind.

But she was also child enough to be devastated that he should arrive in camp for the first time since this time last spring and have not a single word for her other than about the white girls he had thrust at her.

After a brief but hard-fought struggle, the adult in her prevailed. Her father had entrusted the girls to her care. She would keep them safe, as he bade.

But she would also find out what was going on. With a white girl in each hand, she followed him.

Crooked Oak had dismounted and gave the white man's body a shove. The body slid head-first toward the ground and groaned.

He was alive!

Carson would have debated the fact.

This time when he hit the ground, he felt it. He came to in midair and was instantly aware of two things: one, that the back of his head was about to explode, and two, that he was falling. Instinct had him reaching out with his hands to break his fall. It was then that he discovered they were bound at the wrists. He thought, for a fleeting instant, that they were numb, until they met the ground with the full force of his weight jarring down on them. The pain knifed up his arms, across his shoulders, and up into his head, where it sliced behind his eyes and blackened the vision he'd only just regained.

Then his head hit the ground, and he tumbled over onto his back. He heard laughter, and someone calling his name.

Where was he? Cold Harbor?

No, that wasn't right. Petersburg. The siege.

No, not there. It was too quiet for Petersburg, or any other battle site he could think of. He heard no cannon, smelled no smoke.

He opened his eyes to realize that he must, indeed, be dead. Overhead the sky was turning dark, and all around him leering, painted faces stared. It looked real enough. But death was the only explanation for the angel staring down at him. If a man poured enough cream into his coffee, and added just the right amount of bronze and copper, he might come close to matching the color of her skin, but it would take a cool mountain fog to come close to those clear gray eyes. Startled fog, he thought with a touch of hysteria.

Could fog be startled?

Could just the sight of a woman's mouth make a man yearn to taste it?

He was definitely dead if he was thinking such crazy things. And he was going straight to hell for thinking them about an angel. He couldn't, for his soul, take his gaze from hers.

Dead. He was definitely dead.

Winter Fawn blinked at the man sprawled at her feet. He was definitely alive. His eyes were open and staring straight into hers.

For one shocking moment, Winter Fawn stared into the most startlingly blue eyes she had ever seen. The deep blue of a mountain lake, or the summer sky at twilight. Captivating. Mesmerizing. And for that instant, Winter Fawn had the unsettling feeling that she was staring straight into her own destiny.

"Dulaney! Carson Dulaney, can you hear me?"

MacDougall. Carson rolled to his side and looked around. There he stood, big as life and broad as a barn. Innes MacDougall.

Memory rushed back. *Oh, God! The girls!*

He saw them then, with the gray-eyed angel. He was shamed that he hadn't noticed them immediately. The angel—no, not an angel. An Indian. Arapaho? "Megan," he moaned. "Bess."

"Yer lassies be fine, lad, that I promise ye."

The nearest warrior snarled something at Carson and kicked him in the ribs hard enough to knock the wind from his lungs.

By the time he regained his breath, Innes and several of the warriors were involved in a heated argument. As near as Carson could figure, Innes was free, not a captive, which meant he had to be known by these people. Were these the people he'd once lived with? Did he have enough sway with them to get them free?

One warrior, a different one from the one who had kicked him, grabbed Carson by his bound hands and jerked him to his feet. His bound feet. He toppled and fell.

More laughter again.

So, he was to be their entertainment.

Carson had heard stories—who back East hadn't?—of the torture Indians practiced on whites. He had the sinking sensation that he was about to learn about it firsthand.

They got him to his feet again, only this time, instead of letting him fall so they could laugh, they dragged him a dozen yards to a tree, where they tied his hands to a branch almost out of his reach overhead.

"Daddy!" Megan burst from the angel's hold and ran toward him. The woman, with Bess in tow, chased after her. He wouldn't think of her as an angel. He wasn't dead. Yet.

He would have crumpled to the ground in relief at seeing both girls alive and relatively unharmed—if he didn't count the bruise darkening Bess's temple and cheek—but being tied to an overhead branch did not permit him to crumple to the ground. And realizing that they'd been brought among the people who were undoubtedly going to kill him stripped him of his relief.

Megan flung herself at his legs and sobbed. "I'm scared, Daddy."

"I know, baby. I'm sorry. MacDougall!" he bellowed. "I thought you said they were safe, damn you!"

Innes and the gray-eyed woman with Bess reached Megan at the same time.

"Get them out of here," Carson managed through clenched teeth. "Goddammit, man, get them out of here. Don't let them see whatever's about to happen. Promise me. On my father's soul, promise me!"

"Aye, lad, I promise. They'll be safe." To the young Indian woman he said, "Get them away from here. I'll find ye when I can."

"Aye, Da. I'll take them to Grandmother's lodge, then. 'Tis where you'll be findin' us when you've a mind."

When you've a mind? Carson blinked. An Indian who spoke English—sort of—with a Scottish burr?

It dawned on him then that this must be the daughter Innes had spoken of. It fit. Skin lighter than the others, clear gray eyes, and a Scottish burr. As he stood there with the rawhide bindings cutting into his wrists, he thought it was a hell of a time to notice the dignified, confident way she moved, the concern in her eyes, her gentle yet firm touch with Bess and Megan as she led them away.

Bess turned back toward him. "Carson!"

Carson closed his eyes against the plea on his sister's face, the terror in her eyes, her voice. He had to trust Innes in this, because he couldn't bear the thought of anything happening to Bess or Megan. Nor could he bear the thought of them witnessing whatever might happen to him. "Do what Innes says, Bess. Go with her. Take care of Megan."

Bess stared at him a moment, then turned, reluctantly, and let Innes's daughter lead her and Megan away.

As soon as they were out of earshot, Carson glared at Innes. "What the hell happened? Aren't these the same people you said I'd have no trouble with?"

Innes MacDougall ground his teeth. "Aye, that they are." He couldn't believe what had happened. Couldn't believe that Two Feathers, Crooked Oak, and the others had not released Carson the instant they recognized Innes. How dare the bloody bastards attack a friend of his! How dare they not release him and back off at Innes's demand.

Was he not one of them? Had he not lived with them, hunted with them, *had he not married Two Feather's sister, with Two Feather's blessing?*

It was that damn hothead, Crooked Oak. Always wanting to go to war, he was. A dog soldier, and a fierce one. He would use the recent deaths of his friends, if he could, to stir the entire Southern Arapaho tribe to war.

But the bloody bastard wasn't going to get away with capturing Edmond Dulaney's son, Innes vowed. "Not while I have breath in me body."

"What?" Carson asked.

"Just hold tight, lad. I'll get ye oot o' this mess, or die tryin'."

Carson was not comforted. Judging from the looks of those around them, they were all—himself, Innes, the girls—more than likely to die before the sun rose again.

Little Raven sat alone in his lodge, listening to the shouts and cries from without, and praying to Man-Above for guidance. He knew, because the shouts told him, that the six men of the Dog Lodge who had ridden out for vengeance the day before had returned victorious. That they had brought back a prisoner.

What was to be done? He closed his eyes and rocked forward and back, forward and back.

Man-Above, give me wisdom to guide Our People.

Little Raven had been young once. His blood had been as hot as that of those men outside. He understood their need for revenge. He had not been at Sand Creek when the bluecoat, Chivington, had massacred so many that day three autumns ago, but he knew what had happened. He had been with the main body of Our People encamped several miles from the site.

Never again did he want to lead Our People on a flight for their lives as he'd had to do that day. Never again did he want to have to impose upon the Kiowa and Comanche for safety. Our People needed their own land where they would be safe, where whites would not bother them. Where the hot-blooded young men would not be tempted to raid white settlements or accost white travelers. A place where they could hunt their own food without depending on handouts from the bluecoats. A place where the buffalo roamed free and water flowed sweet and swift. Where their children and grandchildren could grow up knowing only laughter and love and safety, rather than hunger and hate and fear.

Peace. That is what he wanted for *Inuna-ina.*

Now the dog soldiers had taken a white captive.

There would be a gathering tonight around the central fire. They would smoke, and they would talk. About what was to be done with this white man.

Man-Above, give me courage, give me strength, give me wisdom.

The council fire flared with the addition of a new log, then settled into a steady flame that warmed those closest and lit the night. Sparks danced crazily on the updrafts of hot air.

Crooked Oak waited impatiently as the pipe yet again made its way slowly from man to man around the circle. He wanted this confrontation over and finished, so he could kill the white prisoner. How was he ever to become a great war leader of Our People if he could not kill enemies?

He would have had the white man's scalp on his lance that afternoon, had it not been for Red Beard. The scalps of the girls, too, although that would not have been as impressive. It wasn't important to him to kill children, except that if they were ever to wipe the white man off the face of Mother Earth, the children would have to die, too.

But Red Beard had been there. The white man was Red Beard's friend.

Crooked Oak hadn't wanted to honor Red Beard's wishes by not killing the captive, but he could not afford to alienate the man just yet. First he must get Red Beard to give him his daughter.

Two Feathers had suggested that Crooked Oak might come closer to his goal of taking Winter Fawn to wife by letting the captive go. But Crooked Oak thought such an action would make him appear weak in the eyes of Red Beard. Weak and too eager to please.

No, he had to prove his honor and valor by standing up for what he believed in, and what he believed in, everyone knew, was killing the enemy. Once Red Beard saw him as a strong man, a brave warrior able to take care of what was his, Crooked Oak would be able to ask for Winter Fawn.

So instead of killing the captive, Crooked Oak had agreed to let the elders decide the captive's fate. This was risky, as Little Raven was always speaking in favor of peace, of leaving the white man alone and staying out of his way. The elders would most certainly encourage Crooked Oak to let the white man go.

Unless he could change their minds.

Careful, he cautioned himself as he glanced at Red Beard across the fire. He would have to be careful. He wanted the white man—the one who was his captive—dead. Wanted it fiercely. One less white man to walk the earth.

But he wanted Winter Fawn, too. She was there, seated behind her father. Firelight flickered copper and bronze across her face as she cautioned the two young white girls beside her to be quiet. Crooked Oak would have felt her presence even if he hadn't seen her. He always knew when she was near. She was that important to him.

His vision had been clear. One day he would be a great leader of Our People, his lance heavy with the scalps of his enemies, and Winter Fawn would be beside him. He must have her for his vision to come true. The only thing standing in his way was Red Beard.

As Two Feathers passed the pipe to him for the second time, Crooked Oak brought it to his lips and drew deeply. As he lowered the pipe and blew the smoke to the winds, his gaze met that of Red Beard. The man appeared calm, but his eyes were filled with anger.

Yes, Crooked Oak reminded himself, he would have to be careful. And if caution did not work, he would have to eliminate this obstacle. For Crooked Oak *would* be a great warrior. He would kill many enemies and lead his people to greatness, with Winter Fawn beside him. He had seen it in a vision. It would come true. He would make it come true. Red Beard would not be permitted to stand in his way.

Across the fire, Innes Red Beard MacDougall saw the flames leap. Not the ones from the pit in the center of the circle of men, but the flames in Crooked Oak's eyes. The man was fair to bursting with anger at having his fun cut short.

Well, that was just too damn bad. As long as Innes had breath in his body, the bloody bastard wasn't gettin' his hands on Edmond Dulaney's son.

O' course, he already had his hands on Carson. The lad was tied several yards away to a tree. It scraped at Innes's pride. He imagined it did that and more to Carson.

The need for a drink threatened to strangle him. Just a small one. A nip would do to steady his nerves, keep his hands from shaking. He kept those hands clasped over his knees so no one would notice their trembling. He couldn't afford to put a weapon like that into Crooked Oak's hands.

Patience, patience, Innes cautioned himself. He would have his drink as soon as this was settled. First he must be patient, be silent until it was his turn to speak. The Arapaho, like any other tribe he'd known, and he'd known a few, thought it rude to just jump into a conversation before the niceties of smoking and silence had been observed.

And it was silent. No talking, no restless movements, except from the two young white girls seated with Winter Fawn in the first row of women at Innes's back. It was a tense silence, a hushed expectancy.

Finally, when the pipe made its way back around the circle again, Little Raven spoke.

"Four suns ago three of Our People rode out to hunt a deer."

A low murmur rose, then quickly fell.

"The bluecoats killed them."

A woman somewhere near the back of the gathered crowd cried out in grief.

"Their women cry," Little Raven said gravely. "They cut their hair, score their flesh."

Another murmur swept through the gathering.

"Yesterday some of our men rode out to avenge these deaths."

Crooked Oak raised a fist in the air and punched the night.

Little Raven turned his somber gaze on Crooked Oak. "Tell us what happened."

Crooked Oak felt his chest swell. To be asked to speak was

a great honor and proved his importance to the band. "We rode for hours," he said, his voice deep and strong. "There were no white men along the track they usually follow. Late in the afternoon we heard the noise of an approaching wagon. We hid behind some rocks and waited. When the wagon appeared, we attacked."

"Yet you did not kill them," Little Raven said.

Crooked Oak met Red Beard's gaze squarely. "No, we did not. Red Beard, who had been traveling with them, said the man was his friend. Out of honor for his position in our band, I stayed my hand. I could have taken the white man's scalp. I had my knife at his head. But I did not."

When Crooked Oak did not continue, Little Raven asked, "Why have you brought the white man here?"

Innes couldn't help the way his chest swelled with emotion. To Little Raven, there was only one white man in the camp, and that was the captive. To Our People, Innes was not white. He was Red Beard. Husband of Smiling Woman. Father of Winter Fawn and Hunter.

Little Raven's continued acceptance of him, when he only visited once a year now instead of living with them, humbled him and gladdened his heart. With a few notable exceptions, he thought with a glare at Crooked Oak, these were good people. He was proud to be considered one of them.

He waited now, knowing that to speak out of turn would make him appear rude and contemptuous of custom. He saw plainly that Crooked Oak did not know how to answer Little Raven's question.

In truth, Innes was correct. Crooked Oak, even several hours since the incident, was not certain what to say. He decided to tell as much of the truth as he could bear. If he strayed too far, Red Beard would surely protest, and Crooked Oak wasn't sure that any but Two Feathers would back him up.

"I did not wish to," he said straightly. "I do not care that he is a friend of Red Beard's. He is an enemy. His kind have spilled the blood of Our People. He has brought his children here to this land." He nodded with his chin toward the two young white girls with Winter Fawn.

"He will claim the land as his own, the way white men do.

He will tear it up, drive off or kill all the game, poison the water. He is an enemy. He should die. I am a warrior. I kill our enemies. I bring him here only out of respect for Red Beard, because he did not wish me to kill the man. I bring him here so that others can make Red Beard see that the killing is needful."

Calmly, deliberately, Little Raven turned to Innes with an inquiring look.

Innes wished again, desperately, for one of the bottles tucked into the supplies he'd carried in on his pack mule. He thought for a moment that it might be to his and Carson's advantage to pass a few of those bottles around. Get all the warriors drunk, then sneak Carson away when they all passed out.

But it was just as likely that after a few drinks Crooked Oak would take it into his head that he should just kill Carson and be done with it. No one other than Innes would really care one way or the other.

So Innes discarded the idea and fought the burning need in his belly. Slowly he looked around the circle of dark, serious faces, not lingering on any one, until his gaze met Little Raven's.

"I cannot say what was in Crooked Oak's heart and mind when I stopped him from killing the son of the dearest friend a man has ever had." A lie, Innes thought, but a necessary one. He'd known exactly what Crooked Oak had been thinking. "I only know that, as the warriors did not realize that I was traveling with the wagon, neither did I realize who was attacking us until I aimed my rifle at the warrior who was about to scalp my friend. Had he not looked up and recognized me and halted, I would have killed him before I even knew it was Crooked Oak. I was defending my friend. There is not a man here who would not have done the same."

A murmur of agreement swelled, then faded.

"I am shamed," Innes continued in Arapaho. "My honor has been stained. I will not say this was deliberate, but it has happened. I swore to my friend that he had nothing to fear from Our People. That if he traveled with me, he would be safe, for I am one of you. Have been one of you for many, many seasons. He trusted me. He believed me. And now he comes to this. He must be set free."

This time the murmur was of protest, and came from only a handful of warriors.

"I would speak," said Bent Old Man. "If we let the white man go, will he not tell the bluecoats what has happened and bring them down on us to kill our women and children?"

People shifted where they sat. Mothers pulled their children closer to them. The murmurs were of anger and fear.

"No," Innes said. "That he would not do. He just spent four years fighting this same bluecoat army that plagues Our People. He has been their enemy, the same as we have. They killed his father—my friend. He would not go to them."

"He fought against his own kind?" Little Raven asked.

Innes shook his head. "Not like you mean. He was of the Gray army and fought against the Blue. Just as Our People fight the Utes."

That comparison they understood. Many faces filled with consideration and turned to study the captive more closely.

But some were not convinced. "He is still a white man," Crooked Oak stated. "They are not to be trusted."

"I am a white man," Innes reminded him. "Am I not to be trusted either? Would you kill me because my skin is not as dark as yours?"

The struggle on Crooked Oak's face was plain. His mind cried *Yes! I would like to kill you!*

Innes could not fathom from where such hatred sprang. He couldn't recall anything he'd ever done to Crooked Oak—to anyone among Our People—to cause such hatred.

But Crooked Oak won his battle with self-control. "You are not white," he said to Innes. "Not in your heart. In your heart you are one of us."

Innes was forced, for the sake of politeness, to nod in acknowledgment of the high compliment.

"Are you willing," Little Raven asked Crooked Oak, "to set your captive free?"

Crooked Oak squared his shoulders. "I am not. White blood must be spilled to avenge the deaths."

"You have spilled his blood," Innes pointed out. "Your bullet struck the back of his head and nearly killed him."

"Yet he still lives," Crooked Oak complained.

"Perhaps," Innes said, "because he is a strong man, a worthy man. Perhaps it is meant that he live."

"Perhaps it is meant that he die," Crooked Oak countered. "Perhaps he is meant to live long enough to give him to the women who lost their men four suns ago."

"If they don't want him," came an old, wavering voice from the back of the crowd, "I will take him."

Heads turned, mouths flew open. The one who had spoken so boldly out of turn was Old Widow Woman. She had seen many more winters than anyone among Our People. She had outlived three husbands and now lived with her youngest son, who was himself no longer young. The gleam in her eye and the grin on her thin, old lips as she stared approvingly at the captive bound to the tree elicited a burst of laughter from the crowd. It was well known that Old Widow Woman would much prefer a man of her own than to live the rest of her days on the charity of her son.

Old Widow Woman's daughter, Sits By Fire, was also widowed and lived with her brother, the same brother who provided for Old Widow Woman. "If you get him, my mother, I hope you remember to share with your daughter."

As unseemly as her words were, the crowd could not help but laugh. Sits By Fire was herself so old that she had no teeth left with which to chew her meat.

The laughter eased the tension that had been building, but soon talk turned again to what to do with the captive. Some sided with Crooked Oak, believing that all whites should be killed—except, of course, for Red Beard, whom they did not consider white.

And praise be to the Holy Faither for that bit o' reasoning, Innes thought fervently.

Around and around the discussion went, along with the pipe. Deep into the night Innes thought that sentiment was swaying slightly in favor of releasing Carson. Despite the shaking in his hands and the twisting need in his gut for a drink—just a small one, that was all he needed—he was elated.

Then Crooked Oak rose to his feet. "I would ask that we consider again tomorrow what to do. I would think on this matter overnight. I would pray on it."

Aye, an' you'll be lookin' for a way to slit the lad's throat afore mornin', Innes thought sourly. ''What is there to consider? What would you do?'' he asked Crooked Oak. ''Kill him where he sits, helpless and tied to the tree? Where is the honor in such a thing?''

''The honor is in the death of an enemy,'' Crooked Oak replied hotly. ''You say you have been shamed by what has happened. What of my shame? I vowed to avenge the deaths of our friends. Instead of acting honorably, we sit around the fire and speak of honor. Like old men who are too feeble to do anything else.''

''There is no need to insult your elders,'' Little Raven said sharply.

Realizing he had gone too far, Crooked Oak unclenched his fists. ''I meant no disrespect. I meant only that I am a warrior of the Dog Lodge. I am supposed to kill our enemies, not talk about it.''

''You are also supposed to protect Our People,'' Innes countered. ''Yet you attacked whites only a few hours from this camp. What if the army finds the abandoned wagon and follows your trail here?''

Another murmur rose from the crowd. This time it was mixed. The dog soldiers would welcome such a thing, for their blood was hot and they were tired of this peace Little Raven kept urging on them. But the women murmured in fear, for they had not forgotten the massacre of so many women, children, and old people of the Cheyenne and some Arapaho at Sand Creek.

A woman called Basket Maker jumped to her feet, panic in her eyes. ''Kill him! Kill the captive quickly, I say. Hide his body and let us leave this place now, before the sun comes up. Let us be long gone from here before they come. They will slaughter us in our sleep. Our children and old people will be helpless against them. We will die! We will all die!''

The knot in Innes's belly tightened, tore a hole that could only be filled by whiskey. He was losing them. Bloody damn and double damn.

''They will not come riding down on us in the middle of the night,'' Little Raven said sharply. ''And we are not defenseless as they were at Sand Creek. Do you think so poorly of our warriors? We will not panic and flee like cowards in the night."

"Like women, you mean," Crooked Oak said with disgust.

The meeting might have gone on all night, but a strong wind came up suddenly and played havoc with the big fire around which everyone sat. Sparks and hot ashes whirled upward in the gusts and were carried through the camp, threatening to set everything on fire. It was agreed that they would put out the fire and resume the discussion in the morning.

"For tonight, the captive will be neither harmed nor set free." Little Raven looked at Crooked Oak, then at Innes. "I will have your word on that, both of you. All of you."

Innes gave his word because there was nothing else he could do. So, too, did Crooked Oak, Two Feathers, and the others.

Hours later the wind had died and Winter Fawn lay awake in her blankets. For once her grandfather's deep, rumbling snore from across the softly glowing embers left in the fire pit failed to comfort her; her grandmother's lighter whistle, accompanied by the sound of lips flapping, failed to amuse. Her troubled thoughts and emotions left no room for comfort or amusement.

First in her heart was the excitement and pleasure over her father's return. Oh, the thrill and joy of seeing him again! The agony of hoping that this time he might stay, this time he might show some small sign of approval, of affection, as he had when she'd been a child. Before the rabbit.

She knew she was setting herself up for another ache in her heart by hoping, but she could not stop herself. Knew, too, that she was too old to be clinging to her father. Grandmother was right; it was time she took a husband and had children of her own. But the mere thought of being given to Crooked Oak made her skin crawl.

He had grabbed her once last fall, in the woods along the creek. She'd never told anyone, too afraid that if her uncle and grandfather knew that Crooked Oak had put his mouth on hers, had put his hands on her breasts, they would force him to take her as wife. So she had kept silent, and kept out of his way as best she could. So far it had worked to keep out of his grasp, but not, apparently, out of his thoughts, for he had spoken to her uncle recently about taking her to wife.

She knew that if she was forced to mate with him she would become one of those sad-eyed women whose husbands beat them, because she would not be able to tolerate his repulsive touch. She would not, in all likelihood, be able to stop herself from trying to push him away. For that he would beat her. Not being a docile person, she would fight back. Not being very large, she would be beaten that much more severely.

No, she could not marry Crooked Oak. Now that her father was here, she must talk to him, must convince him to put a stop to any plans in that direction.

But her father's mind just now was occupied with saving the life of his friend, the captive.

Winter Fawn looked to the blanket beside hers. In the dim glow of the dying embers she could just make out the faces of the two young girls, curled into each other and clinging tightly in their sleep. Tears had left clean marks down their dusty faces. Winter Fawn could not begin to imagine their terror.

Or their pain, she thought, noticing again the raw scrape and dark bruise on the forehead of the older girl, the one her father had called Bess.

The urge to reach over and touch the wound, place her hand on it and let the heat flow, was overwhelming.

What would it hurt? The girl was asleep. Grandmother and Grandfather were asleep. There was no one to know.

Just one touch. Just enough to ease.

As if she were watching someone else, Winter Fawn saw her arm reach out, saw her dark hand press gently but firmly against the pale forehead, the raw, red scrape, the black and blue bruise around it.

Heat flowed instantly from her hand to the girl's head. Pain, both sharp and dull, struck Winter Fawn in the temple. Enough pain that she had to clamp hard on her jaw to keep from crying out.

Enough. She forced herself to pull her hand away. If the touch went on too long, someone would notice.

Suddenly the girl's eyes opened and stared straight into Winter Fawn's. A frown line formed between the girl's eyes. She opened her mouth to speak, but Winter Fawn quickly pressed a finger to her own lips and shook her head. The girl closed her mouth, then opened it again and might have spoken, but something thumped against the outside of the lodge.

"Winter Fawn," came a low whisper from without.

Winter Fawn's eyes widened. Hunter! What was he doing here in the middle of the night, calling to her in English?

"Winter Fawn, come out. Crooked Oak is going to kill the white man, and I cannot find father. You must help me stop him."

CHAPTER 4

Winter Fawn motioned sharply for Bess to remain where she was. She knew the girl had heard Hunter. His words had been unmistakable in the still, quiet night. But the girl stayed where she was and did not make a sound as Winter Fawn quickly and quietly slipped into her clothes, wrapped her blanket around her shoulders against the night's chill, and crept silently from the tepee.

Hunter, appearing as no more than a darker shadow among dark shadows cast by the tepee in the moonlight, touched her arm.

"What's happened?" She whispered in English, as he had done, so that if they were overheard they would not be understood.

Her brother leaned close and spoke low so that his voice did not carry. "Father found me after the council broke up and took me aside. He asked me to make sure horses were ready and his packs from his mule were nearby in case he had to leave in a hurry."

Winter Fawn stifled the low sound of distress that rose in her throat. There was no time for distress, and it was useless. Her father would leave when he wished. But not so soon!

Please, not so soon. He'd only just arrived and she'd scarcely seen him.

"I hobbled the horses in the woods, away from the rest of the herd. Near them I hid his saddle and packs, bridles, rope, water, everything I could think of. But when I came back to camp, I couldna find Da."

"Where did you look?"

"Everywhere I could. But I couldna very well look inside every lodge, now, could I?"

"Of course not."

"I thought maybe he'd gone to talk to Crooked Oak, to try to convince him to give up the white man. That's when I heard them."

"Heard who?"

"Crooked Oak and some of the others. He said he was afraid our father would convince everyone to let the captive go free. He's working himself up into a lather, saying that he's going to go kill the white man now, tonight, and be done with it. We have to do something. The man is a friend of Da's."

"You're right." Winter Fawn clenched her fists at her sides. "We have to get that white man out of here. He won't go without his sister and daughter. I'll get them. Then you take them to the horses while I cut him loose."

Hunter shook his head. "If one of us is going to get caught freeing him, it is better that it be me."

"The only thing that is likely to get us caught is the noise the horses will make if you aren't there to keep them quiet. I dinna have your gift. The horses dinna listen to me."

Hunter might have objected again, but she turned away to get the girls.

She did not have to go back inside the tepee to get them. When she turned, they were there, standing outside the door flap, their pale skin glowing in the darkness, their eyes large and round with fear.

"Come, but quietly." Winter Fawn held out her hand to the little one called Megan. "Go with Hunter, and I will bring your father to you."

Winter Fawn waited until they disappeared into the woods at the edge of camp, then made her way quietly between lodges to the tree where the captive was tied. The moon was so bright she had no trouble avoiding the meat-drying racks, the skins staked out on the ground for tanning.

As if she had needed guidance, the captive's white shirt glowed like a signal beacon in the dark.

Carson heard someone approaching and tensed. Even through four years of war he'd never felt as helpless as he did just then, as he had from the moment that afternoon when Bess had fallen from the wagon and he'd thought they were all going to die. Innes hadn't been quite the protection he had promised to be.

Carson wanted to hate him for that, for giving him such a false sense of security. He wanted to rage at God, at fate, at anything and everything.

But Carson also knew he would be dead if Innes hadn't been with them. He had no doubt of that. The girls might still be alive, but he couldn't even let himself think of what would surely have happened to them at the hands of the Indians who had attacked them.

So much for his determination to never kill another man. He knew that if he had the chance right that minute, he would kill that leering arrogant bastard who had nearly scalped him, and the one who had grabbed Bess. He would kill all six of the warriors who had attacked them. The rage was icy cold in his gut, but hot in his veins.

Now someone was sneaking toward him through the dark, and here he sat, trussed up like a pig waiting for slaughter. The only thing missing was the goddamn apple for his mouth.

The night was so quiet he knew the Indian could probably hear him breathing. When the person stepped from the shadow of the closest tepee into the moonlight, the first thing Carson noticed was the gleam of moonlight along the knife held tightly in a fist.

Carson's heart pounded like a drum inside his chest. He had a choice, it seemed. He might be able to kick with his bound feet if the Indian was stupid enough to get in front of him, but he doubted it would do him much good. There wasn't a thing he could do about that knife. Killing him was going to be disgustingly easy for the sneaking bastard.

He could yell, but he would certainly be dead before anyone heard him.

Okay. This was it, then. He was going to die. He would fight if he got the chance, but as long as he was tied to the tree, the outcome was inevitable. The only question would be how he chose to meet it—cringing, begging for mercy, or with whatever dignity he could muster.

Regrets swamped him, but the largest, the one that nearly choked him, was that he had brought Megan and Bess to Colorado. *Please, God, keep them safe. Help Innes get them out of here alive. Help them find their way back home to Gussie.*

That brief prayer steadied him and slowed his heart. It was all he had time for before the Indian was on him. Only then did he realize . . . it was a woman! He hadn't been able to see her shape because she was wrapped in a blanket.

She bent down and leaned toward his head. In a quiet whisper, she said in English, "I've come to cut you loose."

Carson recognized the voice with its soft Scottish burr. It was Innes's daughter.

"My brother has horses ready, and the girls are with him. I will take you there." Then she slipped behind the tree.

After a slight tug on the rawhide around his wrists, his hands were free. His shoulders screamed with pain as he pulled his arms forward for the first time in more hours than he cared to think about. The blood flowing back into his hands made them throb with agony.

"Where's your father?" he asked in a low, urgent whisper.

"I do not know, but we must hurry." She crept to his feet to sever the last of his bonds. "Hunter overheard Crooked Oak say he planned to kill you this night." Her knife sliced through the rawhide around his ankles. "Quickly. We must go."

To Carson's chagrin, she had to help him to his feet. It took him a minute of leaning against the tree before he could feel anything below his ankles, and the pain of returning circulation had him grinding his teeth.

As she bent down and retrieved the strips of rawhide, Carson heard a noise. An indrawn breath, the shuffle of moccasins along the ground. A quiet word that to Carson sounded like a curse, although it was not spoken in English.

Beside the nearest tepee, twenty yards away, the shadow of a man loomed. A man drawing an arrow back to fire. An arrow aimed at Carson's chest.

Winter Fawn stood and looked toward the shadow. "Crooked Oak, no!"

With a curse of his own, Carson tried to shove her away. "Get down," he warned harshly.

But she didn't get down, didn't duck out of the line of fire. Instead, just as the man loosed the arrow, she committed one of the bravest, most foolhardy acts Carson had ever witnessed. Dropping her blanket, she turned and threw herself at his chest, shielding him from the arrow.

She slammed into him hard. Her breath left her in an abrupt *umph.* In reflex, his arms came around her to hold her. He felt a stab of pain in his side. He stared down at her, and in the moonlight he saw shock, bewilderment, and pain in her eyes.

Another rustle of sound had him clasping her close and looking sharply toward the shadows where the man stood. A second man, big and burly—*Innes*—rushed toward the first, and with a grunt, struck him in the head with the butt of a rifle.

The Indian fell to the ground.

Innes rushed to them. "Damn the bloody bastard," came his harsh whisper. "He's shot me lassie!"

It was then that Carson realized the cause of the sharp pain in his side. "He's shot both of us, but she took the worst of it."

"Both?" Innes demanded.

"Da?" the woman whispered. "Crooked Oak . . . was going to kill him."

"Aye, I saw. You saved Carson's life, lassie. Are ye bad hurt?"

"Aye, I be thinking I am. Hunter and . . . the girls are . . . waiting with . . . the horses. We couldna . . . find ye."

"I'm here now, lassie. Dinna talk. Dinna be movin'." Innes's brogue was thicker than usual. "We'll take care of ye. Shot you both?" he asked Carson again, his voice quiet but tense. "The arrow went clean through her?"

Carson glanced down and even that slight movement drew a hiss from between his teeth. "Clean through both of us. She's pinned to me, and I'm pinned to the tree. But she's got the worst of it. For me I think it's just under the skin."

In the act of pulling the big knife from the scabbard at his belt, Innes paused and cursed under his breath. At least, it sounded like a curse to Carson. It could have been a prayer.

"Lass," Innes said, his voice taut, "if you've a mind to pass out, now be the time for it. I'm going to cut the arrow off back here, then pull you off of it. I willna hurt you more than I have to, but it'll still be bad."

Looking down into her eyes, Carson could not fathom why she was still conscious, but she was. She leaned her head against his chest and raised her eyes to his as she answered her father. "Be gettin' it done, then, Da."

"Aye. Carson, can you hold the shaft steady from your side?"

With another hissed breath, Carson reached a hand between his side and hers. The arrow that pinned her to him left barely enough room for him to grasp it between their bodies. He was relieved to realize he'd been right. While it hurt like a blue bitch, the arrow had skimmed along the outside of his ribs and lay just beneath his skin. That meant his wound wasn't serious. But it also meant the arrow would be less stable when Innes started to work. He grasped it as tightly as he could.

His grip made the shaft move slightly, and the woman pinned to him moaned.

"I'm sorry," he whispered. He could feel now where the arrow exited her body. It must have entered her back at her waist, a couple of inches from her side, for it came out just below her ribs. "God, I'm sorry," he whispered again.

"Ready?" Innes asked.

"All right," he whispered. "Do it."

With a soft curse, Innes snapped the arrow off, leaving about two inches protruding from his daughter's back.

The girl grunted in pain.

"All right, lass, here we go."

Carson held the arrow as steady as possible while Innes pulled her slowly off the shaft. It seemed to Carson that it took forever. Throughout the ordeal, she never took her eyes from his. Something passed between them in those eternal seconds.

A communication, wordless, indefinable. She had been pinned to his chest. They had been joined. Connected. A new connection formed now even as she was being separated from him.

And he thought, *I don't even know her name.*

As the broken end of the shaft slipped free of her flesh, she let out a soft moan and passed out, falling limp in her father's arms.

Innes had his hands full, but Carson had a burning need to unpin himself from the tree before anything else happened. He would have to literally walk himself off of the shaft, but he didn't relish walking himself off the extra six or eight inches that was sticking out of him. He needed to cut it off. "Pass me your knife," he said tightly.

Innes looked up sharply. "Give me a minute and I'll be gettin' ye unstuck there, lad.

"I'll do it." He didn't want to, but he'd dug a bullet out of his own leg once. This couldn't be nearly that bad. "She dropped her knife there by your knee. Hand it to me."

Innes might have argued, but just then his daughter moaned. He handed Carson the knife and gave the girl his attention.

Carson gritted his teeth and, using the knife, snapped the arrow off as close to his body as possible. The arrow jerked and sent searing pain through his side. Before he could think about how bad this was going to hurt, he forced himself to step away from the tree.

It was just a big splinter, he told himself. Nothing more.

During the few seconds it took him to ease himself forward and off the shaft, his stomach rolled, his vision blurred, and cold sweat broke out across his face and down his back. Then, with a final hiss of pain, he was free.

He stood still a moment and took stock. There was pain, but not a great deal. Nothing that would slow him down. There was blood, but again, not much. Not enough to worry about.

Not so with the woman at his feet. Innes had her on her side and had pulled her doeskin blouse up so he could inspect her wounds. Both were bleeding.

Knowing his gray flannel undershirt would keep him warm enough, and not really caring if it didn't, Carson tore off his shirt and handed it to Innes, who ripped it into strips. They made thick pads and pressed them against her wounds hard enough to make her moan even though she was still unconscious. In the moonlight her flesh was paler than his. That such beauty could be so terribly abused appalled him and offended his senses.

"Dammit," Carson swore while slipping her knife down inside his boot. "Why did she do a fool thing like that? She doesn't even know me. She saved my life and I don't even know her name."

"Her name be Winter Fawn," Innes supplied.

"She's your daughter, I take it."

"Aye. Me firstborn, she be. The very image of her mother, God rest her soul."

"I've got a feeling God's gonna rest all our souls if we don't stop this bleeding and get out of here."

They packed more pads against her entrance and exit wounds and used the last of Carson's shirt to wrap around her waist to hold the pads in place as tightly as possible.

Innes knew Winter Fawn would be well taken care of by her grandmother, yet he hesitated to carry her to the tepee. Once he left camp it would be obvious to all that he had helped Carson escape. Because Innes was about to disappear with the captive, her uncle and grandfather would no longer honor his instructions that they not give her in marriage without his consent. Two Feathers would see her wed to Crooked Oak before her wound was even healed.

Oh, yes, Innes had heard the talk. Crooked Oak wanted her. But Innes could not stand the thought of his bonny lass tied for life to that bloody bastard who could think of nothing but war and killing, who took such pleasure in both.

Carson did not know why Innes hesitated, nor did he care. Something compelled him to reach for her and lift her in his arms, ignoring the pain of his own wound. She had saved his life. He still couldn't get over it.

As Carson took her from his arms without a word, Innes considered it a sign that she was not to be left behind. So be it.

* * *

Two Feathers was troubled by Crooked Oak's vow to kill the white man while everyone slept. Such an act seemed dishonorable to him. Where was the glory in killing a man tied to a tree? Killing him when no one would see?

If Crooked Oak was planning to torture and scalp the captive, that was one thing. Then having him tied to the tree made sense. But that was not what Crooked Oak planned. Torture resulted in screaming, and Crooked Oak did not want to wake the camp. He simply wanted the white man dead by his own hand. He did not care if no one knew he had done it.

Two Feathers probably should not care. Crooked Oak was his friend and a strong warrior. They thought alike on the subject of whites and war: they each wanted to use the latter to rid the earth of the former.

But they had given their word before the entire camp that the man would not be harmed during the night. That is what troubled Two Feathers. For not only did such a vow mean that he could not harm the man himself, it also obligated Two Feathers, and every man in camp, to see to it that no harm came to the captive.

He did not want to fight Crooked Oak to save a white man. He, too, wanted to see the man dead. But he preferred to wait and convince the rest of the camp that the man's death was necessary. He did not like this sneaking around in the dark.

Yet sneaking around in the dark was exactly what he was doing. When he could not find Crooked Oak, he left camp and circled around in the woods to come upon the white man from behind, to see if anything was wrong.

He was still more than a dozen yards beyond the edge of camp when he stepped onto the path that would lead him near the tree where the white man was tied. He was not expecting anything this far into the woods, so when the dark shadow loomed up before him, he stumbled backward.

A shaft of moonlight penetrated the overhead branches. In that instant he saw the white man carrying Winter Fawn, and she was covered in blood. The white man had gotten free and was kidnaping her! She might be the daughter of a white man, but she was also Two Feathers's own niece, the daughter of his sister, Smiling Woman. No white man was going to hurt her and carry her away!

As he reached for the knife at his side, Two Feathers opened his mouth to shout a warning to rouse the camp.

Carson recognized the man and his intent. He freed one arm from around Winter Fawn and struck him in the jaw. The Indian's head snapped back and hit the trunk of the tree immediately behind him. He slid to the ground, unconscious.

Ahead of Carson, Innes heard the commotion and turned back. He squatted beside the downed man and grunted.

"Is he dead?" Carson asked.

"Nae, and just as well. I wouldna like to explain to the lass that we killed her uncle."

Saying nothing, Carson held Winter Fawn against him, putting pressure on her wounds as best he could, and waited while Innes bound and gagged the Indian and dragged him deeper into the woods.

"We dinna want the bastard wakin' the whole camp and comin' after us."

"You didn't tie the other one."

"Nae. He's no' aboot to admit shooting at you and hitting Winter Fawn. He'll make his way back to his lodge and wait until morn to be shocked by news of your escape."

Carson said nothing as he followed Innes down the moonlit path through the trees.

The path ended at a clearing beside a rushing stream. Bess, Megan, and a tall, muscular Indian boy of about fifteen rushed forward.

"What happened?" the Indian boy asked anxiously. "Is she dead?"

"Nae," Innes told him, "but she's hurt. 'Twas Crooked Oak wot done it. We hae ta git oot o' here in a hurry. Lad . . . son, I never meant to make ye choose between me and yer mother's people, but if ye've a mind to come away wi' us, they might not be wantin' ye back again, so think careful on it, and think fast."

The boy straightened his shoulders. "I ride with my father. If I be welcome."

"More than welcome," Innes said fervently. "Carson Dulaney, my son, Hunter. Now, let's be gettin' ourselves oot o' here afore Two Feathers and Crooked Oak come to and set after us."

Carson felt the girls moving close to him. "Are you two okay?"

Bess nodded.

Megan said, "I'm scared, Daddy."

Carson's heart squeezed. Both girls looked so terrified. He wanted to take them into his arms and hold them tight and promise that nothing would ever scare them again. But there wasn't time, and his arms were full, and the ordeal was far from over. He couldn't bring himself to make promises he knew he couldn't keep.

"I know you're scared, sweetheart," he told his daughter. "We all are. But we have to be quiet now so we can get away without anyone hearing us. Can you do that? Can you be quiet for us?"

In the moonlight, Megan gripped Bess's hand and solemnly nodded.

Hunter had prepared well. The boy had brought Carson's wagon team and Innes's horse and pack mule, complete with pack, to the clearing.

The pain in the back of Carson's head was making itself felt sharply, along with the new pain from the arrow. He didn't want to have to chose whether Bess or Megan would ride with him. The shape he was in, they were safer riding with Innes and Hunter. Hell, he didn't even have a weapon with which to defend them if the need arose, except for the knife he'd tucked in his boot.

Without waiting, he settled the matter by climbing into the saddle of the nearest horse, with Winter Fawn still in his arms. It wasn't an easy maneuver on any of them, but with gritted teeth, he managed it.

Then he realized he'd taken the only mount with a saddle. The other two horses were his wagon team, and hadn't been wearing saddles.

Innes waved away his concern and mounted one of the team,

then had Hunter swing Megan up to his arms. Innes seated her before him on the horse's withers.

Before mounting the remaining horse, Hunter went to each animal, stroked its neck and whispered into its ear. Maybe it was some Arapaho custom, but Carson wished the kid would hurry. The skin along the back of his neck was crawling.

When the boy went to Innes's horse, Innes leaned down and whispered to his son. A moment later when Hunter whispered into the mule's ear—when the hell was all this damn nonsense going to stop so they could get on their way?—he started fiddling with the packs on the mule's back, then turned back toward Carson.

Carson took back his last thought when he realized that Hunter was handing him his rifle and ammunition pouch. A series of emotions crossed the boy's face. Uncertainty, fear. Pleading. Resignation.

Carson understood. The rifle would be used, if necessary, to kill people Hunter had known all his life, perhaps his friends, perhaps a member of his own family. Yet still, he offered the weapon.

What irony, Carson thought, that an Arapaho boy should have so much in common with hundreds, maybe thousands of men in the recent war, each of whose loyalties had been tested again and again in battle as he faced the horrifying reality that the next enemy he killed might be his best friend, his cousin, his brother. His father. Yet each man stood and fought for what he believed in. As Hunter stood with his father, perhaps against his mother's people.

Carson shuddered, grateful he had never had to face that particular nightmare. In the scant second between his grasping the rifle and Hunter's releasing it, during that instant when it was held by both of them, Carson silently vowed to do his best to see that no one had to die in whatever confrontation might come between him and Hunter's people.

Hunter released the rifle and turned toward his own horse. While he mounted, Carson raised the breech-loading carbine and pulled down on the trigger guard lever. With the hinged barrel now slid forward and tipped down, he inserted a brass cartridge into the barrel, then locked the barrel back into place.

He loaded the roll of percussion caps, then slid the rifle into the saddle scabbard.

He looked up in time to see Hunter hold out his hand to Bess. Without a comment about the impropriety of riding astride, God bless her, she swung up behind the youth and held on. Fear, it seemed, was a good motivator.

"How do we avoid the Coyote Men?" Innes asked his son.

"We cut over the hills beyond the stream and head west, into the mountains."

"Lead the way, then, lad, and be quick about it afore we hae more company than we be wantin'."

"Aye, Da."

Hunter, riding double with Bess, nudged his horse across the stream. Innes waited until Carson crossed. The mule followed, and Innes took up the rear. They entered the woods, so thick and dark it seemed impossible for Hunter to know where they were going. Carson had to trust his mount to follow on its own, for he couldn't see beyond the animal's ears. Couldn't even hear the horse in front of him. The thick woods seemed to absorb sound.

He hoped that meant no one in camp could hear them leaving, either.

When they'd gone about a quarter of a mile, the ground started rising. As the way became steep, the angle of ascent pressed Winter Fawn more firmly against Carson's chest. She moaned and opened her eyes. Seeing him looming above her, and maybe feeling the movement of the horse, undoubtedly startled her. She jerked, then cried out in pain.

Carson leaned down until his mouth was close to her ear. "Easy," he said quietly. "Don't move around, or you'll hurt yourself."

She stilled, but he felt the tension in her body. "Where are we?" Her voice was weak and tight with pain. "Where's my father? My brother?"

"They're here, both of them. Your brother is riding ahead of us, with my sister. Your father is behind us with my daughter."

"Where are we?"

"I don't know." He kept his lips next to her ear so he could speak low enough that his voice would not carry. "Hunter is leading us over the hills west of camp to avoid the Coyote Men. What are Coyote Men?'' Maybe if she talked she wouldn't think so much about the pain, or about the fact that she was being carried away from camp by a stranger.

''Outlooks. No, lookouts. That is the word. Lookouts.''

The darkness ahead suddenly didn't seem quite so dark, and a moment later it was lighter still. The trees were thinning, growing farther apart. Then, abruptly, Hunter pulled to a halt. Carson's horse stopped automatically.

Winter Fawn tensed in his arms, but said nothing as total silence descended on them. Even the horses seemed to be holding their breath.

After a long moment, Hunter must have satisfied himself that the way was clear, for he nudged his horse out into the open. A moment later all three horses and the mule had broken out of the woods into bright moonlight. The ground ahead was broken and rocky, with absolutely no cover as it rose sharply to the top of the hill.

Carson had made many a night march during the war, but his soldiering instincts protested being so exposed. The prickling along the back of his neck grew sharper. He hoped to hell the kid knew where he was leading them.

At least with the moonlight Carson could see Bess ahead of him. She had her arms wrapped around Hunter and was holding on tightly. From the looks of the trail ahead, she would need to.

He looked behind and saw Megan propped astride the withers of Innes's mount. She looked snug as a bug, tucked up against the big man's chest. Innes's arms appeared to cradle her gently yet firmly. As long as Innes could keep his seat without benefit of saddle on the coming steep trail, Megan would be safe.

As for Carson's extra passenger, he would just as soon she passed out again, because the ride to the top of the hill was going to be rough. If they had to have only one saddle among them, he was glad to have it, assuming—hoping—that both Hunter and Innes were more used to riding bareback than he was. At least he stood a halfway decent chance of not falling off the damn horse, adding insult to injury and slowing them all down.

But Winter Fawn, held against him as she was, was going to get jostled and bounced, and it was going to hurt her like hell. She—and he himself—would be better off if she sat behind him, although the horse's kidneys wouldn't thank them for it. But Winter Fawn was too weak to hold on to him, especially on this steep climb.

Hunter's horse lunged up a severely steep spot on the hillside to reach a narrow ledge that led up the face to the top. Carson held his breath, praying Bess would hold on tight, and that she and Hunter wouldn't both slide right off the horse's back.

The two made it. Then it was Carson's turn.

"If you feel like passing out again," he muttered to Winter Fawn, "now would be a good time for it."

But she didn't pass out. He knew by the way she tensed in his arms, and by the occasional quiet, pain-filled moan she tried to bite back. After what seemed like an hour, but which Carson knew was less than ten minutes, they crested the hill and were on top.

Here there was wind, and more trees. They were in the pines now, and above them rose the mountains, blocking out the stars.

Once more he hoped to hell Hunter knew where he was leading them.

Hunter hoped so, too. His heart thundered in his chest with the heavy responsibility of leading his father and the others to safety. Never had he had such an important honor, nor a more harrowing one. Every place he knew of that would make a good hiding place for them was also known by his uncle, Two Feathers, for it was he who had shown them to Hunter.

If he could not find a place for them to hide, someone might die. If Crooked Oak found them . . .

Hunter wanted to spit at the thought of Crooked Oak. To attempt to kill the prisoner after giving his word he would not was dishonorable enough. To injure Winter Fawn in the attempt, even by accident, was unforgivable.

Hunter cursed that he did not have a rifle. Because of the girl hugging his back, he wasn't even able to carry his bow and arrow; it was strapped onto his father's pack mule.

He wasn't certain that he wanted to turn the white man and

his rifle loose on any of Our People, but what he wouldn't give to have Crooked Oak in his own sights.

But first he must find shelter for six people, three horses, and a mule, before daylight.

No small feat this close to camp.

He urged his mount faster. He was sorry for the pain the faster gait would cause his sister, but it could not be helped if they were to make good their escape.

When the horse picked up its pace, Bess tightened her arms around his waist. She knew she was afraid, but was she supposed to feel excitement, too? Fear was the most prominent emotion just then, but confusion pushed at it. She'd never ridden astride before, nor had she ridden bareback. She'd never had to run for her life, never been afraid for her own safety before today.

Well, she thought honestly, that wasn't entirely true. She'd been terrified out of her wits when the Yankees shelled Atlanta. But at least she had not seen their faces. They had not leered at her with paint on their faces and knives in their hands.

Yes, she was afraid now. Surely it was terror that made her mouth go dry, her palms sweat, her heart race.

But there was excitement, too, and she couldn't deny it.

Wait until Aunt Gussie learned of this!

They made it over three more hills without incident, and down into a narrow canyon before the black of night gave way to the gray of predawn. They rode upstream for nearly a mile, then up the opposite bank and out of the canyon into more pines.

Carson cursed again. It would be full light soon, and Winter Fawn needed rest. She needed a new bandage, too. She was bleeding all over his undershirt. He didn't care about the shirt, but with every drop of blood she lost, her strength ebbed.

Hunter led them south when he could, west and higher into the mountains when he couldn't. The sky was light but the sun was not yet up when he led them down another stream, going east this time, following the flow of water. In the patches of sand between the occasional rocky outcropping along the banks, thick stands of willows grew, and now and then, a little grass.

After about a half mile, they came to a shallow cave carved out of the north rock wall eons ago about ten yards from the water. Scattered boulders that had fallen from the rim above partially shielded the west end of the opening. It was the best—the only—shelter they'd seen.

Carson looked around, noting the way the canyon curved up ahead. If anyone came from that direction they'd hear them long before they saw them. They would be able to see anyone coming from the west a long way off. The boulders would help shield them from anyone on the south rim. From the north they couldn't be seen at all.

It would do, Carson thought with a nod. It would do well.

Hunter slipped from his horse and helped Bess down.

Innes dismounted, carried a wide-eyed Megan to Bess, then took Winter Fawn from Carson's arms.

"I can walk," she protested weakly.

"Aye, and I can carry ye. Humor yer ol' Da."

"Is she going to be all right?" Hunter asked anxiously.

"Aye," Innes said. "She just needs a wee bit of rest. See what ye can do aboot that trail we left back upstream, the one a blind man could be followin'."

"Carson," Bess cried softly. "You're bleeding."

Carson looked down at himself. "Most of that is Winter Fawn's. I'm fine. We need a fire. A small one. Can you gather up some twigs for us?"

"Should I take Megan?"

"Okay, but the two of you be quiet, and keep a look out, and don't get out of sight."

Bless Bess's heart, this time yesterday morning she had been in a hotel, in a town, eating a hot meal at a table, and she'd been complaining. If he had told her to do something, she would have whined. Now, here in the wilderness, on the run for their lives, she merely nodded, took Megan by the hand, and walked quietly toward the willows along the stream. He wanted to grab her up in his arms and kiss her in gratitude.

But there wasn't time. Winter Fawn needed seeing to, as did the horses, and they all needed food and sleep.

He found a buffalo robe on Innes's pack mule and laid it out on the ground near the back wall of the cave for Winter Fawn. While Innes laid her there, Carson quickly unloaded the pack mule.

Grabbing his rifle, he led the mule and horses to the stream for a drink. Then he took each animal to a different spot among the willows, hiding them as best he could among the scant cover, while making sure they were within sight and smell of each other. A horse was a herd animal. It was not natural for the animal to be alone. If any of them were very domesticated, they might whinny if they couldn't see each other. He double-checked to make certain each was securely tied. They could not afford for one of their mounts to wander off. In this country, being left afoot was tantamount to a death sentence.

By the time he finished, Bess and Megan had gathered a sizable pile of twigs and small, fallen limbs in the center of the cave, where Innes had directed them. Innes was kneeling beside Winter Fawn, drinking from a silver flask, looking at the blood-soaked bandages, and muttering beneath his breath.

"Is she worse?" Carson asked.

"She's no better, that's for certain."

"You need clean bandages."

Carson and Innes looked up to find Bess standing beside them.

"Aye. Would ye be lookin' through yon pack, there," Innes said to Bess with a nod toward a pack with two brass buckles, "and findin' me blue shirt, lassie? We'll tear that into strips to use, I'm thinkin'."

Bess turned away to do his bidding, and Innes took another pull from his flask. Then he tilted it up to Winter Fawn's lips. She had closed her eyes, but when the liquid in the flask hit her mouth, her eyes flew open. She swallowed, then wheezed and choked. The motion jarred her wound, and she moaned.

"Sorry, lass, but it'll ease yer pain. Take another sip."

When Bess came back a few minutes later, she was carrying several rolls of white bandages.

"Where'd ye be findin' such a thing?" Innes asked with delight.

Bess blushed. "I had on too many petticoats."

"Ach, and a fine lassie ye be to be tearin' 'em up for me daughter. I thank ye kindly."

"Can I do anything else to help?" she asked with a blush.

Carson didn't know where all this cooperation was coming

from after the way Bess had acted on the stage and in Pueblo, but he wasn't about to question the new attitude. "See if you can find a pot in one of those packs and fill it with water. But keep—"

"An eye out. I know."

"A good lass, that," Innes said.

"Yes." Carson watched his baby sister pull a small coffeepot from one of Innes's packs and, after a word to Megan to stay put, she headed for the stream.

He didn't know her, Carson realized. He didn't know this sister of his—his only sister—at all. Perhaps he never had. She'd been around eight when the war started. Up until then they had lived in the same house, but Bess had been under Gussie's wing since their mother had died when Bess was born, while Carson's time had been taken up with the running of the plantation.

Coming home from the war last year to find a twelve-year-old young lady instead of his tiny little sister had been nearly as big a shock as realizing that the one-year-old daughter he'd kissed goodbye the day he'd marched off with the 12th Georgia was suddenly a precocious five-year-old. Add to that the sight of their once gracious home burned to ashes, and it had been almost more than he could handle.

God, he'd missed so much of their lives.

And after all that time, he had then missed the entire next year as well when he had come out West to see about the ranch. Now Megan was six and Bess was thirteen, and he didn't know either of them. And he wanted to. Desperately. They were *his*. A part of him in a way no one else would ever be. His only child, and his only sibling. Even if he had other children some day, Megan would always be his firstborn.

Other children, however, would mean a wife, since he didn't intend to go around siring bastards. But he didn't know if he would ever marry again. If he did, it would be to provide a mother for Megan, and companionship for himself. Never again would he let lust, a pretty face, and a comely shape blind him to reality. God rest Julia's conniving soul.

As a fiancée, Julia Covington had been a delightful tease.

As a mother, a disinterested failure. As a wife, a disloyal, unfaithful, lying, cheating, manipulating—

Of course, he thought with chagrin, that didn't say much for the man who allowed himself to be lied to, cheated on, manipulated, and all the rest.

But that was in the past. Julia had more than paid for her behavior. Carson may have wished he'd never married her—except for getting Megan out of the bargain—but he hadn't wished her dead.

Only Julia would have been egotistical enough to leave her two-year-old daughter with her husband's aunt, travel from Atlanta to Boston *in the middle of a damn war,* and flaunt her Yankee lover beneath the noses of her blue-blooded Yankee friends, just to prove she could.

Ah, Julia.

Maybe he was to blame, Carson thought, for not finding a way to make her happy.

But no, he wasn't going to accept the blame for his late wife's behavior. She had made it clear early in their marriage that she'd only married him to shock her father.

Shock him, she had. United States Senator Thomas Covington had been appalled that the apple of his eye would even speak to a Southerner, much less marry one, and that had been *before* the war.

Carson shook his head, both at Julia and his bitter memories of her, and at himself, for allowing the memories to surface when he needed to be figuring a way out of this current situation.

Whatever happened, he had to make certain Megan and Bess would be safe.

By the time Bess returned with the water, Carson had spread out Innes's bedroll where Megan was already curled up asleep, and he'd started a fire small enough to fit into his cupped hands. What little smoke it produced hit the ceiling of the cave and dissipated.

While Innes tended Winter Fawn, Bess insisted on cleaning and bandaging Carson's arrow wounds. The offer—more of a demand—floored him. Once again he thought, *Who is this young woman?*

When she finished, he borrowed Innes's knife and cut strips

of willow bark to make a tea for Winter Fawn. There was nothing like willow bark tea to ease pain.

Bess crawled into the bedroll with Megan and fell fast asleep. Poor little girls, so tired and afraid.

Carson tried not to watch as Innes helped Winter Fawn sit up, then pulled her doeskin tunic up and bared her ribs, but he couldn't help himself. That beautiful, honey-colored flesh was torn and bleeding. It was a sacrilege. Her face was gray with pain. Dark circles hung beneath her eyes.

For him. Because of him. Because she'd seen the danger and put herself between that arrow and him. "Why?" he heard himself demand. "Why did she throw herself in front of me that way?"

"She isna sure," Winter Fawn answered tartly for herself. "But she's gettin' a wee bit tired o' being talked aboot like she was deaf. Or dead."

She spoke with more energy than Carson would have thought possible, and more of a burr than she'd had the last time she'd spoken. Carson suspected that both were the result of the whiskey. Seeing Innes run a length of thin black thread through the eye of a needle, he realized she was going to need it.

Despite her pain and paleness, there was something regal in the way she held her head and met his gaze unflinchingly.

"Need any help?" Carson asked.

"Aye." Innes insisted that his daughter lie down on her side. "Find something she can bite on. This is going to hurt like a blue bitch."

In one of the packs Carson found a wide leather strap. That would do. He carried it to Winter Fawn and held it out.

She looked at it, at the needle in her father's hand, then swallowed. "Thank you." With a hand that trembled, she took the strap and placed it between her teeth.

While Innes stitched her flesh together, Carson steadied her with a hand to her shoulder. She barely flinched, but her eyes were squeezed shut. The sight of the single tear that slid from one eye burned into him.

The sun was full up by the time Innes finished his task and Winter Fawn rested quietly on the buffalo robe. When the willow bark tea was ready, Carson poured a cupful and took it to her. "Drink this."

Winter Fawn had seen him shave the willow bark, so she knew what he was handing her and was grateful. "Thank you."

"No need."

She tried to sit up. She probably could have managed it, eventually, but this stranger whose eyes fascinated her slipped an arm behind her back and eased her up as gently as a mother tending her sick child.

"I'm the one who owes you thanks," he said quietly, holding the steaming tin cup to her lips. "I'd be dead now if not for you."

Winter Fawn's mind was still stuck on the comparison between him and a mother tending a child, and her lips twitched. She had never seen a man more . . . manly. More masculine. To imagine that he reminded her of a woman was ludicrous.

The tea was hot and bitter, but she knew it would ease her pain, so she drank it as quickly as she could.

By the time Hunter returned from concealing their tracks, she could barely keep her eyes open.

"Sleep," Carson told her softly.

As if she had been waiting for his permission, her eyes drifted shut and sleep overtook her.

Carson watched her breathing slow and deepen as she fell asleep. Her color looked a little better now that she was more comfortable.

God, he still couldn't get over—would never get over—how she had thrown herself in front of him and taken that arrow.

Innes nudged him. "You get some sleep, too. We canna be stayin' here long. I'll take first watch. And drink some of that tea yourself, lad. That head wound, not to mention that newest hole in yer hide, must be painin' ye."

Carson smiled wryly. The wound in his side didn't bother him much unless he moved wrong and pulled it, but his head was a different story. It felt like someone was back there pounding away with a hammer. Maybe a sledgehammer. He followed Innes's advice and drank the rest of the tea before stretching out on the ground beside Bess and Megan. "Wake me in a few hours and I'll spell you."

"Aye, lad. Don't fash yerself." But Innes knew he wouldn't wake Carson. The man was twice wounded and needed time to recover. Hunter would help him keep watch.

Innes's chest swelled with pride when he looked upon his son and his daughter. What they had done this past night humbled him, for he knew they had done it mainly for him. Because Carson was his friend. They had also done it as a matter of honor. That, too, filled him with pride. Little Raven had declared the captive would be safe. That made it the responsibility of everyone in the band to make certain no harm came to Carson. The honor of the band, the honor of Our People, had been at stake. Hunter and Winter Fawn had given much to uphold that honor.

Guilt assailed him. Guilt for having left them so many years ago. Guilt for deliberately keeping distance between himself and the children he loved more than life.

Ah, damn me hide, I'm a bloody worthless bastard, that I am. He pulled the cork on his flask and settled himself where he could watch the stream. It was going to be a long day.

CHAPTER 5

It was mid-morning before anyone found Two Feathers and cut him free.

Crooked Oak had forced himself to remain in his tepee until the cry went out that the white captive had escaped. Only then would he allow himself to emerge.

He assumed that it had been Red Beard who had hit him over the head the night before. When he had come to it had still been hours before dawn and the white man and Winter Fawn were both gone from the tree where they had been.

Fear had nearly strangled him when Winter Fawn had thrown herself in front of the white man. Never, *never,* had he intended to harm her!

But harm her he had.

He hadn't seen her when he first approached. She had been wrapped in a dark blanket and kneeling in the shadows at the white man's feet. Obviously she had been cutting him free, but when he got her back he would teach her a harsh lesson—she would kneel before no man, except *him.*

He had aimed his arrow—unmarked, so it could not be blamed on him—at the white man's heart. Upon seeing Winter Fawn rise up from the shadows, Crooked Oak had tried to pull his shot, but he was already in the process of firing. The only thing he had been able to do was jerk his aim off slightly at the last instant. If he hadn't, the arrow would have struck Winter Fawn in the middle of her back and killed her. Instead, the arrow meant for the white man had pierced her side.

Shock had deafened him to the approach of someone from behind. All he had heard was the sound of Winter Fawn's soft grunt of pain as his arrow struck her.

She was *his,* and he had shot her!

It was all he'd been able to do to keep from roaring in rage and rushing forward to rip out the white man's liver with his bare hands. This was his fault—the captive's. It was Red Beard's fault. It was Little Raven's fault. Damn them all!

Then pain had exploded in his head and everything went black. He woke sometime later to find the white man and Winter Fawn gone. He dared not go after them. No one must ever learn that he had done this thing, or he would be shunned by his own people.

When he came to, he did not dare go near the tree to study the ground for a sign that might tell him if Winter Fawn yet lived, for he could not afford to have his tracks involved if there was blood on the ground. He could not let it be known that he had been anywhere near the captive during the night.

Man-Above, was Winter Fawn still alive?

She had to be. All his dreams of glory depended upon her becoming his woman. She *must* be alive.

Rage boiled in his blood. Fists clenched, he paced back and forth within the confines of his lodge. It was the white man's fault that Winter Fawn was hurt, possibly dead. Both white men—the captive and Red Beard.

Winter Fawn had been cutting the white man loose. She would never have done such a thing had not her father told her to. She was a good and sweet young woman, biddable—although she could be headstrong, he thought, remembering with fondness the way she had rebuffed his attempt to get her alone in the woods last fall. But she would never have gone against Little Raven's wishes by freeing the captive. That was her father's doing. She was far too loyal to Red Beard. It was unhealthy for a woman to show such loyalty to her father. Such gifts belonged to a woman's husband.

That Winter Fawn was not already Crooked Oak's wife was also the fault of Red Beard. Imagine a man not trusting his wife's family to arrange a good marriage for his daughter. Why, such a thing was preposterous!

Crooked Oak had thought that by refusing to give up his captive he could show Red Beard his strength and honor, thereby winning the man's consent for Winter Fawn to become his wife. Now he saw that such a thing was not possible. He would have to take her without her father's permission. Once she was his, everything else would happen as it should, as he had seen in his vision.

But where was she? Was she even still alive? Fear threatened to strangle him. He had to have her! His destiny—his greatness—would not be recognized without her!

By the time he heard the cry go up that the white captive was gone, Crooked Oak had mastered his rage and fear and was able to rush from his tepee to appear properly shocked.

He would go after them, of course, Winter Fawn, her father, and the other white man. Car-son. That was the name Red Beard had called the captive. Crooked Oak would be as shocked and surprised as everyone else that the captive was gone. As disappointed that Red Beard had obviously helped him.

While he wanted—needed—to rage that Red Beard had involved Winter Fawn in his dishonorable act, he knew he could not, for he could not admit that he knew she was involved.

Crooked Oak did not consider that his own act of attempting to kill the white man, after giving his word he would not, was dishonorable. He should have killed the man out on the trail and never listened to Red Beard. The blood of their fallen hunters cried out for revenge!

To Crooked Oak's furious amazement, most of the camp was merely relieved that the white man was gone. What was the matter with them? Where was their pride? Their honor? Whites had killed their people. Their deaths must be avenged! White men must die!

Little Raven took the news of the captive's escape with a

grim countenance, but Crooked Oak suspected the leader was more relieved than any to have the issue over with.

But it was not over, not for Crooked Oak. He had to get Winter Fawn back, and he had to kill two white men.

The excuse he needed to ride after them fell into his hands like a sand plum overripe and knocked loose by a simple breeze. It was a sign from Man-Above when Two Feathers came running from the woods crying that the captive had escaped and had kidnaped Winter Fawn.

"Kidnaped?" Crooked Oak managed.

"Surely not," Winter Fawn's grandmother confirmed with worry lining her face. "But it is true that she is not to be found this day. The two white girls are gone also."

Two Feathers nodded. "He would take his women and children with him. But Winter Fawn! I do not know if she was alive."

"What do you mean?" Crooked Oak demanded.

"She was unconscious. He carried her in his arms, and there was blood."

"He took her?" her grandmother cried to Two Feathers, who was her son. "She was bleeding?"

Crooked Oak placed a hand on the old woman's shoulder. "Do not worry, Night Bird," he told her solemnly. "Be she dead or alive, I will find her. Who rides with me?" he cried out. "Who rides with me to rescue one of our own who has been wrested from us against her will by a hated enemy?"

Little Raven urged caution. "We must smoke. We must consider what is best to be done."

"Consider, *pah.* This is your fault," Crooked Oak said heatedly.

A murmur of shock and disapproval rose from those nearby at Crooked Oak's blatant disrespect of their leader.

Crooked Oak did not care. Damn them for revering and following a man who spoke always of peace, when war was the only answer. "It is on your head if Winter Fawn is dead. We should have killed the white man yesterday. But no, you wanted to smoke, you wanted to *consider.*" He whirled to face the warriors who had gathered. "I go after Winter Fawn. Do I ride alone?"

"No," Two Feathers said vehemently. "I ride with you. We will get her back, my mother. We will not rest until we find her."

"But if her father is gone, too," said Deer Stalker, Winter Fawn's grandfather, "she may have gone willingly."

"No." Two Feathers shook his head. "She was unconscious and bloody. She was limp in the white man's arms. Red Beard would never have hurt her, nor would he allow anyone else to hurt her. You know how fond he is of the girl."

Deer Stalker nodded gravely. "You speak the truth, my son. Maybe Red Beard woke in the night and discovered them gone. Perhaps even now he and Hunter—for he is gone, too—are trailing the white man to get Winter Fawn back."

Let them think that, Crooked Oak thought. When he caught them, there would be no one left alive to say differently. No one but Winter Fawn, but he knew how to guarantee her silence.

"Let us ride," he cried. "We will catch up with Red Beard and help him find his daughter."

"Let us ride," shouted Long Chin.

"Let us avenge this deed," cried Spotted Calf.

The cry went up, and dog soldiers gathered their weapons. The same six who had ridden out for revenge only the previous morning thundered out of camp within the hour. Crooked Oak led them, as he always did. The others, Two Feathers, Talks Loud, Long Chin, Red Bull, and Spotted Calf, would do his bidding. They would find Winter Fawn. They would kill the white man called Car-son. When Red Beard was accidentally killed in the process, it would be considered a tragedy by some. Crooked Oak would secretly celebrate.

He would have to keep his intentions about Red Beard to himself, however. Two Feathers did not like the man, but would never countenance harming him. He was foolish that way, Two Feathers was, letting such a hindrance as honor get in the way of what needed to be done. But Crooked Oak had been getting around his friend's inconvenient streak of honor for years. This time would be no different.

* * *

Carson woke to realize that sleep in no way mitigated the pain in the back of his head. If anything, it was worse. Innes's snoring nearby did not help. Good God, the man was so loud, he might as well be shouting from the rim of the canyon to announce their presence.

Before Carson could roll to his feet, intent on getting to Innes to nudge him awake, Hunter rushed in from outside and rolled his father onto his side. The snoring stopped instantly.

"He was supposed to wake me to stand watch," Carson said.

"There was no need."

"You took my turn?"

"Aye, and I'd best be gettin' back to it."

When Carson rose, the wound in his side reminded him painfully of its presence. Refusing to favor it, he followed Hunter out of the cave. It was just past noon, with a cool breeze stirring the air. Birds chirped and flitted, darting back and forth from tree to tree. The only other sound was the rush and tumble of water over rock.

They should leave soon. They couldn't afford to lay low until dark. The trail last night had been bad enough, and they were still in the foothills. If they had to head higher, the mountains would be suicide in the dark.

"Will you ever be able to go back?" Carson asked Hunter.

The boy looked away toward the far rim. "I don't know. Probably. One day."

"I'm sorry." Carson said.

"There is no need. I do not do this for you. I do it because it is important to my father."

Carson noted that the boy's Scottish burr was absent now. "And your father is important to you."

Hunter cocked his head and looked at Carson. "Was your father not important to you?"

"He was the most important person in my life. I would have done anything for him."

The boy turned back to watch the rim. "We will need to leave soon. You should wake the others."

"I'll check on your sister first."

Hunter looked at Carson again, this time with worry in his eyes. "She is quiet, but I think a fever comes."

With a silent prayer that the boy was wrong, Carson made his way back to the cave and Winter Fawn's side. She was pale again, as pasty gray as she'd been before the whiskey had temporarily revived her. Gently, so as not to wake her, he touched her forehead.

She was warmer than she would normally be, but not terribly hot. Only a slight fever. Considering the seriousness of her wound, he wouldn't have been surprised to find her burning up. But it had only been a few hours, he thought grimly. The fever could rise.

Her skin beneath his touch was soft and smooth, like dark, living silk. Without realizing what he was doing, he let his fingers stroke her cheek. Here she felt like fine velvet, but warm and alive. Or a rose petal heated by the sun.

My, aren't you getting poetic, old son.

Her eyes opened and stared directly into his, gray eyes so deep and dark that for a moment he felt as if he were drowning in them. "How do you feel?" he asked, keeping his voice low.

She smiled slightly. "Like I've been dragged behind a horse for a few miles."

"Only a few?"

"Only a few."

Carson couldn't help himself. He had to ask again. "Why did you do it?"

Her slight smile faded. "I told you, I dinna know. I didna think about it. I knew when I saw him that it was Crooked Oak. Hunter had already told me that he'd overheard him saying he was going to kill you in the night. 'Tis why I came to cut you free. Crooked Oak, I fear, disnae trouble himself overmuch with a wee thing like honor. Had you been killed after Little Raven said you would be safe, it would have shamed us all. I couldna let him do it."

"You saved my life."

"Maybe. Maybe not. We will never know."

Carson shook his head. "You saved my life. I wish you hadn't been hurt doing it."

"So do I."

"I don't know how to repay you."

"I hope you wouldna insult me by trying to pay me for such a thing. It wasna anything I thought of or planned. It just happened."

"How's me lass doin'?" Innes said from behind him.

Carson had been so intent on Winter Fawn that he hadn't heard Innes stir. Bess, too, he noticed, was awake now and watching.

"She's feverish," Carson said.

"Shall I make more tea?" Bess offered anxiously. "Will that help her?"

"It won't hurt," Carson said. "But it's nearly time to head out again, and she shouldn't be moved."

Innes came and knelt at his daughter's side. Feeling her face for himself, he frowned. "I fear ye've got the right o' it, lad. I'll be stayin' behind with her while the rest o' ye—"

"No," Carson said firmly. "You're right that we should split up, but I want you and Hunter to take the girls and go."

Next to the small fire she'd just rekindled, Bess froze and stared at him.

"The hell ye say," Innes protested.

"We all stand a better chance of getting away clean if we split up."

"That may be," Innes said with a low growl in his throat. "But my place is with me daughter. And yours is with your daughter and sister."

"I know that." Carson plowed his fingers through his hair, then winced. Even touching the top of his head made the back of it hurt where the bullet had grazed him yesterday.

God, had it been only yesterday? It seemed a lifetime ago. Yet every time he closed his eyes he saw those painted warriors bursting out from behind the rocks, yelling and shrieking, shooting at him and the girls. Megan screaming. Bess falling from the wagon. The warrior lifting her by the hair. The memories were so vivid that they could have happened only moments ago.

"Look," he said. "I'm the one they want. If they catch up

with us, they're going to start shooting, and they won't care who else gets hurt. Agreed?"

Innes stared at him through narrowed eyes. "Aye, 'tis the way I figure it."

"But if they come upon you and Hunter and the girls, and I'm not with you, chances are better than average that there won't be any shooting. Right?"

Innes frowned, unable to argue.

"He's right, Da."

Again Carson was taken by surprise. He hadn't heard Hunter return. Hell, he thought with frustration. If he wasn't any more aware of what was going on around him than this, he deserved to get shot.

"The one person they won't risk hurting is Winter Fawn," Hunter said. "Crooked Oak would never allow it, and you know he's the leader of that group. He'll be the most likely to come after us."

"Aye." Innes frowned harder. "Not that I like the idea of throwin' ye to the dogs, so to speak," he said to Carson, "but all of us would be safer if you weren't with us. Winter Fawn should go with us."

"Look at her, man," Carson protested. "She shouldn't be moved so soon. She needs rest."

The object of their discussion stirred. "I'm not so feeble that I canna ride," she protested quietly. "But if we split up, I should ride with Carson."

Innes started to protest, but she cut him off.

"If it is plainly seen that I'm with him, they won't take a chance on hurting me. Hunter is right about that. I might be able to talk them out of killing Carson right then and there."

"Now hold on," Carson protested. "You've stuck your neck out for me more than enough."

Winter Fawn put a hand to her neck and frowned in confusion. "My neck?"

"He means you've taken enough risks for him," Innes said.

"That's right. I would never use you to protect myself," Carson claimed.

"You would rather die?" she asked, one brow arched.

"No, I would rather live. I'd rather all of us live. That's

why we should split up. You and Hunter,'' he said to Innes, ''take the girls and get to the ranch. Tell my men there to round up some help and go back for the wagon and supplies, if they're still there. I can't afford to replace them just now. I'll stay here with Winter Fawn until she's stronger, then I'll get her to a doctor.''

''Nae!'' Innes's protest was sharp and swift.

''I don't need a doctor,'' Winter Fawn said.

''I'll not have ye takin' me lass to some town full of whites who'll spit on her because of the color of her skin. Not when sentiments be running so hot these days against the Indians. It wouldna be safe for her. Besides which, by the time she's stronger, she won't need a doctor. Ye're the only white man I'd trust with her, and only because I trusted yer father with me life, and I'm thinkin', hopin', the apple didna fall far from the tree and that ye're as honorable a man as he was.''

''I will protect her with my life, and expect you to do the same with Bess and Megan.''

''Carson?'' Bess asked, her voice shaking. ''You don't mean to leave us.''

''It's the best way, Bess,'' Carson told her.

''Best?'' she cried. ''How is it best? What if—''

''It's the best way to keep us all safe.'' Please, Lord, he didn't want to deal with one of her petulant fits he'd grown accustomed to on the trip west. Not now, when he needed her cooperation more than ever before. ''I know you're scared. We're all scared. But if you and Megan go with Innes and Hunter, I think we'll all be okay.''

''But I don't want to go without you,'' she pleaded, her eyes round with fear.

''And I don't want you to, honey, but it's the only way I can see for us to all stay safe.'' The plea in her eyes was nearly his undoing. But for her sake and Megan's, he had to hold firm. They would be much safer without him. ''If you and Megan go with Innes and do everything he tells you to do, Winter Fawn and I will meet you at the ranch in a few days. Do you trust me, Bess?''

''You know I do.''

"Then believe me when I say that this is the way it has to be."

Hunter approached and stopped several feet away, but he did not look at Carson. His gaze was for Bess. "I will protect you," he said solemnly. "I—my father and I—will keep you safe."

Before Carson's eyes, Bess seemed to change. The lines of fear on her face altered, shifted, became lines of determination. Her trembling lips firmed. Her shaking hands fisted. Her head raised. Her shoulders straightened.

As Carson watched, his baby sister seemed to cross that invisible threshold from child to adult. It was, he knew, a crossing she would make many times in both directions during the next few years as she grew from girl to woman, but this crossing, this time, both hurt him—because it was so very necessary—and made him proud.

At the same time, something private passed between her and Hunter, something that made Carson feel like an intruder, something that made him want to protest.

"All right," Bess said quietly. "We'll go with Mr. MacDougall and do as he says. I'll look after Megan, and we'll be at the ranch waiting for you when you bring Winter Fawn."

Carson nearly sagged in relief. He rose and crossed to his sister, pulled her into his arms and hugged her. "Thank you," he said with feeling. "I'll make it up to you, I promise."

Bess looked up and gave him a shaky smile. "I'll hold you to that. I'm probably going to want a new dress. Especially if we don't get the wagon back. All my clothes are there, you know."

Carson laughed. "A new dress, it is."

"But Carson," she said, frowning. "If having Winter Fawn with you will keep them from shooting at you, then why would they shoot at us if we're all together? She'll be with all of us. Won't that mean they won't shoot then, too?"

"In theory, yes," he told her. "But—"

"But nothing," Innes interrupted. "The lassie's right, lad. We've missed that fine point, we hae, in all our figuring. Since Winter Fawn says she's up to riding, the safest thing for all of us is to stay together."

Carson gnawed on the inside of his jaw. It sounded right to his head, but his gut urged him to separate himself from the others to keep them safe.

"It's settled, then." Innes uncorked his flask and took a drink. "We stay together."

They shared a quick meal of hardtack and jerky, with more willow bark tea for Winter Fawn. Carson didn't know where the trail would take them before they made it to the ranch, but if they climbed much higher into the mountains there might be no more willows. He cut several small sticks and added them to one of Innes's packs.

As they mounted up to leave, Hunter and Innes worked to erase all traces of their presence in and around the cave.

When they rode out they paired up the same way they had the night before. It was the best distribution of weight for the horses. Innes was the heaviest and Megan the lightest, so pairing them up made sense. It would have been better if Hunter and Winter Fawn rode together, as Bess was some few pounds lighter than Winter Fawn, and having her ride with Carson would have eased the burden slightly for his horse. But the difference was slight, and Winter Fawn was not as strong as she thought. Someone was going to have to hold her in the saddle. Hunter was undoubtedly a strong young man, but he didn't yet have the sinewy strength that came with maturity and rock-hard muscles.

In addition to two people, each horse now also carried water, a blanket, and a rifle or pistol. Everything else stayed on the mule, packed tightly so nothing would rattle.

Carson had added another item to his horse's load. He had folded the buffalo robe into a thick pad and placed it over his thighs and the saddle horn to give Winter Fawn a more comfortable ride. She'd said she could ride behind him, but he knew she wouldn't be able to hold on if they had to make a run for it, so had ignored her overconfident assumption.

The trouble for Winter Fawn was that she wasn't merely seated sideways before him, she was surrounded by him. While she couldn't really feel him against her hips because of the thickness of the buffalo robe, she was still more than aware that she was essentially sitting on his lap. Not since she'd been a small child had she sat on a man's lap, and then it had been her father or grandfather or Uncle Two Feathers.

As Carson held her, her right arm and side pressed flush against him. His upper arm and chest were rock hard with muscles. His right arm rested across her thighs, while his left curved around her back like an iron band, yet it was not uncomfortable. Indeed, that was part of her problem. As awkward as her position was, and as badly as her twin wounds hurt—and they hurt worse with every step the horse took—she found that she liked being held this way by this white man. Within the circle of his arms she was snug and warm in her blanket.

She knew she should not be feeling so content. Her gaze should not linger on his profile. Her head should not long to rest against his shoulder. Her nostrils should not drink in the scent of him.

Winter Fawn closed her eyes. She had left her mother's people, with no idea if or when she might return. She had left her grandmother and grandfather to wonder and worry about what had happened to her. A pang centered in her heart. She did not wish them to worry about her.

But to go with her father, she and Hunter both, was a dream come true for Winter Fawn. From the time he had left them during her twelfth spring, she had prayed for his return.

And he had returned, every year. But only for a few days. Then he would start drinking the white man's whiskey and get a faraway look in his eyes, and he would leave. She had never admitted to herself that her father would probably never again live with Our People, but in her heart she knew it was true.

Yet now here she was, traveling with him and his friends to evade pursuit. It was like the grand adventure stories she had heard around the campfires on long summer nights.

Part of her was jealous, perhaps even a little resentful of this man named Carson Dulaney. Her father risked much to help this man. It seemed to the child inside her that her father cared much more for the son of his dead friend than he did for his own son and daughter. And it hurt.

Yet, if Carson were not so important to her father, she would be asleep in her grandmother's lodge this very moment, and in a few days her father would leave them again, and she would not see him until next spring. In that regard, she was glad for this man who held her so gently in his arms. He had provided her and Hunter with the means to be with their father.

"Hang on," Carson told her.

Looking around, she realized they were about to climb up out of the canyon. Hunter had already done so and waited for them above on the bald, rocky rim.

They would be exposed up there, clearly visible to anyone in the vicinity, she thought.

Then she did not think at all. As the horse lunged up the steep bank, agony, sharp and deep, sliced through her side. It was all she could do to keep from crying out as her vision grayed.

By the time the pain settled down again, they were a couple of miles from the canyon.

"I'm sorry," Carson said. As he had the night before, he spoke softly so that his voice wouldn't carry.

"For what?"

"Your pain."

"My pain," she said, feeling her strength ebb rapidly and resenting it, "is no fault of yours."

"Seeing as how you took that arrow meant for me, I kinda think it is."

She wanted to argue with him, but she was suddenly so incredibly tired. Arguing took too much energy, so she said merely, "Crooked Oak is responsible, not you."

"I agree. But that doesn't make it any easier to see you suffer."

"You have a good heart, Carson Dulaney."

"So do you, Winter Fawn MacDougall. Not many people would have risked so much to help a stranger."

"You have already thanked me," she told him. "You are more than repaying me now."

"How so?"

"My brother told me it was you who carried me from camp."

"That was nothing. You were unconscious."

"It was everything. My father might have taken me to my grandmother and left me there."

"She could have cared for you. You would certainly be more comfortable than you are right now."

"Aye, perhaps. But I would rather be with my father. For that, I thank you."

Carson shook his head. "You could have done without an arrow in your back."

"I will survive."

I hope so, Carson thought fervently. He hoped they all survived.

He was still hoping that near dusk that evening when they stumbled smack into a Cheyenne dog soldiers' camp.

CHAPTER 6

Throughout the afternoon they had gradually angled east, deciding to leave the foothills for the plains, where they could make better time, and travel after dark in relative safety if necessary. At dusk, with the light fading fast, they stopped to rest the horses behind a tumble of boulders and juniper at the head of a long narrow valley that disappeared around a bend some two miles ahead.

According to Innes, the valley widened beyond the bend and opened up onto the plains. There, he said, was a better place of concealment where they could camp for a few hours, or the whole night if they chose. Whoever stood watch would be able to see for miles up and down the trail and across the plains, plus back up the valley where they now stood.

Behind them, up in the mountains, thunder rumbled. When Carson glanced west he saw lightning streak from cloud to cloud. He hoped this shelter Innes led them to would keep the girls dry. The storm would catch up with them soon.

The plan was to rest at the end of the valley for a few hours, then hit the trail south again. By this time tomorrow they would be home.

With the animals rested a short time later, they headed out

again, keeping to the tree line along the edge of the valley so as not to leave a broad flat trail through the tall grass. Winter Fawn, Carson noted, had long since given in to her pain and weakness. She was asleep, uncomfortably so, he was sure, in his arms.

He was more than ready for a little sleep himself. How the hell had he lived through four years of war, which equated with four years of little food and less sleep, not to mention flying bullets? He was just so damn tired.

He'd thought after the surrender at Appomattox that he wouldn't have to fight anymore.

With a smirk, he wondered how he had ever come to be so naive. Here he was again, involved in his own private battle.

But no, he acknowledged, it wasn't private. He was but one small part of the larger conflict between the Indians and all of the Americans coming out to the territories. This, to the ones involved, was nothing less than an all-out war. As he understood the situation, the government was trying to push the Southern Cheyenne and Southern Arapaho completely out of the territory, and the tribes did not want to go. It was a powder keg waiting for a match. And here he was, right smack dab in the middle of it.

For a man who had vowed never to fight again, never to aim his rifle at another human being, he'd picked a hell of a place and time to live.

He just wanted peace. Was that too much to ask?

Not that he was ready to sit in a rocking chair for the rest of his life. That wasn't the kind of peace he sought. He expected to work. Wanted to work. The constant struggle to wrest a living from the land was a war in and of itself. But that was a war he welcomed. He could pit himself against the land and look forward to good times among the bad that awaited every man.

The peace he sought was of the soul. Maybe the heart. Peace from killing. Peace from having to be constantly on guard from a bullet. Peace to provide a safe place to raise his daughter and watch his sister complete the transition from girl to woman.

But first, he must survive this new war he'd stumbled into. And he was tired. Soul-deep weary of fighting other men.

Then again, he thought wryly, the fighting in the Colorado Territory had been going on long before he'd arrived. Yet he had chosen to come anyway. He wondered what that said about the man named Carson Dulaney. Telling himself he wanted peace, then coming to a land filled with war.

His head, and his heart, hurt just thinking about it. He would be wiser to keep his mind on the here and now.

And here and now, there was a woman in his arms who had placed herself between him and certain death. He'd seen men on the battlefield do the same. He knew he would have taken the bullet that had killed his father if he'd been looking and seen it coming. Yet, while Carson had a fair respect for women and their struggle to civilize the world—aside from those like Julia, who left some men with an overwhelming urge to smash something—it was difficult for him to accept that a woman would do such a thing.

Yes, some men would do it without a thought. Others would run. She had not run.

It felt odd to hold her, he realized. Good odd, despite the ache in his arms from having held her all night and half the day. It had been a long time since he'd felt a woman's softness against him. A long time since he'd even thought about it. Maybe Julia hadn't completely soured him on women after all, if he could enjoy the feel of Winter Fawn in his arms.

It was almost dark now, more shadows than light. They rounded the bend in the valley, and from behind, the thunder rolled closer.

Up ahead a horse whinnied.

Carson stiffened. It hadn't been one of their horses. He didn't know why, but none of their animals had made a sound louder than a soft blow all day. This had come from ahead of them, in the trees. And that could only mean trouble.

Innes, in the lead, pulled to an abrupt halt, as did Carson, and behind him, Hunter. The muscles across Carson's shoulders tightened. He reached for the rifle in its scabbard.

In his arms, Winter Fawn stirred.

He leaned down to her ear and whispered, "Shh. There's trouble."

As quietly as possible, they started backing their horses and turning around.

Then came the murmur of a man's voice, followed by a shout in a language Carson did not understand.

At the sound, Innes spun his horse around and urged it into a gallop. Carson didn't wait for an invitation to do the same.

Behind them came more shouts and neighs, the sounds of startled horses, and men mounting to ride.

"Cheyenne," Winter Fawn cried softly.

The escapees raced back around the bend and up the valley toward the only cover in sight, the stand of juniper and boulders where they had rested the horses only a short time ago. This time they didn't bother keeping to the tree line but barreled straight up the middle of the valley.

Carson fell back, letting Hunter pass him. Ahead, Megan was protected by Innes's broad back. Winter Fawn, too, was sheltered in Carson's arms. But Bess rode behind Hunter, her back exposed to the pursuers. He angled to put himself between her and disaster if shooting started.

Carson swore silently as he clutched Winter Fawn tightly and urged his horse on. For now his rifle was useless. He couldn't turn and fire at their pursuers while holding Winter Fawn. He crammed the carbine back into the scabbard and wished futilely for his pistol.

The ground stretched out before them, open and bare of anything to use for cover. Behind them the pursuers, shouting and shooting, were gaining. Ahead, the storm raced to meet them.

Finally, in a flash of lightning, the tumble of rocks and juniper appeared out of the shadows. Innes reached the shelter first. Rifle in one hand and Megan tucked beneath his other arm, he scrambled from the horse.

Megan's shriek of fear cut through Carson like a knife. Damn his hide, why had he brought the girls? Why had he let his father infect him with enthusiasm for a land and way of life Carson was obviously ill suited to deal with?

Why did it seem like everyone in this godforsaken territory was out to kill him?

He reached the dubious shelter of the rocks as Hunter leaped from his horse. The mule thundered in right after him.

The sound of rifle fire split the night as Innes cut loose.

The loudness of it shocked Megan into abrupt silence. Hunter took her from his father and handed her up to Bess, whom he ordered to stay mounted. Quickly the boy led that horse and his father's, now riderless, deeper into the thick cover of cedars. Then he dashed back to hold Winter Fawn upright while Carson dismounted.

"I'm all right," Winter Fawn said breathlessly. "Leave me. Do what you must."

Carson took her at her word, grabbed his rifle and ammunition pouch, and crawled up into the rocks several yards from Innes.

The Cheyenne had scattered at Innes's first shot, but they were still out there, slightly darker shadows flitting around other shadows.

Carson would have sworn—had sworn—that there was no cover out there for man nor beast, yet somehow the Cheyenne seemed to disappear before his eyes. But they were still there. He could hear them. Feel them.

While Carson and Innes crouched, rifles at the ready to repel an attack, Hunter helped Winter Fawn shift in the saddle until she sat astride. He led her horse back into the trees where he'd left the others.

In the dark shadows there, brother and sister shared a long, silent look. They did not need words to know each other's thoughts in that moment. The Cheyenne were friends of Our People. Had always been their friends. The two tribes camped together, hunted buffalo together, fought other tribes and white soldiers together. They married each other, lived with each other, prayed to the same God.

Yet their father, to protect Carson and the girls, would shoot them.

The very foundation of Winter Fawn's and Hunter's world was crumbling around them. They had left Our People, and now fought their friends.

But in each other's eyes they read the truth. They would go where their father led them. Anywhere. Any time. His world would become theirs. Maybe someday they would go back to their mother's people. But for now, "their people" would be each other and their father, Innes Red Beard MacDougall of the clan MacDonald from a place called Scotland that was so far away, they could not even conceive of the distance. Winter Fawn and Hunter, in that moment, felt as far away from their own world as their father was from Scotland.

Around them, shadows grew deeper, the gray light darker as night slid down the mountain behind them. Thick clouds rolled in from the west and blocked out the sky overhead. Hunter moved away and whispered into the ear of each horse and the mule. Asking them to be silent, Winter Fawn thought, in awe of her brother's magical ability to talk to horses.

A good thing, too, she thought. She was so tense she must surely be communicating her fear to the poor horse who had carried her extra weight all day.

Bess and Megan sat their horse in petrified silence. Winter Fawn ached for them. She, too, was afraid, but not for herself. Even if the Cheyenne were foolish enough to rush them, she did not believe that she or Hunter would be deliberately harmed. Bess would hold no such belief for herself or Megan. Winter Fawn ached for them.

And she ached for the way Carson worried over them, the blame he placed upon himself for their current circumstances. He had not admitted these things to her, but she read them in his eyes, in the grim set of his mouth. He seemed a good man, this Carson Dulaney. He must be a good man for her father to befriend him and risk so much for him.

The two of them stood now, rifles in hand, to protect their families. She wondered what Carson was thinking just then.

What he was thinking was that the Cheyenne really had disappeared this time. Maybe they hadn't expected to be fired on. Maybe it hadn't seemed worth the risk to cross that open ground and straight into gunfire. Carson didn't care what their reasons were. He was just damn glad they were gone and hoped they stayed that way.

The small juniper grove, studded with huge boulders and flat rocks, butted up against the side of a high bluff. The trees weren't thick enough to completely conceal them, but it was the closest thing to real cover unless they backtracked into the mountains. It would have to do.

Innes crawled down from the rocks, then, after a few minutes, returned. "Hunter is rigging up me canvass tarp for a shelter. It's gonna rain like the great flood any minute. Willna last long, though. It'll just give us a good soaking."

"And wipe out our tracks."

"Aye." Innes grinned. "There is that. Looks like the Cheyenne decided to go look for easier pickings."

"Looks like."

"We might as well all get some rest while we can. I'll take the first watch."

"Only if you promise to wake me for my turn this time."

"Aye, I'll do it. I'm thinking that if things stay quiet, we'd be just as well off staying here until morning."

"No argument here. I'd just as soon not stumble into them in the dark again, in case they haven't gone far."

"My thinking exactly," Innes said.

After a few minutes of assuring himself that nothing more than a bird and a prairie dog stirred out in the open, Carson pushed himself to his feet. "I'll go stretch out for a while. Wake me in a couple of hours."

He waited until he had Innes's agreement, then turned and helped Hunter finish rigging the tarp to keep the girls as dry as possible. Hunter had already cleared a few low branches from three junipers that stood close together. They pulled and tied several waist-high limbs together to form a living tent, then draped the tarp over the branches and tied it in place, anchoring the sides to the ground with the heavy packs from the mule. Beneath the crude shelter they spread Innes's rubber groundsheet, then a blanket.

"Come on, girls," he called softly to Bess and Megan as he approached them in the semidarkness. "Crawl in here and see if you can stay dry. It's going to rain any minute."

Bess and Megan crawled eagerly into the small, living cave. "It's like a playhouse," Megan proclaimed, her blue eyes wide with wonder.

Carson shook his head at his daughter's irrepressible spirit.

"What about Winter Fawn?" Bess asked Carson.

"I'm going to bring her in here with you, so make room."

Carson crossed to the spot where Winter Fawn lay on the buffalo robe. He'd expected to find her asleep, if not outright unconscious, but her gray eyes were open and watching him. He felt her face and found it no warmer than it had been that morning. Relieved, he smiled. "How are you doing?"

"I'm all right. How are the girls?"

His lips twitched. "Megan is inspecting her new playhouse. You've been invited to join them."

"Oh, but you should be the one—"

"I won't leave you out here in the rain," he interrupted.

"Maybe it won't rain. Sometimes it just blows—" A fat, hard raindrop hit her in the eye.

Carson chuckled and scooped her up in his arms. "You were saying?"

When he stood, his side reminded him of the newest holes there. He let out a slight grunt.

"I am too heavy for you to carry. Put me down. I can walk."

"Your wound is much worse than mine," he reminded her. "You shouldn't be up walking around. And you don't weigh as much as my saddle."

"Ah," she said with a slow nod. "So my father has spoken the truth."

"What truth? That you don't weigh much?"

"That white men lie. Your saddle. Hmph."

Chuckling, Carson knelt and laid her on the blanket beside Megan. He ducked out of the shelter and retrieved the buffalo robe and tucked it over the three of them. It was raining in earnest now.

"You'll be careful, won't you, honey?" he asked Megan. "This is Winter Fawn's hurt side. You won't bump into her, will you?"

"Oh, no, Daddy. I might hurt her if I did that."

He leaned down and kissed his daughter's nose. "You're a good girl, Megan Dulaney."

Megan giggled. "You're a good boy, Daddy."

"We can make room for you," Bess told him. "For all of you."

Carson gave his sister a smile. "Thanks, but we'll be fine. Don't worry about us."

"But you'll get wet."

"It won't be the first time. Maybe I'll find a bar of soap in one of those packs and get clean in the rain."

Winter Fawn watched him leave. Through the opening of the shelter she saw him drape a blanket over his head and lay on the ground that was already wet.

She rolled to her uninjured side to make more room for Bess and Megan. The movement pulled on her wound. She bit her tongue on a moan. She lay still, and as one moment stretched into the next, the pain eased.

Thunder crashed directly overhead. Winter Fawn flinched. Megan let out a faint squeak of fright, while Bess clapped her hands over her ears.

The three looked at each other in the dimness of the shelter, and smiled.

"It scared me," Megan said.

"I think it scared all of us," Winter Fawn told her. And if Winter Fawn didn't distract herself somehow, it would scare her again. She hated storms, feared them. To her they meant something terrible was going to happen.

If she let herself think about it she would transmit her fear to Bess and Megan. She would think, instead, of the stories her father used to tell her when she was a child. Stories of a great wide ocean that took weeks to cross. Stories of huge cities full of people and buildings and noise and stench. Stories of white people and their odd ways.

Winter Fawn wondered if she might not have been happier if her father had never told her what life was sometimes like for white people.

He had told her that many white people never knew war, never had to watch their men ride out to fight and die. White people in general did not live at all the way Our People did. They lived in permanent shelters called houses. They did not move from place to place with the seasons, did not follow the buffalo. They stayed in one spot and raised animals and crops for their food.

All her life Winter Fawn had heard these fantastical stories from her father. From the time of around her tenth winter, she began to wonder what it might be like to stay in one place season after season. A home, that was what he had called it. A place that was all yours, where a man and woman raised their children and their children's children. A place to plant seeds in the ground and watch them sprout and grow into food to feed your family. Land that another tribe or the white man's army or white settlers could never take away from you as long as you were strong enough to hold it.

Winter Fawn longed to know what that was like, staying in one place season after season. The little valley where her band usually wintered was her favorite place. She had dreamed of being able to stay there through the seasons. She wanted to know what the cottonwoods along the stream looked like in full summer. Were there wildflowers in the valley? Did it hold the heat in summer, or was there a cool breeze?

She had dreamed of her father taking her to the cabin he'd told her about, where he lived nearly all year, in the mountains called Sierra Blancas. Dreamed of learning all the different seasons of one place.

Maybe she would not like living in one place all the time. Maybe she was too much of her mother's people to live in the way of her father's. But she wanted the chance to know. In order for that to happen, they must elude Crooked Oak and get Carson and Bess and Megan to their ranch.

Being forced to ride into the mountains, then back down through the hills, was slowing them down. Winter Fawn herself was slowing them down because of her wound. Riding in front of Carson as she had been could have gotten him killed just now. He needed to have both hands free to manage the horse and perhaps his rifle. He did not need a weak woman draped across him who could not even sit a horse.

She glanced out of the shelter, but all she could see now was darkness. Inside the tent Megan and Bess had fallen asleep.

No one was watching. No one could see her if they were. This was her only chance. She would not even try what she was about to try if not for the others. She may have slipped many times over the years and done what her father had forbidden her to do, but not for herself. For her grandmother. For Hunter once. For Bess. Never for herself.

This time, if it worked, would be for them, because the weakness caused by her wound was putting them all in danger. It might not even work. She'd never tried it on herself before.

With a deep breath for calm, she placed her hand over the thick pad covering the front wound. Closing her eyes, she concentrated, searching out the wound. She could feel it in her side, of course, and with her hand, but she needed to connect with it in her mind.

Concentrate. Concentrate.

The warmth was there in her hand, but the sharp stab of pain, twice as strong as it had been, broke her concentration. It was all she could do to keep from crying out, the pain was so great.

She took several slow, deep breaths, and, after a moment, tried again.

Once more the pain multiplied to an unbearable level. She clamped her jaw tight and tried to concentrate past it. Sweat broke out across her face. Black spots appeared before her eyes and grew until there was nothing but blackness. She fell headlong into it and passed out.

Innes kept his promise and woke Carson for his turn at guard duty. As Carson stood his watch, the clouds moved out and left the sky clear. He sat in the rocks and shivered in clothes soaked by the storm he had slept through. He thought about a warm fire, hot coffee, a soft bed. Clear gray eyes and womanly curves.

Enough of that. Even if it did warm him better than his other thoughts.

He thought, too, of standing his watch until morning and letting Hunter sleep, but it was a bad idea and he knew it. After only about three hours, by his reckoning, he was already starting to nod off. That's all they needed was for him to fall asleep on watch and let the Cheyenne—or the Arapaho—sneak up on them.

Besides, he thought as he climbed down to wake Hunter,

the kid was young enough that he probably wouldn't miss the sleep. Carson's own twenty-eight years weren't all that many, but on this night every one of them seemed to weigh on his shoulders like a load of bricks.

After waking Hunter, he stretched back out on his soggy blanket on the soggy ground and fell asleep.

He felt like he'd barely nodded off when Innes shook him awake at dawn. "Get everybody up and ready to ride," he said in a low, urgent voice.

Carson sat up, instantly awake. "What's wrong?"

"Riders heading this way. Looks like maybe half a dozen."

Carson swore under his breath and got to his feet.

Hunter led the pack mule from concealment and tied her next to the canvas shelter.

Quietly Carson woke Winter Fawn and the girls. Everyone scrambled to help, even Megan, who held his canteen for him while he saddled his horse.

When the pack mule was loaded, Carson climbed into the rocks where Innes crouched watching the approaching riders through binoculars. Carson could see men on horseback, but as they were nearly two miles away, at the bend in the valley, he couldn't tell anything about them. Except that they were getting closer to this scant hiding place by the second.

"Is it Cheyenne or Arapaho?"

"Arapaho. That be Crooked Oak in the lead."

"Take the girls and Hunter and go," Carson urged.

"The hell you say."

"I'll hold them off from here. If you go now, you should be able to keep ahead of them long enough to get to that far ridge."

"And be down to two guns? And expect me son to shoot at his uncle? Nae. If there's gonna be any shooting at that bunch, it'll be you and me wot does it. I'll not ask that of the lad."

"Dammit, man, you agreed yesterday that if I'm not with you there probably won't be any shooting."

Innes swore. "Winter Fawn can't ride on her own."

"She said they wouldn't hurt her."

"We're all stayin'. If we have to make a stand, better here than out in the open."

This time Carson swore. The hell of it was, they were both right. Carson did not have the right to determine if Winter Fawn stayed or went. But if he stayed, either she would have to stay with him, or Megan or Bess would, because Innes and Hunter could not carry the three females with them on two horses.

They could always put Megan with Hunter, and Bess on Carson's horse, leaving Innes free to carry Winter Fawn. Of course, that left Carson afoot, something he did not care to be with a half-dozen Arapahos after his scalp. Besides, Bess didn't have the skill to ride alone on horseback during what would surely turn into an all-out run for freedom.

One of them could ride the mule, but they'd lose most of the supplies to make room for a rider. And again, Winter Fawn was too weak, and Bess too unskilled to ride alone.

As the sun started up over the trees, Carson crouched beside Innes and watched the riders draw closer toward their hiding place. Even the birds in the trees seemed to know something was about to happen, for they ceased their flitting and chirping.

It grew so quiet that Carson caught himself glancing over his shoulder to be sure Hunter and the girls were still there.

They were, of course, along with Hail Mary and the horses. Hunter was moving from horse to horse, stroking their muzzles and whispering in their ears. Carson wondered what the boy found to say to the animals that he spoke to them so often, and so privately.

"This time he's probably asking them to be quiet."

At the sound of Innes's voice, Carson nearly jumped. "What?"

"You asked what he was saying to the horses."

Carson shook his head. He hadn't realized he'd spoken aloud.

" 'Tis said a horse understands the Arapaho tongue."

"What about you?" Carson asked, returning his gaze to the riders now less than a mile away. "You speak Arapaho. Do horses understand you?"

"Not like they do him. 'Tis a gift he has, the whisperin'."

Down the valley, the riders slowed, but kept coming. They were only a half mile away now. Carson felt sweat gather between his shoulder blades. He felt the back of his head throb.

He felt . . . he felt like a duck sitting in the middle of a pond surrounded by hunters.

He checked his rifle and made sure the percussion cap was over the nipple and ready to fire. The cartridge he'd loaded the night before was still in the barrel.

He glanced behind him and realized that Hunter had moved the horses and mule farther back into the trees again, where they would be harder to spot. Carson hoped that gift of his with horses worked and worked damn good to keep them quiet. He prayed the wind wouldn't come up and carry their scent to the other horses.

Damn, he hated this. As much as he didn't want to fight, this hiding was worse somehow.

Closer and closer the riders came. He could hear their voices now, but couldn't understand them.

If they kept heading in the same direction to ride up and out of the valley, they would pass within two hundred yards. Too close. Too damn close.

Suddenly the warriors pulled their horses to a stop. They were close enough that Carson could easily identify them now. He eased the barrel of his rifle into a notch in the rocks.

The Indians appeared to be arguing among themselves.

"What are they saying?" Carson whispered to Innes.

"They're arguing over which direction they should take. Crooked Oak wants to go back the way they came. The others want to go south, then west into the mountains. Our tracks out of camp led west. They think we kept heading that way."

The argument heated. There was shouting and pointing, and one of the men motioned toward the shelter of the rocks where Carson and the others were.

Carson held his breath. What was that old children's story about the emperor and his clothes? Any minute now someone was going to point out that he was naked. Any minute the Arapaho would spot them, or ride toward the trees to rest their horses in the shade.

He had been in worse situations during the war. Less cover. No cover. Thousands of men shooting at him instead of a half dozen that might or might not notice him. But he hadn't had Bess and Megan with him.

Suddenly one rider—Crooked Oak—broke from the others. With an angry shout over his shoulder at his comrades, he trotted his horse toward the trees.

Carson got him in his sights and waited.

The other riders shouted and galloped off back the way they had come.

A dozen yards from the escapees' hiding place, Crooked Oak drew his horse up. For a long moment he sat there. Just sat there, staring toward the rocks. Staring straight at him, Carson would have sworn.

Then, with a look of disgust, Crooked Oak turned his horse away and rode after the others.

Neither Carson nor Innes moved, other than to turn and watch as Crooked Oak caught up with his friends. In less than a minute they had disappeared around the curve of the valley.

"'Twas a wee bit closer than I like," Innes said as he lowered his rifle, "but it'll do."

Slowly Carson pulled his rifle from the notch. "Let's get the hell out of here before they change their minds and come back."

"You'll be gettin' no argument from me, lad. I'm all for it." Innes turned and signaled to Hunter.

The boy led the animals out of their deep cover. Megan was already mounted.

"Look, Daddy, I'm—"

"Shh," Carson cautioned. Softly he said, "We have to be quiet, honey."

"I'm riding," she said in a loud whisper. "All by myself."

"You sure are." He went to her side and touched her cheek. "And I'm proud of you, honey. Are you ready to go?"

With an irrepressible grin, Megan nodded her head vigorously. Her braids, which Bess had obviously redone recently, bounced.

Innes swung up behind her.

Hunter mounted his horse. He held out his hand to Bess, and offered his foot for her to step on. Carson grasped her waist and gave her a boost up.

Then he turned to his own horse and reached for Winter Fawn.

"No." She backed away from him. "I'm riding behind today."

"You can't, Winter Fawn. You're not strong enough."

"I am not so weak that I canna sit up and hold on. If I grow tired I will tell you."

"We're going to do some hard riding. There may not be a chance to stop."

"Then we shouldna be wasting time arguing about it. I willna let you cradle me again. You need both hands free. Last night we were lucky."

She was right, Carson knew, on all counts. He needed to be able to use the rifle if necessary. He had cursed his inability to do so last night. And they were wasting time. "All right, but if you start feeling weak, you tell me."

"I will tell you."

When he saw how much it hurt her to mount behind him, he regretted giving in to her. But if she could hold on, they would be better off.

Innes led the way out of the rocks and headed south through the woods and over the ridge into the next valley, much smaller than the last one.

The ground they traveled was wet from the rain. It took the hoofprints of the horses and mule deep and held them, a trail of unmistakable tracks for anyone to see. And follow.

Which was exactly what Crooked Oak and the others did when, after finding no sign of the ones they pursued, they decided to go back into the hills to search.

When they came upon the fresh hoofprints in the mud, Crooked Oak instantly recognized the tracks of Red Beard's horse and mule. They were as familiar to him as the tracks of his own mounts. He shouted with excitement. "It is them! Let us ride hard, my friends."

They followed the trail over the ridge, up one valley and down another. Man-Above must surely be smiling upon Crooked Oak again. Now he could catch Winter Fawn, kill the whites, and return with scalps.

Then, with Winter Fawn beside him, his true destiny would unfold for all to see.

Yes, he thought some time later, Man-Above must indeed

be smiling on him. The tracks were so fresh, his prey was only minutes ahead.

Inside, Crooked Oak rejoiced. All would be his!

They crested another ridge and saw them there, Red Beard, Hunter, the white man and his two girls, and Winter Fawn, less than a mile ahead.

Crooked Oak could not contain himself. He let out a wild, shrill whoop. "We ride, my friends! To victory for Our People!"

CHAPTER 7

While waiting his turn to cross the stream, Carson felt the skin on the back of his neck crawl. It was a narrow stream, but the banks were steep and rocky, offering few places to cross. Innes went first, letting his horse pick its way carefully over the slick, shifting rocks in the rushing water, then up the gravel slope on the other side and into the pines.

Hunter followed his father's path. When he left the water and started up the gravel slope, Innes had to retreat farther into the trees to get out of the way. There wasn't room on that small knob of land for more than one horse.

Winter Fawn had yet to say anything. Carson had been surprised and impressed that she had managed to sit upright all morning. He knew she had to be at the end of her strength, as well as in considerable pain, but she had not uttered a single word of complaint.

Carson lifted the reins to urge his horse down to the stream, but suddenly Winter Fawn hissed in a sharp breath and squeezed him hard around the waist. "Look behind us," she whispered.

Carson twisted and glanced over his shoulder. The sight of the six warriors sweeping down on them from scarcely a half mile downstream chilled his blood.

"Hurry," he said urgently. "Get down."

"No! They will kill you!"

He tried to pull her arm from around his waist. "They're likely to kill you by accident trying to get to me. Get down. Now," he ordered sharply.

"If I stay here," she told Carson urgently, "they will come here for me. My father willna leave me. You dinna want them near Bess and Megan. We are all better off if I go with you."

Pausing on the opposite bank, Hunter turned to watch Carson's crossing. But he wasn't crossing. The man was arguing with Winter Fawn. Then, with a glance downstream, Hunter saw the riders and understood. Carson was trying to make Winter Fawn get down. He would take off and lead the warriors away from the rest of them. It was a good plan. But Winter Fawn was not cooperating.

Hunter knew his sister was right. Yes, Crooked Oak surely wanted to kill Carson. What no one had said aloud was that it was very likely that Crooked Oak might not be over-sorrowed if everyone who helped Carson escape—everyone but Winter Fawn—were to be killed. Hunter believed their father was in almost as much danger as Carson.

"Go," he called across the stream. "Take her. We will guard your sister and daughter. Go now, while you can."

From his spot deeper in the trees, Innes could not see what was happening. "What the hell?"

With the warriors drawing nearer every second, Carson knew he had to make a decision immediately. There was no choice, really. If he crossed that stream, they would all be caught. If he took off, chances were good that the warriors would follow him. Bess and Megan would be safe.

Winter Fawn would not.

"Dammit," he said to no one in particular.

Across the stream, Innes had worked his horse up beside Hunter's. The Scotsman squinted and stared at the approaching warriors. "Aye, lad," he called to Carson, "be gone with ye. You take care of my lass, and I'll take care of yours."

Bess, her eyes wide with fear, stared from behind Hunter's shoulder. She sought reassurance from Carson, then looked to

Hunter. When the boy nodded to her, she looked back at her brother. "Go, Carson. Stay safe."

God, Carson thought, when had his baby sister become so brave? What if he was wrong to leave them?

But he wasn't wrong. His instincts told him they would all be safer if he led the warriors away. His only hesitation was Winter Fawn. If she was right that Crooked Oak would come for her—and from all the talk, he had to believe it—then he would not leave her behind. He didn't want to give the warriors any excuse to get near Bess and Megan.

Not that she was cooperating in staying behind anyway. With a final look to Innes, Carson nodded sharply and waited while Innes and Hunter disappeared into the trees.

"Hold on tight," he told Winter Fawn. He lifted the reins and looked back downstream to make certain the warriors saw him.

God, he hoped he was doing the right thing.

"What are we waiting for?" Winter Fawn demanded.

"To make sure they see me and follow."

"If they get any closer, you will end up following them," she cried.

Despite everything, Carson chuckled. If it sounded a little grim, that was to be expected. Outrunning the warriors did not seem likely. Yes, they may have ridden many miles farther, but Carson and Winter Fawn had ridden double, and their horse was carrying the extra weight of a heavy Western saddle. Carson guessed that more than made up for the fewer miles his horse had traveled.

Then there was the fact that the warriors undoubtedly knew this country intimately. They had traveled it, hunted it, raided throughout it. Carson knew north from south and could find his ranch, but since he wasn't about to lead them there, he would need to lose their pursuers, who were, he'd been told, expert trackers. Losing them, he feared, was going to take some doing. He'd been in these mountains before, but to say he knew his way around in them was to exaggerate.

It was a fool's errand if ever there was one. The horse was tired, Winter Fawn was weak and in pain, Carson was a newcomer to the territory, being chased by experts.

He would hope that the warriors would follow him so that Innes could get the girls to safety. He wouldn't, couldn't bring himself to hope for much more than that.

To get to the ranch, Innes would have to head south.

Carson turned his horse north. "Okay, boy, let's see what you've got." He wasn't sure if he was talking to the horse, or himself. With a glance at the approaching warriors, he pulled his rifle from its sheath and held it over his head. With a wild Rebel yell, he loosed the reins and turned the horse north along the ridge, away from Bess and Megan, away from nearly all that was left of his family, toward an unknown, uncertain, and quite likely short-lived future.

But, by God, he wouldn't go down without a fight. For a man who was sick of war and fighting, he was surprisingly eager to stand and fight. This running away, even though it was for the sake of the girls, ate at him.

Ahead, the ridge ended abruptly at a rock wall. With a glance behind to make sure the warriors had taken his bait, Carson guided the animal down the north side and headed out of the foothills and into the mountains.

Winter Fawn held on tight, clinging to his back like a burr on a dog. If she fell off, Carson would stop and come back for her, she knew. And they would be caught. And he would die. She had no fear for her own safety at Crooked Oak's hands. He wanted her too badly to risk harming her. But he would kill Carson. Of that she was certain.

Beneath her the ground fell away one minute, rose sharply the next. The ground was rocky and uneven. She twisted to look behind them for the warriors, and vowed not to do it again when black spots of pain danced before her eyes. She held on tight and did her best to block out the screaming pain in her side.

Carson had no such problem with looking back. As soon as he'd put a hill between him and the pursuers, he hit a small creek that wound between two hills. He followed it as it twisted back and forth. They left it once, then he backed the horse back into the water, hoping to at least delay the others while they figured out what he'd done.

After about a half mile he found what he'd been hoping

for—a patch of gravel that led out of the water. He didn't figure he was fooling anybody, but he would do what he could to slow them down.

Suddenly from behind came the sound of fast hooves scrambling over rock.

They couldn't have caught them so easily!

With blood pounding in his ears, Carson angled behind a pile of boulders that had tumbled down the hillside sometime in the past. Behind their protection, he drew the horse to a halt, then spun him toward the oncoming threat. He raised his rifle and aimed at the spot where they would have to emerge from the tall scrub.

The crashing grew louder. They were making no attempt to sneak up on him, Carson noted ruefully. They were pretty damn certain of their victory over one man.

"Slide down," Carson said quietly to Winter Fawn. "Climb into those rocks and take cover."

"No."

"Dammit, Winter Fawn, do it!"

"I willna," she cried softly, wishing fervently that she was in front of him on the saddle once again. If she was in front, they would not shoot at him. She knew they would not.

Why she felt so strongly about saving this man, she did not know. She had gone to help him, to cut him free, because he was her father's friend. Surely she had done enough, cutting him loose, getting shot for her efforts. Yet something deep inside compelled her to do more.

Something had happened to her when she had been pinned to him by Crooked Oak's arrow. When she had looked up into the white man's eyes, something inside her had moved. Opened up. Taken him in. He had somehow become a part of her. She could no more hide in the rocks and let him face this danger alone than she could stop the sun from its daily march across the sky.

"I willna cower in the rocks while you face them alone."

Carson swore in frustration. He should have thrown her from the saddle when he'd first spotted the warriors.

He had a fleeting wish for one of those new repeating rifles, then there was no time for thought.

The crashing and scrambling drew nearer, grew louder. Winter Fawn's arms around his waist hugged tighter.

Carson's finger slid to the trigger of his Maynard. His palms were damp, but his hands were steady. His hands were always steady during battle. That, at least, had not changed, and he was grateful.

The brush before him parted.

He sighted down the barrel. His finger tightened on the trigger.

Innes's pack mule burst through the brush.

Carson slipped his finger off the trigger and jerked the rifle barrel into the air. "Hail Mary." He wasn't sure if it was the mule's name he was saying, or a prayer. "She'll either keep us alive with the supplies on her back, or get us killed by trailing behind and adding to our tracks, making us more visible."

The mule snorted, then ambled over and lipped the gelding's muzzle. It looked like a kiss.

"She will not trail behind," Winter Fawn said, her voice thin. "I have heard my father say many times that she is faster than the horse."

"What's this?" Carson nudged the mule until he could reach the pouch that had been tied on top of one of the packs. It hadn't been there before. He snared the bag and opened it.

"Bless that Scotsman's red head. He sent us his binoculars."

"This is good?"

"This is damn good." They weren't out of trouble by a long shot. The warriors were still back there, and probably getting closer by the second. But for the first time in a long while, Carson felt as if perhaps the situation was not quite as hopeless as he'd feared. "How are you holding up?" he asked Winter Fawn.

"Holding up what?"

He smiled to himself. "How are you feeling? How's your wound?"

"I am all right."

Carson doubted it, but there wasn't much he could do for her at the moment. They needed to put more distance between themselves and the warriors. It would be dark in a few hours. This was not the type of terrain in which a man wanted to ride horseback in the dark. All they needed was for the horse to stumble on a rock and break a leg.

"Come on, then, Hail Mary. Let's get out of here."

They climbed ever upward, using stream beds where possible to conceal their tracks. Hail Mary followed directly behind the horse like a trained pup. The sun wasn't quite down yet, but the air was cooling rapidly. Mountain peaks loomed ahead, treacherous, forbidding, their tops covered in snow.

Carson had a great respect for mountains. Their majesty was awe-inspiring. He loved their wildness, their strength. He just wished he had more experience in crossing them.

He'd be a fool to head for the peaks. He knew next to nothing about traveling in mountains this early in the year. It would be too ironic to escape the Arapaho warriors, only to die on the mountains due to his own ignorance.

Junipers and scrub oak gave way again to pines. The sun set; shadows lengthened. The air chilled. Against Carson's back, Winter Fawn shivered harder each minute. It wasn't really cold enough for her to be shivering that hard. It had to be caused more by her wound than the weather. He needed to warm her. She needed rest.

In the shelter of some pine trees, he drew the horse to a halt. "Wait here." Taking the binoculars, he swung his right leg over the horse's ears—he was getting damned good at that, he thought with a touch of humor—and slid to the ground.

Hail Mary was right there with them. She hadn't fallen more than a few yards behind since she'd joined them on this trek. Carson unstrapped the buffalo robe and wrapped it around Winter Fawn.

This was the first good look he'd gotten of her face all day. Her paleness shook him. She was nearly as white as Bess or Megan. Even her lips were pale. In the dim light of dusk, the dark, heavy circles under her eyes stood out like half circles of black paint on a warrior's face. She tried to smile at him, but couldn't quite pull it off, and it hurt him somewhere deep inside.

"Can you move up into the saddle?" His voice was huskier than it should have been. "Or do you need help?"

Winter Fawn pulled the buffalo robe snugly around her shoulders, grateful for the sudden warmth, and bit her bottom lip. It stung her pride to realize she probably had not enough strength to accomplish something so simple as slipping up over the back of the saddle and into the seat, but she feared it was true. Yet the thought of him putting his hands on her waist to help her made her want to try the move on her own. In touching her waist, he would not be able to avoid touching her wound, and she feared she would faint if the pain grew any worse.

When she didn't answer or make a move, Carson settled the matter by grasping her gently but firmly by the hips and lifting her over the cantle and into the seat of the saddle.

Winter Fawn sucked in a sharp breath, but he hadn't touched her wound, and the pain had not been nearly as bad as she'd feared.

He placed the reins in her hands. "I'm going to take a look at our back trail. I'll be right back."

Carson forced himself to turn away from the pain in her eyes. He slipped through the trees as quietly as possible until he came to a rocky outcropping that overlooked the narrow valley below. Through the binoculars he studied the area. He knew the warriors were there somewhere. He wanted to know where. If his efforts at disguising his trail were not slowing the Indians down, he would stop wasting his time and just go for speed.

There. What was that? A flash of movement. He lowered the binoculars to gauge the distance and figured it to be a couple of miles. If that was them, he had successfully put a little extra distance between them, but not enough. Not nearly enough.

He raised the glasses to find the spot of movement again. There. That was it. They were about to break through the tree line and into a small clearing barely visible over the next grove.

Deer.

Carson swore in frustration and relief. Frustration that he hadn't found the warriors, relief that they were not as close as two miles. Unless he was just missing them.

Dammit, where were they?

A hawk flew through his view, close enough to appear huge through the binoculars, close enough to startle him.

Great. Now he was jumping at birds.

There. Another half mile back. One, two, three, four riders. Either the other two had turned back, or he'd simply missed them.

Two and a half miles. Not far enough. Not nearly far enough.

Carson jogged back to the horse and mounted behind Winter Fawn. "Are you warmer?"

"I am fine."

He snorted in disbelief. "I think you'd say that if you were half-dead."

"Did you see them?"

"I saw them. Less than three miles back. I'm sorry. I want to build a fire to warm you and make more willow bark tea, but if we stop now, they'll catch us."

"Do not stop," she urged. "Not for me. I am fine."

He didn't believe her, but he did not argue. There was no choice. They kept traveling. Carson pushed the horse as fast as he could over the trackless hills and into the mountains themselves before he found a good—well, not ideal, but acceptable—place to stop before full darkness had him leading them right off the side of the mountain into some deep ravine somewhere.

He found a spot where the land creased between two ridges. Something had happened there a long time ago, some natural disaster. There were a dozen or more uprooted trees, long since dead, scattered like forgotten toys, leaning against each other here, piled one on top of another there. It looked like the aftermath of a small hurricane along the Atlantic coast. Eerie. Solemn.

But it would provide shelter, and, best of all, the arrangement of roots and limbs sticking up in the air would let him rig the canvas, or better yet, the rubber groundsheet, as it would better shield the glow of a small fire from the view of anyone behind them.

At the lower end of the crease, about a hundred yards north, a small creek trickled down the center of an intersecting fold in the land.

Carson wasted no time. It was almost full dark. The sooner he started the fire, the sooner he could put it out. He slid from the saddle, then pulled Winter Fawn down into his arms, buffalo robe and all, and sat her on a fallen pine, the branches of which had been stripped away by time and the elements, leaving a fairly smooth surface.

Next he turned his attention to the mule and stripped her packs, stacking everything inside the perimeter of a triangle formed by three fallen pines. A fourth tree—he couldn't think of them as logs, not with dead roots and branches still attached—lay across two of the others, forming a shelter of sorts that would keep Winter Fawn out of the wind for the night.

While he was unpacking the mule, Winter Fawn stood and left the buffalo robe on the tree. He watched as she made her way across the clearing and into the tree line, where she disappeared in the undergrowth of small pines. Knowing she needed privacy, he said nothing and finished unpacking the mule.

After unsaddling the horse, he led both animals down the slope and watered them, filling the canteen and the coffeepot while there, then picketed the horse and mule near the trees so they could reach the grass there, even though it was still winter-dry. He poured out a handful of grain from Innes's pack for each animal and rubbed them down. They had sure done their work today, and tomorrow would certainly be as bad, if not worse. Mountains in spring could be unbelievably unforgiving.

When he returned to camp, Winter Fawn was back and had gathered a good pile of twigs and small branches.

"I would have done that. You should be resting."

"I will rest when you do."

Now what, he thought wryly, was a man supposed to say to that?

He changed his mind about using the rubber groundsheet to shield the fire. With the trees stacked the way they were, not to mention the slope of the land, the canvas tarp would work nearly as well. He doubted the Indians would come up the side of the mountain in the dark. They didn't strike him as complete fools. No matter how familiar they might be with the area, traveling in the mountains at night was dangerous in the extreme.

Using strips of rawhide and refusing Winter Fawn's attempts

to help, he tied the corners of the canvas to dead branches so that the tarp shielded them from view from the south. While he lit a small fire that allowed only a tiny wisp of smoke to rise, she started rolling out the groundsheet.

"Would you stop?" he said, exasperated.

She looked at him, puzzled and surprised. "Why?"

"Because you're hurt, you're exhausted, and you're feverish."

"Aye, I am all of those things, but helpless I'm not."

"You will be if you don't sit still and get some rest." He braced three sticks to form a tripod over the fire and hung the coffeepot there by a hook, then reached into one of the packs for the willow branches. "As soon as I get this tea going, I want to have a look at your wounds."

Winter Fawn sighed. She knew he was right, she should rest. She was nearly at the end of her strength, and her wounds did need looking at, probably needed a new bandage. The wound in her back felt as if she had pulled it open again.

But it rankled, this new vulnerability and sense of helplessness. She was used to taking care of others, not being taken care of. She was used to doing rather than sitting idle. She was used to feeling well and strong, yet now she was so weak she could barely stay upright, and the pain in her side every time she moved drained her even more.

"I am sorry to be so much trouble," she whispered.

Looking up from shaving willow bark into the coffeepot, he smiled slightly. It changed his entire face, lightening it, softening it.

Oh, she did like that smile.

There was a look in his bright blue eyes that she'd never seen before. It reminded her of the teasing looks shared by young couples just before they disappeared into their lodges for the night.

"I don't doubt," he said slowly, "that you could be trouble if you wanted to."

A new fever, unrelated to her wound, heated her deep inside, flustering her, shocking her. What did he mean by that?

"But so far," he said, turning back to his task and releasing her from whatever spell had held her breath locked in her chest, ''the most troublesome thing you've done is save my life. I find it impossible to complain about that.''

He left the willow bark water to heat, then spread the groundsheet out and added the bedroll on top. As he moved, she noticed how he favored his side.

''You should let me look at your injuries.''

He retrieved the buffalo robe and added it to the bedroll. ''Right after I look at yours.''

Winter Fawn shook her head. She was very much afraid that after the ordeal of having him rebandage her wounds she would be incapable of seeing to him. She was, as her father would say, nearly done for.

''Please,'' she said, hoping that a soft tone would gain her her wish. ''You have been taking care of me for two nights and a day. Let me see to you first.''

''Winter Fawn, you look like a slight breeze would knock you flat.''

''I am tired, aye, but it willna take long to see to your injuries. Then you can see to mine.''

Carson gave in because it seemed to matter to her. Maybe it would ease her mind to see that his wounds were nothing compared to hers. After all, she wouldn't be able to see the pounding he felt in the back of his skull.

He gave her a slight smile. ''Be gentle with me.''

She frowned, then smiled. ''You tease me.''

''I'm begging you,'' he said, still smiling as he pulled the tail of his undershirt from his pants. ''I don't care a lot for pain.''

Winter Fawn checked his bandage and found it to be as clean as could be expected, considering the day they'd spent. There was no sign of fresh blood, no telltale streaks of red to indicate poisoning. Only the bruising around the entrance and exit wounds, and a slight seepage, which was typical.

''I know it hurts when you move wrong,'' she told him, ''but it looks good. Now I'll see your head.''

He turned and sat with his back to her.

''One of us,'' she said, ''is the wrong height.''

He peered at her over his shoulder. ''How's that?''

''Either you are too tall, or I am too short.'' She braced her hands on the ground to push herself to her knees so that she could see the back of his head better.

"Stay," he said. "I'll get shorter." He stretched out in front of her where she sat on the buffalo robe and propped himself up on one elbow. "Better?"

"Hmm," she murmured, reaching for the back of his head. Gently, with the tips of her fingers, she eased thick strands of black hair aside to get a look at the gash. "How did this happen?"

"A bullet creased me. Your father said it was Crooked Oak. That's two I owe that bastard," he muttered, barely loud enough for her to hear.

He had laid the bedding out close to the fire. It was a small fire, but enough to heat the water and give off light. The sky was turning from deep purple to true black. Dozens of stars were already visible. On the mountainside, everything was black. She pulled one of her father's packs close, tilted it toward the light of the fire, and pulled out a rag she hoped was clean. Wetting it from the willow bark tea that was not yet warm enough to steam, she brought it back to Carson's head.

Carson sighed, despite the pain of having the gash washed. The warm dampness felt good, but not nearly as good as her fingers stirring his hair. He couldn't remember the last time someone, a woman, had stroked his hair. She laid her palm against his head and he felt a different warmth, stronger, deeper. The pain seemed to ease as if by magic. If she promised to keep at it for another hour, he just might be willing to die for her.

But she needed looking after worse than he did. With a great deal of reluctance, he bit back a groan and pushed himself up and turned toward her.

Light from the small fire sent flickering shadows alternating with dancing light across her features. In this light she didn't appear so pale, but the dark circles stood out beneath her feverish eyes. He pressed the backs of his fingers to her cheek.

"Damn. Your fever is worse. I should have been taking care of you, instead of the other way around."

"You are making tea for me."

"I'm also checking your bandage." He reached for the

fringed bottom of her doeskin tunic. One look at the fresh blood soaking the pad over her wound in her back had him swearing. "Dammit, why didn't you say something?"

"What was there to say? We couldna stop for a wee trickle of blood."

"Turn your back toward the fire so I can see better." When she did, he unwound the bandage from around her waist. The soaked pad fell away. "You've pulled a stitch or two loose."

"I'm sure I'll be fine with a fresh bandage," she offered quickly.

"If I thought that would do the trick, I'd be the first to agree. But I'm going to have to stitch this again, and neither one of us is going to enjoy it. Do you want me to dig out your father's bottle of whiskey?"

"Nae," she said quietly. "Just be gettin' it done."

Easy for her to say, he thought sourly. She wasn't the one who was going to have to poke a needle through bruised and torn flesh.

No, you idiot, she's just the one whose flesh you're going to poke another hole in.

It wasn't that he didn't know what to do. He'd stitched a wound or two in his day. Hell, he'd even sewn himself up once during the war. But this was different. This wasn't some battle-hardened soldier with skin like leather. This was a woman with skin as soft and smooth as silk. Her flesh was tender.

It was on the tip of his tongue to say that this was going to hurt him worse than it was her, and the thought nearly made him laugh out loud. His father used to say the same thing to him right before he took a switch to his backside for skipping out on chores, or some other transgression, when he'd been a kid. *Believe me, son, this will hurt me much worse than it hurts you.* Humph. One of the more outrageous lies that fathers told their children.

What he wouldn't give to hear his father say those words to him again.

But it wasn't going to happen. Edmond Dulaney was dead and buried, and his son had a woman's tender flesh to sew. And he'd better be getting it done before his beautiful, courageous patient froze to death. It was getting damn cold, and the fire was too small to offer much more than the thought of warmth.

He eased her down onto her side, with her back to the fire. After pulling the edge of the blanket over her, he dug into the packs. It took him several minutes to locate the small pouch he'd seen Innes use. In it he found the needle and thread he needed.

"Do you want the leather strap to bite on again?"

"Nae."

The way she said it, with dread covering her attempt at bravery, made him curse under his breath. He shouldn't have asked. Pride made her refuse.

He thrust the strip into her hands. "Take it anyway. It might not help you, but I'll feel a damn sight better."

Damn, he didn't want to do this. But he knew he had no choice. He had to lean so close to the fire to see to thread the needle that he nearly singed his hair. Then he pulled the blanket aside and bared the back of her waist. "Ready?"

"Aye."

He waited one heartbeat, two, but instead of putting the strap between her teeth, she gripped it tight in one fist.

He touched her back. Her skin was hot. Too hot. Swearing under his breath, he caught the edge of her torn flesh with the needle.

She jerked and sucked in a sharp breath.

"I'm sorry. You can swear if you want." After pulling the thread through, he caught the flesh on the other side of the hole and pushed the needle through.

She let out a small yelp. "Does swearing help?"

"Does for me, when I'm under the needle. One more." He poked the needle through again and pulled slightly to bring the ragged edges of flesh together before tying off the thread.

"Are you under the needle often?" she asked, her voice breathless with pain.

With a small pocketknife from the leather pouch, he cut the thread. "More often than I'd like. There. That's done."

She let out a long, slow breath. "Thank you."

Before bandaging the wound, Carson took another willow twig and peeled it down to the soft inner bark. He cut off a slice no longer than the end joint of his little finger and chewed it to a soft pulp. This he pressed over the wound in her back before covering it with a fresh pad from the remnants of Bess's petticoat.

The wound where the arrow had come out was holding its own, so he decided to leave it alone.

"I'm going to sit you up so I can wrap the bandage around you, but you let me do the work. I don't want you pulling out my fancy stitching."

"All right." Winter Fawn held her breath against the pain to come, but he was true to his word about doing all the work himself. He slid his arm around her shoulders and lifted her.

Winter Fawn was not used to being taken care of. It did not sit comfortably with her to have someone take care of her. Yet if she had to get herself shot and tended to, she couldn't have chosen a better man to do the tending. He was even more gentle with her than her father had been. Wondering where he had learned to chew the willow bark that way, she held her tunic up out of the way while he wrapped the long strip of bandage around her waist three times to hold the pads in place over her wounds.

The tea he gave her was bitter, but hot. She insisted that he drink some, too.

Kneeling between her and the fire, he took the slab of bacon from one of the packs, then pulled her belt knife from his boot.

"Don't fix any for me," she told him as she finished the last of her tea. She reached around him to set the cup next to the fire, then eased down on the bedding, too weak and miserable to sit up any longer. "I'm not hungry."

He turned his head to look at her, but at that angle, his face was in shadow and she could not read his expression. "I don't imagine you are, but you'll eat."

"No, really, I'm not—"

"Yes, really. You haven't eaten anything all day. If you don't eat now, you'll be half-dead tomorrow."

Winter Fawn wanted to argue, but she didn't have the strength, and she knew he was right. She must eat. "You are right. I'm sorry. I do not mean to be so much trouble."

"Humph." He turned back and took another slice of the

bacon slab. "Go ahead and get some sleep if you want. I'll wake you when the food's ready. Girls who save my life are rarely any trouble at all."

"I wish you would stop saying that. You make it sound so . . . noble. It was nothing like that."

"Seemed like it to me." His voice was sharper than he intended, but he still couldn't get past what she'd done. "Noble, brave. Foolish."

"Oh, aye, now you've got the right of it."

Her words were slightly slurred with exhaustion or fever, maybe both. Yet there was humor in her voice. Humor, in the shape she was in. Carson shook his head, amazed.

"Might I be askin' you a question, Carson Dulaney?"

He tossed the bacon into the skillet and set it over the fire. There was no wind yet tonight, so the smell shouldn't carry far. "Sure. What do you want to know?"

"Where is your ranch?"

"Down along the Huerfano. It's got water year-round. Good grass."

"Megan's mother. She must be missing her daughter something fierce. Be she waiting for ye there?"

Her Scottish burr, he noticed, grew thicker with exhaustion, as it did when her emotions ran high. "Megan's mother died three years ago."

"Oh, I am sorry. I didna know."

Carson didn't say anything. He figured that was best. He didn't want to talk about Julia. Didn't want to think about her.

Behind him, Winter Fawn fell silent. He glanced over his shoulder and found her fast asleep. When the bacon was done and the biscuits after it, he hated to wake her. But he'd meant it when he'd told her she had to eat. She would be as weak as a newborn kitten by morning if she didn't.

Looking at her while she slept made him want to touch her. Stroke that soft, soft cheek. Trace the curve of her lips with a fingertip.

Damn fool thoughts.

He woke her and helped her sit up.

"I'm really not hungry," she mumbled.

"I know, but eat anyway." He passed her a tin plate with

a pan biscuit and a slice of bacon, and poured her the last of the tea. She managed, with a great deal of prompting, to eat what he'd given her, but no sooner had he taken the plate from her fingers than she eased back down onto the bedroll. She fell asleep instantly. On top of the buffalo robe.

It took some doing, but he finally got her tucked beneath the warmth of the cover. He figured he'd jostled her pretty good, but she hadn't wakened. Poor girl. Poor foolishly brave girl.

It was too dark to make it safely down the hill to the stream again, so he turned one tin plate face down over the other to keep the bugs out, what few bugs there might be on a night that gave every indication of getting downright cold. He'd wash the plates in the morning.

He checked on the horse and mule, shivering in his undershirt before he made it back to the meager fire. Then he pulled the sticks from the fire until the flames died completely, leaving nothing but glowing coals.

It was a good thing Winter Fawn was fast asleep, he thought as he crawled beneath the buffalo robe, tucking the canteen in with them to keep the water from freezing during the night. He'd heard the Arapaho placed a high value on chastity among their girls and women. She probably wouldn't appreciate sharing her bed with a strange man. Not that he had in mind anything other than sleeping warm. But a man would have to be dead not to have wants around a woman like her. Carson Dulaney might have a few more holes in his hide than usual, but he damn sure wasn't dead.

Around him the mountain was quiet save for an occasional skittering in the underbrush, the far-off call of a wolf, the hoot of an owl. There were so many stars overhead it was dizzying to lay there and look at them. They looked different from here than they had back home. That was one of the first things he'd noticed last year when he'd come west. Maybe it had something to do with the altitude.

Beside him Winter Fawn shivered in her sleep. Without thought, he rolled to his side. Slipping one arm beneath her head and the other over her hips, he pulled her close against him and closed his eyes against the exquisite pleasure of holding her.

This was even better than holding her in the saddle. No need to worry here about keeping her from falling. Here he only needed to keep her warm.

Had a woman ever felt this good pressed up against him? He couldn't remember, but he didn't think so. Maybe she felt so good because it had been so damn long since he'd been with a woman.

It didn't matter, of course. Neither of them was in any shape for him to take advantage of the situation. Even if he had been, he wouldn't. She was Innes's daughter. Innes trusted him, as he trusted Innes with Megan and Bess.

More important than those reasons, Winter Fawn trusted him.

So he held her close against the cold that crept in from the night, and prayed that Megan and Bess were safe and warm.

Three miles down the mountain, Crooked Oak prayed, too. For patience, for victory. For an early sunrise in the morning with good, clear light.

It was not the danger of the mountains at night that had finally halted their pursuit. It was the simple lack of light by which to track their prey. Light had still teased the tops of the taller trees, but deep shadows across the ground had forced them to stop for the night. If they could not see the white man's trail, they could not know if they were still following him, or if he had circled and headed back down the mountain.

Crooked Oak gnashed his teeth in frustration. Like the men with him, he sat huddled around the fire. None of them had come prepared for a cold mountain night. They had ridden out of camp in the heat of the moment, anticipating catching the escapees in a matter of hours. Instead, they'd been on the trail for two days, and still the white man eluded them.

"I am troubled," said Long Chin.

Crooked Oak barely managed to bite back a snarl. Long Chin was always troubled about something.

Two Feathers nodded as though in agreement with Long Chin. "About what are you troubled, cousin?"

Frowning, Long Chin looked across the fire at Two Feathers. "You saw the white man carry Winter Fawn from camp, and from that we assumed he took her against her will."

Again Two Feathers nodded.

Crooked Oak did not like the direction of their thoughts. "Of course she was taken against her will," he asserted. "She was bloody and unconscious, was she not?"

"She was," Two Feathers confirmed.

"Yes," Crooked Oak said. "About this we are all troubled, as we should be. That is why we are here. To find her and bring her back. And to kill the white man. But now his death will not be only to avenge our fallen comrades. Now he must die for daring to take one of our own away from us."

"But today, when we saw them," Long Chin said, "she did not look as though she was being forced. She rode behind him. When she saw us, she did not jump down and run to us for help. She clung to the white man and rode off with him."

A murmur rose around the fire as the others agreed with him.

"You are mistaken," Crooked Oak said heatedly.

Red Bull, who, along with Spotted Calf, could always be counted on to side with Crooked Oak, waved his hand in dismissal of the others. "The white man is no fool. He knows we would not chance hurting her. He surely had tied her hands around him so she could not get down. Would not any of us have done that very thing with a captive?"

"This is true." Spotted Calf nodded slowly. "This is surely what has happened."

Talks Loud grunted. "She did not look tied to me. I say we would have been better off to go back for the white man's wagon instead of chasing him. The goods in the wagon would mean more to Our People than the fate of one girl."

"No!" In a surge of rage, Crooked Oak jumped to his feet. "Winter Fawn is not just any girl. She is mine!"

Talks Loud chuckled. "So you wish, my friend, but her father has not agreed, and is not likely to now."

Crooked Oak ground his teeth and stared up at the stars to keep from shouting that he had no intention of worrying about Red Beard's agreement, for he intended to kill the man. But he swallowed the words. It would not do to speak them in front of Two Feathers. Two Feathers held no true affection for Red Beard, but because of Winter Fawn and Hunter, the white man was considered family. To Two Feathers, family was sacred.

"She will be mine," Crooked Oak said tightly, fists clenched at his sides. "She will be mine."

CHAPTER 8

Winter Fawn woke deep in the night. At first she was startled to feel the heat at her side and a heavy weight draped across her. Then she realized.

Carson.

A slow sigh slipped from between her lips. This, then, was what it felt like to lie next to a man. She'd had no idea anything could be so wonderful. Being held in his arms on horseback had been pleasurable—as pleasurable as possible with her wounds plaguing her. But this, despite the wounds, was a feeling she would treasure for the rest of her life. Such warmth. Such comfort. Yet there was tension in her, too, from lying beside him. A tension she did not understand. If only they could stay like this, she and this stranger whose eyes seemed to hold her destiny, until she could fathom this tight, bewildering yearning that tried to edge out the comfort.

But if they did not get away from Crooked Oak, she reminded herself, her white man's destiny could prove to be tragically short.

Again she thought, *I'm slowing him down.*

She had tried to do something about that last night when they'd been trapped among the rocks. She had tried, and failed.

Or had she failed? She had placed her hand on the front wound. Carson had said it looked good. It had not bled again, nor had any stitches pulled loose as they had in the back. Maybe . . .

She would try again, on the wound at her back this time. She must be stronger. She must not slow Carson down. She must not be a burden to him as he fled for his life. It was not only his life at stake, but the lives of his sister and daughter, as well, for who would care for them without Carson?

It might also mean Winter Fawn's life, she admitted. She had told everyone that Crooked Oak would not harm her, but that wasn't necessarily true. As her uncle, Two Feathers might be counted on to keep her safe. Maybe. Although he'd never been fond of her because of her father.

But Crooked Oak had seen her freeing Carson from his bonds in camp. And today he had seen her clinging to Carson's back as they rode away from the others.

There was every possibility that he would want no more to do with her because she was helping Carson.

That suited Winter Fawn just fine.

But it also meant that her safety lay with Carson. And as long as she was such a burden to him, neither of them was safe.

Yet even with so much at stake, she was afraid to try to heal her own wounds. This was not like the other times, like Carson's head earlier, or Bess's two nights ago, or her grandmother's aching shoulders every winter. Those had been compulsions to her. She had been drawn by a force beyond herself to touch, to heal. This time, it would be deliberate.

She remembered the first time, the rabbit. That, too, had been directed by some unknown force within her. She'd had no idea what was about to happen. She remembered what her father had said about it afterward as if it were yesterday.

Never, ever, do anything like that again! Do ye hear me, lassie? Never!

His voice echoed in her mind. That was the first time she'd ever seen her father truly enraged, and he'd been enraged at her. The memory still had the power to make her tremble. She had been twelve that spring day when he had brought her the rabbits to skin and roast. Her mother had been dead barely a week, and Winter Fawn had become the woman of her father's lodge. But not for much longer, she knew. She would go soon to live in the lodge of her mother's mother, for it was not proper for a young woman, which Winter Fawn was soon to become, to live alone with a man, not even her own father.

Knowing that this time next spring she would not be living with the father she adored, Winter Fawn had eagerly accepted the chore of skinning and gutting the rabbits. She had stroked the nearest one, thinking that she would use the soft fur to line the inside of her father's moccasins before next winter. He always complained in winter that his feet were cold.

Or perhaps she would save the furs until she had enough to line his coat.

She stroked the rabbit's side one more time, then clasped it by the head to bring it closer.

Her palm, pressed against the rabbit's head, began to tingle. At first it tickled, and she thought it was merely the fur, teasing her skin. But then there was heat, and the tingling grew sharper.

She wanted to pull her hand away. The sensation running up her arm felt too much like that she had felt on the hilltop just before the lightning struck and killed her mother.

But she found she could not move her hand.

Then a sense of pain, sharp and centered on her left temple, and fear, overwhelming fear, assailed her. Yet it was not her pain, not her fear, even though she felt them both strongly. They belonged to the rabbit.

Winter Fawn had no understanding of how she knew such a thing, she simply *knew*. The rabbit was not dead. She could feel the wound where the rock from her father's sling had struck its head. The same spot on her head was where the pain centered.

If only she could remove her hand, she knew the pain in her head would cease. But a new knowledge assailed her then. If she removed her hand, the rabbit would die. If she left it there, the rabbit would live.

Such a thing, as far as Winter Fawn knew, was impossible. Yet the knowledge was there inside her, telling her it was true. She tried to look at her father—could he tell her what was happening?—but her eyelids grew weighted, too heavy to hold open. Her heartbeat raced in time with the rabbit's, but her breathing slowed. The back of her neck prickled as though she sensed someone were staring at her.

Gradually the pain began to fade, and with it, the heat in her hand, and the tingling. Her heartbeat and breathing returned to normal while her strength, her energy, drained away. She felt incredibly tired. Exhausted. She could not keep her eyes open. Beneath her hand, the rabbit's eyes popped open, its nose twitched. And in a flash, it rolled to its feet and dashed away into the bushes at the edge of camp. Darkness swirled, and Winter Fawn tumbled down, down, down into its welcoming depths.

When she woke, her father was there. "Father? What happened?"

Because she asked in the language of her mother, which she was most familiar with, her father had answered in kind. "You do not remember?"

With a start, Winter Fawn sat up and frowned down at the lone dead rabbit beside her. "The rabbit, it was not dead. I put my hand on it and felt its pain. It hurt me, but then it didn't, and the rabbit got up and ran away." She looked up at her father, confused. "Did you see, Father? What does it mean?"

Her father had shuddered. When he spoke, his voice was more harsh than she had ever heard. "It means trouble. Never, ever, do anything like that again! Do ye hear me, lassie? Never!"

Hurt by his harshness, Winter Fawn shrank in upon herself. "I didn't mean to do it. I don't know what I did."

"Promise me, Winter Fawn. You must promise never to touch a wound again. Not ever, do you understand? *Promise.*"

"I promise." Her heart thundered behind her ribs. Her stomach knotted. "Don't be angry, Father. I did not mean to take the rabbit's wound away."

Her father had gripped her shoulders tightly. "You must keep this promise, Winter Fawn. You must." His fingers bruised her with their strength. "You must tell no one, not ever."

"Not even Grandmother?"

"No one," he cried, shaking her for emphasis. "Say it. Say you will tell no one."

"It is to be a secret then?"

"More than a secret," he said desperately. "Swear on your mother's soul that you will tell no one what happened here today. No one must ever know. Promise me."

Terrified by the intensity in his eyes, she had promised.

And he had left. The very next day, as thunder had boomed across a sky turned dark and ugly, he had flung his possibles bag over his shoulder, picked up his rifle, and ridden out of camp without a word as to when he would return.

He had not returned. Not that spring, not that summer, nor the next fall or the following spring.

Finally, during that next summer, he came. He stayed three days and left. That had set the pattern of his visits. Sometimes in spring, when their band was camped in the foothills of the great mountains. Sometimes in the summer, when they joined the rest of the tribe along the Arkansas River to hunt the buffalo. He would stay a few days, then leave again.

It was her fault, she knew, although she had never understood why he'd grown so angry, why what she had done had made him leave. She had never dared to ask him about it during any of his brief visits, for fear he might stop coming altogether. She had hoped and prayed that he had forgotten the incident and that someday he would come back to live again with Our People.

He did not know that she had used this strange gift secretly for others. She could not tell him such a thing. She had never done it on purpose. But sometimes, when she was near someone in pain, it was as if she stood to one side and watched herself touch the source of the pain and take it away. There seemed to be no way to stop herself from doing it. Her hand to a wound was like water rushing downhill. Unless something large and forceful were thrown in her path, nothing could stop her. Just as earlier this night when she had pressed her hand to the gash on Carson's head.

She had been certain, to be sure, to pull her hand away before the wound could completely disappear. She had gotten good at that over the years. She had known that she would never be able to explain if a wound were to disappear. Her secret would be out then. She had, against her will, broken her promise to her father to never do such a thing again, but she had kept her word to keep it a secret.

Perhaps some day she would learn why such a wondrous gift must not be revealed. Perhaps some day she would find the courage to ask her father. But until then, she would keep it secret, as he had bade.

Keeping her gift a secret meant she could not heal her own wounds now, even if she were able. Not completely. Carson would surely want to inspect beneath the bandage in the morning to make certain his new stitches had not pulled loose in the night. But she might be able to partially heal it so that she would not slow him down with her pain and her fever.

So she would try again.

He lay against her good side. All she needed to do was get her hand beneath her other side and press her palm against the wound there.

She moved her arm and reached for the wound in her back.

Lying on his side next to her, Carson shifted and pulled her closer.

Winter Fawn stiffened. Was he waking?

His warm breath teased the sensitive skin at her temple. Oh, how wonderful that felt. Then his nose brushed her there and he murmured.

"Carson?" she whispered softly, cautiously.

His knee shifted across her thigh, but his breathing remained slow and deep.

Still, she waited several long moments to make certain he was not awake.

Finally assured that he would not know what she did, she pressed her palm over the pad covering her wound.

Carson woke some time before dawn, startled to realize he was not alone in his bedroll. He stiffened and reached for the revolver he never slept without.

It wasn't there. No revolver.

Heart pounding, he groped beside the blanket and touched his rifle.

Then memory returned, and he relaxed somewhat. The warm form curled into him was not some Yankee come to kill him in his sleep. It was Winter Fawn. Firm yet soft in his arms.

Gently, so as not to wake her, he pressed his hand to her cheek. It was warm, but not hot. No fever.

Thank you, God. He didn't know what he would have done if she'd been out of her head with fever.

Her eyes fluttered open. She groaned softly. "Is it time to leave?"

Carson let out the breath he hadn't realized was locked in his chest. "Not yet. Go back to sleep. I'll wake you."

She needed more rest to recover. Real rest. But they couldn't stay here. He had thought briefly, humorously, last night that he might die for her, but he wasn't ready to sit and wait for Crooked Oak and his men to catch them. He would die if they did. He had no doubt of that. But his death wouldn't guarantee Winter Fawn's safety or health. She would still have to be carried down out of these mountains and back to camp. If, that is, they did not kill her outright for helping him escape.

If she had to be carried, Carson figured it might as well be him doing the carrying. Not back to her camp, but to his ranch. From there, after she was fully recovered, she could decide what she wanted to do.

The thought of watching her ride away from him left him feeling strangely hollow inside in a place he didn't recognize.

Maybe she wouldn't want to leave. Maybe she would want to stay.

Yeah, right, Dulaney.

What did he have to offer her? What, if anything, was he even willing to offer her? A place to live? Why would he think she would even consider leaving her people?

For her father.

The thought teased him. Yes, she might want to stay with her father. But from what Carson knew of Innes, the Scotsman roamed the mountains, did a little prospecting here, a little trapping there. There was a cabin, Carson thought he remembered his father saying once, somewhere in the White Mountains, where Innes stayed part of the year.

Would Winter Fawn and Hunter go there? Would Carson ever see them again? Any of them?

He wished for daylight so he could see her face. But the night was pitch black, the moon having set while he'd slept. But judging by the stars, dawn wasn't far-off. Already a few birds were starting to stir.

The birds weren't the only things stirring. So was his blood, he realized with surprise. If he didn't take his arms from around Winter Fawn and crawl out from beneath the blankets, something else was going to stir. The way he and Winter Fawn were lying, like two spoons in a tray, with her tucked up against his chest and his thighs and his loins, Winter Fawn was quite likely to come awake and feel something of his he'd rather she didn't feel, and slap him in the face. And he would deserve it.

He forced himself out of the warm blankets and into the icy predawn air. The fire he started helped a little, but not much. Damn fine time to be down to his undershirt.

But at least he wasn't wearing a skirt, which allowed cold air to circulate beneath it when Winter Fawn stood, and which bared her thighs when she straddled the back of the horse.

Thinking of skirts, he hoped that Megan and Bess hadn't had to spend a cold night in the mountains. Hell, they didn't even have the buffalo robe or the groundsheet. Only two blankets for all four of them.

Frustrated and angry over their circumstances, and blaming himself, he whacked into the slab of bacon and severed off slices for breakfast. Once it was cooking, he groped beneath the blankets for the canteen, to use the water for coffee.

The back of his hand brushed across something. He turned his palm to it and grasped.

Ah . . . that, uh, wasn't a canteen. It was round and firm, but too soft. It was a butt, and a shapely one. He jerked his hand away.

Winter Fawn sprang upright, her eyes flying wide open. The abrupt action caused her to wince.

She must have pulled her wound, he thought, sorry to be the

cause of more pain for her. The firelight lent an amber glow to her face. He'd never seen a more beautiful face.

"What are you doing?" she demanded.

Incredibly, Carson felt heat sting his cheeks. "Sorry. I was just . . . looking for the, uh, the canteen."

"I am not wearing it."

"I know. Sorry. If you'll, uh, fish it out for me, I'll start coffee."

She frowned. "Fish? Oh." Reaching beneath the covers, she pulled out the canteen from a spot that made it look as though she'd been hugging it in her sleep.

Lucky canteen.

"Here." She handed it to him.

"Thanks."

As soon as he took the canteen from her, she shivered and dove back beneath the buffalo robe.

While he put the coffee on and mixed up a batch of biscuit dough, he heard her shifting around in the bedroll. A moment later he felt a gentle nudge on his arm and turned to find her holding out one of the blankets toward him.

"Take this," she said. "It's too cold for so few clothes."

Carson smiled and wrapped the blanket around his shoulders. "Thank you."

After they ate he insisted on checking her wound again.

"It feels much better this morning."

"Good. But I still want to see it."

She seemed reluctant to let him, but she gave in and turned her back to give him access.

The condition of the wound impressed him. The fine tremor that started in his hand when he touched her skin shocked him. It was a moment before he could speak. "The, uh, willow bark must have done the trick. It looks good. How's the pain?"

"Better," she answered.

Realizing that he was still holding her tunic up and staring at the expanse of smooth bronze skin across her back, Carson dropped the tunic, letting it fall into place, and turned back toward the fire.

They ate in silence, then packed up and headed out as soon as it was light enough to see even a short distance.

"Do you know these mountains?" he asked her.

Seated behind him on the horse, Winter Fawn gripped the saddle rather than the man. Something had happened inside her when he had touched the bare skin of her back that morning. Something hot and wild that she didn't understand. It had made her heart pound and her breath catch as though she had been running for miles. She wasn't sure that she liked it. She wasn't sure that she didn't. For now, she thought it best not to touch him lest it happen to her again.

"No," she told him. "I've heard my father speak of them, but I've never been beyond the foothills until now."

"There's a pass," he said, "north of here."

"To the north, yes. I remember. A wide, easy pass, he said."

"On the other side is Ute territory."

Winter Fawn stiffened. The Utes were old and constant enemies of Our People.

"Will Crooked Oak follow us there?" Carson asked.

"I do not know. With so few warriors, I think not. But he might think the Utes would not be this far east until later in the spring, when more of the snow melts."

"That's my thinking, too. I remember seeing a cabin up here when I was here last summer, but we can't afford to get trapped like that."

He had come to these mountains because they were the closest ones to the ranch. His father had told him that when a man's soul was needy, he could usually find peace in the mountains, if he would only allow himself to sit still and listen.

After the surrender at Appomattox, Carson's soul had indeed been needy. He had gone to Atlanta to see what was left of his family, and while there, realized he could not provide for them in Georgia. The plantation—everything his father and his grandfather before him had worked for—was gone. Only the ranch in Colorado was left. The ranch his father had spoken of with reverence in his voice.

So Carson had ridden west. The ranch had been run-down, neglected, but he'd seen the possibilities. But he'd felt so damn tired. Down deep, soul-deep, weary.

The mountains can heal you, if you'll let them, his father had said.

So Carson had headed for the nearest mountains. These mountains. He'd spent a month roaming them up and down, back and forth, and, a great deal of the time, merely sitting still and breathing in the peace of the place.

He remembered one afternoon when he had ridden up out of a steep, winding, red-and-gray-streaked canyon to find a pile of boulders that had tumbled from higher up the mountain to form what to him, that day, had looked like a bear and two cubs. It had seemed magical. Whimsical, he remembered with a smile. Farther up the mountain, in the next valley, he'd come across an abandoned cabin, where he'd stopped for a while to rest his horse before riding on.

But the cabin, near as he could figure, was too far up the mountain. There was no pass up there. They needed to get over the pass at Hardscrabble Creek. For that, they had to head north. And along the way, he had to make tracking them as difficult as possible.

To this end he stuck to rocky ground when he could, or traveled through pine forests whose floors were covered in deep layers of pine needles, or guided the horse into a creek bed. He marveled, and thanked God, when he realized that the mule walked directly behind the horse rather than off to the side.

At the next ridge Carson used the binoculars to study their back trail. He spotted their pursuers instantly as they crested another ridge. "Damn."

"They still come?"

"Yes," he said grimly, lowering the binoculars. "They still come."

Angling north toward the pass as best he could, Carson kept mostly to the creek beds, going up one stream, then taking a branch out of that one up another, weaving northeast, then northwest, sometimes having to go south before finding another finger canyon heading north.

Around noon they stopped to give the animals a rest.

At least, it felt like noon. It was hard to tell with the clouds so thick. They gathered all morning around the mountain peaks, then rolled quickly down the slopes and seemed to press down on him like lead weight. The smell and the feel of snow to come was a threat he could have done without.

That, and the bastards still dogging his trail. They were still back there, still coming, although there were only three now. He would have felt a hell of a lot better if he knew for certain that the other three had turned back.

Hoping that his zigzagging up and down the streams was slowing the Arapahos down, he took a chance and followed a game trail out of the stream and up the side of the mountain. At a level spot he stopped and concealed himself at the edge of a grove of tall pines. Using the binoculars again, he scanned the area below them.

After about ten minutes he spotted Crooked Oak and two others, right where he'd feared they would be, less than two miles south and gaining on them.

But where were the other three? Had they turned back? Another ten minutes of searching gave him no sight of them.

Twice more during the afternoon he stopped to look again. It was during the second stop that he spotted the other three. His hackles rose. He recognized a pincher movement when he saw one. The other three had gone down the mountains to smoother terrain, for faster traveling. They were now coming at him from about east northeast.

"What shall we do?" Winter Fawn asked.

Carson whirled, startled. He had left her deeper into the trees with the horses and hadn't heard her approach. Damn good thing she was on his side, he thought with disgust. If she'd been one of the warriors, he'd be a dead man.

He gnawed on the inside of his jaw. "They're coming at us from two directions now. If we stay where we are, we'll be caught between them. If we keep angling north toward the pass, the two groups will eventually rejoin each other and continue dogging our trail. If we head east, we'll end up down on the plains, on the Taos Trail where they first attacked me. There's no cover, nowhere to hide, and the warriors aren't riding double. Catching us would be child's play."

What he didn't say was that if they rode down out of the mountains, they wouldn't be far from Pueblo. Toward safety. At least for him. Innes, however, had been adamant that Winter Fawn would not be safe there.

Besides, he still had to get to the ranch. From Pueblo, he

would still have to take the Taos Trail and ride right past the Arapaho camp. Or, he could head west out of Pueblo up Hardscrabble Creek and over the Wet Mountains into Wet Mountain Valley. The eastern edge of Ute country.

"And west," Winter Fawn said, "means higher up into the mountains, toward the snow."

"With the possibility of more snow in the air," Carson added. "Any way we look at it, we need to get over the pass."

They mounted up and headed north. Not as familiar with the Wets as he'd like to be, he estimated that Hardscrabble Creek was just over five miles away. As the crow flies. Unfortunately, they could not travel like crows. They had the land to deal with, and the land enjoyed throwing obstacles in their path.

Carson's concern over the weather grew with every step they took. The temperature dropped, the sky lowered. The wind picked up. He had to get off the side of the mountain, or they were likely to be blown off.

Later in the afternoon he found a wide, shallow stream with banks no more than a foot high. He headed upstream, which led them in a northwesterly direction. More or less.

Gradually the wide banks rose and the stream itself narrowed and cut deeper into the rocky earth, leaving an area of about twenty yards of scattered aspen and pines on either side before reaching the tall banks. The banks themselves grew steeper and higher until they angled several hundred feet straight up from their base.

There was the chance that the stream would end in a waterfall that tumbled down from rocky cliffs above. A dead end for someone on horseback. But Carson noticed deer tracks heading their same direction, and deer weren't likely to get themselves trapped in a dead end canyon.

Of course, the horse and mule couldn't necessarily follow where a deer might go, but the red and gray streaks in the canyon walls were starting to look familiar. If this was the same canyon he had traveled before, he would find the bear-shaped rocks at the point where he would be forced up.

But if he took the side canyon that fed into this one from the north, he would end up in a wide grassy meadow, and maybe reach the pass before dark.

Suddenly the dirt and rock in the embankment to their left exploded. A jaybird squawked and took flight. The sound of a rifle shot echoed between the rock walls.

Winter Fawn sucked in a sharp breath. Her arms, around his waist, tightened.

Carson didn't take the time to look around. He knew the shot had come from atop the right bank. From the Arapahos. *So much for them not shooting at Winter Fawn,* he thought with disgust.

He knew there was no way for the Arapahos to get down to them in the immediate area, but as soon as a way presented itself, they would take it, and he would be dead, and maybe Winter Fawn along with him.

Unless, of course, the warriors improved their aim. In which case he and Winter Fawn might very well be dead that much sooner.

All of this whipped through Carson's mind in the same instant that he dug his heels into the horse and shouted. The horse bolted forward, the mule right on its heels.

Shaken to realize that the Dogmen, including her own uncle, would risk hitting her with a bullet, Winter Fawn hugged Carson's back and held on tight.

Crooked Oak and Two Feathers were shaken as well, and furious at Talks Loud for firing.

Crooked Oak swung out with his own rifle and knocked Talks Loud's weapon from his hands. "You dare!" he cried. "You dare to risk hitting Winter Fawn!"

"What is she but a girl?" Flexing his fingers, Talks Loud spat on the ground as the white man rode out of range. "I ride for revenge. I ride to kill the white man."

Two Feathers nudged his horse up to Talks Loud's other side. "You harm my niece, it is I who will ride for revenge, against you!"

Two Feathers might have lunged for Talks Loud's throat then and there, so livid was he, so shaken that Winter Fawn had nearly been shot, but the sky chose that moment to open up. Tiny pellets of ice, each one as sharp as the finely honed point of a knife, stung and sliced exposed skin. Before the warriors could decide whether to brave the sleet and follow the canyon rim to keep their prey in sight, or make a dash for the cover of trees nearby, the sleet turned to hail.

Round balls of ice the size of peas pounded down on them, bruising skin, bouncing on the ground, making the horses dance in pain. The six riders raced for the cover of the thick pine branches of the forest.

Down in the canyon, Carson and Winter Fawn sought the only close cover available, the scant shelter of a small stand of aspen. As Carson urged the horse toward the dubious cover, he swore. Two days ago Winter Fawn had taken an arrow meant for him. A few moments ago she had nearly taken a bullet meant for him. Now she was shielding his back from the hail and taking *that.* She was even, damn her, covering his head with her own hands.

How many times was the woman going to suffer on his account? He should have been carrying her before him on the saddle. It wasn't the easiest or most comfortable way for two adults to share a horse, but Winter Fawn was still weak from her wound. If he had carried her, he could be shielding her now, rather than the other way around.

The aspens couldn't have been more than seventy-five yards ahead when he'd started toward them, but it seemed to take forever to get there. Hail pounded them like rocks from a giant, angry hand above, bruising, slicing. Carson didn't slow the horse until they were beneath the tree limbs.

The branches weren't thick enough to shield them more than partially, and the leaves had only just begun to unfurl from the fat buds. Hailstones, some the size of the playing marbles he'd had as a boy, tore through the buds, stripping them from the branches, littering the ground with bits of green among the white balls of ice piling up.

Quickly Carson twisted in the saddle and pulled Winter Fawn and her buffalo robe onto his lap.

"Wait," she cried. She struggled out of the buffalo robe and, holding on to one corner, threw it over his shoulder. "Pull it up over your head. It will help."

She was shivering in his arms—from being shot at and pounded by hail—yet she sought to protect him. Swearing again, Carson pulled the thick robe around his shoulders and up over his head, then bent forward and shielded her from the onslaught with his body and the fur.

Beneath them the horse flinched and shuffled each time a bruising ice ball stung through his thick hide. Beside them the mule did the same.

Carson took the time to peer out of his hand-held tent toward the far side of the canyon. There was so much hail that it obscured his vision. He could no longer see the rim clearly, but surely the warriors had sought shelter beneath the pines that grew back some distance from the rim.

"Do you see them?" Winter Fawn asked, her breath catching.

"No. I'm sure they're under cover in the trees."

She looked up at him, her eyes wide, her brow furrowed. "They shot at us."

Carson met her gaze and read the shock in her eyes. "They shot at me."

She looked away and whispered, "But they dinna care that I might hae been hit."

The burr in her voice was thicker than ever. There was nothing Carson could say. The evidence had exploded right beside them when the bullet struck the rocky ground. The shot had come from slightly behind them. She could easily have been hit.

The hail pounded down, shredding buds, ripping small branches from trees, sending geysers of water shooting up out of the stream. It bounced on the ground and covered it in a thick layer of white in no time. Then, about ten minutes after it started, it stopped. Completely. All at once.

"Damn," Carson muttered, silently cataloging dozens of new bruises as he lowered the buffalo robe. "Does this sort of thing happen often around here?"

Winter Fawn's chuckle sounded strained. "Now and then."

"Damn," he said again. "Oh, damn, honey, look at your hands." The backs of her hands were covered in round red spots. "You shouldn't have tried to protect my head." The red spots would be turning blue by tomorrow. Anger surged through him at her newest injuries on his behalf. "Don't ever do anything like that again! If anything, you should have been protecting your own head.''

''My head disnae hae a big gash in the back of it,'' she said tartly.

''No, now it's just got bruises, along with your hands, because you were too busy protecting me.'' He took her hands and lifted them gently to his lips. ''I'm not ungrateful.'' He brushed his lips across the red spots. ''I just wish you hadn't been hurt—again—because of me.''

At the brush of his lips across the backs of her cold hands, Winter Fawn's breath halted. Her heart raced. Heat spiraled through her. Never had she felt anything so tender, so caring, as his kisses on her hands. She had the strongest urge to reciprocate, to press her lips to his big strong hands. To taste his flesh.

Would his heart pound like thundering hooves in his chest, the way hers was?

He lowered her hands to her lap and urged the horse back out into the open as though nothing momentous had happened. But to her, it had. Her palms tingled where his fingers had brushed, as did the backs of her hands where he had kissed her.

The wind, howling down off the snow-covered peaks that were hidden by dark clouds, drove icy rain sideways directly into their faces and beneath the buffalo robe, soaking them to the skin. It smelled like snow, then it was snowing, and Winter Fawn had never been warmer in her life. All because a man had kissed her hands.

Her own uncle, and a man who professed to want her for his wife, had been with whoever had fired the shot that could have killed her. Perhaps Two Feathers or Crooked Oak had fired it, but she didn't want to think so. Still, that any of them would care so little for her was devastating. Yet now, mere moments later, she was so happy she wanted to sing. All because a man—this white man who sheltered her in his arms—had kissed her hands.

Carson was trying not to think about having kissed her hands. About wanting to kiss her lips. He needed to keep his mind on business. The icy rain on the heels of the hail had since turned to snow. Footing for the horse and mule was treacherous, as the hail, large and small, shifted beneath each hoof. But the ground was warmer than the air, and the hail was melting, turning the earth muddy, making the going even more hazardous.

And that wasn't counting the snow. Visibility was dropping as the snow thickened and the wind blew it sideways, directly into their eyes. By the time they'd gone a half mile farther up the canyon and reached the side canyon that would lead them up into the meadow and beyond to the pass, it was a full-fledged blizzard and drifts were accumulating around rocks and along the base of the canyon walls.

They needed shelter. Real shelter, not just a tarp and a buffalo robe. They would never make it to the pass in this weather. If the blizzard kept up, they wouldn't survive a night in the open, not even under the sheltering branches of pines.

They would have to head for the cabin.

Carson prayed he could find it, and find it fast, before the going got even worse. The horse was just about played out. He'd carried two grown people over damn rugged terrain all day on a handful of grain. Now he had this to contend with. When the temperature dropped, this muddy ground would freeze, and ice would coat the rocks.

You just had to come to Colorado, didn't you? See the West. Search for Peace.

Hell, the only peace he was likely to find in the foreseeable future was the peace of the grave if he wasn't careful.

CHAPTER 9

The canyon ended at a rock wall, where the stream shot over the rim above into a pool at its base before tumbling on downhill.

There was a trail to the top. Somewhere. Carson knew, because he'd been up it. Once. A year ago. In clear weather.

But where, dammit? Where?

Then he recalled that he hadn't seen the trail the last time until he'd rounded that big boulder beside the pool. Maybe that was what was left of papa bear, he thought, remembering the rock formations he would find at the top.

"Are we trapped?" Winter Fawn called over the howl of the wind.

"There's a way up," he called back.

She eyed the rock wall and waterfall before them through the blowing curtain of snow. "You are certain?"

"I was here last year. There's a cabin not far from here."

"Shelter?" she asked as a shiver rocked her.

He knew just how she felt. He was doing a little shivering of his own. "Yes. Shelter. If it's still standing."

Thick ice had formed along the rock beneath the waterfall and along the edges of the pond. He urged the horse around the lone boulder and there was the trail, looking more like a mere depression in the snow than a well-traveled game and trapper route. But it was there, that's all Carson cared about.

He rode to the base of it and drew the horse up. The path was steep and rock-strewn, with hail beneath the snow. Asking the horse to carry a double load up that trail was the same as asking for the kind of trouble they didn't need.

"Hold on to the saddle horn," he told Winter Fawn. He swung down from the horse, leaving the buffalo robe around her shoulders.

"What are you doing?" she cried.

"He can't carry us both. I'm going to lead him."

Winter Fawn moved as if to slide from the horse. "Then I will lead the mule."

"The mule doesn't need leading." Forgetting about her wound, he wrapped his hands around her waist and shifted her into the seat of the saddle. "Hail Mary is more surefooted than any horse, and she's got more stamina. And I've got on sturdy boots. You don't. Your feet would freeze in five minutes."

Winter Fawn did not waste her breath arguing, for she knew he was right. Afoot she would be not only useless, but would soon become even more of a burden to Carson than she already was. "At least take the robe." She pulled it from her shoulders.

"No," he said adamantly, shaking his head. "You keep it. It's too heavy to carry on foot. I'll get blankets." So saying, he took two blankets from the bedroll and wrapped them around his shoulders.

After making sure Winter Fawn was covered as much as possible with the heavy robe, he took the reins in hand and started leading the horse up the trail that zigzagged up the rock wall.

The path was narrow, the going slippery. The mule appeared to have no problem at all. Same for the horse. Carson wished he could claim to be as surefooted. He slipped twice and barely caught his balance both times before tumbling off the edge of the trail.

Winter Fawn hated every minute it took to make the climb. Oh, how she hated it. Her mouth was as dry as desert sand. Her heart stopped altogether one minute, then fluttered like the wings of a hummingbird the next. Her hands and feet, relatively warm earlier beneath the buffalo robe, turned to ice. She wanted nothing more than to squeeze her eyes shut and pretend she was somewhere else. Anywhere else. Somewhere warm. And flat.

But she was here, on this trail scarcely wider than the horse's ribs. If she were somewhere else, she would not be with Carson. And she very much wanted to be with him, she admitted. But she did not want to watch him freeze or witness him tumble to his death off the edge of this path.

Oh please. Man-Above, guide his steps, keep him safe.

Carson looked over his shoulder and saw Winter Fawn's lips move, noticed her eyes were closed. He didn't blame her. He'd been doing a little praying of his own during the past few minutes. His toes were going numb, not to mention his bare hands.

When they finally reached the head of the trail and stepped out onto the high shelf, the wind sliced through him like a bayonet. He could no longer disguise his shivering or the chattering of his teeth.

The rock formation was there, right where he had prayed it would be. The cabin was less than half an hour away. On a good day. Since this was damn near the worst day he'd spent since his last battle, he figured it would take them an hour or more to reach their goal.

While waiting for the mule to join them, he stroked the horse's neck and murmured his thanks for a job well done. When Hail Mary reached the top, Carson stroked her also. He checked both animals' hooves and breathed a sigh of relief that neither had picked up any stones.

When he stepped beside the horse to remount, Winter Fawn turned stubborn on him. She refused to scoot up and let him mount behind. Instead, she slid back over the cantle and onto the skirt, where she had ridden for most of the day.

Too cold to argue with her, and considering that she had the warmer wrap, he climbed awkwardly into the saddle. The instant he was seated, she pressed herself to his back and reached around his shoulders with the buffalo robe to envelope him in the meager warmth with her.

They rode into the teeth of the blizzard. The world was reduced to stinging white, not even swirling, but driving directly into their faces.

They kept their faces down.

Carson wasn't sure how he found the cabin in all that white nothingness. He wasn't above believing in miracles just then. But suddenly there it was, gray and squat and abandoned, and as welcome to him in that moment as would have been the mansion at Greenbrier had his former home popped up in front of him.

He dismounted before the cabin and shoved open the door. It was dark and dirty and smelled like the south end of a northbound skunk, and was just about the most beautiful thing he'd ever seen.

He turned back toward the horse and caught Winter Fawn and the robe up in his arms as she was climbing down from the saddle. He thought for a minute that he was weaker than he'd realized. She seemed so much heavier than she should. Then he remembered that the thick hair on the buffalo robe wrapped around her had gotten soaked. It was covered in ice and snow, adding nearly as much weight again as Winter Fawn herself.

He carried her into the gloomy cabin and set her on her feet. He wanted nothing more than to fall with her to the floor and just lay there for a year or two, but he didn't fancy freezing to death, nor letting the horse and mule freeze either.

There was kindling and a few logs beside the rock fireplace. "See if you can get a fire started," he told Winter Fawn.

He went back outside and started unloading the packs from the mule, carrying them in and stacking them along the front wall. Outside there was a woodpile, thank God, at the corner of the cabin.

When the packs, pack saddle, and saddle were indoors, Carson led the animals to the lean-to around the corner. It wasn't much, just three flimsy walls and a roof, but it would help keep the wind off the poor beasts. Their saddle blankets were drier on the top side, having been protected from the rain and snow by the saddles. Underneath, they were damp with sweat. He turned each blanket over and put them back on the animals to help keep them warm.

They needed grain. On his way back into the cabin to get the grain sack from among the packs, he knocked the snow off the top of the woodpile and took an armload of firewood with him.

Winter Fawn had a small fire going. With her teeth chattering as hard as his, she rushed to help him stack the wood beside the fireplace. While he dragged out the bag of grain, she added more logs to the fire.

Carson's hands were so numb, his fingers so unresponsive, that he dropped the bag three times before he finally succeeded in getting it into his arms and out the door. There was a wooden crib nailed crudely to one wall in the lean-to. When Carson opened the bag to pour the grain, his fingers slipped and half the contents of the bag spilled into the bin.

He was tempted to just leave it. God knew the animals deserved it after this day. But he didn't know how many more days the grain would have to last. He couldn't take the chance of running out completely only two days into their trek. With hands that shook so hard they were nearly useless, he managed, after several minutes, to scoop a good portion of the grain back into the bag, leaving enough so each would have enough to last into tomorrow.

When he stepped back out of the lean-to, the wind, if possible, felt stronger, sliced deeper. He lowered his head and staggered into it, the bag of grain held tight against his chest. For safety, so he wouldn't spill the rest. For warmth—it kept the wind off at least a small part of him.

He made it back into the cabin and shut the door. No longer needing to lean forward to walk, he nearly fell on his face without the wind to hold him up.

Winter Fawn noted the grayness beneath his tanned skin and worried. He wasn't moving, except to sway where he stood just inside the door with the bag of grain clutched in his arms and a glazed look in his eyes. Still shivering herself, but not as badly since she'd started the fire, she took the bag from him and set it on the floor.

Then she touched his arm. "Come. The fire is warm."

Slowly he turned his face and stared at her, but didn't otherwise move.

"The fire, Carson," she urged. "It will warm you."

Finally he blinked, and awareness crept back into his eyes. He looked at the fire with the longing of a man seeing a glimpse of heaven. Then he shook his head. "Not yet. We'll need water. We need more wood to last the night."

When he turned back toward the door, Winter Fawn steeled herself for the bitter cold to come and started to follow him. She wanted to stay in the cabin. Desperately wanted to. She was so, so cold. She felt as if she'd been cold her entire life and would never be warm again. But if he was going back out there, she should, too.

"No," he said. "Stay here."

"I can help," she managed through her chattering teeth.

"Your feet will freeze in those moccasins. I'm wearing boots. You stay here. See if there are any dry clothes in the packs."

He was right about her feet. They were already numb, and she hadn't been walking in snow. Outside the door it was piled almost knee-keep.

If she could find dry clothes, she could help him that way. But it hurt to watch him go back out into the blizzard. Not as much as it would hurt to go with him, but it hurt.

"Wait," she told him. "You'll need something to pack snow in for melting." She knew her father always carried bladder pouches for heating water. Quickly she located two.

Carson took them from her and left. As soon as he shut the door behind himself, she knelt before her father's packs and started digging through them again. He always carried a change of clothes. She tried to hurry, but her hands were clumsy, her arms heavy.

Among her father's belongings she found ammunition for his rifle—the rifle he had with him. Her fingers brushed a hard object, and before she even saw it, she recognized by touch the book of poems by the man named Robert Burns. Her father never went anywhere without that book. He used to read aloud from it to her and Hunter. He said he would rather be without his rifle than to lose "Robby's poems."

She found the food supplies, the coffeepot, the skillet, all of which she set next to her on the floor.

There, finally, a green wool shirt, and pair of denim pants she had never seen him wear, and three pairs of heavy wool socks.

Beside her the door burst open. Carson, along with a whirl of snow, blew in on the icy wind. Before she could rise, he had dumped the wood, handed her the two pouches filled with snow, and left again.

Holding the pouches by their leather straps, she hugged her father's clothes to her chest and pushed herself to her feet. She would hang the pouches on the wall for now and warm the clothes at the fire, so that when Carson put them on they would warm him.

Looking down at her wet doeskin tunic and skirt, she realized that she, too, needed dry clothing. Carson did not need a sick woman to care for.

But there were no more clothes. A shirt, a pair of pants, and three pairs of socks. To clothe two people.

It could not be helped. Her mother had taught her that it was all right to wish for more, even, at times, to seek more. But one must first be grateful for that which was at hand. She would take the shirt and Carson would have the pants. They would each have a pair of socks to warm their feet.

She should have removed her sodden garments and put on the dry shirt while Carson was out getting more wood. She could not conceive of undressing in front of him. But the thought of having nothing to cover her legs when the next blast of freezing air swept the room with his next entrance was more than she could bear. She would wait until he was finished coming and going.

She found a nail on the wall beside the door and hung the pouches of snow there, then laid the clothes out before the hearth and started stacking the firewood Carson had dropped to the floor.

Twice more he came and went, looking more gray and haggard each time.

"This is enough, is it not?" she asked, stooping to stack the latest load.

"Yeah." He leaned back against the door and closed his eyes for a moment. "This will hold us into tomorrow."

"I found clothes." She motioned toward the items before the fire. "Not many. We will have to share."

Carson stared down at the pants, shirt, and socks. He was so cold that his mind was slow to realize the ramifications of so few clothes. At first all he could do was dread the effort it would take to remove the wet and half-frozen things he was wearing, and dread equally the moments his bare skin would be exposed to the air in the cabin that had yet to warm much.

When he finally realized that he would be without a shirt and Winter Fawn would be wearing nothing *but* a shirt, he shook his head. Why the hell didn't things like this happen to him when he was in good enough shape to take advantage of them? When he was with a woman he wouldn't feel guilty taking advantage of?

To take his mind off the inevitability of Winter Fawn's bare legs he was certain to get an eyeful of, he gazed blankly around the room. It was tiny, barely eight by eight, with one shuttered window and one door. Along the wall beside the door, the black soot in the rock fireplace spoke of much use in the past. There were three shelves mounted to the wall opposite the fireplace, and in the corner opposite the door, the frame of a bunk was nailed to the wall. There was no mattress, and what was left of the ropes to hold a mattress lay in tatters on the dirt floor.

Crossing the room, Carson peeled the frozen blankets from his shoulders. The ice that been holding them in the shape of his shoulders crackled and fell away as he draped them over one side of the bedframe. He then turned and looked at Winter Fawn, at the snow-covered buffalo robe draping her. The room was warming; snow was melting off the robe and dripping onto the hard-packed dirt floor.

Winter Fawn met his gaze for a long moment, reluctant to part with the robe, fearing the loss of its protection from the cold.

But then, she was so cold already that she doubted taking it off would make much difference. The room *was* warming, after all. Finally she nodded to the question in Carson's eyes. Yes.

She would take off the robe. Taking a deep breath, she let it slide from her shoulders. Its weight, her numb hands, and a frustrating weakness due to her wound and the cold nearly caused her to drop it. Carson helped her carry it to the other bedframe board.

She wondered if she was going to be able to lift the tunic off over her head.

Carson moved to one side of the fireplace and turned his back to her. He pulled the tail of his undershirt from his pants and peeled the shirt off over his head.

Winter Fawn turned abruptly away. She knew he was right. The sooner she got out of her wet clothes, the sooner she would get warm. The tunic was heavy with dampness, but she managed to slip her arms free and lift the doeskin over her head. Before dropping it on the rock hearth, she gave a brief glance over her shoulder to make certain Carson was not looking.

The bandage around his waist made her smile. Not because he'd been wounded, but because it was so similar to hers.

Then her gaze lowered.

Oh, my. With a sharp intake of breath, she quickly turned away, the sight of his trim, muscular, *naked* backside forever carved into her mind. With hands that shook from something more than cold, she pulled on her father's shirt.

Foolishness, she told herself. Pure foolishness to react in such a manner. A breechcloth on a windy day revealed nearly as much as what she had just seen. And she had certainly seen that and more when she and a group of girls had spied on the boys at the swimming hole.

But their skin had been dark and familiar. Carson's was white, his legs covered in dark hair.

The boys at the swimming hole had been that—boys. Carson was a man. A virtual stranger. And they were alone together in this dim shelter with the wind howling like a tortured wolf outside the door. And she herself was about to become half-naked. Maybe those things together caused her heart to race.

She ran a trembling hand down the front of the shirt. The wool was scratchy against her skin, but it was dry, and much warmer than her wet clothes.

The sleeves hung way past her fingers. She had to fold them

three times to get them above her hands. The tail hung down to just above her knees. She thought to leave her skirt on, but it was so wet that already its dampness was soaking into the hem of the shirt. Soon the shirt would be as wet as everything else. Beneath its length she loosened her skirt and let it fall to the floor. Behind her she heard the rustling of heavy fabric as Carson stepped into her father's pants. She heard his harsh breathing. She heard her heart pound in her ears.

"Are you decent?" came his voice.

She looked down at her bare legs. "Nae, but I fear it canna be helped."

Frowning, with one hand holding Innes's too-large pants up to keep from shocking Winter Fawn—not to mention freezing a rather important part of his anatomy—Carson turned. Her legs were long and shapely. He wished fleetingly that he was in good enough shape to appreciate them more fully. But he wasn't, and neither was she. Beneath her bronze skin was a paleness from the fierce cold. She needed to get warm. They both did.

They had the fire, the groundsheet, and the canvass tarp. Those things were not going to be enough. The buffalo robe was too wet to use, and the blankets were stiff with cold. But he hadn't pulled the blankets from the bedroll until after the rain had turned to snow. They were cold, but relatively dry. After finding a length of rope in the pack and tying it around his waist to keep from losing his pants, he grabbed the blankets from the bedframe, shook them out, and held them up before the fire. He was still shaking; the blankets fluttered.

Winter Fawn took the clothes they had both been wearing and draped them where the blankets had been, then she located the bedroll and spread out the groundsheet before the fire. She was shaking less than before, Carson noticed. He, too, was starting to thaw somewhat. But he was still miserably cold, and she had to be, too.

Something hot to eat and drink would warm them. He was about to put down the blankets and start a pot of coffee, but she beat him to it, using the water from the canteen.

Her braids left damp spots where they lay against the shirt, one in front, across her breast, and one down the back. "We need to dry your hair."

She put a hand to the braid draped across her breast. "Yes." With fumbling fingers, she untied the rawhide laces holding the ends of the braid together. Then, with a neat, practiced roll of her shoulders, she flipped the other braid forward and freed it. She reached to thread her fingers through one braid to unravel it.

Carson wanted to stop her. He wanted to do it himself. Wanted to feel those long, silky strands caress the sensitive skin between his fingers. But his hands were still so numb that he doubted he would feel much of anything, and she could get the braids undone easier and faster.

Someday, he vowed silently. Someday she would let him loosen her braids and run his fingers through her hair. Someday she would welcome it.

He looked around the room to make sure he hadn't left something undone. If there was, he had to do it now. Once he sat down, he knew he wouldn't be getting back up anytime soon.

The door. The latch held it shut, but he crossed behind Winter Fawn and put the bar down. Not that he thought for a minute anyone else was out there.

"One good thing," he said more to himself than to Winter Fawn. "Nobody can track us in this weather."

He stood behind Winter Fawn and used one of the blankets to blot the moisture from her hair. She swayed against him.

"Here." He sat on the tarp and took her hand to pull her down beside him. He tucked the second blanket around her bare legs. "That's better."

With the fire inching back the cold, Carson continued blotting her hair until it was nearly dry. Feeling started returning to his fingers, sending sharp needles of pain through them. But he could feel now. Dropping the blanket, he smoothed her hair with this hands, lifted it, fanned it out. Threaded his fingers through it. The braids had left waves and crinkles all through the thick mass. "So beautiful," he murmured.

Her shoulders quivered as another shiver of cold struck her.

He knew the feeling. He was still so cold that his skin wouldn't even raise gooseflesh.

"Until the buffalo robe dries," he told her, "we're going to have to share these blankets to get warm."

She gave him a wry smile. "We had to share last night, even with the buffalo robe. I'm not sure I'll ever be warm again."

"I know the feeling, but coffee will help. Food, too."

At least this time they didn't have hurry to put out the fire to keep from being seen by their pursuers. Nor did they need to keep the fire small. Carson added more wood. After he got the bacon on, he mixed up a batch of biscuits.

"How is your head?" Winter Fawn asked.

Carson paused. "To tell the truth, I'd forgotten about it. I guess it's just so cold I can't feel it."

"It does not hurt?"

"It hasn't hurt since you cleaned it last night."

She smiled and ducked her head.

By the time they had eaten their fill and finished off the coffee, Winter Fawn, he noticed, was barely able to keep her eyes open. "Come here." Lying down behind her so that she was closest to the fire, he pulled her into his arms, enfolding her against his chest, with the blankets covering them both.

Slowly their shivering eased, their teeth stopped chattering. "Better?" he whispered, his arms wrapped around her, his chin resting on the top of her head.

She didn't answer.

Carson raised his head and looked down at her. Light and shadows danced across her profile. Her eyes were closed, her breathing slow and regular. She was asleep.

Unable to stop himself, unwilling to even try, Carson brushed his lips across her cheek. Satiny soft. Warm. Sweet. Closing his eyes, he lay back down and let himself follow her into sleep.

Carson was dreaming. He was asleep and dreaming. How else could he explain the presence of a soft, warm woman in his arms? The bare flesh of a shapely hip felt like silk beneath his fingers. Her thigh was slim and firm. He ran his hand up and down, up and down, ignoring the urge to slide it to the inside of that thigh and up to the heat he knew awaited him. Once there, he knew he wouldn't want to leave, and he hadn't yet had enough of the hip, or the outer shape of the thigh. Hadn't explored her belly, her ribs, the breasts he would find farther up.

But first, the thigh and hip. He wanted more of them. Their silky softness made the tips of his fingers tingle.

Winter Fawn came awake slowly. Wind still howled outside like a tortured soul, while inside the fire burned steadily with a pleasant crackling sound. Soothing warmth surrounded her back, cocooned her, bathed her face. But another warmth, caressing her hip and thigh, excited rather than soothed.

Carson.

It was his hand that caressed her. Her shirt had ridden up to her waist, baring her to his touch.

She waited for the anger over his audacity to rise within her, but there was no anger. She searched inside herself for the shame she should feel over allowing him such liberties, but she found no shame. How could anything so glorious as his hard, callused hand on her flesh, or the heavy heat gathering down low inside her because of it, be shameful?

Winter Fawn was innocent in that she had never experienced a man's lust, or her own, for that matter. But she was not ignorant of what went on between men and women, and she knew this feeling welling up inside her, the swelling in her breasts, the tightening of her nipples, the hollow, moist throbbing between her legs, was lust.

She was not the only one feeling it. She knew what that hard ridge of flesh against her backside meant. He was aroused. He was ready to mate.

The thought sent twin shafts of longing and confusion shooting through her. Longing for this man who awoke feelings in her she had never known before. Not just these feelings of the flesh, glorious though they were, but also feelings in her heart. The feeling of staring straight into her destiny that first time she had looked into his eyes.

And confusion because she was not ashamed to want this man, even though they were not man and wife. And she should be ashamed. She should be repulsed, horrified. That she was not, that is what confused her.

The longing in her was so, so much stronger than the confusion. If she remained very, very still, and very, very quiet, she could pretend she was still asleep, and perhaps he would not stop. Perhaps he would go on touching her.

It was wrong to feel these things for a man not her husband, to want to join with him, to allow this need inside her to grow and grow until it threatened to swallow her whole. She knew, in her mind, these things were wrong. Yet being held in his arms, experiencing his hand on her bare skin, felt so . . . right. As if she had been waiting for Carson Dulaney her entire life. As if it was meant that they be together this way.

His hand did not stop at her hip this time. It slid to her belly. Up, up beneath her shirt, over her ribs, until he cupped her breast in his palm.

Winter Fawn held her breath and bit back a moan of startled pleasure. Oh! It was like nothing she had ever imagined before. If asked to describe the sensation, she would not have been able to. There were no words for the tingling heat, or the sharp tug in her womb when his thumb stroked her nipple. At the next stroke, she could not hold back the sound of pleasure that rose in her throat.

Her low purr pulled Carson from his sleep.

It wasn't a dream. The woman in his arms was no phantom. She was real. She was warm. She was . . . *Winter Fawn.*

"Good God." He pulled his hand from her breast, and it felt as though he were ripping off part of his own flesh and leaving it behind. He squeezed his eyes shut and sat up, burying his face in his hands.

How could he have done such a thing as fondle her in his sleep? He was despicable! He was the lowest form of—

"Carson?"

Oh, God, she was awake, and her voice was quivering. With revulsion? With fear? Anger? He had hoped, prayed, that she'd been asleep and would never know what he'd done. "I'm sorry," he ground out, unable to face her. "I'm . . . sorry."

With a thick Scottish burr, she said, "Ach, now there be somethin' every lass be wantin' to hear."

At her tart tone Carson turned his head and peered at her over his shoulder. "What?"

Anger radiated from her. "I was under the mistaken impression that ye were enjoyin' yerself."

Carson swallowed. "The mistaken—"

"Oh, don't fash yerself," she told him with a wave of her hand. "I don't suppose I be the first woman some man has found wantin'. Or left wantin'." Those last words were muttered under her breath, but loud enough for Carson to hear.

"Wha—" His voice broke. He cleared his throat and started again. "What did you say?"

"Nothing." She gave a delicate sniff and turned to face the fire. "I dinna say aught." Then she looked back at him and tilted her head. "Why is it, do ye suppose, that one man wants a woman, and the woman canna stand him. Then when she does find a man she can stand, one who appeals to her, all he can say is 'I'm sorry.' 'Tis a right odd way o' things, wouldna ye agree?"

The fire crackled as she boldly held his gaze. "Are you trying to tell me you liked what I was doing? The way I touched you?"

She sniffed again, a delicate sniff of disdain worthy of the haughtiest Southern Belles he'd ever known, and turned to stare at the fire. "I'm saying nothing. Me lips, as me da would say, is sealed."

"Yeah, and if he had any idea that I've had my hands on you the way I just did, he'd string me up by my neck and let the buzzards pick my bones clean."

"He isna here, Carson."

"The hell he isn't." Frustration roughened his voice.

"It disnae matter," she said softly. " 'Tis obvious you dinna feel the things I was feeling, or you wouldna have said you were sorry."

"Dammit, don't do this."

"Don't do what?" she asked, surprised, confused.

"Don't put a weapon like that into a man's hands."

"I dinna ken yer meaning. What weapon hae I given ye?"

"Don't tell a man you like the way he touches you."

"And why not, if 'tis true?"

"Because he'll take advantage of you. He'll get it in his head that if you like that, you'll like more."

"And?"

"God, you are innocent, aren't you?"

"If you mean I've never been touched before the way you touched me, then aye. Is that bad?"

Carson closed his eyes and prayed for strength. The strength to resist the sheer temptation of her. "Winter Fawn, a man will lie and cheat and steal, sometimes even kill, to get what he wants from a woman. And once he's got it, he'll walk away without looking back."

"You?" She looked at him with hurt and disbelief in her eyes. "You would do such a thing?"

"I've never met a man who wouldn't, given the right circumstances."

"That is not what I asked. I asked if you would do this. If you would lie and cheat and steal and kill to get what you want from me, and then walk away. Without looking back."

He opened his mouth to say yes, but the lie stuck in his throat. He had never been that type of man. But damn, she shouldn't trust him so much. He wanted her. Wanted everything she had to give. But he wasn't ready to take a wife, and she had no business ruining her life because of him.

"I think," she said quietly, "that you would like me to believe these things of you, but I canna, Carson. I have seen the man you are. If you dinna want me, then 'tis I who should apologize. I shouldna hae said aught when you pulled away from me."

"Not want you?" He nearly laughed with the irony of the situation. With a hand that no longer trembled with cold, he reached out and stroked her cheek. The way she closed her eyes and leaned into his touch was nearly his undoing. "I want you much more than is wise."

"Why?" Her eyes opened slowly. "Why is wanting me unwise?"

"Because," he said bluntly, "I'm not looking for a wife, and you should not give yourself to any man but your husband."

She laughed and pulled away from his touch. "You talk of giving. I had more in mind to take."

At her bald comment, a certain part of Carson's anatomy jerked stiffly to awareness. "Dammit, Winter Fawn, you—"

"Never mind," she told him. "I wouldna take from an unwilling man."

Despite himself, Carson laughed. "Oh, honey, I am anything but unwilling. How many men have you been intimate with?"

"Intimate? You mean, mated with?"

He pursed his lips. "That's as good a word as any. How many?"

She looked away again. "None."

"That's what I thought. That's how it should be. When you take a husband—"

"You mean when my uncle or my grandfather or my father chooses a husband for me, whether he be to my liking or not."

"They would not choose someone unworthy, would they? Someone you truly couldn't love?"

"My uncle chose Crooked Oak. Love? There is not even a liking between us. Not from my side."

"Your father wouldn't agree to Crooked Oak. Not now."

"I know not what is in my father's mind. I see him for a few days every spring, and that is all. He canna abide to be around me longer than that."

Carson stared, stunned. "Why do you say that? He loves you."

Her smile was sad. "Perhaps. But still he leaves. I fear he will marry me off to the first man he sees, just so he will not need to worry about me."

"I think you're wrong about that."

She eyed him from the corner of her eye. A sly smile played across her lips. "He might even try to give me to you. He likes you."

"Oh, no." Carson shook his head vigorously. "Oh, no. I've had one wife. I don't need another one."

Winter Fawn laughed. "I see panic in your eyes. Do not worry, Car-son Du-la-ney," she said, giving his name the halting pronunciation of her people. "I willna let him talk you into such a thing, since ye be so reluctant. I dinna want a husband who doesna like to touch me."

Carson opened his mouth to again deny the charge, then

snapped it shut. What the hell was he thinking, to try to convince her how much he liked touching her? He was supposed to be talking her—and himself—out of such behavior. He had no business trifling with Innes MacDougall's daughter. The man would cut off Carson's balls and ram them down his throat.

The wind howled and the storm raged for more than twenty-four hours. Outside the cabin, snow piled in drifts, and the supply of firewood dwindled.

Inside, the cabin retained a meager warmth. Their clothes dried. The buffalo robe also dried, allowing Carson and Winter Fawn to keep at least the semblance of distance between them.

But when they slept, their bodies ignored the restraints Carson placed upon them. In sleep, Winter Fawn instinctively sought his warmth and nearness. Carson shifted closer to her softness. More than once they woke in each other's arms.

Each time, Carson quickly retreated. And each time, it grew progressively more difficult to remember why he should. Constantly he had to remind himself that she was Innes's daughter; Innes trusted him. She was innocent, and Carson felt duty-bound to see that she remained that way.

There wasn't much to do in the cabin but eat, sleep, pace the dirt floor, and brave the blizzard for more firewood. Whenever he had to go out for wood, Carson also checked on the horse and mule. He took them water they'd got from melting snow, and gave them more grain.

Their second morning in the cabin they woke, as usual, in each other's arms. But this time something dragged Carson's attention from the heat in his loins and the woman in his arms. Something was different. Something . . .

Frowning, he raised his head and stared at the door.

In his arms, Winter Fawn stiffened. "What is it?" she whispered.

"Shh. Listen."

Winter Fawn half rose, barely registering that for once, Carson held on to her rather than turning her loose. Were they out there? Had Crooked Oak somehow managed to find them? She strained for a sound that would tell her. All she heard was the pounding of her own heart. "I hear nothing," she whispered.

A slow, wide grin curved Carson's lips. "That's because there's nothing to hear."

"Wha— No wind! The storm has stopped!"

"Sounds like it." With a laugh, Carson stood and swooped her up in his arms. In one stride he was at the door and flinging it open.

Dazzling sunlight reflected off the snow-covered landscape and nearly blinded them. Icy air stung their nostrils. Winter Fawn's eyes stung from both. She looped her arms around Carson's neck and hoped he wouldn't realize he was holding her. She liked being in his arms. "It's beautiful," she said, looking out at the fantastic shapes the wind had carved into the snow.

"And dangerous," Carson added lightly. "Never forget that beauty can be dangerous." He looked down at her, his blue eyes as bright and dazzling as the sky. His head lowered toward hers.

Winter Fawn's breath backed up in her lungs.

"Beautiful." His breath brushed her lips. "And dangerous." Closer, closer he leaned. "Like you."

She forgot all about the cold and the blinding snow. Her fingers flexed against his neck. "I am not dangerous."

"Aren't you?" came his husky question. Then his lips took hers softly.

Winter Fawn felt her breath glide smoothly out of her body. She felt her bones weaken and turn to water. Had she been on her feet, she knew she would have felt the earth tilt beneath her. She felt his mouth, warm and firm against hers, and it was glorious. Never could she have imagined the dark taste of him, the way her heart would race, the way her mind would empty until there was only him, only his lips, his tongue, his teeth gently nibbling on her.

She understood so much in those moments when he kissed her. She now thought she knew what had put that look in her mother's eyes, the one that made her smile as though she had swallowed the sun. That look of secret happiness whenever Smiling Woman had looked at Red Beard.

Winter Fawn also understood that this kiss, though it had yet to end and she prayed that it might never end, had already changed her life. She would never be the same again, never look at Carson the same, as a stranger she was coming to know. He was inside her now, a part of her she would carry with her forever. Her life was no longer solely her own.

Nor was her body her own any longer. Every time he looked at her now, she would remember this kiss, and her bones would melt. And she would want him to kiss her again.

How could she miss his warmth and kiss when he had yet to release her? She tightened her arms around his neck and kissed him back, determined to take all he would give her, fearing this was all there would be from this reluctant white man.

But reluctance was the farthest thing from Carson's mind just then. He was lost. Lost in the kiss, in her warmth, her open responsiveness. Lord, but she was responsive. He wanted to take her down right then and there on the snow and find out how she would respond to something more than a kiss. He wanted all of her. Wanted to simply gobble her up.

"Oh, yeah," he whispered against her lips. "I was right, honey, you are dangerous."

"I think," she said breathlessly, staring up at him, "that you are dangerous, too."

Carson might have kissed her again. He wanted to, badly. But something else drew his attention away, and hers, too.

The wind was rising. But this was not the icy wind from the north, bringing another blizzard. This was a warm, moist wind, strong from the west.

Winter Fawn raised her face into it and sniffed. "Chinook."

"What?"

"The wind. It is called a Chinook wind. It will melt the snow."

Carson glanced around at the four-foot drifts against the side of the cabin, and others blocking the trail that had led them there. "In a few days, if it keeps up," he said skeptically.

Winter Fawn shook her head. "Today. It has already begun. Look." She pointed toward the roof of the cabin.

Carson followed her gesture, amazed to see water dripping

from the eaves. Amazed further that he had been so wrapped up in her, in kissing her, that he hadn't heard the rushing plops.

With Winter Fawn still in his arms, he stepped back into the cabin and put her down. If the snow was going to melt, they would need to leave.

CHAPTER 10

The snow melted so rapidly that bare patches of ground appeared across the valley before noon, growing larger each passing minute. Drifts shrank. Water stood in low-lying areas, and trickled downhill wherever it could.

Carson and Winter Fawn left the cabin shortly after midday and headed north for Hardscrabble Creek and the wide pass that led through the Wet Mountains to Wet Mountain Valley. The warm Chinook wind had swept the pass clean of all but the deepest drifts by the time they reached it that afternoon.

Winter Fawn had started the trip the same way she had the day the blizzard had struck, by holding on to the cantle rather than Carson as she rode behind him. Her wounds were much better now, and she was stronger. But that was not why she tried to sit up straight and manage without him.

It was the kiss.

Or rather, the way Carson had been able to put the kiss out of his mind the instant he stood her on her feet. He had kissed her until her head had spun, then simply walked away and started packing their gear. She had been breathless. Her entire life had been altered. Yet he appeared to be completely unaffected. Because of that, she was reluctant to hold on to him.

The first steep incline disabused her of that idea rapidly. She had to wrap her arms tightly around his waist to keep from slipping off the back end of the horse.

"How long will it take us to reach your ranch?" she asked him.

He turned his head slightly to answer. "We should get there tomorrow afternoon."

Tomorrow afternoon. "Do you think my father and the others will be there?"

"I hope so. I expect they got there before the blizzard hit, if it even hit there."

The sun was going down. She would spend this one last night on the trail with him, then they would reach her father. And after that? She had no idea what would happen.

Her life should have been predictable. Or as predictable as that of any of Our People. Her family should have found a good man to be her husband, a man she could respect and love. She should have lived with him and borne his children. Every spring she would have taken down her lodge, packed her belongings, and gone with her band to join the rest of the tribe to follow the buffalo for the summer. Every fall she and her children and husband, should he still be living, would have come back to the foothills for the winter.

From season to season, she would have known what to expect.

Now she knew nothing about her own future.

Her father had ridden into camp, and Winter Fawn had helped free his friend. She did not know if she would ever be welcomed back. What was her grandmother thinking about her leaving? What would Crooked Oak and Two Feathers say when they returned to camp empty-handed?

So many questions, and no answers. She didn't even know if she would go with her father, wherever he might go. He had not wanted her before. Why should he want her with him now?

Besides, she was a grown woman and should not be clinging to her father or counting on him to take care of her.

And what of Hunter? Was he asking himself these same questions?

But it was not the same for a man, even one as young as her brother.

By the time Carson stopped for the night, Winter Fawn still had no answers.

"You're awfully quiet tonight," he said, pouring the last of the coffee into their cups.

Her only answer was a soft murmur.

"Is something wrong?" Carson gave a short laugh. "You've been forced to leave your people, your friends, your home, because you helped a stranger."

His words only served to remind her of the uncertainty of her life.

"You've been shot, shot at, hailed on, frozen half to death, had nothing to eat for days but a little poor food. That ought to be enough, but why do I get the impression there's more?"

All Winter Fawn could offer him was a slight smile and a shake of her head. "You are right. That is enough. I'm just tired."

"Is your wound bothering you?"

She shook her head again. "No more than it should. Not much, really."

He took a sip of his coffee and looked up at the night sky. "I've never seen wounds heal as fast as mine have. And yours. Must be the mountain air."

She ducked her head. "Aye. That must be it."

They spoke no more as they finished their coffee. Carson wondered at her pensive expression, the frown line between her eyes. But then, she had plenty to frown about. On top of everything he had named earlier, she had to worry about a man, a virtual stranger, who couldn't keep his hands or his lips to himself.

Was that what concerned her tonight?

It concerned the hell out of him. He hadn't wanted to stop kissing her this morning. That realization rocked him. Yet, with the way he'd been reacting to her from the beginning, he supposed it shouldn't. He wanted her. It was as simple and as complicated as that.

Had he upset her, scared her this morning when he'd kissed

her? She hadn't looked scared or upset. She had looked like he had felt—like she wanted more.

Damn. He didn't even want to think about that.

He was going to have to sleep beside her one more night. It would be too cold to sleep apart. They would have to share the blankets and buffalo robe. Not to mention the groundsheet; melting snow made for downright wet ground.

As he put out the fire, he steeled himself for the amazingly enjoyable torture of lying next to her one last time. Tomorrow they would reach his ranch. Her father would be there, and even if he wasn't, there were beds in the house, beds in separate rooms. No more need to sleep beside her. No more excuse.

When he had delayed as long as he reasonably could, he crawled beneath the blankets and found her lying with her back to him. Tension seemed to radiate from her.

"Winter Fawn?" he called softly.

After a pause, she answered. "Aye?"

Carson lay on his back, not touching her. "Have I done something to upset you?"

The soft sound of the blanket shifting accompanied her movement as she turned onto her back. "Of course not."

"Good," he said. He was quiet for a long moment, waiting for her to turn her back against him again. When she didn't, he started to wonder about things he shouldn't be wondering about. Things like, had she liked his kiss as much as the look on her face that morning had led him to believe? Or had he misread her. Did she like lying next to him as much as he liked lying next to her?

Around and around the questions went, and all the answers he came up with told him she would welcome his touch, and more.

There couldn't be any "more." But he could hold her this one last night, couldn't he? Deliberately hold her, rather than waiting for it to happen in their sleep.

"Are you cold?" *Say yes,* he silently urged. *Say yes and give me an excuse.*

"No," she whispered.

Carson swallowed. Disappointment tasted sharp on his tongue. She wasn't cold. He'd given her the perfect opportunity to snuggle up next to him if she wanted, and she hadn't taken it.

"Not too much," she finally added.

Oh, God. "Come here," he said, slipping his arm around her and gently inviting her closer.

With a breathy sound that might have been a sigh, she rolled to her side and scooted closer, until she pressed flush against his side. Her head nestled into his shoulder as if the spot had been made specifically for that purpose. Her small, bruised hand rested on his chest.

Carson let out the breath he hadn't known he'd been holding. He tightened his arm around her and pressed his lips to the top of her head. "Sleep warm."

"Aye, I will, now."

If he wasn't mistaken, that was a smile he heard in her voice.

He went to sleep with a smile of his own, and a nice, warm tingling in his loins.

He woke in the grayness of predawn with Winter Fawn's knee pressed against his hard-on, and the rest of her sprawled across his chest. When she arched her neck and opened her eyes to look at him, he forgot all the reasons why he should not pleasure them both with a kiss.

What reasons?

It was only a kiss. That's all he wanted. Just a quiet, good-morning kiss.

With one hand at the back of her head, he pulled her lips closer to his. With his other arm, he held her firmly against his chest. And then he kissed her.

It started out the way he'd planned, a quiet good-morning kiss. A soft sharing of breath, a gentle brush of lips. Then her tongue tentatively touched his lower lip and Carson felt his blood catch fire. He deepened the kiss, taking her mouth with his like a plundering marauder.

He felt her hands clutching at his head. He heard the soft whimper that came from her throat.

Too much. He was taking too much, pushing too hard, too far. With more effort than it should have taken, he pulled his mouth from hers, astounded to realize how hard he was breathing.

"I'm sorry," he managed.

"No," she whispered forcefully. She shifted upward along his chest until their lips brushed.

The movement forced her thigh more fully against his groin. Blood rushed there, pooled, heated. He bit back a groan.

"Don't stop." It was not a plea she spoke, but a demand, as, this time, her mouth took his with fierce hunger.

Ah, God, he could taste the hunger in her, feel it feed the craving in him even as that craving grew stronger. He took her kiss and gave in return. His hands roamed up and down her back, up, and down, then up beneath the soft doeskin tunic, over the bandage at her waist, to bare flesh. Smooth. Soft. Silky flesh. Warm and living. He couldn't get enough of it, of her. He wanted to just gobble her up, swallow her whole until she was inside him, a part of him that would always, always be there, warm and exciting and giving.

She shifted atop him and he raised his thigh between hers to keep her from slipping off. God, she was hot. Through his denims and her doeskin skirt he could feel the searing heat between her thighs.

Winter Fawn, too, felt the heat. The heat, and so many other things. Something was there, something she could not define, just beyond her reach. Something she instinctively knew she wanted. Had to have.

Her blood rushed to that secret place between her legs and created a deep, powerful throbbing. So deep and powerful that she pulled her mouth from Carson's and, gasping for breath, stared down at him in shock.

With his hands on her shoulders, Carson raised his thigh more firmly against the heat between her legs.

Heat gushed through her. The throbbing deepened. With a soft cry, she shifted and pressed against him even more.

"Yes," he hissed, his breath as harsh as hers. "Feel it. Let it happen."

What? she wanted to cry. Feel what? What was happening? But she could not ask because she could not speak. Her words, along with her breath, were locked in her throat. All she could do was move against him, clamping her thighs around his. The sensations felt like colors—brilliant shades of red—like fire.

Each movement against his leg brought them into sharper focus, intensified them, heightened them, until she thought she could not bear another moment without exploding. Or screaming.

An instant later, she did both. The explosion was inside her, shocking in its intensity. The scream was breathless. On and on, the sharp ripples slammed through her, rocking her. Changing her. Forever.

Carson watched her face as it happened. A deep shudder wracked him. Watching her pleasure was the most arousing thing that had ever happened to him. He was torn in two with the need to raise her skirt and bury himself inside her, feel her inner muscles clamp around him and give him the same sort of pleasure she had just found. Yet, if he sought his own pleasure, he would miss the chance to soothe her, to ease her back to the world, back into herself.

Not to mention that she was the daughter of a man who trusted him to keep her safe. Even from himself.

No, he would not—could not—take his pleasure. But pleasuring her was proving to be fulfilling in its own right. He was man enough, he hoped, to give unselfishly to this woman who had already given him so much.

Gently he eased her back down onto his chest and wrapped his arms around her. He held her there, stroking her back, her hair, her arms, praising her with whispered words.

When Winter Fawn once again became aware of her surroundings, the first thing she realized was that Carson held her safely in his arms. She was wrapped in a cocoon of warmth. She could almost feel the caring in his embrace.

The second thing she realized was that the hard ridge of his arousal still pressed beneath her thigh. Slowly she pushed herself up on arms that were alarmingly weak and looked down at him in the gray light. "Why did you do that?"

His expression was tender, yet somber. "Because, for all you've given me, this was something I could give you."

Winter Fawn felt a squeezing sensation around her heart. "Payment? You give me this for payment?"

"No." His arms tightened around her. "I didn't mean it that way. I just wanted to give you something."

"But you did not take anything for yourself. Is this not something that is to be shared between a man and woman?"

"Between the right man, and the right woman."

The squeezing around her heart tightened painfully. "And I am the wrong woman?"

"I am the wrong man. Don't think for a minute that I didn't get anything out of this."

"You dinna get what you should have." She rubbed her thigh against him and watched his eyes close, felt his chest heave.

"Stop that," he said with a low groan and a short laugh. "I got what I wanted." His eyes opened and stared into hers. "I've never . . . watched a woman find her pleasure before. There was nothing unselfish about it. It was something I'll remember for the rest of my life. Thank you for giving me this."

Winter Fawn did not know whether to laugh exultantly, or weep in despair. She laid her head on his shoulder. "You are a generous man, Carson Dulaney."

"I'm a selfish son of a bitch." There was a smile in his voice. "Don't ever forget it."

"I won't." She knew he meant for her to never forget he was selfish, but what she meant by her answer was something else entirely. Never would she forget this morning and the man who had shown her what it was to experience her womanhood.

Before the sun was up they were on their way. They followed the creek west and up toward its source. Snow clung to the north-facing sides of the canyon, but the warm wind and sunshine of the day before had cleared the south-facing wall. Gradually the canyon widened into a grassy valley bordered with tall pines. The creek narrowed until it was nothing more than a stretch of wet grass instead of a flowing stream.

Then there was no more evidence of the stream, and they crested the pass and started down the drier, western side of the Wet Mountains.

Winter Fawn had never seen the Wet Mountain Valley. Bordered on the west by the high, snow-packed Sierra Blancas, the valley stretched south as far as the eye could see, thick with cottonwoods still winter-bare along the creeks, and wide wetlands of willows.

Our People, she knew, would love it here. The western slopes of the Wet Mountains were drier than the valley floor and looked to have good ground for a small village here and there.

But there were the Utes to consider. This was their territory. She also suspected that this valley would be colder and get more snow than the small valley where Our People wintered on the other side of the Wets.

But the Utes would not come today, or anytime soon. There was too much snow in the Sierra Blancas. They would wait for an easier time.

With her arms around Carson's chest, Winter Fawn leaned against his back and watched a herd of deer, unafraid of the intruders approaching, amble toward a stream.

Carson confused her. The things he had made her feel that morning had been so incredible, she could not fathom why he would deny himself those same feelings. Perhaps it wasn't the same for a man.

Winter Fawn nearly laughed aloud. She had always heard that it was the man who enjoyed the intimate encounters, and the woman who must endure. Perhaps she and Carson were made backwards.

He said she should wait to give herself to the man who would be her husband. What man would that be? Certainly not Crooked Oak. Never Crooked Oak.

If she did not return to her grandmother's lodge, how was she to ever get a husband? The usual way was for a man to choose the girl he wanted and make arrangements with her male relatives.

Slowly Winter Fawn raised her head from Carson's shoulder. Her mother had not waited for a man to make an offer for her. Smiling Woman had told the tale often when Winter Fawn had been a child. She had come across the white man in the forest.

Winter Fawn smiled fondly. Her mother had seen the white man and had thought he was smiling at her. Right then and there, she had fallen in love with his smile.

Smiling Woman had not been in the habit of falling for a

handsome smile, nor had she been in the habit of approaching white men. But she had felt drawn to the big man with hair the color of flames. And the hair was not only on his head, but his face as well!

It was only as she had neared him that Smiling Woman had realized the man was not smiling, but grimacing in pain. His foot was caught in the steel teeth of a white man's bear trap.

Using a stout pine branch, she had pried his foot free and helped him back to the village. There she helped her mother and the medicine man nurse him back to health.

And then, Winter Fawn thought with a soft smile, Smiling Woman had pursued Red Beard shamelessly. "I knew," she had told her daughter years later, "that I would welcome no other man but him to my blankets."

Mother, Mother, I fear that I know just how you felt.

But no, Winter Fawn told herself, she was not in love with this white man. She knew naught of love. She would do both him and herself far better service by keeping an eye out over her shoulder to make certain Crooked Oak had not found their trail and followed them to this peaceful valley.

Crooked Oak and his men did not follow. When the blizzard had struck, they had ridden before it down the mountains and returned to camp. They were cowards, Crooked Oak thought with scorn. Children, to run and hide from a little storm. He was furious at their behavior. Even more furious with himself for accompanying them. He should have let them go and followed the white man on his own.

Now he might never find Winter Fawn. At least, not alive. That fool white man had headed straight into the teeth of the blizzard. In the spring they would probably find his body, and Winter Fawn's.

Crooked Oak rained down every curse he could think of upon the white man's head. *How am I to achieve my rightful greatness among Our People without Winter Fawn?*

Winter Fawn was part of his destiny. Nothing was possible if he did not have her.

She could not be dead. He would not let himself believe that

all his plans were in vain, that his sacred vision had been false. She was alive, and he would find her if he had to search clear into Ute territory; if he had to search alone.

"Come," he said to the men gathered in his lodge—the same five men who had ridden with him. The same ones who had turned away from the storm and made for home like children afraid of the dark. "Surely it is warm enough for you now," he said with a sneer.

No one said anything as they followed him out of the lodge into the sunshine. They had all argued viciously as they had huddled around Crooked Oak's fire while the storm had raged. All but Crooked Oak had fallen sullenly silent the next day when the warm Chinook winds came.

"Where do you intend we go?" Two Feathers was the only one among them brave enough to speak directly to Crooked Oak. "Do we try to pick up their trail again?"

"Yes. But first we go get the wagon." What heros they would be, Crooked Oak thought, when they returned to camp with a wagonload of goods for everyone to share. There might be food, clothes, who knew what. "Our People will welcome the goods and supplies. Perhaps there is ammunition."

"We should split up," Talks Loud stated. "Some go for the wagon, the others after the white man and Winter Fawn."

"We stay together," Crooked Oak said sharply.

"Crooked Oak is right." Red Bull nodded. "The wagon is on the white man's road. If there is trouble, six of us are stronger than three."

The others concurred. Cowards, Crooked Oak thought. Were they not Dogmen, the fiercest of warriors? It would take more than a dozen white men to best three Dogmen.

But he did not discourage them in their fear. He did not trust any but himself to see the job done. Talks Loud would keep too much of the loot for himself and not share it with the others. Two Feathers would see the goods fairly distributed, but if Crooked Oak let him, and took off after Winter Fawn, then he himself would get none of the supplies.

Besides, how was everyone to remember that he was the one responsible for these gifts if he was not present? The original idea for revenge, which had led to the attack on the wagon, had been Crooked Oak's. He had led the attack. Now he was leading the search. Our People must not be allowed to forget who had done all of these important things for them.

He could return with the wagon, then resume his search for Winter Fawn.

"Let us go for the wagon," he said again. "Then, the woman."

It took only a few hours to reach the spot where they had surprised the white man. When they arrived, Crooked Oak swore viciously. The wagon was gone.

Could nothing go right?

It was the white man's fault. All white men. From the instant he had ridden from behind the rocks and confronted the one called Car-son, everything had gone wrong.

Remember the vision.

Yes. He must remember the vision. He would have his revenge against all whites. He would lead Our People in a great war and rid the land of their enemies. He would become the White Killer, the greatest warrior, the greatest leader of all nations.

Winter Fawn was the key. Not the wagon, not the white man, but Winter Fawn. With her at his side, the prophecy would come true and everything would be his.

Without her, there would be nothing.

He turned his horse back toward the mountains. Let the others follow or not. His path lay clear in his mind now. He would find Winter Fawn.

Innes MacDougall took another drink from his bottle of Taos Lightning and counted off the days again, starting with the day their ragged little group of escapees had gotten separated.

He had gritted his teeth in frustration when he'd realized Carson and Winter Fawn had been spotted by the warriors. He'd feared they were all in for it for sure. But Carson had done what he'd said he wanted to do, and that was lead the warriors away from his daughter and sister. In his place, Innes would have done the same.

"But dammit, lad," Innes muttered, looking out across the

grasslands to the buttes beyond. "Did ye hae to take me lass wi' ye?"

The answer, of course, was yes. If Carson had stopped long enough to put Winter Fawn off the horse, Crooked Oak would have caught him. Innes knew that.

It dinna help.

But Innes had never been one to fail to take advantage where he could, as long as it dinna harm a body what dinna deserve to be harmed. With the warriors taking off after Carson and Winter Fawn, the way had been clear for Innes to ride out onto the plains and get Carson's wagon. The lad had sunk a fair penny into the goods he'd bought in Pueblo. There was no sense leaving them for some scalawag to carry off for his own.

They had reached the wagon near sundown and made it to the safety of Colorado City that night.

He had told Carson he did not want his children in a town, but mostly he'd meant his daughter. Whites might scorn Hunter's Indian blood, but they wouldn't necessarily think of him as easy prey, or available goods, the way they would a young, beautiful Arapaho woman. Still, Innes had taken the precaution of waiting outside town until dark before entering Colorado City.

That was day one.

From Colorado City to the ranch—day two.

Now here it was, near sundown, and they'd been at the ranch for three days. Waiting. Watching. Praying.

Five days. Five days since Carson and Winter Fawn had led the warriors away from the rest of their party. Five bloody days. Why, a body could walk all the way to Denver and back afoot in that length of time.

There had been a storm in the mountains. That had Innes worried. Carson was a good man, and smart, but he wasn't used to mountain storms. Wasn't used to mountains at all.

"Any sign of 'em?"

Innes turned to find Beau Rivers, one of Carson's hands. "Nae. Nary a sign."

"I wouldn't fret," Rivers said in his lazy Southern drawl. "The cap'n's been in tight spots before. He'll show up, you mark my words."

Innes took another drink from his bottle. "Aye," he said in hopes of convincing himself. "He'll show."

From the bluff on the south side of the river, where Hunter had gone in search of higher ground from which to watch, came a shrill Arapaho cry of victory.

Innes whirled and saw his son pointing toward the north. He looked in that direction, squinting, searching. There! A small dust cloud. Was that them?

"What'd I tell ye?" Rivers slapped Innes on the back and let out a wild Rebel yell. "Hey, Frank! The cap'n's comin'!"

Winter Fawn's first view of Carson's ranch came with the cresting of a hill.

With a low "Whoa, boy," Carson pulled the horse to a stop. "We made it."

Winter Fawn peered over his shoulder. To the left and right of the hill where they sat, a line of low bluffs stretched out and curved away on either side. Below them lay a long, narrow valley thick with lush grass and cradling the river called Huerfano. The Orphan River. Thick stands of cottonwoods lined the banks, and across the river, the grass stretched out to a line of fifty-foot bluffs dotted with cedar.

On a slight rise this side of the river sat a log cabin that she supposed was what whites called two-story. She had never been inside such a building and wondered that anyone would want to live in a place where people walked above their heads.

Near the house stood a barn built of flat boards, like the houses she had seen in Colorado City once when her band had ridden near on the way to their winter camp in the hills. Fences around the barn held a number of horses. A smaller log house sat off to the west beyond the corrals.

And there, in front of the main house, stood a big, broad-shouldered man with flaming red hair and beard.

"Aye," she said in response to Carson's comment. "We made it."

As eager as she was to see her father, Winter Fawn felt sadness well within her. These next few minutes were likely to be the last she would ever spend alone with Carson.

He turned his head and looked at her, and she read her thoughts in his eyes. After a moment, he spoke again. "Are you ready?"

Winter Fawn gazed at him as though it were her last chance to look upon his face. She felt that somehow, it was. Everything would be different now. She didn't know where she would go or what she would do. But she would remember these few days with Carson for the rest of her life.

Slowly, she nodded. "I'm ready."

The door to the house banged open, and Bess and Megan rushed out to join the men in the yard. "Is it them?" Bess cried.

Megan jumped up and down. "Is it Daddy and Winter Fawn?"

"Girls! Come back!" Mrs. Linderman dashed from the house and grabbed each girl by the arm. "You must come back inside. It might be Indians."

Innes shook his head in disgust. According to Rivers and Johansen, Carson had hired the widow woman in Badito, just down the river, to tend the house and take care of the girls. Innes had never seen a more useless creature. The woman was scared of her own shadow. And he damn sure dinna care for her refusing to let Hunter step foot in the house. Chased him away from the door with a frying pan, she did, shouting and calling him a murdering savage.

Innes had had an idea to stick around for a time and help Carson get the ranch on its feet. But if the woman stayed, Innes would take his children and leave. He had no tolerance for people who had no tolerance. He didn't care if her husband had been scalped right next to his own outhouse. He was sorry for the man, and the woman, but the deed hadn't been done by Hunter, and the woman had no call to go a'screechin' every time she saw the boy.

Wee Megan pulled free of the Linderman woman's hold and darted out toward the incoming riders. "It's Daddy!" she cried. "It's Daddy and Winter Fawn!"

"Carson!" Bess ran after Megan, waving frantically. "Carson!"

Beau Rivers chuckled. "Think they're glad to see him?"

"Probably not near as glad as he is to see them," Innes said, going by his own feelings at seeing his daughter safe on the back of that horse.

There it was again, that huge lump that rose in his throat, as it always did the first time he saw her after having been away from her. Ach, but she looked so like her mither, she did. So very beautiful, so very special.

To be sure, Smiling Woman's skin had been darker, her face more round. Her eyes had been deep brown, while Winter Fawn's—Hunter's, too—were the same gray as his own. There were other differences as well, if he cared to dwell on them. But this was Smiling Woman's daughter, and no mistake. His daughter. He did not stop to think that as a young woman raised in the way of Our People, it was not proper for her to embrace a man, not even her own father. He thought only of how worried he'd been, how fair glad he was to see her. He saw only the delight in her eyes when she spotted him.

Then he saw the way she clung to Carson, and a prickle of unease stole up his neck. What was this? She did not hold on to the cantle, as she could have. She was not grasping his sides, as might be logical, nor even wrapping her arms around his waist if she were afraid of falling off.

No, his lass was doing none of those things. Her arms came up beneath Carson's and her hands reached up and splayed across the man's chest. It looked, to Innes's stunned gaze, entirely too much like a caress.

The prickle of unease turned into a flush of rage when Carson dismounted and turned to lift Winter Fawn from the horse. He didn't merely grasp her and lift her down. First their gazes met, and lingered. Then his hands slid up her sides, practically brushing her breasts—ach, but his own wee daughter was a grown woman, with *breasts*—before clasping her beneath the arms. Placing her hands on Carson's shoulders, Winter Fawn looked down at him as though . . .

Ach, but Innes refused to even finish the thought.

Carson pulled her from the horse, and she ended up flush against his chest. Their gazes were still locked on each other.

What the devil is going on here?

And then she was there before Innes, and he forgot his suspicions, his questions. He swept her up in his arms and twirled her around and laughed to keep from bubbling and making a fool of himself.

"Da!" she cried. "Oh, Da, 'tis glad I am to see ye."

"And I you, lass, and I you."

Carson turned, stunned at the feeling that ran through him at the sight of Winter Fawn in her father's arms. If he wasn't mistaken, what he felt was jealousy. Good God!

He hadn't wanted to let her go. Their time alone together was over. There would be no more sharing of blankets for them. No more kisses. Never again would he see the pleasure of climax fill her face.

"Daddy, Daddy!"

Turning his gaze from Winter Fawn to Megan, Carson swooped his daughter up into his arms and squeezed her tight. "How's my girl?"

"We missed you, Daddy."

"I missed you, too, sweetheart. Bess . . ." He held out one arm and hugged her close to his side. "I missed you both."

"Are you all right?" Bess asked, her brow creased. "You took so long getting here, we were worried."

"We're fine. We would have been home sooner, but we had to sit out a blizzard."

"Really?" Megan's eyes widened. "What's a blizzard?"

"It's lots of snow and wind and freezing cold."

Megan wrinkled her nose. "That doesn't sound like fun."

Carson laughed. "No, blizzards aren't any fun at all." He set her back on her feet and turned to greet his men. "Beau, Frank."

"Cap'n." Beau shook his hand.

"Good to see you, Captain," said Frank Johansen.

"Same here," Carson said, shaking his hand. "Everything all right around here?"

"Pretty quiet," Beau told him as Hunter joined Innes and Winter Fawn.

"Mr. Dulaney." Mrs. Linderman, her back as straight as a board, marched up to him. "That," she said pointing at Winter Fawn, "is a squaw."

"I beg your pardon?"

"One murdering savage was bad enough. Now you've brought another."

Carson blinked. "What did you say?"

"You hired me to give a proper upbringing to your daughter and your sister, both young and impressionable girls. I cannot be responsible for their well-being if they are allowed to mix with savages."

Carson took a slow, deep breath and looked around. No one but Mrs. Linderman would meet his gaze. Hunter was sneering at her; Winter Fawn stared at her. Everyone else looked at either the ground, the sky, or off into the distance. No one said a word.

"Very well," he said to the woman. "Beau, is that my wagon?" He nodded toward the familiar-looking Yankee blue vehicle parked next to the barn.

"Yessuh, Cap'n. Mr. MacDougall said you'd be glad to have it back."

"That I am." Carson squinted toward the western horizon. "Looks like we've got a couple of hours yet before full dark. That should be enough time for you to hitch up the team and take Mrs. Linderman back to town."

A slow grin spread across Beau's face. "Yessuh, Cap'n," he said with a snappy salute.

Mrs. Linderman sputtered in shock. "You can't mean to fire me."

"Yes, Mrs. Linderman, I can. I'm sorry to put you out of work when you need the job, but I'm sure you'll find another position shortly."

"Why . . . why . . . how dare you!"

Carson's voice hardened. "I dare damn easy. I won't have my sister and daughter exposed to such prejudice as yours—"

"Prejudice?" the woman shrieked. "Prejudice? From a rebel Southerner who fought a war and killed his own kind so he could own dozens of slaves? And you call me prejudiced, when it was murdering savages like these that killed my husband?"

"I'm sorry about your husband, Mrs. Linderman, I truly am. And you're right, my family did own slaves. But I know now that wasn't right. And no one I know fought a war for the purpose of owning slaves, nor, I might add, did anyone from the North fight to free the slaves. The war was about states' rights, if you'll recall, and it's over. The war is over. I won't have another one fought on my land to satisfy your sense of decency, and I won't have my *guests* insulted by anyone in my employ."

Her thin, wrinkled cheeks quivering with rage, the woman stuck out her withered chest. "You'll be sorry, Mr. Dulaney, you mark my words. Those savages will murder you in your sleep if you're not careful."

"Daddy?" Megan tugged on Carson's arm. "What's a savage?"

"They're not savages," Bess said hotly.

Mrs. Linderman glared at Bess, then at Carson.

"I believe you have some packing to do," he said coldly.

A few minutes later Beau Rivers snapped the traces and the team pulled the wagon out of the yard and onto the road toward Badito.

Winter Fawn left her father's side and went to Carson. She placed a hand on his arm. "Carson, what have you done?"

His gaze, when he turned it on her, was fierce. "I won't have you or your brother insulted."

"But—"

"But nothing," Innes said, interrupting. "He did just what I was hoping he'd do, the ol' biddy," he added under his breath.

"He did what should have been done," Bess told Winter Fawn. To Carson she said, "I tried . . . she wouldn't listen to me. She said I was too young to know what was what. But I'm not too young, Carson."

"I know you're not, honey." He took a deep breath, then let it out. "I hope you're not, because I just fired our housekeeper. That means you're in charge."

Bess's eyes widened and her mouth gaped. "In charge? Me?"

"I'm sorry," he said at the dismay in her voice. "I know

it's a lot to expect, but it's just until we can find a new housekeeper."

Bess swallowed, then squared her shoulders. "I'll do my best."

In that instant, Carson thought she looked about eight years old. What the hell had he done, putting the responsibility for their home on her shoulders? The house, the cooking, the cleaning, the laundry, Megan. The list seemed endless to him. But the petulant young lady from the stage seemed to have disappeared. He wasn't about to discourage this new Bess who was willing to try.

"I know you will," he told her. "I promise it won't be for long. There's bound to be other women looking for work besides Mrs. Linderman."

Bess was nearly beside herself with fear and excitement. Mostly fear. Mistress of the house! Oh! What to do first? Food! "You and Winter Fawn must be hungry. We have some stew and corn bread left from supper. Mrs. Linderman didn't know how to make corn bread. I made it myself from Aunt Gussie's recipe."

Innes stepped forward. "And mighty fine corn bread it was, Miss Bess. If you wouldna mind, I'd like a word or two with Carson while you show Winter Fawn where she can wash up."

While Bess and Megan hurried toward the house, and Hunter helped Frank take care of the horse and mule, something in her father's voice made Winter Fawn pause.

CHAPTER 11

Carson's gaze lingered on Winter Fawn as she paused halfway to the house.

"I trusted you, by damn I did," Innes said with a growl.

Because he had been staring at Winter Fawn, remembering the feel of her in his arms, wanting her, knowing he shouldn't, Carson flushed.

Innes swore.

Reminding himself that he hadn't done Winter Fawn any true harm, Carson met Innes's gaze. "What do you mean?"

"I mean, ye bloody bastard, I trusted ye wi' ma daughter. I trusted ye wi' more'n just her life, but wi' her virtue as well."

Carson felt himself flush again. "Are you accusing me of taking advantage of her?"

"Aye, that I am."

"Da!" Winter Fawn cried, rushing back across the yard. "How can you say such a thing?"

"How can I not?" Innes cried. "Do ye think I canna see the way ye look at each other?"

"Wanting is not the same as doing," she said hotly.

"Wantin'? Wantin', she says! What do ye know of wantin'? 'Tis a child ye be, too young to be talkin' of wantin'."

"Innes—" Carson began.

"Too young?" Winter Fawn interrupted, her voice low and quivering. "You've had no idea of my age for years. You left me." Her hands balled into fists at her sides. "You rode away and left me. Why should you care what I do?"

"Why should I care? Ye gods, lass, you're ma own flesh and blood."

"Yer own flesh and blood, am I? Left to wait on yer whim before I'm allowed to grow up, to become a woman, to have a family of my own. Ye may want me to stay a child, Faither, but 'tis a woman I am, full grown."

"Wot be this, wantin' ye to remain a child. I never!"

"Then why did you forbid Grandfather and Two Feathers from accepting a marriage offer for me?"

"And glad ye should be of it, unless it be Crooked Oak ye be wantin' for your husband."

Winter Fawn let out a string of words in Arapaho that Carson could not understand, but which turned Innes's ears red.

"*That's* what I think of Crooked Oak," she cried. "But there are other men. I have passed twenty winters. Other girls my age have husbands and children of their own. But me, I live in my grandmother's lodge, like a child, because my father canna be bothered to see to my future."

"Ye dinna ken of wot ye speak, lass."

"And ye dinna ken that I am a woman, not a child. If I want a man, I will have him."

"The hell you say!"

"Aye." Her eyes narrowed to angry slits. "I do say."

She whirled toward Carson, taking him by surprise. Which was nothing compared to what she did next. She grasped his face in both hands, pulled his head down to hers, and kissed him full on the mouth, a deep, hot kiss that took his breath.

She broke off the kiss quickly and turned back to her father, whose face nearly bled, there was so much blood beneath his skin.

Carson's own face was flaming, although for a different reason. How could he want her so damn much, with her father standing right beside him?

What game was she playing? The damn woman was going to get him killed.

"You accuse Carson," she told her father, "but he has done nothing wrong. I am as I was before, untouched. Not because I wanted it that way, but because he is an honorable man who wouldna betray the trust of a man he called friend. You should be ashamed of yourself."

With that, she turned away and marched into the house.

When the door slammed behind her, Innes eyed Carson. "Innes," Carson began. "I don't—"

"Ach, we'll say no more on it. The lass is too damn much like her mither to suit me. Ye just be sure an' keep yer hands to yerself, or ye'll be answerin' to me, lad, that ye will."

When Winter Fawn entered the house, Bess was waiting for her. The girl's eyes were huge. She said nothing for a long moment, and Winter Fawn wondered what was expected of her in Carson's home. The silence stretched out.

Finally Bess blurted, "You kissed him."

Winter Fawn wasn't sure what to say. Warily, she nodded once.

"What was it like? Oh, you must tell me."

Winter Fawn let herself relax and smile. This she understood. Younger white girls, it seemed, were no different from the young girls of Our People.

"Was it simply fabulous?"

"I dinna ken this word, fabulous, but it was . . . exciting."

"Oh." With a sigh, Bess clasped her hands together over her chest. "Oh."

"Now you must tell me something," Winter Fawn said.

"What?"

"What is it like to be the woman of your home?"

Bess laughed nervously and plucked at her skirt. "I have no idea. I've never done it before. But I guess I'm getting ready to find out." She laughed more easily this time.

Winter Fawn laughed with her.

"The first thing I must do is see to our guest. You're my first guest," she added with a giggle.

By the time Winter Fawn had made use of the soap and water Bess provided, Megan had returned from the privy behind the house, and Bess had set the table for two.

Carson stepped through the front door, not sure what to expect. He found the three females talking and laughing and not even noticing his arrival.

He took advantage of the moment and looked around the house his father had built, wondering what Winter Fawn saw when she looked at it. Did she compare it to that cabin in the mountains and find the house enormous? There must be so many things here that were foreign to someone who had lived all her life in a tepee. Wooden doors to extra rooms, the narrow staircase to the second floor. The iron cookstove. Oil lamps. The table and chairs at the kitchen end of the great room, the horse-hide sofa and wooden rocker at the opposite end, by the fireplace.

Everything must look strange to her.

And what about Bess? What did she see when she looked at her father's home? It didn't begin to measure up to the gracious elegance of Greenbrier, nor even the quiet dignity of Gussie's home in Atlanta. But then, Bess hadn't lived in either of those houses in years, and he wondered how much of them she remembered. And missed.

Still, the Martins—with whom the girls and Gussie had been living since the middle of the war when Gussie's husband, Oliver, had been killed—had a nice house. Polished oak floors, carpets, wallpaper, velvet drapes, imported furniture, landscapes and family portraits on the walls.

Did Bess find her new home lacking? She could have no understanding of how hard their grandfather had worked to build this place for them. He'd gone into the mountains and cut the trees himself for every wall, dragged them down the mountains. No telling how many trips, how long it had taken. The plank flooring had been hauled all the way from Denver, as had the cookstove and every stick of furniture. The rocks for the fireplace had been gathered by their grandfather right there on the ranch. Edmond Dulaney had lifted every log, set every rock, hammered every nail himself. He'd even put in an indoor pump so they could have water right at the sink in the built-in counter in the kitchen.

When Carson looked around the house, he did not compare it with what they had once had. When he looked, he saw a man's hopes and dreams, a man's love for the family who thought he had abandoned them.

"There you are, Carson," Bess said brightly. "Come wash up. Your supper's ready."

The meal was silent except for the occasional scrape of spoon against bowl or the creak of Carson's chair as he shifted his weight. The table sat ten. His father had had big dreams.

Bess seated Carson at the head and Winter Fawn at the foot, then brought a tablet and pencil and sat next to Winter Fawn.

"What are you writing?" Carson asked, feeling isolated at his end of the table.

Bess looked up and smiled. "I'm making an inventory and planning meals and chores. How is the corn bread?"

Carson laughed. "It's great, and you know it."

"Of course it's great. Aunt Gussie said it was Mama's recipe."

"Do you miss her?" he asked softly.

"Yes," she said with feeling. "I wish she could have come with us."

Carson pursed his lips. "I don't think she would have enjoyed our little adventure."

Bess giggled, turning from young lady to little girl in the blink of an eye. "We might not have had such an adventure if Aunt Gussie had been with us. She would have scared those warriors off with one of her looks." Bess arched one brow, looked down her nose, and puckered her lips, in so perfect an imitation of Gussie in one of her disapproving moods that Carson broke out laughing.

"Oh, Winter Fawn." Bess placed her hand on Winter Fawn's arm. "I wish you could meet our Aunt Gussie. You would love her."

Winter Fawn's lips twitched. "She sounds like an interesting person."

"Oh, she's simply wonderful."

Carson was still looking at Winter Fawn, unable, unwilling,

to take his eyes from her, when Bess jumped up from her chair as though someone had set it on fire.

"Oh! A fine hostess I am." She rushed to the counter and grabbed a large kettle. Pushing it up beneath the water pump, she began working the handle. "If I don't get this water heated, it will be midnight before Winter Fawn can have a bath."

A vivid picture of Winter Fawn, dewy wet and naked and lounging in a bathtub, seared Carson's mind. On top of that kiss she'd given him outside earlier, it was more than enough to make a man sweat.

Because thinking of the kiss made him uneasy, he tried to block the memory. She hadn't kissed him because she'd been suddenly overwhelmed by passion. She had kissed him to shock her father, to make him angry.

Ordinarily Carson wouldn't care why a beautiful woman kissed him, he would just be glad that she did. But this time it bothered him. He wanted Winter Fawn, there was no doubt of that. But he'd been used before to get a father's attention. He'd be damned if he would stand still for it again.

So he tried not to think about it. But that left the bath, and he didn't dare think about *that.*

"A heated bath?" Winter Fawn stared at Bess. "I have heard of this."

"Oh, my stars." Bess blinked like a baby owl. "I hadn't thought, but it makes sense that you would never have had a hot bath in a tub. Oh, Winter Fawn, you just don't know what you've been missing. You're going to love it."

Winter Fawn looked uncertain. "You must heat the water over the fire? 'Tis a lot of work for you for me to have this warm bath."

"No," Bess said hurriedly. "No, it's no trouble. And after you see how wonderful it is, you'll probably be in here heating your own water. Just wait."

"If you're sure it isna too much trouble."

"I'm sure. Carson, there's more room in your bedroom, so that's where we've been keeping the tub. You won't mind if she bathes in there, will you?"

An invisible fist tightened around Carson's throat. Another

one clutched his groin. Dewy wet and naked and lounging in a bathtub *in his bedroom.*

He had to clear his throat twice before he could speak. "Uh, no. I mean, I don't mind. That's . . . that's fine."

As far as he knew, no man had ever finished a meal and escaped a house as fast as he did right then.

How strange it felt to sleep totally alone. Of course, she wasn't asleep, but she should be, Winter Fawn acknowledged. How lonely white people must be if they all slept away from each other every night. There was no comforting snore from Grandfather nearby. No soft snuffling from her grandmother. No family close at all, since her father and Hunter had made their beds in the barn.

In the room next to her Bess and Megan lay asleep. Down on the first floor, there was Carson.

But here in this room high above the ground, on a mattress stuffed with straw and raised knee-high off the floor by a wooden frame with legs, there was no family close at hand. There was only Winter Fawn, and she could not sleep.

Yet it wasn't only missing her family that kept her awake, it was also the bath. When she'd been a child and heard her father talk of a hot bath in a tub she had thought he'd been teasing her. Now she knew that he'd been telling the truth. Yet as wonderful as he had made it sound, his words had not come close to describing the incredible pleasure of immersing herself in hot water for the first time in her life.

It had been like nothing she had ever before experienced. The only thing that compared was the feel of Carson's warm hands on her bare skin. That was what she had thought of as she had been surrounded by the liquid heat of the water. Carson. His heat. His touch.

Loneliness, that was what kept her awake this night. No, it was not her family she was missing. It was Carson.

When sleep finally claimed her, she dreamed of him.

* * *

A hot bath was the first of many new experiences for Winter Fawn. The next morning she came to realize that white people ate at regular times throughout the day. All of them, together. Such a thing certainly made it easier on the woman responsible for cooking in that she could plan her day around when meals were expected, but still, it seemed strange. What if one were not hungry when the regular time came?

She voiced this question at the breakfast table the next morning when she first realized how firmly whites believed in such a system.

Her father chuckled. "You'll get used to it."

"I will?" She blinked. Did that mean she would be around white people long enough to become accustomed to eating by the sun instead of when hungry?

"Aye, if you've a mind to," her father said.

Winter Fawn glanced at her brother, who sat next to her, but he was so intent on devouring as many of Bess's biscuits as possible that he paid no mind to the conversation around him. Her father was likewise occupied.

From the opposite end of the table, Carson met her gaze. "Your father has agreed to stay and help us get the ranch on its feet."

"On its feet? I dinna understand."

Carson smiled. "Sorry. We have a lot of work to do to make the ranch profitable. Your father says he'd like to give staying in one place a try for a while and help us."

She looked at her father, her heart pounding. Staying in one place? "Is this true, Da?"

"Aye," he said around a mouthful of biscuit. "I was thinkin' you and your brother might want to stay, too. You're half white. 'Tis time—past time, I'm thinkin'—for the two of you to learn white ways."

They would stay. Winter Fawn looked down at her plate, the fork feeling awkward in her hand. She wanted very much to stay with her father. She wanted just as much, if not more, to remain near Carson. But what of Our People? Was she never to go back? Did she want to?

"Give it time," Carson said quietly.

She looked up to find him watching her with understanding

in his eyes. Did he know her so well, then, that he could see how she was pulled in two directions?

"I'm sure your father would understand if you decided you didn't like it here and wanted to go back to the Arapaho. As for us—" Carson glanced at Bess and Megan, including them in his statement. "We hope you and your brother—your father, too—will stay as long as you want, as our guests."

"Ach, now," Innes said. "There'll be none of this guest business. MacDougalls earn their keep, they do. I can do whatever needs doin', fix whatever might get broke."

"There's plenty around here to fix," Frank added.

"No foolin'," Beau agreed, laughing.

"Winter Fawn," Innes said, "can sew and cook and all sorts of other things to help the young lass run the house. And Hunter, why, you'll be findin' no better man to work your horses. He's got a gift, does the lad."

"A gift?" Bess asked, her gaze locked on Hunter. "What kind of gift?"

Hunter stopped eating long enough to look at her. If Winter Fawn did not know what a cocky young man her brother was, she would almost swear he was blushing. " 'Tis nothing," he murmured, looking back down at his food.

Winter Fawn nearly choked. Modesty? From Hunter? Even their father, who was not around often enough to know either of his children well, raised a brow at Hunter's response.

"Nothing, is it?" Innes said with a chuckle. "I'll tell you, Miss Bess, 'tis nothing short of magic, is what it is. All he has to do is whisper in a horse's ear, and the animal will stand on his head, if the lad asked it of him."

Megan, seated directly across from Hunter, stared at him in awe. "Really? I've never seen a horse stand on its head before."

When presented with the prospect of helping Bess around the house, Winter Fawn had feared that she would feel much as a second wife, having to take orders from and bow to the wishes of a jealous head wife. Only for them, there was no husband.

But such was not the case. Bess eagerly accepted Winter Fawn's help.

Not that Winter Fawn felt especially helpful. There was so much to learn! White people, it seemed, went to a great deal of trouble to create work for themselves.

A fire pit did not have to be scrubbed. A cast-iron stove, it seemed, did.

A lodge with a dirt floor did not have to be swept clean of dirt. A wooden floor did.

A trade blanket and a buffalo robe did not show soil. White sheets of cotton did.

Moccasins did not require polishing. Leather shoes and boots did.

The list of chores for a white woman was apparently endless.

White men, however, also worked, she discovered. The men of her tribe were responsible only for hunting, protection from enemies, and the care and acquisition of weapons and ammunition. The rest of their time was spent gambling, racing their horses, or sitting around watching their women work. White men had to build corrals, dig wells—why was a mystery, since there was a river so close at hand—herd cattle, and any number of other chores that apparently kept them as busy as any woman.

Everything was new and, at first, strange to Winter Fawn. Learning to use the cookstove, the unfamiliar foods, boiling water over a big fire outside to wash clothes and bedding. Dusting, sweeping, breakable plates.

But Winter Fawn did not mind the work. For once, she felt truly needed. There was far too much for Bess to manage on her own. Especially when trying to keep a six-year-old girl entertained and out of the way. Not to mention taking care of all of Megan's little scrapes and bruises. The child could get into trouble so fast it was amazing.

"Megan, I'll swan," Bess said, exasperated when Megan rushed in from outside tearfully begging Bess to pull out her newest splinter. "I'm buried in bread dough right now. See if Winter Fawn can help."

"Help what?" Winter Fawn asked, having just finished changing the bedding upstairs.

"Kiss it," Megan cried, holding up her tiny forefinger. "It hurts."

"Here, let me see." Winter Fawn seated Megan on a chair at the table, then knelt before her. A thin sliver of wood protruded from the tip of the finger. "How did you manage to do this?"

Megan pouted. "The porch grabbed me."

"It did? Well, we'll have to be having a talk with that mean ol' porch, won't we?" While she spoke, she quickly caught the splinter between her fingernails and pulled it free. A tiny drop of blood oozed out of the hole.

"You're supposed to kiss it and make it better."

Winter Fawn smiled. She remembered her own mother kissing her skinned knees to make them better. She raised Megan's finger to her lips and placed a kiss on the hurt spot. Then she pressed the finger into her palm.

Megan tilted her head and watched. "What are you doing that for?"

Winter Fawn felt the heat, the tingling, the slight sting on her forefinger. "Making sure the kiss won't fall off."

Megan's eyes grew large in her face. "Does that work?"

"Sometimes." She released the finger. "There, is that better?"

"Oh, yes! Thank you, Winter Fawn." She threw her arms around Winter Fawn's neck and hugged. "You're the best hurt-kisser ever."

Feeling the child's arms around her neck warmed Winter Fawn's heart in a way nothing else could have.

As the days passed, a deep bond was formed between the three females. Winter Fawn sometimes feared she was growing to care too much for Bess and Megan. They became the sisters she had never had. When it was time to leave the ranch, she would miss them terribly. But she did not try to stop herself from loving them, for they needed her even more than she needed them.

Bess was grateful for an older woman to rely on, even though that woman knew little about white ways. And Megan was starved for attention. The three became inseparable.

Winter Fawn was so happy with her new life that the thunderstorm took her completely by surprise. It struck late one night when she was fast asleep. It began with the low rumble of distant thunder and hurled her, still asleep, back in time until the spring of her twelfth year.

Over the trickling sound of the creek came a faint rumbling. Startled from her daydream, Winter Fawn looked up. The sky overhead, what she could see of it above the tall cottonwoods lining the creek, was cloudless. Not thunder, then.

Could her uncle and the other men of the band be moving the horses?

No, it was too soon. They had only started packing this morning. Her mother had told her they would leave at midday on their journey to join the rest of the tribe. There was time yet before Winter Fawn needed to go help her mother dismantle the tepee.

With an exaggerated sigh, Winter Fawn trailed her fingers in the icy waters of the creek and felt them instantly start to numb. She did not want to move. She liked it best here in this spot in the foothills of the great mountains. She liked it best when it was just her band.

Her father had told her many times about the white man's custom of most people living in one place year-round. It had sounded impossible to her young ears the first time he had told her. Did the white man have some sort of magic to make the buffalo come to them, then? How else did they manage such a mystery as staying in one place all year?

But the white man, her father had told her, did not live off the buffalo. He instead raised cattle and other animals, grew crops, and bought other goods in towns.

Impossible, she had thought. But, being a white man himself, her father should know.

Now, facing her twelfth summer, Winter Fawn wondered what that might be like, staying in one place all year. She thought it sounded fine.

But they did not live in the white man's world, and it was time, as happened every year when the snows melted, for her band to journey out onto the plains and join with the rest of Our People. Arapaho, the whites called them. Southern Arapaho.

Someday she thought she would like to know what it was

like to not have to move constantly. To know upon awakening how far she was from water, that her favorite tree stood not far away, that the same bald hill stood in its same spot as always.

Someday . . .

The rumble sounded again, and this time she knew it was thunder. She glanced up to see dark, angry clouds boiling across the sky.

Maybe they wouldn't take down the tepees just yet. Maybe the women would wait until the storm passed. Maybe by then it would be too late to start out today, and the band would spend one more night in Winter Fawn's favorite spot.

She thought about following the creek back to camp, but that would not be fair to her mother. The creek wound and twisted and snaked around rocks and hills on its way to the river. It would take much longer to follow it than to simply climb the bald hill behind her. Camp was just on the other side.

"Goodbye, creek," she whispered as she pushed to her feet. "Goodbye, tall willow." A tree grew strong and sturdy by staying in one spot. So, too, she thought, might she.

But it was not to be. Not now. For now it was time to go. Already the wind was whipping the branches and the sky looked dangerous. Winter Fawn hurried away from the creek and toward the hill.

As she left the trees and neared the hill, she heard her mother's voice calling her name. Looking up, she spotted her standing at the top of the hill, waving.

"I'm coming, Mother!"

She should have returned sooner. It was not fair to force her mother to come looking for her. Winter Fawn began to run.

This side of the hill was not steep, but once on top a person could look out over the tops of the trees lining the creek, for the hill, with no trees of its own, was the tallest thing around. When Winter Fawn reached the top where her mother waited, she paused.

"Hurry, child, a storm comes."

"Just one last look," Winter Fawn pleaded.

Smiling, her mother turned with her to take a final look at their winter home. "One look, to last until next autumn." Winter Fawn's mother always smiled. That was why she was called Smiling Woman.

As they stood atop the bald, flat-topped hill and gazed at the small valley nestled in the foothills of the mighty mountains, Winter Fawn felt a sudden prickling along her arms. The sensation spread until it felt as though every hair on her body were standing on end. It tickled.

Laughing, she glanced at her mother.

Smiling Woman was no longer smiling. She was looking up at the clouds, her eyes wide, her breath coming fast.

"Mother?"

"Run," her mother cried.

"What? Why?"

"Run, child!" Smiling Woman grabbed Winter Fawn's hand and began to run toward the far side, toward camp.

Stumbling in her mother's wake, Winter Fawn felt the prickling along her skin intensify. Now it did not tickle. Now, it hurt. It stung like a thousand bees. "What's happening?"

"Run!"

As they neared the edge, where the bank cut sharply down, Winter Fawn tried to slow. It was steep there and she had no desire to fall.

But Smiling Woman would have no slowing. Screaming now at Winter Fawn to run, she planted her feet in the gravely dirt and flung her daughter over the edge of the hill.

For one horrifying instant, Winter Fawn hung suspended in the air, staring in shock at her mother standing on the hill. While she watched, helpless, arms flailing, a bolt of lightning reached from the dark sky and struck Smiling Woman.

Before Winter Fawn could even scream her mother's name, her mother was thrown into the air, her body arced like the curve of a bow, before slamming back down to earth. Then Winter Fawn herself dropped like a stone from the sky. She hit the ground hard, felt the sharp scrape of rock against flesh and tumbled down the steep slope. She screamed. And screamed, and screamed.

The harsh effort of her own screaming brought her upright

in bed. What in her sleep had been a scream was no more than a harsh exhale. Her throat was locked and could make no sound.

Icy sweat soaked the nightgown Bess had given her. Terror and anguish clutched her throat. Every flash of lightning outside her window made her flinch in terror.

She would not think of her mother. Would not allow herself to remember the bolt of lightning that had struck and killed her mother right before her eyes.

Yet how could she not remember, when the nightmare was so fresh and vivid and every few seconds the room filled with another flash of light as bright as midday, and the thunder sounded like the end of the world?

Winter Fawn buried her face in her shaking hands and prayed for the storm to stop.

Think of something else. Anything else.

Carson. She would think of Carson. Had the storm awakened him?

Don't think of the storm!

What about Bess and Megan? Were they frightened of the jagged lightning, the crashing thunder?

Don't think about the storm!

Carson, she reminded herself. She must think about Carson.

Deliberately she let herself remember the taste of his lips, the way the hard calluses on his fingers and hands felt scraping tenderly across her skin.

She saw him many times throughout each day, yet there was always someone else about. Her father, her brother, Beau, Frank. Bess, Megan. Always someone.

Except two days ago when he had forgotten his leather work gloves. The men were mounting up to ride out and check on the cattle after breakfast when Carson had come back inside for his gloves. Bess and Megan had gone outside to wave them off.

Winter Fawn had heard the front door open and thought it was the girls returning. She had turned from checking Bess's bread dough with a guilty smile curving her lips. She had learned from Bess one of the greatest delights of the white world—stealing a pinch of raw, yeasty dough while it was rising.

"The trick," Bess had said with mock seriousness, "is to not get caught doing it."

Now Winter Fawn had been caught. Not by Bess, however. By Carson.

He looked as surprised to find her there as she was to see him. He glanced from her fingers, which were still in her mouth, to the large bowl of dough on the counter, then back to her. "Caught you," he said with a teasing grin.

His grin, as it always did, backed the breath up in her lungs. She tried to laugh at his teasing, but couldn't quite manage it. Quickly she took another pinch of dough and held it out to him. "If you have some, too, then you canna tell on me."

As he walked toward her, his grin disappeared. He stood before her a long moment, staring into her eyes, holding her captive as if she were tied to him with braided rawhide. Slowly he leaned down toward her offered fingers. His lips parted, his mouth opened.

Winter Fawn held her breath and waited for that instant when his mouth would caress her fingers. Her heart pounded in anticipation. Her own lips parted, yearned for the taste of his.

Gently he closed his mouth over her fingers. With his tongue, he captured the dough and stroked it into his mouth. But he did not straighten and leave. He lingered, running his tongue over and around her fingertips, sucking on them, stealing her breath, all the while still holding her captive with those vivid blue eyes.

Then slowly, reluctantly it seemed, he pulled his mouth away and straightened. He brushed her cheek with one hand. "You've been working hard. How's your side?"

"It's . . . fine."

His gaze lowered to her lips. He leaned toward her.

Winter Fawn sucked in a sharp breath. He was going to kiss her.

Outside a horse neighed, a man shouted. Megan giggled.

Carson straightened abruptly and moved away. "I forgot my gloves."

He disappeared into his bedroom, then quickly left. Before he closed the front door behind him, he looked back at her.

Just looked, that was all. But with such heat in his eyes that she nearly cried out and ran after him.

How dare he, she thought now, her fists clenched in the sheet. How dare he lead her on that way and make her think he wanted her as much as she wanted him, then treat her that night as if nothing had ever happened between them.

Something *had* happened between them. Something wonderful, that last morning on the trail, before they reached the ranch. He had given her the most precious gift of all, the gift of her own pleasure as a woman.

How could she want more from him, how could she care more each day for the man he was, the way he loved his sister and daughter? How could she be falling in love with a man who wanted her one minute, but not the next?

Two days after the storm, four days after he had gone back into the house after his gloves, and Carson was still unable to forget the pull of her.

He had had no intention of getting near her that morning. A smile, a word, that was all that was necessary. Yet he had been drawn to her as if he'd had no will of his own.

Or as if he had thrown out all common sense and let his will have its own way.

It was only physical, this need he felt for her. He had teased and tormented himself with imagining what it would have been like if they had made love that morning on the trail, if he had buried himself inside her instead of holding back.

He had to quit thinking about it, dammit. She was his guest. Her father was his friend. She deserved better than a roll in the hay, and that was all he really wanted.

Wasn't it?

"You expectin' any company, Cap'n?" Beau asked.

Carson hadn't heard that particular tension in Beau's voice since their last battle during the war. He looked up sharply and followed the man's gaze. "No," he said grimly, "but it looks like we're about to have some."

From around the bend in the bluffs to the east, a large gray cloud of dust boiled into the air.

"I make it around twenty riders," Beau said, squinting at the dust cloud.

Carson grunted in agreement, then swore. Had Crooked Oak managed to track them here and gone back for more warriors? Damn.

"Beau, you and Frank take the barn."

"Yessuh," Beau said quickly, as if the war had never ended and Carson was still his captain.

"Innes, get Hunter and come to the house."

"Aye," he said slowly, eyeing the approaching cloud. "That I will, lad, that I will."

Carson sprinted to the house. He burst through the door and reached for his rifle, which rested on pegs above the door.

"What is it?" Winter Fawn asked quickly.

"Company." He glanced around, making sure all three girls were there. From the looks on their faces, he knew they realized he hadn't meant *invited* company. Being raised during a war gave even Megan an understanding he wished he didn't need to be grateful for.

His mind scrambled for the safest place to put the girls. Every room in the house had at least one window. He didn't want them near a window. "I want you upstairs, but stay in the hall and out of the bedrooms."

"Can we help?" Bess asked tightly.

"You can bring me the box of ammunition from the bottom of the wardrobe in my room, but hurry." A glance out the front window showed the dust cloud was nearly at the bend.

Winter Fawn came to the window. "Is it Crooked Oak?"

"I don't know."

"Where are my father and Hunter?"

As if in response to her question, the front door burst open and Innes and Hunter rushed inside. Innes carried his rifle in one hand, ammunition pouch in the other.

"Hunter," Carson said when Bess brought his ammunition. "Get the girls upstairs. Stay with them. Keep them in the hall and away from the windows."

Hunter did not bother getting insulted over being sent to watch the girls rather than take part in the fighting. If that was Crooked Oak out there, Hunter wouldn't mind putting a hole or two in him, but otherwise, he would not—did not think he *could*—fire on any of Our People.

"Come." He took Bess by the arm and Megan by the hand and led them up the stairs into the short, dim hallway.

"I'm scared," Megan complained with a whimper. "Is it the Yankees? Are the Yankee Bluebellies coming?"

Bess brushed a shaking hand over the girl's hair. "No, honey, it's not the Yankees. That war is over, remember?"

"I want to stay with Daddy."

"You will be safer, and so will he," Hunter told the child, "if you stay here and let him do what must be done."

Megan slid to the floor and started crying, loud, racking sobs. "I want Daddy!"

Bess was scared, too, and wanted Carson. She tried to soothe Megan, but it was Hunter who got through to the girl.

"Your tears are an extra weapon in the hands of your enemy."

The statement was complex enough to give both Megan and Bess pause.

Megan sniffed and looked up at him as he crouched beside her on the floor. "My enemy? You mean the Bluebellies?"

Hunter shrugged. "Any enemy."

"But a weapon is a gun or a knife," Bess said. "A tear can't be a weapon."

"It can. If your enemy knows you are frightened and crying, he becomes stronger. It is what he wants you to do."

Megan sniffed again and looked to Bess, who nodded. Megan looked back at Hunter. "But nobody but you and Bess knows I'm crying."

"If your father hears you, he will know. Your tears will hurt and weaken him, when he needs to be strong. He needs to know you are strong."

The child's face was pale, her eyes wide. "Oh. Am I strong?"

"Aye, you are." He looked up into Bess's eyes. "You are both very strong."

Bess felt pride swell within her at Hunter's praise.

Megan sniffled again. "Will you keep us safe, Hunter?"

Hunter looked down at the tiny girl solemnly. Her belief in him was humbling. "I will do my best, lassie."

"Where's Winter Fawn?" Megan asked.

"She is downstairs."

"I love Winter Fawn." Megan smiled, her tears and fear forgotten for the moment. She reached up and patted Hunter on the cheek. "I love you, too, Hunter."

Hunter felt his chest swell with pride that the little one and her sister should trust him so much.

Downstairs things were not so cozy. Carson glared at Winter Fawn. "Get upstairs with the girls."

"I willna. Surely there is something I can do to help."

"Dammit." Carson took another look out the window, saw the dust cloud advance closer to the point. He glared back at Winter Fawn. "I will not have you taking another arrow or bullet meant for me."

"Bullet?" Innes stiffened.

Winter Fawn ignored her father and glared back at Carson. "The bullet missed."

"What bullet?" Innes demanded.

She glanced past Carson out the window and frowned. "That canna be Crooked Oak. He wouldna come riding in that way, would he?" She looked to her father. "He wouldna be so bold or foolish. He would sneak up on us."

Carson and Innes frowned and looked out the window again.

"Aye, lass, I think you've got the right of it. He wouldna chance losing so many men in such a direct attack. He wouldna shout his approach with such a cloud. He would sneak in over the bluffs and try to take us by surprise."

Carson didn't have to think long to realize Winter Fawn and Innes were surely right. But if not Crooked Oak, then who? The Cheyenne hadn't been reported this far south in years. Utes would come from the west, not the east. The Navaho, if they broke free of the reservation, would come from the south.

Who, then?

CHAPTER 12

Carson's answer came a moment later when the first riders appeared past the point of the bluff. ''Army.''

Carson had surrendered at the end of the war and gave his loyalty oath in good faith. To him the war was truly over. But he couldn't help his instinctive reaction at the first sight of all those blue uniforms headed his way. He gripped his rifle tighter and raised it toward the window.

Then he let out his breath and lowered the rifle.

The war was over. Had been over for a long time.

Behind him Winter Fawn sucked in a sharp breath. She, too, had an instinctive reaction to the sight of all that blue, and it was every bit as tense as Carson's. ''What do they want?'' Bluecoats inevitably meant dead Indians.

''Well I'll be damned.'' Carson startled them with a laugh. ''Isn't that just like her.''

''Who?'' Innes leaned toward the window for a closer look.

''Girls?'' Carson crossed to the foot of the stairs. ''Girls, you can come down now. I've got a surprise for you.''

Quickly he ushered everyone outside and pointed toward the advancing party.

''Yankees?'' Bess said uneasily. ''That's your surprise?''

"Bluebellies!" Megan squeezed Carson's leg with both arms. "Don't let them get me, Daddy!"

Carson put his arms around both girls. "I had pretty much the same reaction, but I'll remind you what I reminded myself, girls. The war is over. That's our army now. Those are our soldiers. And no, they aren't the surprise. Look at that buggy. Ever hear of an army with a fancy buggy like that?"

"Oh!" Bess covered her cheeks with her hands. "Oh, my stars." Suddenly she was jumping and laughing with excitement. "Look, Megan! Look!"

"Who is that?" Innes asked.

"Innes, Winter Fawn, Hunter," Carson said with a flourish, "you're about to make the acquaintance of Mrs. Augusta Dulaney Winthrop."

Megan squealed with delight. "Aunt Gussie! Daddy, it's Aunt Gussie! She came, she came!"

They'd been wrong in their estimate of the number of riders involved in raising such a large cloud of dust. Rather than the twenty Beau and Carson had estimated, there were only a dozen. It was the buggy wheels that were responsible for the rest of the dust.

The troopers filed into the yard and the sergeant driving the buggy pulled it to a halt before Carson and the others. "Cap'n, suh!" The sergeant's face split in a wide grin around a chaw of tobacco. "Uh, beggin' your pardon, Captain Trimble," he added to the Cavalry officer riding next to the buggy.

"Captain," Carson said with a nod.

"Sir, I am ordered to deliver Mrs. Winthrop to the Dulaney ranch."

"You've come to the right place. I'm Carson Dulaney."

The officer nodded. "I'm Captain Trimble."

"Pleased to meet you," Carson offered. "You from Fort Reynolds up near Pueblo?"

"We are."

"You've had a long ride. You and your men are welcome to get down and take your ease. There's water in the trough or at the river for your mounts. Your men can refresh themselves at the well."

"Thank you." Stiff-backed, Captain Trimble gave the order and dismounted.

Carson turned back to the buggy. "Anderson, you old rebel," he said with a laugh. "I didn't recognize you in all that blue."

"Didn't recognize you without your gray, either, boy."

"I declare, if you two are quite finished," said the woman beside the sergeant, "it's been a long trip and I would like to get down."

Anderson rolled his eyes.

Her eyes were Dulaney blue and twinkling, her hair, despite her forty-eight years—only thirty-some of which she would admit to—was glossy black. She wore it in a soft bun at the back of her head, and it showed off the pure, clean lines of her round face. She held her head at a dignified angle, but flirted with her twirling parasol.

Carson's grin nearly split his face in two. "Yes, ma'am." He rounded the buggy, grabbed her by the waist, and twirled her in a laughing circle.

Augusta Dulaney Winthrop shrieked and laughed. "Put me down, you crazy scoundrel."

After another vigorous twirl, Carson set her on her feet, then pulled her into his arms for a big bear hug. "Lord, woman, it's good to see you." He pushed her back and held her at arms' length so he could look her up and down. "What are you doing here? You said . . . Oh, damn. Mrs. Martin?"

Gussie gave him a sad smile. "I'm afraid so. Lucille passed away three days after you and the girls left."

"Damn, Gussie, I'm sorry." Lucille Martin had been Gussie's closest friend since they got their first corsets. They'd shared their first tea parties and debutantes' balls. Lucille had tended Gussie's miscarriage, and Gussie had helped Lucille bury the Martins' three-year-old son when he died of the croup. After Oliver, Gussie's husband, was killed in the early part of the war, Gussie, Bess, and Megan had gone to live with Lucille for the duration. "She was quite a woman," Carson said.

"Yes." Gussie blinked moisture from her eyes. "I'll miss her till the day I die, but she's not suffering anymore, that's what matters."

Carson gave her another squeeze, then led her toward the house. "Hey, girls, look who's here."

With squeals of laughter, Bess and Megan besieged their favorite—and only—aunt. The entire Dulaney family, late of Atlanta, Georgia, now stood within a five-foot square of Colorado grass.

After the initial burst of hugs and kisses, Bess and Megan chattered one atop the other like two magpies.

"You'll never guess what happened to us, Aunt Gussie!"

Megan jumped up and down. "We got captured by Indians!"

"And Hunter and Winter Fawn and Mr. MacDougall saved us and helped us escape," Bess added breathlessly. "Oh, Aunt Gussie, it was terrifying. But it was exciting, too, and you'll just love Hunter and Winter Fawn and Mr. Mac. Come meet them."

Bess took Gussie by the hand and dragged her toward the covered porch. "Here they are. Aunt Gussie, this is Winter Fawn, her brother, Hunter, and their father, Mr. MacDougall. This," she said to them, "is Aunt Gussie."

Gussie Winthrop smiled brilliantly at the three wary faces before her, her mind spinning like a top. Captured? Indians? Escaped? Good gracious! It was clear to her that she was desperately needed here. She should never have let Carson and the girls travel without her.

"I'm so glad to make your acquaintance, all of you," she told them. "And so grateful that you were there to help Carson and the girls. I am deeply in your debt."

Carson had followed. Gussie's words relieved him greatly. He knew that if someone helped her or hers, Gussie became their devoted friend and servant for life, but he hadn't been certain how she would react to meeting Indians. Now he was. Winter Fawn and Hunter would receive no cold shoulder or ugly names from Gussie, as they had from Mrs. Linderman.

Carson went into the house and brought the wooden rocker to the shade of the front porch. "Here, Gussie, sit and rest. Bess, how about something for Aunt Gussie to drink?"

Bess jumped to attention like a soldier receiving an order. Soon orders were flying from her mouth as she eagerly exercised her role as woman of the house. Innes and Hunter were to carry in Aunt Gussie's trunks. Winter Fawn and Megan were asked to bring water for the troopers. Beau and Frank were to help the soldiers with their horses and setting up camp.

Gussie watched it all with a twinkle in her eye.

"The housekeeper I hired didn't work out. Bess agreed to take over until we made other arrangements."

Gussie smiled as Bess dashed into the house. "So I see." Her gaze turned serious. "Are you all right? Truly?"

"Truly," Carson said, patting her hand. He turned to Sergeant Anderson and Captain Trimble. "Of course, we wouldn't have had any trouble from the Southern Arapaho if the army hadn't killed some of their men in retaliation for something the Cheyenne did."

Anderson flushed and looked away.

Captain Trimble's eyes turned cold and hard. "My orders were to question any Indians in the area in order to find the ones responsible for the massacre of the Johnson family over on the St. Charles River."

"But you knew the ones you were after were Cheyenne."

"The Southern Cheyenne and Southern Arapaho are close allies, Mr. Dulaney. Where there's one, you'll find the other."

"Aye." Innes strolled up and pulled his flask from the leather pouch hanging from his belt. "They're together a great deal, the two tribes. There were even a few Southern Arapaho at the Cheyenne camp at Sand Creek a few years back."

Bess bounded out the front door and onto the porch. "Here you go, Aunt Gussie."

Captain Trimble made as if to respond—hotly—to Innes's comment, but Carson stopped him with a sharp look. "Thank you, Bess."

"Yes, thank you, dear." Gussie didn't understand the significance of Mr. MacDougall's comment, but she had no trouble at all detecting the tension in the air, nor did she miss the look Carson gave the captain. With the cool cup of water from the well in her hand, she sat back in the rocker and took a long sip.

"I just didn't have the heart to stay in Atlanta any longer." Using her fan to stir a breeze over her face, Gussie pushed with her toe and set the chair to rocking. "With Lucille gone," she said sadly, "there didn't seem to be any point."

Carson squeezed her hand. "I'm sorry about Lucille. But we're glad you came, Gussie."

Carson meant his words. Aunt Gussie had always been one of his favorite people. She'd lost a child, her husband, her brother, and now her best friend. He couldn't stand the thought of her being alone, without family. Now that she was here, she wouldn't have to be alone.

And now that she was here, there would be someone to help him raise the girls. Thank God. Yes, he was glad Gussie had come. As far as he was concerned, she was home.

A side benefit to her presence was that now it would be virtually impossible for him to spend any time alone with Winter Fawn. Aunt Gussie had the eyes of an eagle. And that was for the best. If a sense of loss filled him, that was his problem.

Gussie smiled through her sadness and gazed at Bess and Megan, who were gathered close around her as the afternoon waned. "I declare, I missed all of you so much, I just couldn't stay away."

"We've put your things in the room next to Carson's," Bess said. "I hope that's all right."

"I'm sure it will be fine." Gussie smiled brilliantly. She motioned toward the soldiers lounging around the yard and turned to Carson. "It was good of you to invite them to take their ease. I declare, I had no idea so many Southerners had joined the Union Army."

Carson chuckled. "It's not the Union Army now, it's just the army, Gussie."

"I know." She let out a sigh. "It still takes some getting used to. But imagine my delight," she added with a smile, "to learn that some of these boys served with you and your father. Why, the sergeant even knew my dear Oliver, God rest his soul."

"Yes'm." Sergeant Anderson, seated on the porch steps, nodded. "Met up with him two or three times in the early days of the war."

While Carson, his aunt, and several of the soldiers talked

about the war and old friends, Winter Fawn thought to make herself scarce. Being around the bluecoats made her nervous. She did not like the way some of them looked at her, neither those who leered, nor those who sneered.

But Carson saw her step from the porch and called to her. "Come." He held out his hand. "Sit with us."

How could she graciously turn down such an invitation? Especially with her father nudging her in the back. "Do it, lass. You, too, Hunter. Go."

Innes saw the reluctance on his children's faces. Ach, but he had surely neglected this part of their education too long. Had neglected *them* too long. They were half white. They shouldna be fearin' white men. Soldiers. He should have introduced them to the white world long ago. He should never have left them.

In the wee hours of that night, when everyone else was long since bedded down, Innes MacDougall drank himself to sleep.

The whirlwind that was Carson's Aunt Gussie did not strike full force until the next day.

It started out as any other day, with Carson the first one up in the house.

As was her habit, Winter Fawn awakened at the first sound of his stirring. She lay in bed and listened to his firm, confident strides as he left his room and crossed to the front door. He wasn't loud, but sound carried inside the log walls of the house. A moment later the front door opened and closed. In two hollow-sounding steps he was across the porch.

She wondered, as one boot sounded on the porch steps before he stood on the ground, which stair he used. There were three from the porch to the ground. Did he step on the top one, then skip the next two, or use the middle one on his way down?

Shaking her head at her foolish wonderings, she tossed back the covers and rose from the bed. A few minutes later she was dressed, her hair was brushed and rebraided, and she was downstairs lighting the lamp in the kitchen, firing up the stove, and putting on the first pot of coffee for the day. This was her favorite task. She enjoyed being the only one up in the house for this half hour of solitude before Bess woke.

As was her habit, she crossed to the front window and looked out at the rosy tint on the eastern horizon.

Things would change now that Carson's aunt had come. Winter Fawn didn't know in what way, but the certainty of change, the uncertainty of her own future, was within her.

Turning from the window, wishing that turning from her unsettled thoughts were as easy, she carried the lamp into Carson's bedroom and made up his bed. The sheets were still warm from his body; they carried the scent of him. She closed her eyes and inhaled, wishing it was him beneath her hands and not just cotton.

Having been built for a large man, his was the largest bed in the house. Why, there was room enough for two, even if one of them was the size of Carson.

The thought should have brought a blush to her cheeks. Instead, it brought a yearning in her to be the one to share this bed with him. Sometimes, when he looked at her, she could almost see that same wanting in his eyes.

But other times he treated her as though their lips had never touched, as though his hands had never caressed her bare flesh. As though his thigh had never pressed between hers and sent her soaring.

With a heaving sigh, Winter Fawn finished making the bed and picked up the lamp. As she turned away toward the door she paused. He'd left his hat behind. She lifted it from the peg on the wall next to the door and took it with her back to the kitchen. The felt was soft and stained with the sweat of his brow. She rubbed the brim lightly across her cheek.

In these quiet, solitary moments, she allowed herself to imagine what it would be like if this were her home. If Carson was her man. If she had the right to walk outside in the bright light of day, hand him his hat, tease him for forgetting it, then kiss him. In front of anyone who might be watching.

She wondered what it would feel like to move the braided rug closer to the fireplace rather than before the sofa, or hang a painted hide on the wall.

No one would care, of course, if she moved the rug. Chances

were good that no one would even notice. But it was not her rug, not her floor upon which it lay. She did not feel as though she had the right.

As for the painted hide, the thought made her smile. What would these white people think of that?

She placed the lamp on the counter in the kitchen and held Carson's hat in her hands. He would be back later for breakfast. The sun wasn't even up yet. He wouldn't need his hat this early. She would not take it out to him, no matter how great the temptation to use it as an excuse to see him. He had not given any indication lately—ever—that he would welcome such personal attention from her.

By the time Bess came downstairs, Carson's aunt was stirring in her room, and Winter Fawn had a big pot of oatmeal on the stove. The coffee was done; Winter Fawn moved it to the back of the stove where it would stay hot.

"Good morning," Carson's aunt said cheerfully.

Bess rushed forward and gave the woman a hug and a kiss on the cheek. "Good morning, Aunt Gussie."

"I must have been more tired from the trip than I realized, to have slept so late. Why, I declare, the sun is coming up. Winter Fawn, child, whatever are you doing?"

Warily Winter Fawn glanced at Bess, then back at the girl's aunt. "Stirring the oatmeal?"

"Land sakes, you're a guest. You aren't expected to cook."

Winter Fawn tried to stifle it, but the irritation rose so swiftly there was no stopping it. The woman had arrived yesterday. Winter Fawn had been here for more than a week. Just who was the newcomer here?

But the truth was, this woman was family. Winter Fawn was not. She swallowed her irritation as best she could. "I dinna mind, Mrs. Winthrop."

"Gussie, please, child. Call me Gussie. Or Aunt Gussie, if you prefer."

After a short hesitation, Winter Fawn nodded. "All right. Gussie."

Gussie beamed at her. "Good. But I meant what I said. As Carson's guest, you should not be working."

"She's been helping me, Aunt Gussie," Bess explained.

"And I'm sure she's been a big help. But I'm here now, so she need do nothing more than relax and enjoy herself."

"I couldna," Winter Fawn exclaimed in horror. "Da and Hunter help Carson. The least I can do is help around the house."

The woman took the spoon from Winter Fawn's fingers and gave the oatmeal a vigorous stir. Smiling, she said, "We'll see, child, we'll see."

"Mrs. Win—Gussie," Winter Fawn said slowly. "I am no' a child."

Gussie laughed heartily. "Do forgive me. At my age, everyone seems like a child to me. I meant no disrespect, I assure you. And I must say, I just adore that Scottish burr in your speech. It's simply delightful."

Completely disconcerted, Winter Fawn stepped aside and made way for Gussie before the stove.

"If you're still of a mind to help," Gussie said, "you two girls could set the table. I assume that Mr. Rivers and Mr. Johansen will be joining us?"

"Aye," Winter Fawn said, looking at Bess for a clue as to what was happening.

Bess merely smiled and turned to get the bowls from the cabinet.

While the girls set the table, Gussie continued to rattle on. She was quite certain that she made no sense whatsoever to them, for she certainly made no sense to herself. But she didn't know what else to do but talk and keep busy. If she stopped talking, stopped doing, she was very much afraid she would break down and weep. She had never believed in public displays of grief, yet she felt the terrible anguish over Lucille's death building inside her.

She had thought—hoped—that the trip west would ease her heart, and for a few days it had. There had been so many new sights, and she was here now and overjoyed to be with her family again, even if this rough homestead was not what any of them were used to. Since the war, she had learned the hard way that people—family, friends—were so much more important than fine things or nice houses.

Gussie wasn't sure why losing Lucille seemed so hard on

her. The death certainly had not come as a surprise. Lucille had been ill for months, and they had both known what was coming. And Lord knew, Gussie had lost others, and probably would again. But she had dreamed of Lucille last night, of their girlhood together, and now tears threatened to choke her. All she knew to do was keep busy, and so she would.

Lord, but she was carrying on like a magpie. She couldn't seem to stop, nor did she have any idea what she'd been saying.

Winter Fawn had never heard anyone talk so much in her life. She sensed in Gussie a frantic need of some sort, but could not imagine what it might be. And it was none of her business.

By the time they had the table set, Megan had come downstairs. As was the custom they had established during the past days, the child carried her hairbrush to Winter Fawn.

Winter Fawn led her to the sofa and carefully undid yesterday's braids. Using the brush, she gently eased the tangles out, then rebraided the soft black tresses, using the lengths of pink ribbon that Megan had brought downstairs with her to tie the ends.

This was one of Winter Fawn's favorite things to do. Someday she would have a daughter of her own whose hair she would braid. Or perhaps a son, she thought with a smile, who would think it unmanly to let his mother braid his hair.

"There." After tying the last bow, Winter Fawn lifted the end of one braid and tapped it against Megan's little nose. "You are all beautiful again."

Megan giggled, then pressed a tiny kiss to Winter Fawn's cheek. "Thank you, Winter Fawn."

Winter Fawn closed her eyes briefly to savor the sweet affection. "You're welcome."

The men came in a short time later and took their places around the table.

"Carson," Gussie said when everyone was seated. "Would you say grace, please?"

Innes paused with a biscuit halfway to his mouth. His eyes bugged. He dropped the biscuit as though it were on fire. His face turned as red as his beard.

"Yes ma'am," Carson said with a smile.

Grace, Winter Fawn quickly realized, was a prayer. She was

ashamed to realize that she had not given thanks to Man-Above in days, and she had so much to be thankful for. Until coming here it had been her habit, as it was with all of Our People, to give thanks throughout the day for all the blessings, the small as well as the large, that came her way.

By asking Carson to pray, Gussie had raised herself a notch in Winter Fawn's estimation.

After the prayer, everyone grabbed for food as if someone had fired a shot to start a race.

Innes eyed the new woman carefully before deciding it was now safe to eat. A fine-looking woman, she was, but soft, he figured. Those dainty white hands had never seen hard work. She wouldna last a month out here afore wantin' to hie herself back to civilization.

"I do hope," Gussie said, looking around the table, "that y'all will forgive me, but I am used to taking charge of a household. I will undoubtedly make a few suggestions to change the way things are done. If I overstep my place, Carson dear, please do tell me."

"Aunt Gussie, your place is wherever you want it to be."

"Why thank you, dear heart. But you're used to my ways, you and Bess and Megan. I do not wish to offend the others."

"Miz Winthrop," Beau said dramatically, "I do hereby grant you permission to change me any way you want."

"Why thank you, Mr. Rivers. Perhaps you'll allow me to give you a haircut."

Innes snickered, expecting to see a look of horror on Beau's face. But instead, the man beamed a smile at her.

"Allow it? Miz Winthrop, I will become your servant for life if you cut my hair."

Gussie chuckled. "How you do go on. Whenever you have time, you just come on up to the house and I'll make sure my shears are sharp. Mr. MacDougall, I could trim your beard for you."

Innes choked on a piece of biscuit. *Bloody hell, you could, woman.* "Dinna fash yerself on my account, ma'am. My beard and I hae grown accustomed to each other." *There. That should put her in her place.* If there was one thing Innes didna care for, it was a meddling female.

"I declare," Gussie said with a smile. "It would be no trouble at all for me to trim it so that it's short and neat."

Innes saw the determination in those blue eyes and panic slid up his spine. Grabbing his bowl and spoon, he stood and backed away from the table. "I'll, er, just be takin' this out onto the porch to finish."

Beau, Frank, and Carson roared with laughter as Innes made his escape.

Soft? Had he thought her soft? She was too damned bossy to be soft. Bloody, bossy woman.

During the next several days, Winter Fawn's ambiguity regarding Gussie continued to grow. She could not decide if the woman was a gift from Man-Above, sent to make life wonderful, or a curse placed upon her by some evil spirit. All she knew was that until Gussie's arrival, Winter Fawn had felt useful, needed. She'd felt a part of the ranch. An important part, she admitted.

Now she felt . . . useless. In the way. Terribly, terribly unneeded.

Gussie never gave any indication that she did not genuinely like Winter Fawn. While she did occasionally cluck her tongue when Innes came in smelling of the contents of his flask—the clucking of the tongue, Winter Fawn learned, indicating disapproval—she was unfailingly kind and warm to Winter Fawn, and to Hunter.

All I need do, Winter Fawn repeated to herself, *is tell her I want to feel useful.*

No, that would not work. She had tried that. Perhaps it was the word "want" that was insufficient. Perhaps if she told Gussie that she *needed* to feel useful, the woman would relent and share some of her work.

But Winter Fawn had yet to find a way to say the words that would not cast fault on Gussie for taking away her chores. Winter Fawn did not want to hurt Gussie. Even though by taking over the braiding of Megan's hair each morning Gussie had unknowingly hurt her.

And she could not say anything to Bess, because Bess was

so very pleased to have her aunt with her, taking over the responsibilities, teaching her, shooing her off to spend time simply being a child.

As miserable as she was, Winter Fawn did not know what to do. She stood on the porch and gazed off toward the bluffs to the north and east. Maybe it was time to consider returning to Our People.

Carson saw her there on the porch when he walked from the barn to the well for a drink of water. He saw her unhappiness in the way her shoulders sagged, had seen it the past few days in the shadows in her gray eyes. Was Gussie working her too hard? Had his aunt said or done something to upset her?

The way Winter Fawn stared out toward the northeast worried him. Was she thinking of leaving? Returning to her people?

The thought tied his stomach in a knot. She couldn't leave. He wasn't ready for her to leave. Might never, he realized slowly, be ready for her to leave.

He wasn't in love with her. Of course he wasn't. So why should the thought of her leaving make cold sweat break out between his shoulder blades?

He liked her. He enjoyed her company.

When was the last time you shared her company?

Now he was being stupid. He shared her company every day, every time he stepped foot in the house.

Shared. Yes, shared. With a half-dozen other people around all the time. He wanted her alone. He wanted to touch her, hold her, kiss her. Every day he fought back the wanting. Every day he told himself it was a passing thing that he would get over. Yet every day it grew inside him, the need to make her his.

But it was only physical, he was sure of that. And therein lay his problem. She was not a woman to be used for a quick roll in the hay.

What if that's all she wants from you?

The question brought him up short. She had been willing enough in the mountains. Eager, even.

And hot.

Oh, yeah, she had been hot. Hot enough to singe the willpower right out of him, otherwise he would never have done what he did that last morning on the trail.

Maybe he'd been holding himself back for nothing. She was a grown woman. Should she not be allowed to make her own decision about who to give herself to, and when?

She had wanted him once. Maybe if he could get close to her again, make her want him again, she would not get that sad, faraway look in her eyes that made him think she was leaving.

He hung the dipper back on its hook and straightened his hat. He didn't have much time to waste. He and the men would be heading out before dawn in the morning to round up more cattle to brand. They might make it back tomorrow night, and they might not. He could not leave without at least talking to her for a few minutes. Alone.

He crossed the yard and stood just on the ground at the edge of the porch. Their positions, with him on the ground and her on the porch, made her a few inches taller. He tipped his head back and found her gray eyes there, dark and pensive, waiting for him.

"You're all alone," he said.

Winter Fawn gazed at his sweat-streaked face and knew she had never seen a more handsome man. "So are you."

His smile came quickly. "I am. But you're the one who usually has a little shadow following you around everywhere."

Winter Fawn couldn't help a smile of her own, but it faded quickly. "Your aunt insisted that Megan take a nap."

His smile, too, disappeared. "Are you unhappy here, Winter Fawn?"

She supposed she should not have been surprised by his question, not with the way she had been moping around feeling sorry for herself. She felt ashamed. He had so much on his mind trying to get the ranch going. Her father had explained enough of the white man's ways that she thought she understood about cattle and branding and money and land rights—although how any one person thought they could own the land, she could not fathom. But white men thought it, and acted on it, so she supposed that meant they had to worry about it. Carson did not need to worry about her, too.

"I am fine, Carson."

"You looked sad just now." He stepped up onto the porch and towered over her. With a gloved hand, he stroked her cheek. "I don't want you to be sad."

The look in his eyes took her breath away. It was the same look he had given her in the predawn light that last morning on the trail. She read the memory of what had happened there in his eyes. Without thought, she gave in to the yearning in her heart and leaned toward him. His name was a whisper on her lips.

He leaned down closer, until his breath brushed her cheek.

From inside the house, Megan's voice rang out. "Winter Fawn, where are you?"

Carson straightened and dropped his hand to his side. "One day," he said softly, "there will be time for us."

The promise in his voice, his eyes, stayed with her long after he walked away.

CHAPTER 13

The men had been gone for three days.

With them gone, there was less work to be done. Winter Fawn was more miserable than ever. Not only was she almost totally idle for the first time in her life, but she missed Carson. Every night she lay awake remembering the promise in his eyes that day on the porch.

What did it mean? What would happen when he returned?

Was he all right? Did he have enough to eat? Was he warm at night?

The questions raced through her mind over and over until she thought she might scream in frustration.

The fourth night of his absence, thunder rumbled in the distance, teasing her with the threat of another storm. Closer and closer the thunder sounded, until she knew it would soon be directly overhead.

Knowing she would not sleep, she tossed the covers aside and crawled from the bed. The cotton gown fell to her ankles, and she ran her hands down the soft fabric. While she preferred the feel of soft fur against her bare skin, white people did not sleep in furs, nor, she had determined, did they bare their skin anywhere outside of the bath tub. Since she felt obliged to adhere to white ways while in a white man's house, she was glad the gown Bess had given her was so comfortable.

The thunder came as a sharp clap now rather than a low rumble, and was accompanied by a flash of lightning. The storm was getting closer. Maybe if she were not upstairs, with the feeling of being perched high in the air, she would not feel the presence of the storm so much.

Although why she should think so was beyond her. One could not be closer to the earth than in a tepee, and she had never felt safe there during a storm. But anything was worth a try.

Tiptoeing downstairs as quietly as possible so as not to wake Bess, Megan, or Gussie, Winter Fawn made her way through the darkness to the sofa. She curled up there and, for something to do, she undid her braids and used her fingers to comb her hair.

The thunder was almost constant now. Her fingers, when she saw them through a flash of lightning, were bent like talons. With a conscious effort, she relaxed them and forced a deep breath into her lungs.

It was only a storm. She was safe inside these sturdy walls. It couldna hurt her.

But it was not for herself that she feared storms. At least, not her own safety. It was her heart that was in danger of breaking, because she greatly feared the loss of another loved one. Her mother. Her father.

Her father had returned, but he always left again.

Storms took people away.

He was out there now in the storm, her father. Along with her brother. And Carson.

Man-Above, keep them safe. Please do not take one of them into the storm.

Carson was ten yards from the house when the sky opened up and dumped on him. Cursing, he sprinted the rest of the way to the porch.

At least they'd finished. They had beat the brush and rounded up fifty-four head of cattle. There were more out there, and he would find them. But for now, they'd slapped the Double D brand on another fifty-four head.

They'd had plenty of men to hold such a small herd during a storm, but he was glad they hadn't needed to. The damn critters could run from here to kingdom come, as far as he was concerned. They now wore his brand; he would find them again. There was no need to hold them.

They wouldn't go far, anyway. Carson's father had chosen this spot along the Huerfano because of the layout of the land. The surrounding bluffs formed a natural barrier—albeit sometimes miles away.

He hit the front porch and nearly slipped on the wet wood. Cursing again, he removed his hat and shook the water off as best he could before pushing open the front door.

As he stepped inside, thunder crashed and a flash of lightning over his shoulder illuminated the room. He shouldn't have been able to hear the small intake of breath over the fury of the storm. He shouldn't have, normally wouldn't have bothered to look toward the sofa. But he did hear, did look, and everything inside him tightened.

Huddled into the corner of the sofa, Winter Fawn sat with her knees beneath her chin, both hands covering her mouth, and her eyes as wide as saucers.

Quickly Carson closed the door and rushed across the room. He crouched on the floor before the sofa. "What's wrong? What's happened?"

Her head jerked back and forth and a tiny whimper escaped her throat.

Carson put his hands on her shoulders. Her violent trembling alarmed him. "You're frightened. Talk to me, Winter Fawn. Tell me what's wrong."

He couldn't see her now; the room was as black as the inside of a cat. More than worried, he tugged off his gloves, then found her ice-cold hands, where they covered her mouth. As gently as he could, he forced her hands from her lips. "Honey?"

"I'm s-sorry." A deep shudder wracked her. "It's nothing."

"What's nothing?" he asked, trying to keep his voice low and smooth.

"The s-storm I . . . don't like . . . s-storms."

"Ah, honey." Forgetting his wet clothes, he sat next to her on the sofa and pulled her onto his lap. "Ah, honey," he said again. She didn't like storms. Who was she trying to fool? She was plain-ass terrified. She shook against him like a fall leaf barely hanging on in a high wind. "You're safe here, I promise. The storm won't hurt you."

Her swallow was audible. "I know. I'm sorry. I'm all r-right." Carson held her for a long time, running one hand up and down her arm, the other stroking her back. Slowly it dawned on him that all she wore was a thin nightgown. He wished he hadn't realized that.

Her tremors eased as the storm slackened.

"There," he whispered in her ear. "Hear that? The thunder's moving off. No more storm. Only rain." His lips brushed her temple. "It's only rain now. You're safe."

The small taste of her skin was not enough. He kissed her temple again, then her cheek, her jaw. When she turned her head, their lips brushed. Settling there, his mouth on hers, came as natural to him as breathing. With the music of the rain falling from the roof mixed with the soft sounds of their breathing, he kissed her.

Everything inside Winter Fawn stilled. Everything except her heart, which suddenly raced faster and pounded harder than a racing herd of buffalo. Starved for the taste of him, she opened her mouth and welcomed the invasion of his tongue, stroking it with hers, reveling in the soft groan that came from his throat.

With fingers trembling from eagerness now, rather than fear, she touched his face, his hair, and held his head in her palms.

Carson wanted to swallow her whole. He lost himself in the kiss, in her warm welcome. Had a woman ever responded to him this way? No, never. This was not something he would be able to forget. He wanted more of her. All of her. Without thought to where they were or what could happen, he twisted on the sofa and took her down until her back was pressed against the seat and he felt her breasts against his chest.

Suddenly a sound penetrated the heated fog in his brain. The creak of a floorboard.

He sprang upright just as the door to Gussie's room clicked open.

"Carson?" his aunt called.

The hand he slid over Winter Fawn's mouth served not only to keep her silent, but to keep her hidden from Gussie below the back of the sofa. "Sorry, Gussie, I didn't mean to wake you."

"I didn't know you were back. What are you doing sitting here in the dark? Let me light a lamp for you."

It was too dark to see her, but from her voice he determined that she remained in the doorway to her room. "Don't bother," he said quickly. Beneath his hand, Winter Fawn lay as rigid as a board. "Go on back to bed. I just want to sit here a minute before turning in."

"I could put on some coffee if you—"

"That's all right. I don't want anything. Good night, Gussie," he added, hoping, praying she would take the hint and go back to bed.

"Well, if you're certain you're all right, dear. You sound a tad odd. You might be coming down with something."

"I'm just tired," he told her, letting the weariness of his bones creep into his voice. "That's all."

After a long moment, she finally said good night and closed her door.

Feeling as though someone had pulled his spine right out through the top of his head, Carson fell limp against the back of the sofa. His hand slipped from Winter Fawn's mouth.

God, that was close.

Then the irony of the situation settled over him. He was a grown man, the father of a six-year-old, and he was sitting in his own house. And he'd felt like an eight-year-old caught with his hand in the cookie jar.

Winter Fawn was grateful for the shock that had held her immobile beneath Carson's hand. From all she had observed, and from the things Carson had said, it was no more proper in the white world than it was among Our People for an unmarried woman to be seen kissing a man. For any woman to be seen kissing any man not her husband.

Not that young couples did not usually find a way to steal a kiss now and then. That's what she felt like now, a young girl having barely escaped being caught stealing a kiss with a young warrior.

Ye feel that way, lass, because you did just barely escape. She did not know whether to giggle like that young girl she might have been, or cry for the woman she was, who could not have the man she wanted.

Carson's fingers touched her arm and pulled her up until she sat leaning against him with his arms around her. When he whispered in her ear, his warm breath sent shivers down her spine.

"Lord, I don't want to let you go."

"Then don't." She turned and slipped her arms around his waist. "Don't let me go, Carson. Never let me go."

"I have to," he said softly. "I won't have you exposed to talk because I couldn't control myself and took you right here on the sofa in a house full of people."

Winter Fawn shivered again. No, she did not want that either. In her eagerness for his kiss, his touch, she had not thought of the consequences. If he had not reacted so quickly, his aunt would have known she was here with him.

"Damn, I got you all wet," he said, fingering the side of her gown. "Go on back to bed, honey, and get warm."

She did not want to go. She did not want to leave him. But she knew she must. "Kiss me again, and I will go."

With a soft groan, he complied. He kissed hard and fast, as if he could not get enough of her. Then he pulled away.

Long after she went back to bed, Winter Fawn lay awake, running a finger back and forth across her lips. She could still taste him there, a dark and dangerous flavor that made her yearn for more.

Carson, too, lay awake long into the night. For the first time in his life he felt an envy for men like Innes who spent most of their time in a fog, courtesy of the flask that seldom left his hand.

The next morning at breakfast, Carson could not keep his eyes off Winter Fawn. He wanted to reach over and touch her, stroke her cheek, press his lips to hers. Last night she had been alive and on fire in his arms. This morning she would not look at him.

Winter Fawn could not bring herself to look at him. She was afraid, very much afraid, that she might beg him to kiss her again, right there in front of everyone.

This wouldna do. From the beginning it had been Carson saying they should not, could not make love, and her trying to make him forget the restrictions he had imposed upon them. But last night, as she had lain in bed and listened to the rain drum against the roof, she had remembered again that final morning on the trail, when he had taught her the pleasures of her own body.

She had wanted that pleasure again, with him, wanted to bring those same sharp, hot feelings to him. She had wanted it when he came to her on the sofa. Had Gussie not interrupted them, it might have happened. They might have made love right there.

And then what? Would they sneak around and hide, as though what they shared was something dirty? Or would he openly claim her as his lover.

His whore, you mean.

There. The word had finally formed in her mind. He had never offered her marriage. Had in fact been emphatic that she save herself for the man who would be her husband.

And he had been right. As much as she wanted Carson, she could not bring herself to become his whore. Such a thing was simply not done among Our People, nor, from what she knew, was it acceptable among whites.

What was she to do? Man-Above, what was she to do?

Carson was staring at her, watching her every move. She did not dare look at him for fear of weeping.

Look away, she silently begged him. *Please do not look at me so.*

But Carson couldn't help it. Something was wrong, terribly wrong, but he didn't know what. Was she sorry about last night?

Don't let me go, Carson. Never let me go.

She couldn't be sorry. The woman who had so desperately whispered those words against his lips could not now be sorry.

Suddenly the other men were pushing back their chairs and standing, heading for the door. Carson looked down to find his plate empty, but for the life of him he could not remember what he'd eaten.

"Carson?"

He blinked and looked up at Gussie.

"Might I have a word with you before you get busy for the day?"

Carson felt his gut clench. Had she realized Winter Fawn was with him last night? Had she guessed what they were doing? Had she heard them?

He squared his jaw and nodded. "Certainly." He would not be scolded like a schoolboy. He was the head of this family now, and if he wanted to kiss a woman, he would kiss a woman, by damn.

He saw Gussie's eyes flick toward Winter Fawn, then back to him and ground his teeth. He wouldn't have her passing judgment on Winter Fawn over this, by damn.

"Let's go out onto the porch, shall we?" Gussie asked.

"Yes," he said, scooting his chair back and rising. "Let's." He followed her onto the porch and closed the door behind them. The sun was just creeping up over the horizon, but the sky was light.

Gussie clasped her hands together at her waist. "I don't know quite how to broach this subject. I realize it's none of my business, but . . ."

"What's none of your business?" he asked tightly, sure he was going to regret it.

"Well, it's Winter Fawn."

"What about her?"

"Oh, now, see? I've upset you already and haven't even had my say. No—" She held a hand up, palm out, to forestall his interruption. "I must say it. The poor girl simply must have new clothes, Carson."

Carson blinked. "Pardon?"

"The doeskin is beautiful, but it's becoming dreadfully soiled, and as near as I can tell, she has nothing else to wear."

If ever a man felt like a fool, it was Carson Dulaney in that moment. Twice the fool. Once for jumping to conclusions about what Gussie had to say, but mainly for not realizing himself that Winter Fawn had no other clothes.

"I don't know your financial situation, Carson, dear. I'm not sure that it's any of my business. Please don't take offense, but if money is tight, I have a few dollars I brought with me. Enough to purchase some fabric for a dress for her, if the settlement I passed on my way here has any. Or perhaps her own father should—no." She sighed. "I'm sure that man doesn't have two cents to rub together. His son could use some clothes as well. I'm sorry if I'm butting in—"

"Gussie, Gussie." Carson grabbed her hands and squeezed them gently. "Stop apologizing. I'm the one who should be apologizing, to Winter Fawn and Hunter for not realizing . . ." He shook his head at himself. "I should have done something about this the minute we arrived. Today's what, Wednesday? How about we all go to town Saturday and do some shopping. And you save your money to spend on yourself. I'm not rich, but I can afford what we need."

"Bless you." She returned the squeeze on her hands. When Carson stepped off the porch and headed for the barn, Gussie stood for a moment looking out at the sunrise. She was proud of herself. That she was noticing and thinking of others meant she was putting her grief over Lucille behind her. Lord above, but Lucille herself would have scolded her good for neglecting the needs of others while wallowing in her own self-pity.

That was behind her now. Gussie squared her shoulders and turned toward the door.

"Mrs. Winthrop?"

At the sound of Mr. MacDougall's voice, Gussie paused. Now here was a man she didn't know quite what to think of. Try as she might to find something good about him, she could come up with nothing other than the fact that he seemed to have sired two beautiful children. He reeked of whiskey, even early in the morning. He wore those disreputable buckskin pants that looked stiff enough with grime to stand on their own, and that hair! Bushy red and grimy, all over his head and face, and way, way too long. She was still itching to get her scissors into that mess.

He stopped at the foot of the porch steps and looked up at

her with narrowed eyes. "I've got a bone to pick with ye," he said with a snarl.

Gussie's back went ramrod straight. "Indeed?" The nerve of this—this *foreigner*—to speak to her so!

"Aye, *indeed.*"

"And that would be?"

"My lassie, Winter Fawn, was happy until you came. She felt useful and needed. Now all she does is wander around looking like she's lost her best friend. What have you done to the girl is what I'm wantin' to know."

"Done to her?" Gussie's eyes widened. "I assure you, Mr. MacDougall, I have done nothing but try to make her days here as pleasant as possible."

"And what, might I be askin', is yer idea of pleasant?"

Gussie wasn't sure why she was even conversing with this ill-mannered man.

No, that wasn't true. She spoke with him as politely as possible because he was Carson's friend, had been Edmond's friend. And because what he was saying genuinely distressed her. Now that she thought of it, Winter Fawn did seem rather listless, but not having seen her any other way, Gussie had assumed she was merely a quiet young lady. If Gussie had done anything to make her sad . . .

"Well, I've taken over all the chores so that she is free to do whatever she wants."

"Ye *what?* Ach, it's no wonder then that the lass be at a loss. She's never been idle a day in her life. She's used to being needed, to keeping busy. Ye've made her feel useless, that's what ye've done."

The denial she wanted to utter died on her lips. She could see now that he was right. By taking away the work Winter Fawn had been doing, she had left the girl—young woman, she amended—with no sense of worth. Why, if anyone had ever done such a thing to *her,* she would have cried herself to sleep.

But Gussie saw something else, too, something other than this particular mistake of hers. She saw the love that this man had for his children. Perhaps here, too, she had misjudged.

"Mr. MacDougall—"

"Innes. My name be Innes."

There were some lines Gussie was not prepared to cross, not with this man. Perhaps he had more good points than she had realized, but he was still too depressingly unkempt for her liking. "Mr. MacDougall," she said firmly. "I can see now that what you say about Winter Fawn is true, and I am deeply sorry for being the cause of her unhappiness. I assure you I will endeavor to correct the situation at once."

The sun was full up now, and it threw half his face in shadow, but not so much that she couldn't tell that he was peering at her from one eye.

"Endeavor to correct?" he repeated warily.

"That's right."

"Well, then, see that ye do." With a sharp nod, he stomped off toward the barn while Gussie stepped into the house.

"Is there a problem?" Carson asked Innes when the man reached the barn.

Innes pulled his flask from the pouch on his belt and took a swallow. Jamming the cork back in, he let out a gust of breath that would have knocked over a horse, if one had been close enough.

"What's it mean, this word *endeavor?*"

Carson shrugged. "Try."

"Hmph. Try what?"

"Try. Endeavor means to try."

"Oh. Aye. Hmph. Any objections if I go huntin' today?"

"Innes." Carson shook his head. "I've told you before that you don't owe me anything. You're free to come and go as you please."

Innes squinted one eye. "Is that a no?"

Innes rode west to do his hunting, and Hunter rode with him. Carson, Beau, and Frank spent the day cutting trees in the hills to the north for firewood and snaking them back to the ranch. They came back to the house for the noon meal, then went back to the hills for another load of logs. When they brought the last logs down for the day, they were hot, dirty, and tired.

While Beau and Frank cleaned up at the bunkhouse before coming in to supper, Carson headed for the house.

He rounded the corner, heading for the front door, and came up short at the sight of Winter Fawn. There she stood, as she had the other day, staring off toward the northeast.

He made himself walk the rest of the way to the edge of the porch. "You scare me when you do that."

She must have heard him coming, for she didn't jump as if surprised by his voice. She merely turned her head and looked at him with solemn, curious eyes. "When I do what?"

"When you stand there all alone and stare off in the direction of your village."

"They would have gone by now, somewhere out along the Arkansas to gather together with the rest of the tribe and hunt the buffalo."

"You miss that," he said flatly.

"No, actually. I dinna miss packing up and moving the village out onto the plains. Da used to tell us stories of white men who lived in the same place season after season. I've always wondered what that would be like."

"Then why do you look as if you want to go? You said not to let you go," he reminded her. "Yet I get the feeling you're the one thinking of leaving."

Her smile, slight as it was, was sad. "I do not know what I will do. I canna stay here forever."

"Why not?"

"Would you?" she asked.

"Last night you—"

She looked away, off into the distance again. "Last night was a mistake."

"No." He leaped onto the porch and grasped her arm. "It wasn't a mistake. You didn't think so at the time."

Again came that sad smile that tore at his insides. "I didna think at all."

"Are you saying I took advantage of your fear of the storm?"

"Nae." She shook her head and gently pulled her arm from his grasp. "I'm saying that when you touch me, all I can think about is touching you, and my mind is no longer my own."

Carson's heart knocked against his ribs. "Believe me," he

said with feeling. "I know just what you mean. We can have more of that, if you stay. Remember how good it was that last morning in the mountains?" He touched her cheek, the corner of her mouth. "I want to give you that again. It can be even better the next time."

"Please." Her eyes slid shut. "Do not say such things to me."

"Why? Why are you talking of leaving? I thought you wanted . . . I thought you liked the things you feel when we're together."

"Like them?" She opened her eyes and met his gaze. "I crave them. I want them—you—so much that I canna think of aught else."

"Then why—"

"You are the one who kept reminding me that I must wait for the man who will be my husband. Is that man you, Carson? Are you asking me to be your mate, your wife? Or are you thinking I'll make a good wh—"

"Don't say it!" He gripped her arms and shook her twice. "Don't you dare say it. *Never.* I've *never* thought of you that way. Damn you for even thinking it."

"If I'm to be neither your wife nor your whore, then are we to be merely friends?"

Carson stared at her. Hard. He couldn't believe the turn in the conversation.

"Friends do not do the things we have done together. At least not among Our People. Do they among whites? Would your aunt and your sister and your daughter understand if I were to be that kind of friend to you and you to me?"

"What is this?" He turned loose of her arms and stepped back. "I've been blind-sided once by a woman and ended up married and wishing I wasn't. I won't make the same mistake again."

"I do not know this word, blind-sided. I was merely explaining why I canna stay here. I knew you didna want me for your wife, Carson. But you've made me realize what the alternative would be, and that would be as unacceptable to me as my becoming your wife would be to you."

Carson took a slow, deep breath, then let it out. This was

not Julia, northern beauty, trying to get him, Southern planter, to the altar just to shock her father. This was Winter Fawn, and she would leave him if he didn't stop her. Maybe not today, maybe not tomorrow, but soon. One day he would wake up and she would be gone.

The thought was intolerable.

What the hell. She was beautiful and he wanted her. He had planned to someday marry to provide a mother for Megan. He couldn't expect Gussie to spend the rest of her life raising his daughter.

"Did you mean what you said about wanting to live in one place instead of roaming the prairie?"

"Aye, I think I would like that, but such a thing is not possible for me," she said, looking off into the distance again.

"It is possible. I think you're right—we should get married."

Winter Fawn gaped and stared at him. "I never said we should do such a thing."

"Why not? Think about it. I need a wife, Megan needs a mother. You need a home. We want each other. That's more than most people have going for them when they get married."

"You say nothing of love."

She made a direct hit with that one. He didn't want to love a woman. That way lay heartache. "Neither do you," he responded.

Winter Fawn closed her eyes and tried to breathe. So. He didna love her, but would marry her to keep her from leaving. She supposed she should accept his offer. Or rather, send him to her father, as was the way of Our People. But to live with him day after day and never have his love . . .

At least if she had married Crooked Oak, she wouldna care that he didna love her.

With Carson, she knew she would care too much.

"Nae," she told him. She did him the courtesy of opening her eyes when she spoke, but she tried her best not to see his face. "I dinna want a man who willna marry me, but I willna marry a man who disnae love me."

* * *

The band of Southern Arapaho led by Little Raven had left its winter encampment and joined the rest of the tribe along the banks of the Arkansas. There was much revelry as old friends were greeted, new children were shown off, exploits bragged about.

Little Raven kept a close eye on the warriors whenever they gathered, for fear they would speak more of fighting than of finding the buffalo. But with Crooked Oak gone, it was fairly easy to keep even the dog soldiers from doing anything drastic.

Crooked Oak could stay gone, as far as Little Raven was concerned. Little Raven did wonder what had become of Winter Fawn, but he assumed she was somewhere with her father and brother. This is what her uncle, Two Feathers, now believed, which was why he had left Crooked Oak and returned to Our People. Long Chin and Talks Loud had come with him. They said that Crooked Oak was determined to find her, even though they had searched the mountains for weeks and found no sign. Red Bull and Spotted Calf had remained with Crooked Oak.

Little Raven was confident that one day Winter Fawn would return to let them know what had happened to her. She would not leave her grandparents to wonder and worry.

For now, Little Raven must decide what to do about the message he had just received. The white fathers wanted another peace council. They wanted the Arapaho, the Cheyenne, and others to gather at Medicine Lodge Creek in the place they called Kansas. No doubt they would want Our People to confine themselves to a reservation, as had happened with other tribes. Little Raven did not care for the idea of a reservation, unless it meant that the whites must stay away. If there was game and good water and no whites . . .

Ah, but how was he ever to convince the Dogmen that another treaty was better for the tribe than going to war?

Man-Above, guide me. Send me a sign. Should we go to war? Or should we make peace?

CHAPTER 14

''I wonder if we can grow squash here.'' Gussie tapped the blunt end of her pencil against her chin.

Carson looked up from the poker hand he held. The family, except for Megan who was in bed, was seated around the table after supper. Bess and Winter Fawn were each bent over an article of clothing, plying needle and thread to mend various tears. Carson and Innes were teaching Hunter the finer points of five-card stud.

''Planning a garden?'' Carson asked.

''Yes.'' Gussie smiled. ''We certainly need one, but I'm not sure what will grow well here. I suppose the merchant in town can advise me. I thought,'' she said, glancing at Winter Fawn, who sat across the table from her, ''that we could purchase seeds when we go to town Saturday, and that perhaps Winter Fawn might not object too strongly to being in charge of our garden.''

A big smile slowly lit Innes's face. ''Ach, that be a fair good idea.''

Winter Fawn looked up, skeptical. ''I know nothing of gardening.''

''Oh, but you could learn,'' Bess offered. ''Aunt Gussie can teach you, and I can help.''

"Certainly," Gussie added. "And think what a useful skill you'll possess."

Winter Fawn glanced down at her mending. "I will be glad to help in any way I can, but gardening is not something I can do once I return to Our People. We do not stay in one place long enough to grow anything."

Reaction to her calm statement came swiftly.

Innes looked thunderstruck.

Hunter merely watched her, his face expressionless.

"Return?" Bess cried. "Oh, Winter Fawn, you wouldn't leave us, would you?"

Carson slapped his cards face down on the table so hard the globe rattled in the lamp. "You're not going back," he protested. "Good God, woman, they tried to kill you. Twice!"

Winter Fawn kept her gaze steadily on her sewing. " 'Twas you they tried to kill. I merely got in the way."

"Winter Fawn," Bess cried again. "Say you don't mean it. You can't leave us. We need you!"

Finally Winter Fawn looked up at Bess with a half smile. "I canna stay here forever. This is your home, your place in the world. I must find mine."

"This would be yours," Carson said, his eyes narrowed, "if you'd just marry me, like I asked."

Winter Fawn stiffened. She could not believe he said such a thing. To her it was private, between the two of them, not a thing to be discussed around the table.

"What's this?" Innes roared.

"Carson!" Bess jumped up and hugged his neck. "You proposed? And no one said anything?"

"She did." Carson's mouth twisted down at the corners. "She said no."

"But . . . but *why?*" Bess wanted to know of Winter Fawn. "Oh, it's perfect. It's the answer to everything. When you marry Carson, you'll be my sister for real."

"Bess . . ." Winter Fawn was at a loss. Was she to tell them all, straight out, that Carson did not love her? Was she to humiliate herself in such a way?

"You asked my daughter to marry ye without talkin' to me first?" Innes demanded.

"If she'd been agreeable," Carson said, his words clipped, "I would have come to you. Since she wasn't, there's not much point, is there?"

Innes pushed back his chair and stood. "Let's be takin' ourselves a little stroll, lass." It was not said as a request. He held his hand out to Winter Fawn.

Reluctantly, she stood.

"Take my shawl, dear," Gussie told Winter Fawn. "It's there on the peg by the door. I declare, the nights get downright chilly out here."

As Winter Fawn turned away from the table, Bess gripped her hand. "Change your mind, please. Stay here forever with us."

Winter Fawn tried to speak, but couldn't. She followed her father onto the porch and out into the yard.

The air was cool, the star-studded sky black. She took a deep breath and let it out, silently praying for strength, for help.

Her father took a drink from his flask. The fumes stung her eyes and pinched her nostrils.

"So, the lad asked ye to marry him."

As far as Winter Fawn was concerned, his comment required no response from her.

"What? Ye've nothin' to say?"

She heaved a sigh. "Aye, he asked me."

"And ye turned him down."

"What is this?" she cried. "Not too long ago you were telling me to stay away from him."

"That was different. Now we're talking marriage. Lass," he said, his voice softening in a way she hadn't heard since she was a child. "I've seen with my own eyes that he appeals to ye."

"He disnae love me, Da."

"He said as much?"

" 'Tis what he didna say that tells me."

"Ah, so now ye be readin' his mind, is that it?"

"No," she said crossly. "I asked him right out if he loved me. He didna answer. That was answer enough, do ye no think?"

"Few enough marriages start out with love, lass."

"Yours did. You and Mother loved each other."

Innes felt the squeeze around his heart at the mention of Smiling Woman. God, but the lass had the right of it. He and Smiling Woman had loved each other like there was no tomorrow. Now their daughter stood before him a grown woman. Never had he been more unsure of himself. Never had he missed Smiling Woman's wise counsel more than at this moment.

"Aye," he said finally. "That we did. But . . ."

"But I should settle for less?"

"Tell me, lass, what would have happened if Carson Dulaney and his family had never come along?"

Winter Fawn looked at him warily. "What do you mean?"

"Ye said yerself that other girls your age are long since married, with children of their own. If things had no turned out the way they had when I came to the village this time, Crooked Oak would have offered for you."

"Ye wouldna have accepted!" she protested.

"No him, nae. But there would have been other offers. Chances are I would have accepted one and you might already have a husband. Aside from yer mother and me, I know of no other marriage among Our People that was not arranged by the girl's family. Is this not true?"

"Aye," she said reluctantly. "So?"

"Most of those couples were not in love when they married, yet many came to love each other. Do ye think I wouldna have accepted an offer and arranged yer marriage if Crooked Oak hadna attacked us? Lord, lass, 'tis time ye took a husband."

"You wouldna arrange a match with Carson," she said, horrified. "Da, you wouldna."

Innes narrowed his eyes. "And why wouldna I? Why shouldna I do that very thing? He's a good man. He can provide for you. With him ye'll be safer than with any man in the tribe."

"Da—"

"Nae, dinna fash yerself, lass. I'll no force the issue. Not just yet. Not if ye promise me ye'll think on it. Ye may think he disnae love ye, but from what I see, I'm thinkin' maybe he just disnae know it yet."

"Nae." She shook her head. "He likes me well enough."

Innes hooted. "Aye, and ye dinna mind lookin' at him too much yerself. Lass, ye must have a husband soon. This world is no place for a woman alone."

"I'm not alone, Da. I have you. Unless," she added with a touch of hurt in her voice that she could not disguise, "you're going to leave me again."

"Nae, I'll no be leavin' ye, lass. Not apurpose. But I'm old. I canna provide for ye forever. Carson can. Promise me ye'll think on it."

To please her father, Winter Fawn gave him the promise he sought. She only wished she did not want so badly to be Carson's wife. She wished she did not want so badly for Carson to love her.

Saturday morning they headed out for town. Carson drove the wagon, with Gussie sitting next to him. Winter Fawn had insisted on riding in the back with Bess and Megan. Hunter and the men accompanied them on horseback.

They were nearly there when Innes cursed and drew his horse to a halt.

Carson drew the team up and called back, "What's wrong?"

Innes dismounted and lifted the left forefoot of his horse, then lowered it. "Loose shoe," he called back. "I'll be seein' about it in town."

Carson gave a nod, then, when Innes remounted, urged the team forward.

Badito was a small, dusty town that served the needs of the outlying ranches up and down the Huerfano. It sat at the point where the Yellowstone Creek emptied into the river, just below the southern tip of the Wet Mountains. Just north rose a pointed peak, small compared to other mountains, but isolated so that it stood out, especially when coming from the east. Word was that it rose to over eight thousand feet above sea level.

The town boasted two saloons, a combination livery and blacksmith shop, a general store, a post office, and a few scattered houses.

As they rode into town, people stepped into doorways and peered out windows to watch.

Carson pulled the wagon to a stop next to the general store and helped Gussie down. Innes was there for Winter Fawn and the girls. Winter Fawn walked past Carson and joined Gussie without looking at him.

"You ladies get whatever you need in the store," he said to Gussie. He wanted to remind her not to forget material for a dress for Winter Fawn, but hell, it was she who had noticed the need in the first place. He didn't figure she needed reminding. He didn't figure Winter Fawn would appreciate his saying anything, either. She didn't seem to appreciate much of anything he did or said lately.

He turned toward Hunter. "While we go see about that horseshoe, why don't you go with them and pick yourself out some shirts and denims?"

Hunter looked to his father. When Innes nodded, the boy, face expressionless, followed the ladies toward the store.

Carson turned away and accompanied Innes down the sun-baked street toward the livery.

Winter Fawn sighed as he walked away. She did not know what to do. She wanted so much to be with him, to stay with him. But she wasn't sure she could bear knowing he did not feel the same.

Yes, he had asked her to marry him. But she feared that was more a matter of convenience for him. A woman to share his bed and be a mother to his daughter.

She had had an ache in her heart for days. Now it moved to her head and throbbed behind her eyes. This heaviness of spirit was not like her. With an effort, she shrugged it off and turned back to follow Gussie and the girls into the store.

The door to the store stood open. As Gussie stepped near, a woman came out and blocked the way.

Winter Fawn stiffened.

"You!" cried Mrs. Linderman. "Mr. Hernandez doesn't allow savages in his store. We don't allow savages in this town."

Having never been exposed to hate before, Winter Fawn was at a loss.

Not so, Gussie. "I declare, I'm pleased to hear it." In an elaborate gesture, she looked around at Winter Fawn, at Bess and Megan and Hunter, then up and down the street. "It must be working. I don't see a single savage in sight. How do you do? I'm Mrs. Winthrop, late of Atlanta."

Bess had trouble holding back a giggle.

Mrs. Linderman made a low, snarling sound of rage in her throat and stomped away down the street.

"My, my," Gussie said beneath her breath. "What an unpleasant woman."

"That," Bess informed her, "was the housekeeper Carson fired."

"I always knew that boy had a good head on his shoulders." Gussie lowered her parasol and stepped through the doorway and into the dim interior of the store. "Girls, shall we get busy? I declare, it's been simply ages since I've shopped. I've a terrible need to spend some of Carson's money."

It was the most unpleasant hour of Winter Fawn's life. She could not indulge her fascination with all the wonderful sights and smells in the store, for everywhere she turned, she felt the shopkeeper's eyes, narrow and suspicious, on her. Two women swept their skirts aside when she or Hunter neared, as though the material would be contaminated beyond redemption if it should brush against one of them. Another man stared at her every bit as intently as the man behind the counter, but his look was not suspicious; he looked at her as though she wore no clothes, or as though given half a chance, he would rip her clothes from her body and not care in the least that she might object.

She was not even aware of what Gussie was buying, so miserable was she.

And Bess, bless her, was not enjoying herself either, for she had obviously appointed herself Winter Fawn's guardian and refused to leave her side.

I do not belong here, Winter Fawn thought. How could Carson want to marry someone his own kind hated? If he married her, would they not soon come to hate him, too? And Megan, and Bess, and anyone else close to him?

She was right to refuse him.

She watched dully as Gussie helped Hunter select three work shirts and two pairs of denim pants like the ones Carson wore.

"Take these." He handed the pile of clothing to Winter Fawn. "I'm getting out of here."

Eyes wide, she watched her brother desert her and step out into the street.

Hunter was sorry to leave his sister in that place, but he figured that Carson's aunt could handle anything that might happen. If he had stayed there a moment longer watching those men stare at Winter Fawn, watching the women draw their skirts aside, he would have done something foolish, like draw his knife and flourish it before the next person to insult his sister.

And foolish it would have been. The only thing that had stopped him was knowing that Winter Fawn would have been humiliated by such an act. She was well able to stand up for herself. He'd seen her do it a dozen times. Why she did not spit in their faces, he didn't know.

That was not true. He did know. Her spirit was troubled by Carson's offer of marriage. She should just accept and be done with it. She would give in eventually. It was what she wanted; it was what was best for her. Why their father was allowing her to make everyone miserable, he did not know. Grandfather would not have put up with such behavior.

But maybe in the white world things were different.

Shaking his head, he stepped into the shadows of the livery stables, and directly into more trouble.

"What did you say?"

Hunter had never heard Carson's voice so quiet and cold before, nor had he ever seen his eyes look so hard.

The man he spoke to wiggled a finger in his ear. He was half a head shorter than Carson, with lank, greasy hair that was probably brown when clean—if it was ever clean—but looked black. He wore denim pants, with suspenders over a red flannel undershirt, and his hands were grimy.

"The squaw," he said. "You let me have her for a couple o' hours and I'll loan you the use of my plow so's you don't need no new handle on yours."

"Why, you—"

"Okay, okay," the man said quickly. "Maybe a couple o' hours is too much. An hour. I'll just take her out back here—"

Innes let out a low groan and lunged. "Why, you filthy-minded—"

"Oh, no." Carson caught Innes at the last minute before his hands closed on the man's throat. "Allow me." He rammed his right fist into the man's mouth.

The man grunted in surprise and pain. Blood spurted from his busted lips. "What was that for?"

"For the hell of it." Carson hit him again.

This time the man went down, out cold.

Innes scowled. "I thought you said you came west because you were tired of fighting. Now look at ye."

"I'm not all that fond of fighting," Carson said, prowling through the tools on the workbench for the one he needed to pull the shoe from the horse, since it looked like they were going to have to serve themselves. "But what I actually said was that I was tired of killing. I meant with guns. Fists are different."

"Ah." Innes let out a satisfied sigh. "A man after my own heart."

As neither man had yet to notice Hunter, he slipped back out the door and returned to the store. He knew that neither his father nor Carson would tell Winter Fawn what had happened, but Hunter would. The livery man was a danger to her. She should be made aware.

In the noise and confusion of loading their purchases into the wagon and getting ready to leave a half hour later, Hunter managed to get Winter Fawn aside and tell her what had happened.

What he told her only served to harden her resolve. She must leave. She was bringing Carson and his family nothing but trouble. First the woman, Mrs. Linderman, then the men and women in the store whom Gussie had to stare down more than once, and now this.

No, she could not stay and cause more trouble.

But where would she go? She doubted her father would take her to join the tribe for the summer. He wanted her to stay and marry Carson.

The thought of leaving her father brought almost as much pain as the thought of leaving Carson.

Where would she go? How would she live?

The questions plagued her all the way home.

At some point during the trip she realized that she and the girls were now sharing the wagon bed with not only the supplies purchased in town, but also a crate of baby chicks. They were cute and fuzzy, but could not hold Winter Fawn's attention. Nor could the cow that was following them, although Winter Fawn did think to wonder why a cow would follow them home. Then she saw the rope that tethered it to the back of the wagon. Why would a man who raised cattle go to town and buy a cow?

The question didn't matter, as it had nothing to do with her.

It wasn't until they all sat down to supper at sundown that Winter Fawn noticed Carson's hands. The sight of his knuckles, bruised and swollen and covered with deep scratches, roused her sharply from her introspection. "What have you done?" she cried, dismayed.

Beneath the table, a foot knocked hard against her shin. Startled, she looked across at her brother. He frowned at her and shook his head slightly.

"I declare, Carson," Gussie exclaimed. "You should have said something."

The fight, Winter Fawn realized. Carson had injured his hands fighting over her, and she wasn't supposed to know about it.

"Did you hurt your hands, Daddy?" Megan asked, her little brow furrowed with distress.

"Just a little accident," Carson said. "I've had worse."

"Indeed, I'm sure you have." Gussie turned to Winter Fawn. "As soon as you're through eating, dear, would you be so kind as to heat some water for him to soak his hands in? Just hot enough to soothe, mind, not scalding. Cold water first, though, for twenty minutes. Then the hot."

"Yes, ma'am," Winter Fawn said automatically. Her hands ached to touch, to ease Carson's pain. Pain suffered on her behalf.

"And I'll get the iodine for you to dab on those scratches," Gussie added.

"Ooh, Daddy, that ol' iodine'll sting. You oughta just have Winter Fawn kiss it and make it better."

Winter Fawn's hands trembled at the thought of kissing his knuckles. As if drawn by force, her gaze rose until she was looking directly into his deep blue eyes.

"I should, huh?" he asked Megan. His voice was low and intimate and sent a shiver down Winter Fawn's arms.

"Uh huh," Megan said cheerfully. "She can kiss it real good so it don't hurt."

"So it *doesn't* hurt, dear." Gussie's voice sounded slightly strangled.

"How about it?" Carson asked Winter Fawn softly, never taking his gaze from hers, holding her, trapping her, making her heart pound hard and fast. "Will you kiss it and make it better, so it won't hurt?"

Innes cleared his throat loudly.

Winter Fawn jerked as if shot. She jumped up from her chair. "I'll go get some water."

Blindly she placed the large soup kettle beneath the spigot and pumped the handle for all she was worth.

He was out of his mind, looking at her that way, talking to her that way. In front of everyone! Making her breath catch and her hands shake. Making her want to touch him.

Ach, but the man is a menace.

She pumped so hard and fast that the water nearly overflowed the kettle. She had to dip part of it out into a bucket to avoid sloshing it all over the counter. When she finished, she wrapped a dish towel around the wire handle of the kettle to keep it from cutting into her hands.

"That's too heavy for you." A long arm—Carson's—snaked over her shoulder. "I'll get it." He grabbed the kettle and carried it to the table.

Winter Fawn turned, her mouth gaping. "I am not so weak that I canna lift a pot," she protested.

"I never thought you were." Carson plunked the kettle down on the table, then sat and placed his hands in the water.

Gussie and Bess were looking at each other. They appeared to be trying to keep from laughing. They were not having much success.

Hunter was making a serious study of the fork on his empty plate, while Innes beamed at Carson as though he were a treasured child who had just taken his first step.

Winter Fawn wanted to scream at them all. Instead, she turned back to the counter. "I will heat water to follow the cold."

"Use the warm water in the reservoir on the stove, dear," Gussie suggested.

"Nae." She checked and found a number of hot coals still glowing in the stove. She added one piece of wood for a small fire, then started pumping water into another pot. "Then you'll have to heat more to wash the dishes. This will do."

Aye, she thought. This would do. To pour over Carson's head.

But when she carried the warm water to the table a short time later and lifted his hands from the cold water to inspect them, she forgot her irritation. As her fingers brushed across his bruised and battered knuckles she could feel the pain there. Her hands were drawn to it as the sun is drawn to the western mountains each evening.

She felt the heat grow in her hands, felt the aches and pains in her own knuckles, took them out of his flesh and into her own. Healing him. Healing—

"Lass," her father called.

By the sharp tone he used, he must have been calling her repeatedly. She had not heard. She had been lost in—

Oh no! Quickly she released Carson's hands. *What have I done?*

Holding her breath, she watched Carson flex his fingers.

Not gone. The marks of his fight were not gone. She hadna gone so far as that, to remove all sign of his injury. It would be all right. No one would know.

"Thank you," Carson said, slipping his hands into the warm water. "They already feel better."

With a low cough, Innes left the table, left the house in such a hurry that the front door slammed shut behind him.

Nae! Winter Fawn thought frantically. He couldna do it. Her father couldna leave her again, the way he did over the rabbit.

With panic squeezing her chest, she bolted after him.

Those around the table stared in surprise.

''Is something wrong?'' Bess asked.

It wasn't lost on Carson that it was Hunter his sister questioned. But Hunter merely frowned and shrugged. Carson started to rise.

''Sit, dear,'' Gussie told him in that kind voice that had pure steel running through it. ''Finish soaking your hands. Whatever is going on, I'm sure Winter Fawn and her father do not need our help.''

Outside deep twilight had settled in. Winter Fawn finally spotted her father in the gathering darkness beside the barn, his flask tipped up to his lips. ''Da!''

With a curse, he lowered the flask and turned as if to stalk away, but Winter Fawn ran and caught him by the sleeve.

''Nae,'' she cried, holding on when he tried to jerk free. ''Nae, ye willna do this again, not without so much as a word. Ye might as well put a knife to my heart as leave me again that way.''

Innes stared at her, dumbfounded. ''Ach, what stuff and nonsense is this? I dinna ken what yer talkin' aboot.''

Winter Fawn let out a long cry, one that had been held deep in her soul since the spring of her twelfth year. ''Dinna tell me it is so unimportant to ye that ye canna recall riding out of our lives without a word, without a thought. Do yer own bairns mean so little to ye, then?''

''Lass,'' he cried. ''What are ye sayin'?''

''Ye canna deny ye saw what I did just now, with Carson's hands.''

He looked away quickly. ''Nae.'' His voice lowered. ''I canna deny what I saw, what ye did.''

''The last time . . .'' Her voice broke over the words, the pain of saying them aloud. ''With the rabbit. You said, never do it again. Then ye left. Ye left and ye didna come back, Da. Ye didna come back. Dinna leave again, Da.'' A sob broke free of her will. ''Dinna leave me again.''

''Lass.'' Innes had not seen his daughter cry since the day her mother was killed. It shook him. ''Ah, lassie, I swear, I didna leave because ye healed the rabbit. Ach, but I know ye couldna help that, any more than ye could help what ye did just now yonder wi' Carson's hands. I wish ye *could* help it, for I fear it will be the ruin of ye, but it has naught to do with my leaving."

"Ye were so angry." She sniffed. "That time over the rabbit. Ye were appalled at what I'd done. The next day ye were gone."

"Aye, I left ye. I'm no proud of it, but I canna deny it, lass. But it had naught to do with the rabbit, I swear to ye. Naught at all."

Winter Fawn stared at him, stunned. If he spoke the truth . . . "Then *why,* Da? Why did ye leave us?"

"Ach, lassie, I couldna stay. Dinna ask me why. It was nothing that ye could help, but ye'll only blame yerself anyway."

"Oh." Winter Fawn felt as if the earth had just tilted beneath her feet. "Then I was right. Ye left because of me."

"Nae, not like ye mean." Innes cursed. He'd gone about this all wrong. All he could do now was bare his soul and tell the truth. "I left because I'm a weak man and a coward."

"Nae!" To Winter Fawn, her father was the strongest, bravest, smartest man alive.

Well, maybe next to Carson.

"Ye've never been weak, Da, nor a coward."

"That's a daughter's love for her da speaking, and I thank ye for it. But the simple truth is, I couldna face another day with all the reminders of yer mother. Her loss was eating me alive. I wasna strong enough, am still not, to live without her. Ach, lass, ye look so much like her it fair takes me breath away."

His words came as a shock to her. Everyone who had known her mother missed her. But they all went on, lived their lives, as was expected.

"Nae, Da, I canna help what I look like."

"I know that, lass. It's not yer fault I left. I canna get over that I shouldna hae sent her out into that storm," he said with anguish. "I should hae gone myself."

"But if anyone is to blame for her death," Winter Fawn cried, " 'tis me. I knew a storm was coming. I should have returned to the lodge sooner on my own."

"Ye were but a child, lass. Ye couldna know the consequences."

His words could not wipe out Winter Fawn's many years of self-blame, nor could she believe that her healing of the rabbit had not sent him away. He'd been so angry, so very angry with her.

He placed his hard, rough hand on her cheek. "Ah, lass."

She could not recall the last time her father had touched her face. She turned in to the touch, rubbing her cheek against his palm.

"I know ye canna help the way ye look so much like her. I do not blame ye for it. Please dinna be blaming me for hurting when I'm reminded of her. She was my life."

"Oh, Da." A tear slipped down her cheek. It was past time, years past time for him to let her mother go. But looking at the pain in his eyes, she could not bring herself to say the words. When he turned away and walked toward the river, she let him go.

The wind picked up, stinging cold against the tears on her cheeks. She walked away from the barn and stopped halfway to the house, facing the wind, letting it dry her face. Hoping it would blow the confusion from her mind as well.

Every time her father looked at her and saw her mother in her face, the pain must surely be crippling. No wonder he stayed only a few days with Our People each spring. The miracle was that he came to visit at all.

All these years, she had thought it was something she had done that had driven him away. Now she understood. It was not a deed, not the healing of the rabbit, it was her mere existence.

It was said that Hunter, too, strongly resembled their mother. Was that a double burden for her father, or did he not think on it because Hunter was male?

Man-Above, what was she to do? For so long she had dreamed of living with her father. The three of them, her, Hunter, and Innes Red Beard MacDougall. A family. Together.

Now that could not be. As she stood there in the dark and stared blindly at the light glowing through the front window of the house, she mentally let go of her dream and allowed the wind to carry it away. Then she wiped another tear from her cheek.

No more tears. She must think. She must plan. She could not remain with her father. She could not stay with Carson. The only place left for her was with Our People.

A coldness settled in the pit of her stomach at the thought that her uncle and grandfather might force her to accept Crooked Oak. She would not do it. She would run away before allowing herself to be tied to him for the rest of her life.

But to where would she run?

Was there some other man among Our People she might find acceptable? Or perhaps among the Cheyenne. Yet the thought of any man but Carson touching her brought a cry to her throat that she barely stifled.

Yet she could not stay with him now. Even if she were willing to accept him without love, her staying would only bring him the scorn of his neighbors. She could never do that to him. He would grow, in time, to hate her.

And if her own father could not tolerate her gift of healing, how would Carson ever be able to accept it when he learned of it? He would learn, eventually. She would not be able to hide it from him forever.

Why not? whispered a small voice in her head.

Indeed. She paused. No one else knew, and all these years she had been unable to keep from using the gift when confronted with someone else's physical pain. Her grandmother thought she knew, but there was no proof.

No. She could not keep such a secret from Carson.

Her only choice, it seemed, was to return to Our People. Yet she did not know where they might be. She did not fool herself into thinking she could find them on her own while they roamed the plains in search of buffalo as they did this time every year.

In the fall, then. She would stay here through the summer. In the fall she would be able to find the place where they established their village for the winter to come.

The decision settled over her shoulders like a mountain of weight, but she could think of nothing else to do.

* * *

By the time Winter Fawn returned to the house, Carson had sent everyone off to bed. Maybe without such an avid audience Winter Fawn would talk to him, tell him what the hell had just happened. One minute she'd been caring for his hands, the next, running out the door after her father.

Gussie had helped him shoo Bess and Megan upstairs, but his aunt had not wanted to go to her own room. "It seemed a private matter to me," she told him. "Between her and her father. Perhaps you shouldn't interfere, dear."

"You mean maybe it's none of my business?"

She smiled slightly. "You always did speak more bluntly than I did. Yes, maybe it is none of your business."

"If I can change her mind, Gussie, I plan to marry her. Everything about her is my business."

Gussie raised her brow. "I have no doubt you'll succeed with the former. As to the latter, Winter Fawn just might have something to say about that."

Carson considered that as just another instance of women not always making sense. He was just relieved that she had let it drop and had gone to her room.

When the front door opened and Winter Fawn stepped inside, Carson stood alone beside the table, waiting for her. He was prepared to demand an explanation, to badger, to cajole, to tease it out of her if possible. Whatever it took to find out what had sent her running a few moments ago.

She met his gaze, then looked away. "I am sorry for running out like that. I needed to speak with my father. Did someone put the iodine on your knuckles?"

"What happened?" he demanded. Her explanation of needing to talk to Innes wasn't going to wash. "What's going on?"

"Nothing you need to be concerned about."

He stepped closer and smelled the night wind in her hair. His voice softened. "I'm concerned with everything about you. Talk to me, honey. You looked so hurt. Was it something I did?"

"Of course not. You did nothing at all."

"You're not going to tell me what's going on, are you?"

She shook her head. "It is an old story, between my father and me. If you do not need the iodine, I will say good night."

At a loss, Carson stood as if rooted to the floor while she crossed the room and mounted the stairs.

Behind her closed door, Gussie eavesdropped shamelessly. She waited until she heard Carson retire to his room, then slipped silently out and toward the front door.

This was all that Scotsman's fault. He had done something to upset Winter Fawn, and when Winter Fawn was upset, it hurt everyone else in the family. Augusta Dulaney Winthrop was having none of it. She was going to find that disreputable weasel and give him a piece of her mind.

Before stepping outside she lit a lantern and carried it with her. She did hope the man was not in the bunkhouse with the other men, but if he was, so be it. She would drag him out by the ear if need be.

Something told her, however, that he would be doing his drinking alone this night, so she went to the barn before chancing waking the other men.

At the first stall, Gussie paused and raised her lantern. The milk cow blinked big, brown cow eyes at her, then lowered her head and went back to her dozing.

Satisfied that the cow was fine, Gussie went from stall to stall. Most were empty of everything but the new baby chicks, who objected with frantic *cheeps* to the light and the intrusion.

There was no sign of Innes. She was debating with herself about climbing the ladder to the loft when she heard what sounded like a man's voice from the one stall she had missed. She turned back and raised her lantern. When she leaned over the stall's half door, noxious whiskey fumes stung her eyes and offended her nostrils.

Quickly she pulled the lantern back for fear the small flame might ignite the fumes wafting from the open flask in the man's hand and blow the whole barn to kingdom come.

The man moaned and threw one arm over his eyes.

Well, didn't that just figure. Drunk as a skunk, and twice as ugly.

He mumbled again.

"Mr. MacDougall," she called.

"Nae, love, come back to me."

Gussie reared back and pressed a hand to her chest in outrage. Love? *"Mr. MacDougall!"* He must be more drunk than she'd thought!

"Smiling Woman . . ."

I declare. Wasn't Smiling Woman the name of his late wife?

"I canna go on without ye."

He was drunk as a skunk and talking to his dead wife. Why, as near as Gussie recalled, the poor woman had been dead nigh on eight years. Of all the fool things.

"Mr. MacDougall," she called sharply, "wake up. Wake up, do you hear me?"

But Innes was too far gone in drink to hear anything but his own confused mutterings.

This, Gussie decided, could not be allowed to continue. Spotting the bucket of water the men kept with which to wash, she marched over and raised her lantern to peer inside. Six inches of water remained in the bucket, with a disconcerting combination of grease, scum, horse hair, and three dead bugs floating on the surface.

"Perfect."

Careful not to touch anything but the bail, she lifted the bucket and carried it back to the stall housing that fool, drunken Scotsman. There she hung her lantern on a nail, took the bucket in both hands, and emptied the contents, with as much force as possible, directly into Innes MacDougall's face.

He surged up from the straw sputtering and coughing and swinging his arms at some imagined foe.

"What the bloody hell!"

"I'll thank you to watch your language, Mr. MacDougall.

He gaped up at her in shock. "What hae ye done, ye interfering ol'—"

Gussie clucked her tongue. "Gotten your attention is what I hope I've done."

Rising to his feet, he swayed and grabbed for the side of the stall for support. "Aye, ye've done that, right enough. What I be wantin' to know is why?"

"I am appalled, sir, I truly am."

"Aye, me, too. Be gone wi' ye, woman, and let me be."

"Let you drown in your whiskey and wallow in your self-pity, you mean. You should be ashamed of yourself, you should. How is your poor wife supposed to ever find peace in the hereafter if you keep calling to her and begging her to come back? Of all the foolish, selfish things."

In the soft glow of the lantern, Innes's neck and face flushed dark red. "Ye don't know what yer talkin' aboot."

"Oh, don't I? Do you think you're the only person who ever lost the one who meant the world to you? Well, you're not, Innes MacDougall."

"You know all about it, do ye?" he snarled.

"I lost my own Oliver nigh on four years ago. Oh, I know," she said fervently, "I know what it's like, I do. But you have to learn to let go," she said earnestly, "for her sake as well as yours. Not to mention those two fine children of yours. Your drinking and misery is making them miserable."

When he merely stood there and blinked at her, she got mad again. "If life's not worth living, shooting yourself would be better than all this whining and self-pity."

"Fine. Where's my gun?"

Aghast, Gussie clapped her hand over her mouth. "Oh, no! I didn't mean it, I swear. You wouldn't—" She narrowed her eyes and glared at him. "No, you wouldn't. You're too blamed stubborn, aren't you?"

"Aye, I've been called stubborn a time or two. You, on the other hand, are just plain mean."

"Well!"

Innes threw his head back and laughed. Laughed! She couldn't believe it!

"I never," she cried.

"I'll bet you have, Gussie Girl." He winked at her.

Gussie closed her eyes and prayed for patience. "Mr. MacDougall, I simply do not know what to do with you. You defy all logic."

"Then why don't you just go on back to the house and leave me be."

"Yes." She gripped her skirt in her free hand and raised the lantern in the other. "I believe I'll do just that. You know, Mr. MacDougall, you may never find another woman to love the way you loved your wife, but you've got two children who've been thrust into a world they don't understand. They need you. But they need you whole and sober. Think about that, why don't you?"

Innes watched her flounce out of the barn, the light from the lantern bouncing all around her.

Damn woman. Who did she think she was, throwing water in his face, telling him how to live his life? He hadn't been doing so bad on his own, had he?

Says who, laddie?

He winced at the sound of his own voice in his head. All right, so maybe he spent more time drunk than sober. He wasn't hurting anybody, was he?

Only yerself, laddie, and the bairns.

He hated it, that voice in his head. Almost as much as he hated that bloody woman, come traipsing in here with that ripe, soft body, reminding him how long he'd been alone, how long she'd been alone. Smelling of sweet flowers and looking at him with those damn blue eyes that saw straight through him.

Damn her.

"And damn me." She made sense. There was the rub.

CHAPTER 15

Breakfast the next morning was a grim affair. Even Megan was subdued, picking at her food more than eating it.

Carson didn't trust himself to say two words in a civil tone. Everything was going wrong.

He had come west seeking peace, looking for a spot of earth that wasn't scorched by war. Yet he'd been attacked before reaching the ranch, exposing Bess and Megan to more danger than they should ever have to know about, let alone experience. The only peace he had found since returning to Colorado had been in the arms of a woman who now wanted nothing to do with him.

He hadn't planned to marry again. Now that Gussie was here, he didn't feel pressured to find a new mother for Megan. But now that he'd changed his mind and decided to marry, Winter Fawn wouldn't have him.

He'd met the man his father had spoken so highly of, and liked him. But now, because of some secret no one would reveal, Innes was hiding out instead of joining the rest of them for breakfast.

And what the hell were Gussie and Winter Fawn looking so guilty about?

Then there was Bess, who was drawing close enough to Hunter these days to have Carson worrying. She was too damn young, and so was Hunter.

How had he ended up in charge? How had he ended up responsible for all these people, all these problems, a ranch to run? Near as he could recall, he'd been climbing trees with his best friend, Charles Binkley, from River House, and turning his fingers purple throwing ripe mulberries into Mary Lou Throckmorton's pretty blond hair. He wondered now why he'd done such a stupid thing.

Then, before he knew it, someone was putting a gun in his hand telling him to shoot anything in blue, and now, here he was.

He had blinked, that's what he'd done. He'd blinked and the world had changed on him.

But looking at the people around the table—his beautiful daughter, his sister, his aunt, Beau and Frank, Hunter, Innes wherever he was, and Winter Fawn, who had such a hold on him it was frightening—they needed him, and he needed them. For the life of him, he couldn't think of a single thing he would change.

Except Winter Fawn's heart. If he could change that, if he could make her love him—

Good God. Did he want her to love him? He wanted her to marry him, but love?

It's what she asked of you.

It was true. The night he'd asked her to marry him, she had asked if he loved her. Was that why she'd turned him down? Because he hadn't answered? Because he hadn't said yes?

"Where's Da?" she now asked her brother.

Hunter shrugged and grabbed another biscuit from the plate being passed around. "Busy."

"Doing what?" Carson asked. Conversation seemed a better idea than wallowing in his own morose thoughts.

"In the barn," Hunter said with another shrug.

So much for conversation, Carson thought.

They were sipping the last of the coffee when he heard the plop of hooves and the rattling of chains approach the front of the house. Curious, he rose and went to the door.

Innes opened it from the outside before Carson reached it.
Carson stared. "Do I know you?"
"Real funny, ye are, lad."
Innes MacDougall had cleaned up, to the point that he was nearly unrecognizable. His hair was still wet from washing, as was his beard, which was now trimmed close to his jaw instead of hanging four or more inches long. He had on a new yellow shirt and new denim pants, and boots instead of his usual moccasins.
"Da?" Winter Fawn's eyes nearly swallowed her face.
Carson happened to glance at Gussie. She rose slowly from her chair with a smile so big he was afraid her face would split.
"Mr. MacDougall, good morning," she said with a peculiar note in her voice. "We missed you at breakfast."
Innes was probably unaware that he was mangling the hat he held. "Mrs. Winthrop. If ye'd show me where ye want the garden, I'll get started on the plowing."

By noon the garden was plowed, and an irrigation ditch ran from the river to the newly turned soil, a dam of board and mud holding back the water until it was needed.
Innes inspected his work with a satisfied smile. He hadn't plowed a field since his youth. He'd hated it back then, but this time he got a kick out of it. It was the first productive thing he'd done in years and it felt damn good.
He reached up to tug on his beard, only to find there wasn't much left to tug on since he'd trimmed it that morning. Scratching his jaw through what was left, he wondered if he oughtn't to just go ahead and shave the thing off.
And he found himself wondering what Mrs. Winthrop would think of that.
Ach, pure foolishness to wonder what a woman would think. Grumbling to himself, he took the horse back to the barn and unhitched the plow.
The planting began that afternoon. Gussie showed Winter Fawn and Bess where to plant which seeds, and how to do it. Megan "helped," too. Winter Fawn realized immediately that

this planting was hot, dirty work, but she did not mind. It felt good to sink her hands in the soil and think that something might grow from her labors.

"We're a little late, I think," Gussie said, "with the chives and garlic and onions, not to mention the peas, spinach, and turnips. They might not do well. The green beans and potatoes might take, and the radishes. They sprout and grow so fast, maybe they'll be ready to harvest before hot weather sets in. If not, I suppose the chickens will . . . oh, dear."

"What is it?" Winter Fawn asked. "Am I doing it wrong?"

"No, dear. I was just wondering how we're going to keep the chickens from scratching the seeds up and eating them."

Winter Fawn pictured the fuzzy little creatures that had ridden home from town in a crate in the back of the wagon. "Can they do that when they're so tiny?"

Gussie smiled. "I don't suppose they'll be a problem just yet. But we'll have to rig some type of fencing before they're too much older. If that squash takes, why, I've seen one hen ruin a dozen hills of squash in under an hour." She tapped her finger against her cheek in thought. "Yes, we'll need fencing."

Late that afternoon Carson paid a visit to the new garden and found Gussie alone there. "Where are the girls?"

Gussie smiled. "Can't you hear them?"

He turned his head away from the wind and heard shrieks of laughter from the direction of the river. "They're swimming?" He tugged on the brim of his hat. "Can they swim? That river's pretty swift, and it's ice cold. I'd better—"

"You'd better stay away from there, that's what you'd better do." She laughed at the way his brows climbed up. "Planting is dirty work. They're bathing, and they don't need an audience. Winter Fawn assures me she is a strong swimmer. She won't let anything happen to Bess or Megan."

He wished she hadn't told him. He knew Winter Fawn would take care of the girls, but the thought of her doing so while wet and naked was enough to have sweat popping out across his face. "Oh. Uh, okay. Sure." The sound of Winter Fawn's laughter was something he had not heard in a long time. It started an ache deep in his chest.

"Well?" Gussie waved a hand out toward the new garden. "What do you think?"

Carson chuckled. "It looks like long rows of wet soil to me. Are you sure there are seeds in there?"

"Oh, go on with you." She playfully swatted his arm. Then she smiled and looked back over the garden again. "Mr. MacDougall did a fine job with the plowing and the irrigation ditch and the dam."

"Innes is just full of surprises these days. I'll just . . . uh, go tell the men to stay away from the river."

Winter Fawn enjoyed herself at the river so much that she hated to go back to the house. But they were all hungry, and the sun was sinking, and Megan was so tired, the poor little thing, even though she would not admit it. She had worked and played as hard as Winter Fawn and Bess. Winter Fawn suspected that the color in the child's cheeks was as much from feverish exhaustion as from the sun.

"Come," Winter Fawn said. " 'Tis time to return."

They traipsed back to the house through the tall lush grass. At the edge of the garden, they stopped to look. Winter Fawn slipped an arm around each girl. "We did something here today."

Bess chuckled and braced a hand against her lower back. "Yes, we nearly killed ourselves."

Winter Fawn shared in the laughter. "Aye, we'll all be stiff and sore for the next few days. But just think. If something grows there—"

"If?" Bess protested. "Of course something will grow there. Everything will grow. You'll see."

I hope so. Winter Fawn thought she would like to see something grow in the ground from a seed she planted.

With her arms still around the other two, they turned toward the house. Carson stepped away from the back wall.

Winter Fawn nearly stumbled at the sight of him. Her first

instinct was to run to him and share the joy of this day, the thrill of working with the soil, the fun of playing in the river.

He wanted to marry her. The hot look in his eyes made her knees weak. He wanted her, and she yearned for his kisses, the feel of his hands on her body once more. But she wanted his heart, too, and he did not love her.

It was wiser, she knew, to keep him at a distance. If she gave in to him, he would grow to hate her. He would not long tolerate the prejudices of his neighbors.

But it hurt, turning away from him. Deep inside it hurt.

Carson watched the delight on her face fade away when she spotted him. Dammit, she wouldn't even look him in the eye.

"Bess, Megan, why don't you two run on into the house and help Aunt Gussie. I need to talk to Winter Fawn."

He saw the refusal building in Winter Fawn's face.

"Please," he added.

When the girls were gone, Winter Fawn folded her arms across her chest and looked away toward the mountains in the west.

"You worked hard today," he offered.

"We all did."

"And you enjoyed it."

"Perhaps."

"I heard you laughing. I haven't heard you laugh in a long time. It sounded good."

When she said nothing, Carson was tempted to grab her and shake her. *Talk to me dammit.* But he didn't.

"Your father says you agreed to think about marrying me."

"My father says too much."

"Are you thinking about it?"

The quick flash of pain across her face hurt him, but it told him she cared. If she didn't care, none of this would hurt her. Relieved that he hadn't completely lost her yet, he scrambled for something to say.

Finally, slowly, he spoke. "You asked me the other night if I loved you."

Her sharp intake of breath assured him that he had her attention. "It is not important."

"I don't believe you. If it wasn't important to you, you

wouldn't have asked. You wouldn't have said you couldn't marry a man who didn't love you. I didn't answer you that night because I didn't know what to say."

"It was a simple question. Yes or no would have served."

"But for me it's not a simple question," he said. "I don't trust love, Winter Fawn. Not the kind of love you meant. I mean, love for a child, a parent, that kind of love I understand. I accept that. But what passes for love between a man and a woman . . . I've just never seen it work right. Mainly I just trust what I can see and touch."

"What about Megan's mother?" Winter Fawn asked quietly. "Did you not love her?"

"Yes. I thought so. But it didn't make either of us happy. It just got in the way."

"It got you a beautiful daughter."

"No. Love didn't get us Megan. That was sex. Sex, I trust. I understand it. We could have that, you and I. It would be good between us, Winter Fawn. Better than good. I can make you happy if you'll give me the chance."

Finally, finally she met his gaze. "You ask me to give you, and sex, a chance. Yet you give love no chance at all. What happened with your wife that makes you so distrustful of love?"

It was human nature to protect oneself against pain, and Carson was not immune to such instinct. He had humbled himself before her more than with any other person. Yet still she pushed for more. He could not give her what she wanted.

With a shake of his head, he said, "That was a long time ago, and it's not something I care to talk about."

Winter Fawn had not thought her heart could ache worse, but she'd been wrong.

"This isn't about Julia and me," he said. "It's about me and you, the two of us. It's about the future, not the past. I'm asking you to give us a chance, Winter Fawn."

"A chance for what?" she cried softly. "Do you not see the future you speak of, Carson? Have you already forgotten how you scraped your knuckles in town? How long will you want a wife who is scorned by all your neighbors? How long before you come to hate me for it?"

"I don't believe you said that. Do you think I give a damn what those small-minded people think?" he demanded.

"Do you want their hate for me to fall on Megan? On Bess?"

"It won't happen," he protested. "Not if you give us a chance. Give those people in town a chance to know you."

"Me?" she cried. "Why do they not give *me* a chance? They have judged me and condemned me because of the color of my skin. Now I know you cannot love me if you can suggest that the burden be mine. And you are not thinking of your family, of the hurt that could be done to them. And what if we had children? Do you want children with Arapaho blood? You ask if I have thought of marrying you. I have thought of little else for days, and I see no way for either of us to be happy. If you search your heart, you will know I speak the truth. You canna deny it."

"Deny it?" Lord, had a woman ever made him so furious? "Why should I bother denying it, when you've got everything all figured out? You have all the answers, and they're all bad ones. But you forgot one thing, and it's something *you* can't deny."

She stood before him, half-defiant, half-wary. "What?"

"This." Before she could protest, before she could slip away, he pulled her to his chest and took her mouth with his. No soft, exploring kiss this time, no gentle giving. He took. Hard and fast and deep, he ravaged her mouth with his, claiming her. She was his, by damn, *his.*

And he was bruising her. Appalled at his own harshness, he gentled the kiss and slid his arms around her, feeling her heart pound in rhythm with his. When her hands moved to his shoulders, he nearly sagged in relief. She still wanted him. This magic that happened between them was still there, still real. She felt it, too.

Slowly he eased his lips from hers and looked down at her face. Her eyes were closed, her lips parted.

When her eyes fluttered open he saw the hunger in them.

"Deny that," he whispered. "If you can."

Trembling, she stepped back and pressed a hand to her lips. "I must go in now. I must . . . help set the table."

Carson fought the urge to grab her again and never let her go. In his arms was the one place where she did not argue.

Instead, he let her walk away and tried to calm the fury, the pain rising inside him like a sickness. If she could walk away from him this way, he could not hide from the truth.

He was losing her.

During the next few days Winter Fawn tried to act as if nothing was wrong.

Gussie insisted on making a dress for her from some of the fabric she'd bought in town. At first Winter Fawn had been wary, until Gussie assured her that she would not strap her up in one of those awful things Gussie wore beneath her dresses. A corset, she called it.

Once that fear was dispensed with, Winter Fawn eagerly agreed to the new dress, but insisted on helping. She was good with a needle and thread. Her own steel needles had been given to her by her father many years ago. But along with everything but the clothes she had been wearing for so long now, the needles had been left behind. She hoped her grandmother, who had her own needles, would find someone to put them to good use.

Gussie and Bess had both brought needles with them, and they were smoother and finer than hers.

The blue gingham dress she and Gussie designed was made in a simple, wraparound fashion with long sleeves and a decorative collar.

"Oh, it's lovely," Bess claimed. "And the color is perfect on you."

Winter Fawn ran her hands down the skirt, loving the crisp feel of the new fabric. "I'll be afraid to wear it," she said with a smile. "I'll get it soiled." She was also afraid the new dress would draw Carson's attention.

"That," Gussie proclaimed, "is why you need another dress, of the dark green this time, I think. And an apron. That will help protect them."

So, even as Winter Fawn strengthened her resolve to return to Our People in the fall, she took another step into the white world. She lived in a log house on a ranch, took heated baths in a tin tub, cooked on an iron stove. She sewed by the light of a glass-globed lantern. She wore a white woman's dress. And like any white farmer, she studied the furrows in the turned earth every day for a sign of something green.

"Something other than grass," she muttered, yanking out yet another interloper in the garden. The grass, it seemed, did not wish to remain plowed under. It knew where it wanted to grow and did not care that Winter Fawn had other plans for that particular patch of soil.

Every morning as soon as it was light Winter Fawn walked the garden, careful to step only between the rows where the precious seeds were planted. She pulled grass, checked the moisture level, carried water in a bucket if one area seemed too dry while the rest of the garden was still damp from the last irrigation.

Hunter stood by one afternoon watching her bend and stoop and inspect. "Da says you must have patience."

She laughed. "Does he say where this patience is supposed to come from?"

Her brother smiled. "Nae."

Winter Fawn strolled to the end of the row and stood beside him. "You are content here." She made it a statement rather than a question, because she could see the truth of it in his face each day. He and their father were nearly inseparable, and Winter Fawn was glad for them.

"Aye," he said. "That surprises you?"

"Nae." She shrugged and watched a hawk glide high above the river.

"You would be content, too, if you could settle your differences with Carson."

Winter Fawn shook her head. "It's not that simple. Doesn't it bother you the way they treated us in town?"

"Nae, why should it? Do you remember when we were children we talked about how we wanted one day to see the world our father described to us, the world beyond the one we knew?"

"Aye." Across the river now, the hawk dove for its prey. "I remember."

"Then after he left, we dreamed of going with him, of him coming for us one day to take us with him."

"Aye, but we never thought about how the whites would treat us."

"I don't understand why you care about that."

She shrugged again. "Maybe for myself I don't, although I find it hurtful to be despised for nothing more than the color of my skin."

"Do not Our People think of whites in the same way? Have we not raided the white man's settlements and ranches and farms, stolen his cattle, sometimes even his children? Killed him and carried his scalp on our lances with pride? Simply because he is white?"

"No," she told him. "Not simply because he is white. At least not at first. It was because the whites keep pushing us away from our hunting grounds, telling us we have no right to go where we will. Killing off all the game so we go hungry."

Hunter nodded as though giving her the point. "Still, can you not see beyond your hurt and ignore those people in town?"

"Perhaps," she admitted. "But how long can I ignore the fights Carson will get into because of me? How long before those people turn on Megan and Bess and Gussie for befriending us? Nae, I canna accept that. I canna be responsible for that."

Hunter frowned at her. "You are not responsible. They are," he said with a wave in the general direction of town. "And I will tell you this, sister, it is not your place to make decisions for Bess and the others, including Carson. They can make up their own minds if they want to deal with those people or not."

Deep into the night Winter Fawn thought about Hunter's words. In the end they only served to confuse her more.

More than a week had passed since the seeds were buried in the soil behind the house. Winter Fawn was about to decide that the entire effort was a miserable failure, yet she could not stop herself from making her daily trek outdoors as soon as they had cleaned up after breakfast. The sun was usually just breaking the horizon by that time. It was not, perhaps, the best light by which to discover tiny green sprouts, but she would stand and wait for the sun to rise, for the light to come.

Today, as the light grew stronger, she stood with her arms around herself to ward off the morning chill and stared out over the rows. *There!* What was that? It looked like . . . like moss. They had not planted moss, she was sure of that.

Stooping for a closer look, Winter Fawn's eyes widened. Slowly, tentatively, she ran one finger over the tiny green growth.

Radishes.

Oh! Oh! "They sprouted. Oh, my. They sprouted." They didn't look like radishes, but they would. Oh, they would! She knew what they were because she had made herself memorize the location of every type of seed they had planted, and Gussie had said the radishes should be the first to sprout. There were dozens and dozens, so tiny and tender, like a small green blanket over the soil.

"Look at them," she breathed.

Behind her came a low chuckle. "We'll make a farmer out of you yet."

On her knees and totally oblivious to the dirt she was grinding into her new dress and apron, Winter Fawn turned to smile up at Carson in wonder. "Aren't they beautiful? There are so many!"

Carson laughed. "You'll thin them down to give them room to grow."

Her eyes widened in horror. "Thin them down?" She didna like the sound of that, no, not at all. "You mean . . . *kill* them?"

This time Carson's laughter boomed and echoed through the trees along the river beyond the garden.

Gussie, Bess, and Megan rounded the house just then, on their way to have their own daily look.

"Gussie," Winter Fawn cried. "Gussie, come look! We have radishes! Carson says we must kill some of them to give them room to grow. He canna mean it! After all our work?"

As gently and matter-of-factly as she could, Gussie explained the concept of thinning to Winter Fawn.

Winter Fawn did not like it, but she saw the sense in it and resigned herself. But pulling up so many of those tiny, beautiful seedlings was one of the hardest things she had ever done in her life. It *hurt.*

But soon she was too busy in the garden to worry about those small plants she was forced to pluck from the ground. The emergence of the radishes, it seemed, was a signal to the rest of the seeds that it was time to send down roots and sprout leaves. Winter Fawn spent hours thinning, pulling grass and weeds, irrigating. She spent even more hours simply standing beside the garden and staring at it in growing wonder. It was a miracle, this business of gardening.

Sadly, she acknowledged that when she returned to Our People in the fall, she would never be able to plant another garden.

Maybe she wouldn't return to the tribe. Or perhaps when they moved out onto the plains again next spring she would simply stay in their winter valley and plant a garden there.

Alone?

The mere thought of living her life alone, even for only the spring and summer seasons, brought an unbearable ache to her heart. She could not live alone, with no one to talk to, no one to love. It was not the way of Our People to live alone. It was not her way.

Shaking off the depressing thought, she vowed that if this were to be her only garden, she would work to make it the best it could be.

Standing at the corner of the house, Carson thought he could almost read her thoughts as her expression changed from delight to pride to sadness. Damn her stubbornness.

Hell, if she wouldn't marry him, maybe he could hire her to be his gardener.

He tugged on the brim of his hat and strolled toward her. "It looks good," he told her.

She took a deep breath. "Aye, it does, doesn't it? Of course I've never seen a garden before so I have naught to compare it to, but to me it is a beautiful, miraculous thing."

"If the corn does well," he said casually while tension tightened his shoulders, "we should plant a couple of acres of it next year."

"Perhaps you should."

"Don't," he said sharply. "Don't exclude yourself that way, as if you won't be here next year. I won't let you go, Winter Fawn."

She turned on him with anger in her eyes. "Am I as a horse to you, that you think you can control me? Own me?"

"That's not what I meant and you know it."

"I will chose my own staying and leaving, and you will have naught to say about it, Carson Dulaney."

Dammit, he thought as she stomped away from him. He always managed to say the wrong thing to her. He either made her mad or sad, no matter what he said.

They should stop talking. They did much better together when they didn't talk.

He didn't think of her as his property, like a horse. But she was still *his,* by damn. All he had to do was figure out a way to make her realize it.

CHAPTER 16

Two nights later, a sharp crack of thunder woke Carson sometime after midnight. For one unguarded moment, before he was fully awake, he thought it was cannon fire. He bolted upright and, for three beats of his heart, he didn't know where he was.

Then he heard the loud roar of rain pounding on the roof.

Home. He was home on the ranch in Colorado. No cannons. No war. No piles of dead bodies. It was only thunder, only a storm.

As his pulse slowed and his mind cleared, his first thought was to worry about Winter Fawn's garden. His second was to worry about Winter Fawn herself. She was frightened by storms. Had the thunder and lightning awakened her?

The thought of her huddled in the corner of the sofa with her hands ice cold and shaking with terror drove him from his bed. He would check on her, he thought as he stepped into his pants and fastened them. It wouldn't hurt to check on her.

As he stepped out of his room, a shaft of lightning revealed her right where he feared she would be, huddled in a tight little ball in the corner of the sofa.

"Ah, honey." Sitting next to her, he slid his arms around

her. "You're freezing." It was like putting his arms around a block of ice. A shivering block of ice.

"I'm all r-right." Her teeth were chattering. "I d-didna mean to w-wake ye."

"You didn't wake me, the storm did. Come here." He scooped her into his arms and stood. "Let's get you warm."

His only thought in taking her to his room and climbing beneath the covers with her was to warm her. She was too shaken for anything else, and her terror certainly did not arouse his passion. But it was sweet, so damn sweet, to feel her curl into his arms and snuggle her cold nose into the crook of his neck.

"That's it," he whispered against her ear. "Get warm, honey. I've got you now. The storm won't hurt you." He kept talking—speaking low but not whispering, knowing Gussie wouldn't hear his voice over the noise of the wind and rain. He talked about anything and nothing, hoping the sound of his voice would ease her.

"You should see your brother work those mustangs. Have you seen him work with horses? I guess you probably have. I've never seen anything like it, myself."

While he spoke, he absently threaded his fingers into her braids, undoing them.

"That boy can take an ornery, green-broke mustang that would just as soon kick and buck as eat, and he can have him trotting around the corral with a saddle, bridle, and rider like it was some old gray mare taking the family to church for the hundredth year in a row. It's sheer magic what Hunter can do with a horse."

With her hair freed from its braids, it spread across his hands like heavy silk. He brought a handful up to his face and inhaled the smell of flowers. "Are you getting warm yet?"

"Aye. Thank you."

"Feel like talking?" he asked quietly.

"Are you running out of things to say?" There was a smile in her voice.

He chuckled. "Just about." He sobered and brushed his nose across her cheek. "You're not scared anymore, are you? I promise you're safe."

She rolled onto her back and let out a long breath. " 'Tis not for myself that I fear storms."

"Then what? Talk to me, Winter Fawn. Tell me."

She was silent a long moment before speaking. "My mother was killed by lightning. I saw it happen."

Carson tightened his hold on her. "How old were you?"

"Twelve. I was playing at the creek, but I should have been helping her pack. She came after me. If she hadn't come after me . . ."

"It wasn't your fault. You have to know that."

"A week later Da got on his horse and rode out. There was a storm then, too. He just rode away and didna come back for two years, and then only for a few days. I hate storms," she said with feeling. "Storms take people away."

"Ah, honey, I'm sorry." He kissed the delicate skin beside her eye. "Come to think of it, it was storming the night my mother died, too."

"How old were you?"

"I was fifteen. It was the night Bess was born."

"Oh, no. Bess never knew her mother at all?"

"No. Nor our father, either, really. He just couldn't find it in himself to go on after Mother died. He lasted until Bess was about four, then he heard about the gold rush out here, and that was the last we saw of him until he came home to fight in the war."

"Our fathers, it seems, have a lot in common."

"That's what Dad told me. He said that was what drew him and your father into friendship. They had lost their wives and run out on their children, and they both felt guilty as hell about it."

If he hadn't had his face so close to hers he might not have heard her small *sniff.*

"Winter Fawn?" He brushed a finger across her cheek and felt wetness. "Now I've made you sad. I'm sorry." He pulled her close and stroked her back. It was then that he realized she wore a thin nightgown, and nothing else. And she was in his arms. In his bed.

His body's response to the realization was swift and unmistakable. He shifted away to keep her from feeling his arousal.

"No," she whispered, pushing her thigh firmly against him. "Don't go."

Carson barely stifled a moan when she pressed against him. "You don't mean that."

"I do." She kissed his chin, his jaw, his cheek. "Give me something else to think about the next time it storms. Something other than my fears."

Her light, feathery kisses, her knee against his groin, and her hand splayed across his bare chest. Simple things, yet they had his heart pounding and his lungs wondering what happened to the air in the room.

A clap of thunder directly overhead shook the house.

Winter Fawn flinched and latched on to Carson.

"I won't have it said that I took advantage of your fear."

She pressed herself flush against his chest. "Then show me how to take advantage of yours."

God, the feel of her breasts against him was heaven. "You're doing just fine without my help."

"I canna do it alone," she protested breathlessly. "Show me, Carson. Show me how to make you feel the things I felt that morning in the mountains."

He knew he shouldn't. She was afraid, vulnerable. But when the next flash of lightning lit the room and he saw her face, he saw no fear there. He saw a hunger to match his own. With a low groan, he gave in and kissed her.

She responded instantly, honestly. The taste of her, the feel of her tongue sliding against his, played havoc with his mind, not to mention his body.

Easy, easy, he warned himself. He had to think. There was something . . . did this mean . . . ?

No, he couldn't fool himself into thinking her eagerness for him meant that she had changed her mind and decided to marry him. This might be his one chance to make love with her. Fear of losing her drove him on, when reason should have stopped him.

But there was no room for reason, no time for thought. There was only Winter Fawn and the storm, both driving him on, pounding in his blood. He kissed his way down her neck and lower until, through the thin fabric of her gown, he found one tight, beaded nipple.

When his mouth closed over the tip of her breast, Winter Fawn nearly screamed, the pleasure was so startling, so intense. She had wanted to feel what she had felt before, but this was more, so much more. And she wanted it, wanted it all, for she feared this might be the only time he would give in to her need and his.

When he pulled his mouth away, she moaned in protest. "Don't stop."

Instead of answering, he kissed his way down the slope of her breast and up the other until he reached that peak. This time when he latched onto her and suckled, she arched clear off the bed. It was magic. He suckled at her breast, and she felt it in her womb, a hot tingling, a yawning emptiness that demanded filling.

She whispered his name and ran her hands frantically over the hot, smooth skin on his back.

His name on her lips touched something deep inside Carson. God, how he wanted her. And she was his. For this night, this moment, she was his.

With hands that weren't quite steady, he pulled her gown up and off over her head. Now he could feel all of her, and he did, tracing his hands greedily across her flesh. "God, you're so soft. So perfect."

He didn't give her the time or opportunity to speak. He had to taste her mouth again, wanted it, needed it. Was starved for it.

He felt her hands at the waist of his pants. She fumbled at the fastenings. He tore his mouth from hers and tried to see her face in the darkness.

"Are you sure?" he asked. "Be sure, Winter Fawn."

Her hands cupped his cheeks. "I have never been more sure of anything in my life. This is right, what we do here. I feel the rightness of it."

God, so did he, and he hoped he wasn't just fooling himself. He hoped she thought it was so right, so good between them, that she never wanted to leave him. But he couldn't bring himself to say the words for fear of her answer.

He reached for the fastenings on his pants, undid them. He pushed the pants down and kicked them off onto the floor.

Now there was only flesh against flesh, and it was exquisite. His blood pumped hotter, his heart beat faster. He ran a hand over the curve of her hip, down the outside of one thigh, up the inside. He tortured them both by stopping short and moving to the other thigh. Down the inside, up the outside. Then he took her mouth with his and made the trip in reverse.

Again and again he stroked his hand between her thighs, each time going higher, closer to the core of her. She began to move, to shift against his hand, to whimper against his lips.

"Is this what you want?" he whispered, trailing one finger up to touch the heat of her.

Winter Fawn gasped and arched into his touch. "You know it is. More. Please." She flexed her hips again. "More."

It was a plea Carson could not resist. He cupped her between her legs and felt her scalding heat. He tested her with one finger and found her ready.

Shifting and settling his hips between her thighs, he tensed at the thought of hurting her.

She flexed her hips and made him forget.

He eased into her, grinding his teeth to keep from taking her in one violent thrust of need. He couldn't . . . couldn't.

Winter Fawn felt him there at her entrance. There was fear of the unknown. There was a slight discomfort that took away some of the pleasure. But there was something else, something stronger than either of those. A primitive need inside her, a hollow emptiness that throbbed and begged to be filled by him, with him.

And then he thrust more fully into her, and the pain surprised her. She tensed against it, even as she tightened her arms around him.

"Easy, honey," he murmured, his breath coming hard against her ear. "If you can relax, it'll feel good again."

Carson said the words to reassure himself as much as her. She was so tight. He'd never been a woman's first before. The thought aroused a mixture of feelings in him. Pride, humility. Honor that she would trust him with this most precious gift.

Fear that he might wake up any minute and find that she was only a dream.

He felt her muscles gradually relax and pushed himself farther inside her. This time she took him more easily. But she still wasn't there, wasn't mindless with wanting him, and that's where he wanted her. It was where he wanted himself. Mindless. So he wouldn't have to think about what might happen tomorrow.

Very deliberately, he drove them both wild with a fierce, hungry kiss. Soon he didn't have to try for mindlessness. It was upon him before he realized it. She was kissing him back and moving beneath him. She was taking all of him, and giving him back more than he'd ever dreamed possible.

He had come to this ranch looking for peace. He'd searched for it in the ruins of their plantation, across the plains, and into the mountains. And it was here all along, inside the woman who gave herself to him. Winter Fawn was his peace. And she was burning him alive, heating his blood, stealing his breath, and teasing him with the release to come.

He pulled away, then thrust again. In and out, faster, harder. She met him thrust for thrust. Even over his own excitement he could feel the climax build inside her. Higher, higher they climbed together toward the peak.

And then they were there, flying off the edge of the earth into blackness that was somehow filled with brilliant colors. Flying higher, holding tighter, until there was nothing to cling to but each other.

Much later, when Carson's mind cleared, he realized he must be crushing her. Holding her close, he rolled to his side and took her with him. She was as limp as a wet dishrag.

Alarmed, he stroked her face. "Winter Fawn?"

Her chest heaved on a long, quiet sigh. "Hmm?"

He chuckled and relaxed. "Just checking to see if you were still alive."

She answered his laugh with one of her own. "I'm not sure. Am I supposed to be?"

* * *

Twice more they made love to the sound of rain drumming hard on the roof. Each time, he surrounded her, filled her, and took her to the stars and back in his arms. Each time, he filled her with glory. Each time, she fell more deeply in love with him. And each time, her heart broke a little bit more.

Was there no hope for them? No way for her to set it in her mind that her giving in to him would not hurt him or his family? Would not, in the end, end up ripping her own heart out?

Joining their bodies together seemed to be the only way to still the fearsome questions inside her, so each time he came to her, she welcomed him.

It was nearly dawn when Winter Fawn finally admitted to herself that she must return to her bed or risk offending Gussie and shocking the girls.

Carson climbed from the bed with her and pulled her close. It felt glorious to be held against him this way. The hair on his chest teased her cheek; the hair on his thighs, her legs. The kiss he placed on the top of her head was so sweet and tender it brought tears to her eyes.

''I must go,'' she whispered.

''Winter Fawn, if we were mar—''

''Shh.'' She placed her fingers over his mouth. ''Do not say it, please.''

He twisted his head away from her hand. ''You told your father you'd think about it.''

''Aye. And I am. I will.''

''We could have this every night, if you'd let us.''

Winter Fawn closed her eyes and lay her head against his chest again. Nothing would please her more than to lie in his arms all night, every night for the rest of her life. She wanted it so badly.

Was he right? Could it work between them, even if he didn't love her?

Was Hunter right that she should let the others make their own decisions? That she should not worry about the consequences?

It was all so painfully confusing. ''I must go.''

She meant to plant a brief kiss on his cheek, but he turned his head and captured her mouth with his.

That fast, and her knees were weak with wanting him again. Before she could give in, she broke free and pulled open the door. She was halfway to the stairs when she heard him.

There was laughter in his voice. "You might want this."

With a gasp, Winter Fawn raced back and grabbed her nightgown from his fingers.

Winter Fawn had never felt more awkward or shy in her life as she did later that morning when the men—Carson—came in for breakfast. One look at him, at the knowing, intimate look in his eyes, and she felt the blood rush to her face. She did not dare look at him again. Nor did she dare look at anyone else, for fear they would read in her eyes all that she and Carson had shared during the night.

She was not ashamed of her night with him. But it was too private a thing to share with anyone. She wanted to hold it to herself and keep the memories safe. For those memories might be all she had one day soon.

"Lass?"

She looked up at her father. "Aye?"

He stared hard at her for a moment, and she felt her face heat. He looked at Carson, who met his gaze squarely.

"By damn," Innes muttered. He looked back at Winter Fawn. "By bloody damn."

He knew! One look at her face and her father knew.

"You!" He jabbed a finger at Carson's chest. "Ootside, mon." He stood so fast his chair toppled over. He paid it no mind as he stomped out the door with a final, "Now!"

Carson gave Winter Fawn a slight smile and a shrug. "Excuse me, ladies." He carefully placed his fork beside his plate, and then laid down the red-checkered napkin that had been on his lap.

"Carson," Winter Fawn said, "no."

He reached over and patted her hand. "It'll be all right. Don't worry."

"What on earth?" Gussie looked from Winter Fawn to Carson. As Carson rose and followed Innes outside, her mouth opened, then closed. Her face went carefully blank.

"What's going on?" Bess asked.

Megan frowned. "Is Mr. Mac mad at Daddy?"

"Just never you mind," Gussie said. "Eat your breakfast."

Winter Fawn could not sit still while her father berated Carson for something she had urged. She tossed down her napkin and raced after them. They were several yards from the house, squared off at each other like two rams about to butt heads.

"Ye bloody bastard," Innes bellowed, right before he punched Carson in the jaw.

"Da! No!" she cried.

Carson stumbled back beneath the force of the blow. He put a hand to his jaw, then wiggled his jaw back and forth to see if it still worked. "Feel better?"

"No, by God, I don't. Did she change her mind? Are ye getting married?"

"Da! Stop it. You've no call to talk to him like that."

"No call? The bloody bastard takes advantage of ma own wee lassie, and I've no call?"

She advanced on her father. "I'm no a wee lassie, and haven't been for years. You lost the right to your outrage long ago when you rode away and left us to be raised by Grandmother. And if there was any advantage taken last night, it was me doin' the takin', not that it's any of your concern."

He looked Carson up and down.

Carson was hard-pressed not to whoop with laughter. It really wasn't funny. Really it wasn't. He'd just been caught, albeit not directly in the act, of doing unspeakable things with the man's daughter. But Winter Fawn's claim of having taken advantage of him, and the shocked look of disbelief on her father's face, nearly did him in. Giving Winter Fawn a quick wink, he held his hands out to his sides and told her father, "I would never contradict a lady. What can I say? She overpowered me."

Winter Fawn clapped a hand over her mouth to keep from laughing. It wasn't funny, she told herself. It was horrible! It was the most embarrassing thing that had ever happened to her.

"I somehow doot that," her father snarled at Carson.

Funny, horrible, and embarrassing the situation might be, but her father had not been there for her since the spring of her twelfth year. She would not tolerate his condemnation of Carson, or of herself. "*Doot* it all you want," she said heatedly. "But 'tis the truth."

"Ye'll be marryin' him now, and that's a fact. If he'll still have ye."

"I'll have her," Carson stated firmly.

Winter Fawn ignored him and gaped at her father. "I'll be doin' no such thing. Not on your say-so, I won't."

"Winter Fawn." Carson grasped her arm.

She shook off his hold. "I'm not saying no to you, at least not right now. I told you I'd think about it. But I'm saying no to him."

"I knew I should have left you with your grandmother that night you were shot," Innes muttered. "None of this would have happened then."

"No, I would have grown old and died alone, because you forbade Grandfather to accept any offers for me."

"Lass . . ."

"Carson, would you leave my father and I alone for a while?"

"If you're sure that's what you want."

She met his gaze and tried to offer him a smile. "Aye, I'm sure."

After a long look into her eyes, Carson nodded once and walked back to the house.

"For the life of me," Innes said, "I can't decide which one of you is leadin' the other on. If ye gave yerself willingly to him, ye ought to be willing to marry the man. Ye gods." He shook his head and looked to the sky as if for guidance from above. "Listen to me talk to ma own daughter about giving herself to a man."

"I'd rather not listen to any of it," Winter Fawn told him darkly. "You've humiliated me in front of everyone."

"Ye shoulda thought of that afore ye went and did the deed," he protested. "Why would ye do that if ye dinna plan on marrying him? Did ye no stop to think ye could be with child now?"

Winter Fawn froze. Man-Above! She hadna thought of that at all.

"Ach, I see that got yer attention, it did. Now, will ye marry him willingly, or do I have to get ma shotgun?"

Winter Fawn frowned in dismissal of his threat. "You wouldna shoot me and we both know it."

"Nae, but I might shoot him."

"Da, be serious."

"I'm being dead serious, lass. This willna do. This just willna do at all. I'll no hae ma own bairn make a whore of herself when she could be a honest wife to the very man she's so hot after if she wasna so all fired stubborn."

His words stung like a lash on tender flesh. "Do ye think I dinna want to marry him?" she cried.

For the first time since realizing what had happened between his daughter and the man he called friend, Innes's look softened. "Ye love him, don't ye?"

"Aye," she said miserably. "I'm so confused, Da. I dinna ken what I should do."

"Ye're making it much more difficult than it has to be, lass. Just marry him and let everything take care of itself."

"Aye, I might be able to convince myself to do that, but . . ."

"But? But what?"

Winter Fawn closed her eyes for a moment and took a deep breath for strength. "He disnae know about that thing I'm not supposed to do, but that I do anyway, and that I'm not ever supposed to talk about."

"Oh. Well? So maybe he disnae need to know."

Her eyes flew wide. "You would have me keep that kind of secret from the man I marry? 'Tis . . . why, 'tis dishonest."

"Then tell him."

"Tell him?" she cried. "My own father canna accept it, and you expect him to? Why, Da? You've never told me why this gift I have is so terrible that I must never let anyone know."

Innes looked away and would not meet her gaze. "It just is, that's all."

"Why?" she demanded. "I've done what you said. I've kept it a secret all these years. I've stood back and watched people suffer needlessly because you said I must never heal again. Why?"

"Because I dinna want people looking at ye and calling ye a freak," he said hotly.

Winter Fawn frowned. "What is a freak?"

" 'Tis something unnatural. An abomination. Like a two-headed calf, or a man with a third eye in the middle of his forehead."

"You're making that up."

"Nae. 'Tis true enough. That's how people treated ma grandmother when I was a lad. Like she had an extra head, or an extra eye. They whispered about her, called her a witch. They despised her and ostracized her. But when one of them was hurt or sick, they came running fast enough, begging her to make things right. And she did, bless her soul, because she couldna turn away from suffering. Then the minute the bastards was well again, they wanted nothing to do with her. Fair broke her heart they did, over and over. It finally killed her."

Winter Fawn hugged herself against a sudden chill from within. "What happened?"

"She gave too much of herself, that's what happened. It works for you the same as it did for her. I saw that right off. When you touched that rabbit, you took its pain into yourself. You felt what it was feeling, didna ye?"

"Aye," she said slowly.

"And with Carson's hands. You felt the pain in them, and when you felt it, it left him."

"Aye."

"The worse the injury, the more it costs ye. Do ye remember passing out, that time with the rabbit?"

"Nae."

"Well, ye did. Ye were too young to be healing that kind of wound. If I'd had any idea ye'd inherited that damned bloody curse I never would have brought those rabbits near ye. Ye keeled right over. Ye were out for several minutes. Scared ten years off ma life."

She shook her head. "I dinna remember that. Is that what happened to her? Your grandmother?"

"Aye. She was too weak to take on that bairn that had fallen from a carriage. The child was too far gone, but she had to try. It was too much for her. She collapsed and never woke again."

Winter Fawn swallowed a lump of emotion. "And the child?" she asked softly.

"It died, too. Now do ye see why I canna accept it in you? Why I dinna want ye doing it? It'll be the ruin of ye, lass. I swear it will. Dinna let it happen."

"You think . . . Carson would think of me as, what did you call it, a freak, if he knew?"

Innes shook his head. "I dinna know, lass. But ye're better off not findin' oot, and that's the truth."

She was silent for a long while, looking out toward the river and the mountains. "Well then," she said finally. "I guess it's a good thing I never agreed to marry him."

CHAPTER 17

Carson didn't like secrets. He despised having to keep them, and despised even more when he knew one was being kept from him.

Not little secrets, like birthday and Christmas surprises. Those were innocent fun. The ones he hated were the kind that hurt, the kind that ruined lives.

There was a whopper being kept from him these days by Winter Fawn. Her father was in on it, too. Whatever the two of them had talked about the morning after Carson and Winter Fawn made love, it had made an impact on Winter Fawn. She was now more withdrawn than ever from him. It was as if that night together in his bed had never happened.

He had demanded that Innes tell him what the man had said to upset her. Innes had shaken his head. "Whatever the lass does is up to her. I apologize for hitting you, and for some of the things I said. She's a woman grown and can make her own decisions. If you want to know what's in her head, you'll have to ask her."

Yet when Carson tried to talk to her, she said nothing. Literally.

"What's wrong?" he had asked.

"Nothing."

"What are you thinking?"

"Nothing."

"What are you planning?"

"Nothing."

"What can I do to make things right again?"

"Nothing."

"What do you want from me?"

"Nothing."

As each day passed, she slipped farther and farther away from the intimacy they had shared. She treated him with the same reserved courtesy she did Beau and Frank. It was driving him crazy. Maybe Innes had the right idea with that flask of his.

Carson watched carefully whenever he was around the house—it was disgusting how often that was, when his work was out on the range with the cattle—but Winter Fawn treated Gussie and the girls as she always had. The four of them were always together, doing something, planning something.

Now Gussie was planning another trip to town Saturday. "The merchant was woefully lacking in fabric choices," she explained over breakfast Friday. "I had to place an order for material for curtains. I couldn't use the same thing for the windows as we used for Winter Fawn's dresses, now, could I?"

Megan giggled. "That would look funny."

"You should have said something," Winter Fawn claimed. "I could have made do with one dress."

Gussie's eyes twinkled. "I don't mean to sound condescending, dear, but have you ever seen window curtains?"

"That depends." Winter Fawn's lips twitched.

"Depends? On what?"

"What does condescending mean?"

"It means . . . smugly superior. As though I were belittling you for never having seen curtains. Which I'm not," Gussie assured her quickly.

Winter Fawn laughed. "I take no offense at the question, as long as you take none at my assumption that you've never seen a tepee. There are no windows. So, no, I've never actually seen curtains. But I understand the concept."

"Then think again, dear," Gussie said with a smile. "The green is lovely on you, but would have been dreadful on the windows. I asked him to order in three different fabrics. You girls will have to help me decide."

Winter Fawn shook her head. "I have no experience with curtains. I thought I would stay home and bake bread while the rest of you make the trip."

"Oh, Winter Fawn, you have to go with us," Bess protested.

"Of course you'll go," Gussie said, as if there were no question.

"Gussie," Carson said. "If Winter Fawn doesn't want to go, she doesn't have to. She wasn't exactly welcomed with open arms the last time. I don't think I blame her."

"What nonsense," Gussie proclaimed. "Why should you care how those people act?" she asked Winter Fawn. "I declare, if I can survive a two-day escort of Bluebelly Yankees, you can survive a trip to town."

Carson swallowed his irritation with his aunt's typical high-handed tactics and strove for a reasonable tone. "Maybe she doesn't want to be hurt, Gussie."

"Maybe," Winter Fawn said, making a serious study of the last piece of corn bread in the bowl just beyond her plate. "Maybe she doesn't like to be talked about as though she were not here."

"Oh, dear, I'm sorry," Gussie said quickly. "You're right. How terribly rude of us."

"It's all right," Winter Fawn assured her. It was Carson her words had been meant for. "I've changed my mind. I will go to town with you after all."

"Oh, wonderful." Gussie beamed.

Let Carson see, Winter Fawn thought. Let him see again how they treat her, and how they will treat him and his family when she is with them. Maybe then he will agree that she should leave.

* * *

The alley beside the mercantile, where Carson had parked the wagon the last time, was blocked by a large freight wagon with a six-mule team. Carson pulled up directly in front of the store and set the brake.

Beau and Frank had ridden in with them. It was payday, and tomorrow was their day off. They had come to lose their money in the nearest card game, and if any was left, there were women to be had at the saloon. They wouldn't make it back to the ranch until Sunday night.

But Carson wasn't ready to cut them loose just yet. It looked like every hand from every outlying ranch and farm was in town for the weekend.

"Beau, Frank, if you two don't mind—"

"And even if we do," they said in unison. It was an old joke among them from during the war. Captain Dulaney's "if you don't mind" generally prefaced a direct order.

"Right." Carson smiled. "Water the team for us, then hang around and keep an eye on things while we're inside." He intended to stay close this time. No one was going to get away with insulting Winter Fawn today. "Knowing Gussie, we might need your help loading up when she's through shopping."

"Why, Carson Dulaney," Gussie protested. "How you do go on. I only intend to purchase a few items."

"Yeah, like Noah only intended to take a few animals on the ark."

Gussie swatted his arm, then demanded he help her down from the wagon.

"Do you know about Noah's Ark?" Bess asked Winter Fawn as they climbed down from the back of the wagon.

"Da told us. He used it to tease us one fall when it rained for days without stopping. He told us we needed to build an ark before it was too late."

"I wish I had all those animals like Noah," Megan said.

Bess took her niece's hand and they and Winter Fawn followed Gussie into the mercantile. "Why, you've got baby chicks, and we've got horses, the milk cow, and all those cattle."

"You forgot Hail Mary."

"Mrs. Winthrop." Mr. Hernandez stood behind the counter

polishing the top of a glass case that held a row of pocketknives. "You are right on time. Señor Gonzales, here," he motioned to the man leaning on other side of the counter, "just delivered that fabric you ordered."

At the sight of Gonzales, Winter Fawn turned quickly away and began a careful survey of the saddle blankets piled on a shelf.

"Wonderful." Gussie smiled at Mr. Hernandez and nodded to the man named Gonzales. "Are you a tinker, Mr. Gonzales?"

"No, Señora." With one dark hand, he pulled off his sombrero. "I am a freighter. I haul goods from Pueblo."

He was also a trader who often did business with the Arapaho. Winter Fawn had recognized him instantly. She had no desire that he recognize her. What if he traded with Our People again and mentioned that he had seen her? Would Crooked Oak come? Would her uncle?

You're being ridiculous, she told herself. Looking for trouble where there was none. After all this time, Crooked Oak had given up. No woman was worth so much time or trouble.

Still, she caught her brother's eye and made a slight motion toward Gonzales.

Hunter gave a slight nod and stepped into the shadows of the back corner of the store.

Winter Fawn ambled that way slowly, so as not to draw attention to herself. She was so intent on reaching the relative safety of the back corner that she did not hear the man approach.

"Excuse, Señorita. I know you, *sì?*" He repeated his question in Arapaho.

Winter Fawn was at a loss. What should she do? It was too late to hide.

Just then her father entered the store, and Gonzales recognized him, too.

"Ah, the white Arapaho, Red Beard MacDougall."

"Gonzales, you old horse thief," her father greeted good-naturedly. "Still charging double what yer goods be worth?"

"Me? I am such a poor trader I am lucky I do not lose the shirt off my back."

Innes laughed heartily. "Aye, and ye're a worse liar than you are a trader."

Outside someone shouted, then people started rushing toward the end of the street. A young boy barreled his way through the crowd and raced into the store.

"Is Mrs. Vickers here?"

"No, son, she left about ten minutes ago. What's going on out there?"

"Her girl fell in that abandoned well down the street.

"Little Juney?" Hernandez cried.

"Yeah. Juney's pa sent me to find the missus." Since she wasn't there, the boy raced outside again.

Mr. Hernandez hurried from behind the counter and made for the door. "Mrs. Winthrop, ladies, Dulaney, you'll have to excuse me."

"Sir," Gussie called out. "Am I to understand a child has fallen down a well?"

"It appears so." He didn't wait for more conversation. The look in his eyes was part worry, part avid curiosity.

"Carson." Gussie put a hand to her chest in dismay. "Is there anything we can do to help?"

"I don't know. I'll go find out."

She gave a sharp nod of approval. "We shall come with you." Gathering the girls, Hunter, and Innes along as though shooing her flock of baby chicks, Gussie herded them all outside and down the street to where the crowd had gathered. She led them straight through the dozen or so people there until they stood almost at the edge of the well.

The old well was nothing more than a hole in the ground. A wide board had evidently been used to cover it but was now pushed aside.

Two problems became readily apparent. First was the child herself, no more than four years old. She was unconscious and could not help herself. She lay ten feet down on a narrow dirt ledge; the hole next to her looked bottomless. If she came to and moved, she would surely fall deeper into the shaft. To make matters worse, one leg lay at an awkward angle and looked broken.

The second problem was the well shaft.

"It's narrow," said the man from the livery. He was Abe Vickers, the girl's father. "But I think . . ." He stopped and swallowed. Greasy sweat coated his face. It was more than apparent that the sides of the shaft were crumbling. One wrong move and the child could be buried, or pushed off the ledge and into the blackness below. "I think I can get down to her."

"Nae, man," Innes said. "Ye'd never be able to bend down and lift her—it's too narrow. And ye canna get below her, because it narrows even more."

Vickers plainly wanted to argue, but it must have been obvious to him that Innes was right.

"Oh, my baby!" A distraught woman with brown curly hair and freckles pushed her way through the crowd.

Vickers caught and held her before she could throw herself down into the hole with her daughter. "Stay back, Martha. The sides could cave in."

"What are we going to do?" she wailed. "Abe, what are we going to do? She's dead, isn't she. I just know it."

"She ain't dead," Vickers told her. "I seen her breathin'. She ain't dead, Martha. Just get that out of your head, you hear?"

"What about a ladder?" Mr. Hernandez asked. "I have an eight-footer. Would that work?"

Vickers looked ready to cry. "There's roots sticking out partway down. You'd have to run the ladder down the middle of the hole instead of at the side, and then there's even less room."

While everyone stood around trying to decide what to do, Winter Fawn studied the hole. It was narrow, but she would fit. The mother was obviously too upset to be of any help, and none of the other women looked willing. All of the men were too big. Even the older boys, the ones who looked like they were trustworthy enough for the task, were too broad-shouldered.

"Da, I can do it."

"No!" This, from Carson.

"Then who else?" she cried. "I'm the only one here small enough, without being too small. You can lower me down on a rope."

"For heaven's sake, Martha," Mrs. Linderman cried. "Look at her. She's an Indian. A savage! She'd probably kill poor Juney on purpose."

Winter Fawn whirled on the woman. "I'm no in the habit of killing helpless babes, but I find I'm in the mood to cut out a wagging tongue if it doesn't be still."

Mrs. Linderman turned pasty gray and nearly swooned.

To the child's parents, Winter Fawn said, "I can get to her. If I canna lift her out myself, I can tie the rope around her and you can pull her up."

Confusion warred on Vickers's face. "You would do it?" He looked from her to Carson, to Innes. Everywhere but at his wife.

"Aye," Innes told him, "she will do it because she disnae know what an ass ye be."

Vickers's face flushed crimson.

"I do know," Winter Fawn said coldly. "Hunter told me what he said. But it disnae matter. 'Tis the child that matters."

Winter Fawn quietly walked to the edge of the hole and sat down with her legs hanging down into it.

"Winter Fawn." Carson took a step toward her, then looked at the crumbling edges of the hole and stopped. She could see that he wanted to protest, but they both knew there was no one else to go after the girl. "You'll be careful."

"Aye."

He looked at her another silent moment. She felt the need to say something, to tell him she loved him, but that seemed like a desperate act, as though she feared she was about to die. In truth, she wasn't much afraid for herself. With a rope around her waist she would be safe enough. If anything went wrong, they could pull her out. It was the child she was concerned with.

But she did love him, and wanted to tell him. In the end, she said nothing.

Carson opened his mouth, then closed it. There was nothing he could say. What she was about to do should be safe enough. That he had a bad feeling about it was his problem. He would not put fear into her mind at a time like this. Finally he gave her a single nod and turned away. "We need a rope."

"And a horse," Hunter said. "we can tie the rope to the saddle horn. She'll be safer that way than if we lower her ourselves."

"Safer?" Vickers protested. "I don't know of a horse in the area that's trained for that kind of work, unless you got one yourself. Who the hell are you, anyway?"

"I'm her brother. The horse requires no training. Just—"

"Here's a horse, mister." The boy who had been sent to find Mrs. Vickers led a buckskin gelding toward Hunter. "He's got a saddle an' all. Will he do? He's even got a rope." There was a coiled rope tied to the saddle.

Hunter took the reins from the boy. His eyes were on the horse's face when he spoke. "He'll do fine, lad. What's your name?"

The boy swallowed. "It's Jimmy. Are you really a savage?"

Hunter smirked. "Nae, I'm half Arapaho. Thank you, Jimmy. Is this your horse?"

"Golly gee, no. All I gots is an ol' mule named Sally, and she's not even really mine."

"A mule's a fine, noble animal," Hunter told him. "Smarter than a horse, more surefooted."

"Really?"

"Really." Hunter kept his gaze on the horse, communicating silently through his eyes and his touch. "Who's horse is this?"

"It's Mr. Haley's. He won't mind. He's over in the saloon gettin' drunk. It's okay, isn't it, Mr. Vickers?" the boy asked earnestly.

Jimmy desperately hoped it was okay. It was his fault Juney was down in that hole. All he'd wanted to do was look down there, see if there were any neat snakes. If he hadn't pulled the board away, Juney never woulda fallen down there when she tripped. He supposed he'd have to tell, but he figured everybody was plenty busy enough just then. He'd tell later.

Vickers shifted from one foot to the other. "I guess. He's pretty docile."

While Carson took the rope from the saddle, Hunter stroked the horse's neck and whispered to him in the language of the Arapaho.

Jimmy's eyes bugged. "What'd ya say to him?"

"I'm praising him, and telling him what he has to do."

"Does he understand? Mr. Haley tells him to do stuff all the time and it don't seem like it ever does any good."

"That's because he probably tells him in English. Most horses don't understand English."

"But they understand Arapaho?"

Hunter stroked the horse's neck and smiled. "Some do, aye. This one understands just fine."

A few feet away, Carson checked the knot at Winter Fawn's waist one last time. "It's good and tight. You'll be all right."

She touched his arm. That small, brief contact brought with it the urge inside him to grab her and carry her as far away as possible from this hole in the ground.

"I am not afraid, Carson."

I am, his mind screamed. "You don't have to do this, you know. We'll figure something else out. You don't have to prove anything to anyone."

"Is that what I'm doing? Trying to prove something?" Winter Fawn stilled and searched inside herself. "No," she said slowly. "I dinna think so. I'm doing it because I seem to be the only one who fits in the hole."

"Ready?" Innes asked.

Carson stood and checked the loop around the saddle horn. "All right. We're ready."

Hunter spoke into the horse's ear, and the animal backed up until there was no slack in the rope. Then he nodded to Winter Fawn.

Winter Fawn carefully braced herself against the sides of the shaft and lowered herself an inch at a time. Beneath her hands and feet, earth crumbled and fell on the child and down into the black hole next to her.

She had to bend and twist herself to get past the gnarled roots of some nearby tree. In some places there were holes in the sides of the shaft, worn there by water, or left when a rock finally gave way and fell. Some were shallow enough to make convenient footholds. Others were so deep she could not see the end of them. Like small tunnels snaking off from the shaft.

Winter Fawn grimaced. She wished she hadn't thought of the word snake. She uttered a quick prayer that there were none in this hole.

Why did white people have to dig holes in the ground? Why

did they chose to live where such a thing was necessary for water? There was water aplenty in the river.

Above, Carson and Innes were calling advice.

Winter Fawn ignored them. She had to concentrate on what she was doing. She had no desire to lose her footing and fall on the child, or have the rope cut into her waist by the force of her full weight dangling from it.

With every clod of dirt that fell on the child below her, Winter Fawn prayed the girl would not awaken.

The farther down she went, the less light there was. Yet when she finally reached the child, she had no trouble seeing that the girl's leg was definitely broken. From up above, it hadn't been as obvious.

Winter Fawn looked up to see a half-dozen faces peering down at her. "Please." She waved her hand, motioning them away.

"Let's get back," Carson said. "We're blocking her light."

She offered him a smile and a nod, then braced herself to get Juney. Before she picked her up, however, she looked up again. Only Carson and Mr. Vickers were there now. As small as the hole was, and the way she had to bend and stoop to reach the child, all they would be able to see for a moment would be her own back.

Satisfied, she leaned down and wrapped her hands gently around the girl's leg.

Pain, instant and crippling, shot through her own leg. She bit back a cry and forced herself not to reach for it in reflex.

Concentrate. Let the pain in. Take it from the child. Heal her. Heal her.

The girl's leg was cold. Winter Fawn's hands were hot. Hot with the force of the gift she never wanted but could not deny. Sweat beaded across her brow and between her breasts. Her head grew light. The pain in her leg increased.

Then, the pain eased slowly, and her hands began to cool. When the pain was gone and the temperature of her hands felt normal, she knew the girl's leg was mended.

Of their own accord, her hands moved to the girl's head. There was injury there. A large knot, but nothing serious on the inside. She pressed her hand there until she felt the heat, the pain. Until both eased, and the child stirred.

''Mama?''

''Nae, Juney, but your mama is waiting for you. Be still now, so I can pick you up and take you to her.'' She only hoped she had the strength to lift her and climb out of the hole. Healing the leg had left her trembling with weakness.

The girl's eyes blinked open. ''Who are you?''

''My name is Winter Fawn.''

The girl giggled. ''That's a funny name.''

Winter Fawn scooped her arms beneath the girl. ''Is it, now? Can you put your arms around my neck?''

As the child complied, Winter Fawn saw a long angry cut down one forearm.

The injury was minor. She forced herself not to reach for it to heal it. She could not afford a further drain, even a slight one, on her strength. Nor could she afford to have the girl telling tales about her. Besides, she thought the child deserved a reminder of her adventure, and it would give Mrs. Vickers something to fuss over. When a child fell unconscious down a hole in the ground, a mother needed to fuss.

''Hold on tight now,'' she cautioned. ''Up we go.''

Slowly, inch by inch, Winter Fawn started up the shaft the same way she had come down, using the sides to brace herself. Except now she had a child hanging onto her, and she needed one arm to hold her in place, and two more to help her climb.

A touch of hysteria bubbled up inside her. Why, she wondered, couldn't freaks have an extra arm instead of a head or eye?

The crumbling of the walls was worse this time. She placed her hand on a rounded rock, thinking it would be more stable. It shifted beneath her weight and rolled out from under her hand.

Winter Fawn cried out and slammed her shoulder and the side of her head against the wall. At the impact, Juney screamed and tightened her hold, nearly strangling her.

Had the hole been any wider, they both would have fallen.

Up above, Carson and Mr. Vickers swore.

"Are you all right?" Carson demanded.

Trying to catch her breath and calm her racing heart, all Winter Fawn could do was nod her head. By the time she was able to straighten and loosen Juney's strangling hold, she realized that she hadn't heard the rock hit bottom. Maybe she had just been gasping too loudly.

Then she did hear something, and it stopped her heart. The buzzing hiss of a rattlesnake.

Where? Where was it? Below? Above? She couldn't tell. The sound echoed along the shaft and sounded as if it came from everywhere.

All right. All right. No choice. She had to move. Up was the only choice.

Up above, the men swore again.

Carson's throat closed. *Rattler!* He wanted to caution her not to move, but she couldn't stay there. He wanted to snatch her up from that hole, but he couldn't reach her. He wanted to shout at Hunter to back the horse up as fast as he could and jerk her free of the trap she was in. But such a sudden movement could cause the snake to strike.

Christ, it could already have bitten her.

"Winter Fawn?"

Without looking up, she shook her head and braced herself to move. The hissing rattle of the snake grew louder.

Now, Winter Fawn thought. *Now I am afraid.* It threatened to paralyze her, this fear. She could not let it. *Move. Ignore the snake and get out.*

She pushed herself up.

From below, over the buzzing of the snake, came the distant sound of a splash. The falling rock had finally hit bottom. The sheer distance was every bit as terrifying as the snake. Yet the snake was the more immediate problem, and she still didn't know where it was.

Dinna think about it. Just move.

One inch. Then another. And another.

All around her the rattle sounded until it filled her head. The urge to scream built. She clenched her teeth together and inched up a little farther. Almost there. Just a little more.

"I've got her," Carson called.

Suddenly Juney was pulled from her arms. Winter Fawn sagged in relief.

It was then that the snake struck.

Winter Fawn cried out.

"Shit." Carson passed the little girl to Vickers. "Hunter! Back the horse. Now!"

The instant he could reach her, he pulled her from the hole and into his arms. "Did it get you? Winter Fawn, look at me. Did the snake bite you?"

Winter Fawn closed her eyes and swallowed. "Aye."

"Jesus. Where?" His hands raced over her frantically. "Where?"

"My left leg." Her hand was shaking when she pulled her skirt up to her knee and twisted her leg to show him the back of her calf. Four punctures showed in the rawhide legging attached to her moccasin.

Hugging her daughter tight, Mrs. Vickers approached. "Is she all right?"

"No." Carson bit back another curse and used his bandanna as a tourniquet just below her knee. "I knew I shouldn't have let you go down there." Not too tight, but tight enough, he hoped to stop the flow of venom. "I knew something would go wrong."

As gently as he could, he pulled the legging and moccasin off. God, his hands were shaking. She was bleeding freely from all four puncture wounds. The fangs had sunk in deep, and the spread of the bite was wide, indicating a large snake.

"Innes!"

"Right here, lad. Ach, lassie."

"Dear Lord," Mrs. Vickers cried. "Oh, you poor girl. My Juney's leg wasn't broken after all. She barely has a scratch, and now you're hurt."

"She's all right, then?" Winter Fawn asked.

"Yes, thanks to you. Why, you saved her life."

Carson pulled his belt knife free. "Hold her," he told Innes, "so I can get to her leg."

Mrs. Vickers stepped back, and her husband wrapped his arm around her while they watched solemnly.

After being passed from one man to the other, Winter Fawn twisted in her father's arms to look at the bite. She instantly wished she had not. The back of her leg was already red and swollen for inches around the bite marks. When Carson leaned over her with his knife, she swallowed and looked away.

Carson wished he could do the same, but he could not. Gritting his teeth, he made a short cut over each puncture wound. God love her, she only flinched once. Then he bent down and placed his mouth over the cuts and sucked. The coppery taste of her blood filled his mouth. He turned his head and spat, then repeated the process over and over.

"You'll want to make her as comfortable as possible," Mrs. Vickers said. "Please, bring her to our house. She can have our bed while she recovers."

"That's kind of ye," Innes said.

"Thank you," Winter Fawn managed. She wasn't feeling well at all. "But I want to go home."

Finished with her leg now, Carson wiped his sleeve across his mouth. Winter Fawn swallowed. Her blood was smeared on his cheek.

"It's a long way back to the ranch." Carson knelt beside her and took her hand. "You'll be better off without making that trip just yet."

She looked into his eyes and saw fear there. Fear for her. "I'm going to be sick, aren't I?"

He reached for her and pulled her from her father's arms into his. "I'm afraid so, honey."

"I might even die," she admitted.

"No," he said forcefully. "No."

"Ach, so ye do care, then," she teased.

"Care? I think the damn snake got you in the head. You know I care."

"Then take me home, Carson."

He opened his mouth to object, but she cut him off.

"Please. If I'm going to be sick, or . . . or die, I'd rather do it at home."

Carson closed his eyes and rested his forehead against hers. For a long time, it seemed to her, he just held her and rocked her, as though she were a wee bairn.

"Innes," he finally said. "Get the wagon. She wants to go home."

CHAPTER 18

''Remember awhile back when I said I didn't trust love?'' Carson shook his head in confusion. ''I'm beginning to wonder if I knew what I was talking about. I'm not so sure now that I've ever been in love.''

He smoothed a strand of hair from Winter Fawn's cheek. Her skin was still too hot. ''Compared to what I feel for you . . . this is so much stronger. It fills me up until I think I'll burst with it. It devastates me. It terrifies me.''

He gave a short laugh. ''There. I said it. What I feel for you is so damn strong it terrifies me. I can admit that now, because I've found something that terrifies me even more. Even more than having you walk away from me. And that's having you not wake up.''

As was the case for the past three days, Winter Fawn made no response. She lay in his bed, and just now she was quiet. He didn't know if he preferred that, or her thrashing and moaning when her fever rose. Watching her suffer tore him up inside, but seeing her lie there so still, eyes closed, chest barely moving, scared him. It looked too close to death. Too damn close.

''Please, God, don't take her.''

If she wanted to leave him when she got well and return to

the Arapaho, he wouldn't try to talk her out of it. Would even help her go if he had to. If she really wanted to go.

"Just don't go like this," he whispered. "Not like this." He could survive if she walked away from him. He had no choice. He had a daughter and young sister to raise, an aunt to care for. But if Winter Fawn died—

Don't think it. Don't even let the idea into this room.

"But I don't think you have any excuses left for not marrying me." Maybe if he said it aloud, she would somehow hear, and believe. "I can say the words now. I love you. As for your other excuse, about how people in town treat you and how that might affect the rest of us, you can forget that."

He threaded his finger through her limp ones and squeezed her hand.

"You pretty much took care of that problem Saturday when you went down that well after the little Vickers girl. You're a hero now. Heroine, I guess. Three families have sent out food so Gussie wouldn't have to cook while taking care of you, and Abe Vickers has ridden out once to see how you're doing. He brought some new yellow gingham that Hernandez sent with him to replace the dress you ruined. Vickers is coming back in a day or two to check on you again. Said he'd bring his family. His wife wants to thank you again in person. No, I don't think you have to worry about folks in town anymore."

Carson laughed. "Except maybe Mrs. Linderman. I don't think she'll ever get over you threatening to cut out her tongue."

He squeezed her hand again and lay his head down on the edge of the bed. "I think that's when I finally realized I loved you."

Innes entered the house quietly. Across the room, the door to Carson's bedroom remained closed.

Gussie looked up from where she sat beside the window sewing the new dress for Winter Fawn.

"Any change?" Innes asked.

Gussie read the pain and fear in his eyes. Her heart went out to him. She set aside her sewing and rose to place her hand on his arm. "Her fever is down some, and she's resting quietly."

"But she hasna awakened."

"Not yet."

Innes closed his eyes and took in a slow, deep breath.

"She's going to make it, Innes. You must believe that."

He opened his eyes and looked at her. "You're a good, kind woman, Augusta Winthrop, to take such good care of me lass like ye're doin'."

"If I'd been blessed with a daughter, I would have wanted her to be like Winter Fawn. She is a fine young woman, Innes."

"Bless ye for saying that, Gussie. I'll just stick my head in the door and see her for a minute. Is Carson still in there?"

"He won't come out."

Squaring his shoulders against finding his daughter still in a coma, Innes crossed the room.

Hunter knew his father had gone to the house to see about Winter Fawn. It shook him to think of her lying in there, sick and helpless and maybe dying. Winter Fawn could not die. It seemed impossible to him. She was always there for him, had always been there.

He'd been only seven when their mother had died and their father left them. Seven and frightened. But Winter Fawn had been there, and he had clung to her. She had never left him. She sang to him, played games with him, tended his scrapes and bruises. She had made sure he never forget the English their father had taught them. And when he discovered he had a gift with horses, she had encouraged him.

To think of losing her was not possible. He had complete faith in her strength. She would recover and be fine. She had to, because he could not imagine life without her. He would be lost not knowing she was somewhere near, not being able to count on her when he needed her.

But he *did* have faith in her strength. Deep inside, where all things important rested, he knew she would be fine. He would go to the house later and visit her.

First he wanted to see what Bess was doing. He'd spotted

her down by the river an hour ago, and he could still see her there, sitting beneath a cottonwood on the grassy bank.

It was unusual for her to be idle for so long. Bess was always busy, and almost never alone.

He finished brushing down the gelding he'd been working with and turned the horse out into the corral.

It took him several minutes to walk the distance to the river. During that time he kept his gaze on the pale pink of Bess's dress. It did not move.

Halfway there he stumbled to a stop. What if the dress didn't move because Bess wasn't in it? What if she was taking a swim? Maybe he should just go on back—

He'd been watching her dress through the trees for nearly an hour. She wouldn't be swimming that long. The water in that river came directly from melting snow up in the mountains and was freezing cold. If she was in the water all this time, she would be a nice shade of blue.

He didn't like it. Something could be wrong. If she wasn't swimming, if that was her sitting there, she hadn't moved in much too long. Sitting still was not like Bess.

In or out of her dress, she could be in trouble.

Hunter sprinted the rest of the way to the river. Before he got there he could see that it was her sitting there. He slowed for the last few yards.

"Bess?"

She was crying. Sitting there with her knees up, arms wrapped around them, and her face buried against them, crying softly.

Hunter dropped to his knees beside her. He knew she'd heard him, but she didn't look up. What should he do? Should he leave her alone?

Then panic set in. Had his sister died and no one told him?

"Bess!"

She sniffed and rubbed her face against her dress. "I'm sorry."

"Is it Winter Fawn? Has . . . has she—"

"No! Oh, Hunter, no. I'm sorry. I scared you and I didn't mean to. She hasn't . . . I mean, there's no change. She seems a little better, but I'm afraid to hope." She sniffed again and looked down at her knees. "I'm just plain afraid. That's why I was crying."

Her eyes and nose were all puffy and her hair was coming down from the pile of curls on top of her head. She was just about the prettiest thing Hunter had ever seen.

"Of what are you afraid?"

"I . . . Oh, I'm so ashamed." She buried her face in her hands again and cried.

He wanted to touch her, to give her comfort. It was a new experience for him, and he wasn't quiet sure what to do about it. "There is no shame in tears," he told her.

"It's n-not that," she managed between sobs.

"Nor in fear," he offered. "Everyone is afraid now and then. It's nothing to be ashamed of."

"Oh, Hunter, I'm so afraid for Winter Fawn. And Carson won't leave her side, and he won't eat or sleep, and Megan cries all the time and Aunt Gussie works so hard and worries, and your father is so sad, and if Winter Fawn doesn't get better, I don't know what we'll do without her, because we all love her and if she's not here you might leave." She turned and threw herself against his chest. "And I don't want you to leave and that's so selfish of me and I'm so ashamed of it, but I can't h-help it."

As her hot tears soaked through his shirt to his skin, a new warmth began inside him. His chest swelled, and maybe his head, too, a little. She cried because she did not want him to leave. No one had ever cried over him before.

His arms came around her and pulled her closer. "I'll not leave you, Bess." And suddenly he knew it was true. Down in that secret place inside himself, he knew. He might come and go for a short time now and then, but his place was here, with these people. His father, Carson, Gussie, wee Megan, Frank and Beau, and this blue-eyed girl he felt closer to than anyone else, who tied his stomach in knots with her tears. "I won't ever leave you."

* * *

It was hot in the darkness. She didn't like it there. But fighting to be free of it didn't seem to help. She didn't know which way to go to get back to the light.

Then she heard the voice. She couldn't make out the words, but they seemed to call to her. Desperate to be free of the suffocating blackness, she struggled toward the voice. Who was it? What was he saying?

He?

Yes. A man's voice.

Carson.

Carson. With his thick black hair and his brilliant blue eyes and his kisses that stole her breath. *I'm coming, Carson.*

But the darkness was too thick, like stew. She slipped back down into it.

The next time she surfaced, she came all the way awake. It was dark, there, too, but there was a candle burning on the small bedside table.

What was she doing in Carson's room? In his bed? Had they made love again? She ached all over.

Then she saw him. He had pulled a chair up next to the bed and leaned over with his face against her hip.

"Carson?" Why was her voice so weak? She wet her lips and tried again. "Carson?"

At the sound of her voice, Carson jerked upright. Her eyes were open! "Winter Fawn?"

"Why do I hurt?"

She was lucid. *Thank you, God.* "You've been sick, honey, but you're going to be fine now." Relief weakened him, but he had to hold her, if only for a moment. He carefully slipped his arms around her and placed his head beside hers. "Thank God, you're going to be just fine."

Gussie could not wait until breakfast to tell Innes the good news.

She had awakened to the sound of voices from Carson's room and had rushed in without even bothering with her robe.

Now that she was dressed, she rushed to the barn, where Innes was in the habit of sleeping. She didn't know why he didn't bunk with the other men, but she suspected, being a loner like he was, that he preferred his privacy.

With lantern in hand, for it was still dark out, she tugged open the big barn door and stepped inside. "Innes? Innes!"

Puzzled at getting no response when light was already glowing from the bunkhouse window, she started toward the last stall on the right. Maybe he was already up and out in the corral, but she would check here first.

At the stall, she raised her lantern and peered inside. Disappointment flooded her. Irritation stiffened her spine. He was drunk again, drunk as a skunk and talking to himself. She thought he'd been doing better about his drinking, but apparently she'd been mistaken.

"Poor lassie," Innes muttered.

Ah. This was about Winter Fawn. Gussie was torn between anger and sympathy, but either way, she could alleviate his concern about his daughter. She reached for the stall door.

"What good is that bloody curse of healing," he cried out, "if she canna even heal herself?"

Gussie froze. What in the world was he talking about? What was this bloody curse of healing?

"Heals the child, and this be her reward."

Heals the child?

Gussie gasped. Could it be? She had peered down into that well herself and been certain the little girl's leg was broken, yet when the child was pulled up, the leg was fine.

Heals the child?

She shook her head, sure that she was being fanciful. Innes was drunk and rambling, that was all.

Wasn't it?

"Innes! Wake up. Do I need to get the slop bucket to wake you?"

"Huh? Wha—? Who's there. Gussie?" Then his eyes flew open and he seemed to sober instantly. "What is it? Ma lass—"

"Is awake and hungry," she said, unable to keep from smiling widely.

"Hallelujah. Thank ye, Lord."

* * *

Winter Fawn recovered rapidly. Neither Carson nor Gussie would accept anything less. They cosseted her, babied her, would have spoon-fed her if she had allowed it. When she tried to get up the first day she awoke, Carson had threatened to tie her to the bed.

"You don't know how sick you've been. You need to rest."

It had been a wee bit humiliating to realize just how much rest she had needed. Her weakness during those first few days had both alarmed and frustrated her.

But it had been three weeks now, and she was fine. Even Gussie had stopped hovering.

If Carson still watched every move she made whenever she happened to be within his eyesight—and if he happened to go out of his way to get her in his eyesight more often than not—she was not inclined to complain about it.

She was not inclined to complain about much of anything these days. She had come too close to dying. She now looked at the world differently. At herself, at her life. At Carson.

She loved him. Now that her blinders were off, she knew that he loved her, too, whether he admitted it or not.

The people in town were no longer a concern. They accepted her now, as was proven when the Vickers family had come last week to assure themselves that she was recovering, and to thank her—so profusely that she'd been embarrassed—for what she'd done for their daughter.

There would always be people who scorned her because of her Indian blood, but no longer would she allow them to have a hold on her emotions or the decisions she made.

And she was taking Hunter's advice and letting Carson and the others make their own decisions about wanting her in their lives.

Never had Winter Fawn felt more loved and more accepted. She felt as welcome here as she had been in her grandmother's lodge, and it was a heady feeling to admit and accept that.

* * *

Crooked Oak had returned to the big camp along the river on the chance that Red Beard had brought Winter Fawn back to her grandmother. But there was no word of Winter Fawn, and Crooked Oak had not been greeted with warmth.

He would show them. He would show them all, when he found her. And he would find her if he had to search every white settlement, every farm, every ranch. She was out there somewhere, and she belonged to him. He would have her.

Another vision, that was what he needed. But he did not wish to take the time away from his search.

Man-Above decided to smile upon him by having his path cross with that of the Mexican trader Gonzales. If nothing else, Gonzales would give him a bottle of whiskey.

And Gonzales did. That, and more. Neither spoke the other's language well, but between the few words and phrases they did know, with a little sign language thrown in, Crooked Oak was able to determine that Gonzales had seen Winter Fawn in the town called Badito at the southern tip of the Sierra Mojada.

"My good friend!" Crooked Oak was ecstatic. "I am in your debt." He scarcely took the time to finish off the whiskey before he urged Red Bull and Spotted Calf to mount up and ride. Now he would not have to search every settlement, nor every house. Only those along the upper Huerfano.

Soon. Soon he would have Winter Fawn, and his destiny would unfold.

Winter Fawn had not yet told Carson that she had changed her mind and would marry him. She was grateful that he had not pressured her for an answer. But she would tell him. Soon. Just as soon as she found a way to tell him about her gift.

Would he be able to accept her then, as her own father had not?

He had to. He simply had to.

Her chance to explain came sooner than she expected. Sooner than she wished.

Saturday evening they had an early supper, finishing just after sundown. It was just Carson, Hunter, and the females, since the rest of the men had ridden for town. Innes had said he would be back later that night, but Beau and Frank would probably not return until Sunday evening.

It was Winter Fawn's turn to wash the dishes. Gussie was doing something in her room, and Bess was out on the porch talking to Hunter. Megan was bored. She wanted to help Winter Fawn.

"Well, then, that would be fine. Let's drag a chair over to the counter so you can reach the dishpan."

Megan's eyes grew big and round. "I get to stand on the chair?"

Uh oh. "Only for special reasons, and only if you have permission and someone else is with you. I'll be havin' yer word on that, lassie."

Megan giggled. She loved it when Winter Fawn put a little extra burr in her words. "Ye've got it, lass."

"Wot's this I'm hearing?" boomed Carson with his own imitation. "Has ma hearth an' home been invaded by foreigners?"

"Aye," Megan crowed.

"Off with ye." Winter Fawn shooed Carson away with a dish towel. " 'Tis wimmen's work we're aboot here, mon."

"Ach, run oot o' me own kitchen." He winked, then strolled off toward his room.

"There now." Winter Fawn brushed her hands against each other and turned back to the dishpan. The water should still be warm enough to wash the dishes, yet cool enough for Megan's tender young hands.

"Up ye go." With great fanfare, she helped Megan up onto the chair and tied the dish towel around her waist for an apron. "Here's the stack of plates. Remember, now, one plate at a time, and carefully."

"I remember."

"And don't forget to count." Having her count each plate as she washed it had been Gussie's idea to help Megan learn her numbers.

"I won't. This is number one."

Winter Fawn bit back a smile at the look of total concentration on Megan's face. So earnest she was, so intent on getting each plate clean.

"You're not supposed to watch me," Megan complained.

"Sorry. I forgot." Winter Fawn turned partly away and busied herself gathering the utensils from the table. From the corner of her eye she watched as Megan, tongue peeking out from between her teeth to help her concentrate, finished washing the first plate. Gripping it tightly in both hands, she lifted it from the soapy water and over into the second dishpan, this one of clear water for rinsing.

Having succeeded, she propped her tiny fists on her hips and gave a sharp nod of approval. "I did it," she whispered. "Now, number two."

Plate number two went into dishpan number one. Megan used the dishrag to scrub every inch of it a dozen times. She got so carried away once that water splashed into her face and down the bodice of her dress, making her giggle. When she was satisfied that the plate was at last spotless, she whispered one of Gussie's sayings. "As clean as clean can get." Then she held the plate up to make sure.

And, Winter Fawn knew, to see her own face reflected in the sparkling clean surface.

Winter Fawn saw the accident coming, but wasn't able to move fast enough to prevent it. Megan's hands and the plate were both slick from the soapy water. The plate slipped from her grasp and shattered against the rim of the dishpan. Pieces of plate scattered across the worktable, the floor, and into the dishpan, sending up a small geyser of water.

Megan shrieked and started crying. "I didn't mean to," she wailed. "I didn't mean to."

Winter Fawn embraced her and lifted the girl's hands from the dishwater. "Of course you didn't, lassie. 'Twas an accident, that's all. Hush now, don't cry. You'll make your pretty blue eyes all puffy and red."

Megan hiccupped and sniffed. "It just slipted."

"I know, I know. Sometimes that just happens."

"I cut my hand."

"Here, now, let's have a look." Already holding the child's hands, Winter Fawn turned them over to check. Blood oozed from a slice across the palm of her right hand.

"Oh," Megan wailed. "It hurts."

"Nae." Winter Fawn quickly slipped her hand around and covered the cut with her own palm. She felt the heat instantly, and the sting of the cut as the pain shifted from Megan to her. "You're not hurt, not at all," she crooned, hugging Megan to her with her other arm. "That silly ol' number two plate just scared you, that's all."

Megan's tears stopped instantly. "Oh, it's hot."

"Aye, hush now. There," she said as the pain faded away. Cupping Megan's hand in hers, she held it up. "See? There's no cut there. You're not hurt at all."

Megan stared at her hand, then at Winter Fawn. There had been a cut, and now there wasn't. Winter Fawn quickly dipped both their hands into the dishpan to get rid of the blood. She used her apron to dry Megan's hand, then placed a kiss where the cut had been.

"Is it magic?" Megan asked, her face and voice filled with awe.

Unease crept across Winter Fawn's shoulders. What could she say to keep the child from talking about it? Obviously telling her there had been no cut would not work. The girl had felt the sting and seen the blood.

Of course, since there was no trace of a cut, and the blood had disappeared into the dishwater, no one was likely to believe a story about magic. But if she talked about it, Winter Fawn would be reduced to essentially calling Megan a liar, and she knew she could never bring herself to do such a thing.

"Aye," she whispered. " 'Tis magic, and a secret. If you tell anyone, it will never work again."

"I mustn't tell?" Megan whispered, her eyes wide. "Not *anyone,* not *ever?*"

"Not anyone." Winter Fawn kissed the tip of her nose. "Not ever."

"Okay," Megan said with a grin, no longer whispering. She peered over Winter Fawn's shoulder. "We mustn't tell anyone, not ever."

"So I heard," Carson said carefully.

Winter Fawn whirled to find Carson and Gussie standing beside the table looking wary, confused.

"I declare," Gussie whispered.

Panic seized Winter Fawn by the throat. Here was her opportunity to explain, finally, to Carson, yet all she could do was run.

''Winter Fawn,'' he called as she flew out the door.

She did not pause. Ignoring Hunter and Bess's startled expressions, she leaped from the porch and ran. With every pounding step, the word *freak* echoed through her head. Around the side of the house, past the garden, toward the sheltering trees along the river where the shadows of dusk gathered and offered concealment. Visions of two-headed men and three-eyed women waited for her, sprang out to point at her. *Freak. Freak. Freak.*

''Winter Fawn!''

She closed her eyes and leaned panting against the wide trunk of an old cottonwood. She had not outrun him. Foolish to think she could.

''Winter Fawn, talk to me.'' He placed his hands on her shoulders.

They were strong hands, warm hands. Powerful, capable. Yet they could be tender and gentle, too. Clever enough to drive the breath from a woman's lungs and all thoughts from her head. Despite her fears, she felt her knees turn to water from wanting him.

''What just happened in there? What's going on? Why did you run?'' With a gentle tug, he turned her until she faced him. ''Talk to me.''

She swallowed around a lump of fear. ''What would you have me say?''

He dropped his hands and stepped back. ''You can start with telling me what just happened with Megan.''

The distance he placed between them felt as wide as a canyon. One by one she felt her emotions shut down. Better that than to feel the yawning emptiness of realizing that she might never be able to cross that canyon and reach him again. He might very well not want her to. ''I don't know what to say.''

In the deepening shadows Carson saw the light fade from her eyes. She was withdrawing from him again. Farther this time, faster. More completely. He grasped her shoulders again. ''Don't do this.''

She blinked up at him as though he were a stranger. "Don't do what?"

"Don't shut me out."

She smiled slightly. "I love you. Did I ever tell you that?"

His heart skipped one beat, two. Never had he expected to hear those words in a tone that meant goodbye. "No, don't."

Frowning she cocked her head. "Don't love you?"

He recognized that blank look in her eyes now, and it terrified him. He'd seen it before in the eyes of men in battle, men who had seen too much, men who could no longer accept what was happening around them so they closed themselves off in their minds where the horror could no longer touch them. To see that same look in Winter Fawn's eyes now made no sense. And that scared him all the more, because he didn't understand what put it there. He gripped her shoulders tighter. "Don't leave me," he said fiercely, pulling her to his chest. "Whatever's wrong, we can fix it. Don't shut me out, don't leave me."

She was trembling. "I'm so frightened."

He held her closer. "Of what, honey? What scares you so much?"

Her arms slipped around his waist and held him hard. "The thought of losing you."

"No." He kissed her forehead, her temple, her cheek. "You'll never lose me. Never," he added fiercely as he took her mouth in a kiss so possessive that she had to know, had to understand that she was his no matter what, and nothing would ever change that. Fear sharpened the edge of his passion and the kiss turned more fierce, went beyond possessive. He plundered, he ravished. With his mouth, his hands, he branded her as his.

"Yes," she whispered harshly when he left her mouth to devour her neck. "Love me, Carson, love me."

"I do." He took her down right there on the ground and ran his hand up her skirt. "You know I do."

When he touched her there between her legs, she cried out. Frantically she fumbled with his belt buckle.

He tasted his way up her jaw and to her mouth and pushed her hand away. In seconds his pants were undone and pushed down, her skirt up to her waist.

Carson had one thing on his mind. Possession. If he couldn't get through to her any other way, he prayed this would reach her, prove to her that he wanted her in his life, that he loved her and would not easily let her go.

Their bodies joined, and primitive instincts ruled. It was hot and hard and fierce. No pretty words or soft touches. Only racing hearts and pounding flesh. Hotter. Harder. Faster. Flashes of light. Yawning darkness. Something powerful just out of reach. Coming closer. Closer. Until it was there in their grasp. It exploded around them, within them, and when it turned and slammed into them they cried out together.

When they could breathe again, when they could think, Carson levered himself up and pulled her onto his lap. "God, I'm sorry. I never meant to . . ." He kissed her eyes, her nose, her lips. "You deserve better than the hard ground for your bed. Are you all right?"

Still reeling, Winter Fawn nodded. "I think so."

Carson smoothed a hand across her cheek. "Now do you understand what it's like for me? You're a part of me, you're inside me, a part of every thought, every breath. Do you hear what I'm saying? I love you."

This time when she looked up at him, there was no blankness in her eyes. They glowed with warmth and love. "I like the way you make your point."

"I'm glad." He kissed her, this time with all the tenderness that was in him. "I *love* you. Whatever is wrong, we can face it. We can fix it, or we can learn to live with it, but I won't let it come between us. Talk to me. Please."

"Yes," she said quietly, with what sounded like resignation. She pushed herself to her feet and shook out her skirt.

Carson joined her, and after straightening and fastening his pants, he waited.

Winter Fawn took his hand and gripped it tightly. "I don't know where to start."

"How about with a broken plate and a cut hand."

She sighed heavily. "Yes. That is as good a place as any. Megan cut her hand."

Carson drew in a steady breath. He had seen it, seen the blood. "I looked at her hand after you left. There was no cut."

"I know."

"But I saw blood. You have some on your apron."

Winter Fawn looked down. In the glow of the rising half moon, the smear of blood on her white apron was plainly visible. "Yes, there was blood."

"But then there was no cut. I don't understand."

Winter Fawn's heart squeezed. No more evasions, no more hiding the truth from him. "There was a cut, and then there was not, because I healed it."

Confusion gave way to denial on his face. "What do you mean, you healed it?"

"Do you remember when I held your hands after you'd fought with Mr. Vickers?"

Denial turned to wariness. "Yeah."

"Remember how they ached, and then I held them? You said my hands were hot. And then your hands didn't hurt anymore."

"Of course. I'd been soaking them in cold water. Naturally your hands would feel hot after that."

"And the pain?"

"The cold water took care of that. You can't mean you think you somehow healed my hands, or Megan's cut. Good God," he whispered. "That *is* what you think."

"If you have another explanation for Megan's cut disappearing," she said gently, "what is it?"

He shook his head. "I don't know. But what you're suggesting . . ."

"Remember in the mountains, the night before the blizzard, when I cleaned the wound on the back of your head?"

"What about it?" His tone said he didn't really want to know.

"Remember how warm my hand was when I touched the wound? Remember how the pain went away and didn't come back?"

Carson was finding it more difficult by the minute to breathe. Everything in him protested what he was hearing. "What you're suggesting is impossible."

"Aye," she said quietly. "I know."

"Winter Fawn, you've been ill. It hasn't been that long since you were out of your head with fever. Maybe—"

"You would rather think I am crazy than believe me?" She pulled away from him. "Yes, of course you would. Because then you wouldn't have to accept the truth. You wouldn't have to accept what I am."

He reached for her hand again and held tight when she would have pulled away. "What is it that you'd have me believe you are?"

"A freak. That is the word for someone who is not normal."

"Honey, you're not a freak. There's nothing wrong with you that a little rest—"

"No!" She pulled free of his grasp and stepped back, holding out a hand to keep him from reaching for her again. "You asked me to tell you why I ran from you tonight. The least you can do is listen to me."

"I'm listening."

"Nae, you're not. You're hearing my words, but you're not listening. A few days after my mother died, Da brought me a pair of rabbits to skin and roast for his supper. When I reached for the first one, I put my hand over the spot on its head where Da had hit it with a rock. When I took my hand away, the wound was gone, and the rabbit got up and hopped away. Before you tell me I only imagined it, ask my father. He was there, he saw it. He saw it, he told me to never do it again, and he left. He left Hunter and me to be raised by our grandmother because he couldna accept that I have the same healing gift that his grandmother had."

Carson tried to speak, but couldn't. Just as well, because he had no idea what to say. What she was telling him was too farfetched to be believed.

"You don't believe me."

"I . . . I can't."

"Remember little Juney in the well?"

"Of course."

"You—everyone—thought her leg was broken."

Carson squeezed his eyes shut. He could see again the tiny girl at the bottom of the deep hole. The leg bent at an awkward angle. Broken. No other way for it to bend like that.

"You're asking me to accept the impossible."

"I'm asking you to accept me."

"To accept that you can somehow heal wounds just by touching them?" he cried.

"Yes," she hissed back.

"Prove it." He pulled his knife from the sheath at his belt.

"What are you doing?"

He rolled up his left sleeve and cut a long slice down his forearm. He had to convince her of the truth, that she was imagining things. That what she claimed was simply not possible.

"Carson, no!"

He held the arm out to her. Blood oozed from the gash. "Prove it. Heal me."

With a cry, she seized his arm, clasping her palms against the cut.

"Wha—?" Carson couldn't get the rest of the word out. Her hands were hot against his skin. Abnormally hot, as hot as if she were still suffering the fever that had nearly killed her three weeks ago. The pain seemed to flow out of his arm directly through her hands. She whimpered as though in pain herself.

Suddenly he knew that somehow she was. His pain became hers. He could see it etched on her face.

He lowered his gaze, and shock froze his heart in his chest. She had rolled the sleeves of her dress up so she wouldn't get them wet when washing the dishes. Her forearms were bare. As he watched, a thin line of blood appeared on one. The left one.

It was madness. It was impossible. It was . . .

Finally she released his arm. When he looked, there wasn't a mark on him, nor on her. There was blood, on each of their left forearms. But no cut. He had deliberately sliced himself with his own knife. The knife was still in his hand. He had not imagined the cut, the pain, the blood.

Now, all but the blood was gone. He stared at her in shock. "How?"

"I don't know. Da says his grandmother had the same . . . ability. I think of it as a gift. He calls it a curse."

"Christ." He ran his splayed fingers through his hair. Then something slammed into his back and pitched him forward into darkness.

Winter Fawn gaped as Carson grunted and pitched forward. The arrow sticking out of his back made no sense. "Carson?" In a daze, she knelt beside him. "Carson?"

Then reality burst through her. *An arrow!* "Carson!" As she reached for the arrow, her gaze darted frantically toward the river .

Who? Where?

Crooked Oak. She saw him jogging from beneath the trees along the river, not a dozen yards from where she and Carson had just been.

She tried to scream, but there was no air in her lungs. With all her strength, she gripped the arrow with both hands and tore it from Carson's flesh. She threw it aside and slammed her hands over the wound, one hand atop the other for extra force and heat.

Instantly the pain struck her in the back. Carson's pain. She cried out against it and felt a wave of dizziness. *Concentrate. Get past the pain. Heal the wound.* She'd never tried to heal so bad a wound before, except her own, that time in the mountains. She'd never faced so much pain from another.

Then something slammed into the back of her head. Before everything went black, one thought flew through her mind—*not enough time.* She hadn't had enough time to heal him.

CHAPTER 19

Winter Fawn came to lying on her side on the ground. Pain throbbed at the back of her skull. Groggy, but remembering the arrow she had torn from Carson's flesh, she reached for him.

"Good."

Crooked Oak!

"You are awake," he said.

She gasped and sat up, then gasped again as pain lanced behind her eyes. There was a small fire, she realized. On the other side of it sat Red Bull and Spotted Calf. She did not see her uncle. The only other person there was Crooked Oak, who loomed above her.

Crooked Oak, who shot Carson.

"What have you done?" she cried. "You killed him!"

"Yes." Satisfaction was plain on his face and in his voice. "If you had not cried out," he added with disgust, "I would even now have his scalp to decorate my lodge. But there was only time to kill him. I shall need to take other scalps to make up for missing his."

It couldn't be true, she thought frantically. Carson could not be dead. *Man-Above, do not let him be dead.*

But the arrow had sunk deep. She had made everything much worse by ripping it out. So much worse. And then everything had gone black. She lifted a hand to the back of her head and felt a large, tender lump. Merely disturbing the hair there hurt.

Crooked Oak must have hit her. She had been unconscious.

He had killed Carson.

Winter Fawn's heart and soul cried out in anguish. The pain was too deep for tears. Like a wounded animal crawling into a den to lick its wounds, she retreated to the den of her own mind where the truth could not touch her. Nothing could touch her. She was empty. She did not exist.

"You do not weep or wail." Crooked Oak crouched beside her. "This is good. You will be glad to be my wife. But you gave yourself to that white man," he said between his teeth. "For that you must be punished." So saying, he backhanded her across the face and knocked her down.

The blow jarred her from the nothingness she had fallen into inside her mind. With a snarl she rolled to her feet and sprang at him.

She took him by surprise and they tumbled to the dirt. She used her nails to scratch, her teeth to bite. She kicked and gouged and hissed like an enraged cat.

Crooked Oak could scarcely believe what was happening. He managed to grab her hands, and she sank her teeth in his arm. He howled with pain and outrage. "Harm me, will you?" With his fist he punched her in the jaw. She fell limp across his knees.

Across the fire, Red Bull licked the grease of the quail he'd just eaten from his fingers. "She must have had a fondness for the white man."

Spotted Calf grunted. "He will beat it out of her, as he should."

Crooked Oak waited until his breathing calmed, then pushed her to the ground. Seething with rage, he bound her hands and feet with strips of rawhide. The whites had tainted her. She would not be allowed to display such temper again. He would school her in the proper ways of a good and obedient wife. Nothing in the prophecy said that she had to accept him, only that he walk by her side.

* * *

Gussie was worried. Carson had followed Winter Fawn outside, and they'd been gone for hours. It was after midnight and they had yet to return.

Megan had been so excited about the "magic," running on and on about how they weren't supposed to tell anyone.

Gussie couldn't blame Carson for wanting an explanation. She wanted one herself. At the sound of the plate shattering she had dashed from her room. She had seen the blood. After Winter Fawn and Carson had gone, she had examined both of Megan's hands herself. There was not a mark on the child.

How long would it take for Winter Fawn to explain? Where was she? Surely Carson had found her quickly. There was no real place to hide except the barn, and that took mere minutes to search.

When first Winter Fawn then Carson had raced out the door, Bess and Hunter had come inside and asked what was happening.

Gussie had been hard-pressed not to explain, but what could she have said? How did one explain the inexplicable? She held her breath and waited to hear what Megan would say. The child, bless her, was incapable of keeping a secret.

But all Megan said was, "I broke a plate."

Gussie had finally hinted that Winter Fawn and Carson were having a slight disagreement, and that the two should be left to work things out on their own.

And they should. But it had been *hours.*

Unable to wait any longer, fearing something terrible had happened, Gussie donned robe and slippers and carried a lantern onto the porch. They had headed around the house toward the river. Could one or the other or both have fallen in?

Oh, dear, she didn't know what to do. "Carson?" she called softly. "Winter Fawn? Are you out there?"

She was going to feel like a ninny and an old busybody if they were standing behind the house kissing. And if that's what they were doing for all this time, she was going to give them both a piece of her mind for worrying her so.

Stepping off the porch, she started around to the back of the house.

She almost tripped over Carson.

"Oh! Carson!" Nearly dropping the lantern in her haste, she knelt beside him and gaped at the blood on his back. "Carson?" *He cannot be dead. Dear Lord, not Carson, too, please, God, not Carson.*

With a trembling hand she touched his shoulder. It was warm. Thank God it was warm. "Carson, can you hear me?"

He groaned.

He's alive! Thank God!

She had to get him into the house and see how badly he was hurt. But where was Winter Fawn? Gussie stood with the lantern and make a circle around Carson, but saw no sign of her. She needed help, yet she hadn't heard Innes return from town yet.

"Hunter!" Stumbling through the grass, she ran toward the bunkhouse. "Hunter!"

He rushed out to meet her, and the two of them, with a little help from Carson himself, who was coming around, got him into house and onto his bed.

"Winter Fawn," he moaned and tried to push himself up.

"No." Gussie pressed him back down. "You mustn't move."

Carson blinked his eyes open. "Where's Winter Fawn? What happened?"

"You've been hurt," Gussie explained, tearing open the back of his shirt. "Can you tell us what happened?"

"We were talking." Gradually, through the fog of pain, he remembered. "We were talking and something slammed into my back. That's . . . all I remember."

"You have a hole in you. You've been shot, Carson."

"I didn't hear a shot," Carson said.

Hunter leaned over and inspected the wound. "Not gunshot," he said tensely. "An arrow, and it's been ripped out of you."

"Oh, my!" Bess rushed into the room. "I heard voices. What— What happened to Carson?"

"Help your aunt," Hunter ordered tersely. "I'm going out to look around."

"Hunter." Gussie stayed him with a hand to his arm. "You'll be careful."

"Yes, ma'am."

Gussie turned back to Carson. "Bess," she said over her shoulder, "put some water on to heat."

While Bess did that, Gussie fetched clean rags and her medicine box. She used her scissors to cut the rest of Carson's shirt away. So much blood. Dear Lord.

But when she began cleaning the wound, she was amazed. It wasn't nearly as deep as she had feared.

"How bad is it?" Carson asked.

"Well," she said, putting a smile in her voice for his benefit. "If I had my way it would keep you in bed for a week, but I suspect you'll be up and about in no time. I'm amazed, truly. There was so much blood, I feared it was much worse."

"Winter Fawn," he whispered.

"Don't talk, dear, just rest while I take care of you."

"I remember. Winter Fawn . . . her hands. The heat. That's why . . ."

Gussie paused, then resumed cleaning gently around the wound. There would be time for explanations later. She didn't want him thinking about Winter Fawn and what might have happened to her. Gussie refused to think about it herself. Not now, when Carson needed her.

"Here, Aunt Gussie." Bess placed a bowl of warm water on the bedside table.

"Thank you, dear. Move the lamp a little closer, please."

Gussie made short work of cleaning the wound and stitching it closed. Carson was even able to sit up on his own while she wrapped a bandage around his chest to hold the padded cloth in place over the wound.

Hunter barreled back into the house, his face pale. In his fist he carried a bloody arrow. "Crooked Oak," he spat. "I recognize the markings on the arrow."

"Winter Fawn?" Carson demanded.

Hunter's eyes were fierce. "He took her. I followed the signs to the river and lost them there. But he'll take her back to the tribe with him. They'll be easy enough to find."

"Why would he take her there where she has friends and family who would help her?"

"Because he's an arrogant fool," Hunter spat. "I'm going to saddle my horse."

"You're not going alone," Carson stated flatly.

"Carson, you can't," Gussie cried.

"You're in no shape to ride," Hunter claimed.

Carson pushed himself to his feet. He swayed a moment, and the pain was bad enough to make him want to fall down, but he settled for gritting his teeth and steadied himself. "I can ride."

Gussie was able to delay them long enough that Innes returned before Hunter left the house to saddle the horses. When he learned what had happened, he exploded with rage. It took several minutes to calm him enough so that he was coherent.

"I'll saddle you a fresh horse while I'm saddling ours," Hunter said.

"Nae," Innes said forcefully. "You'll no be goin', lad."

"What do you mean I'll no be goin'? She's my sister."

"Aye, but think, lad. If shooting starts, how many of Our People are you going to be able to look in the face and kill?"

"I can shoot that bloody bastard Crooked Oak right between the eyes and smile while I'm doin' it."

"Aye, as could we all. But there will be others. Your uncle."

Hunter stared furiously at his father.

"Someone has to stay here, and we canna any of us leave afore light or we'll lose the trail for sure."

The argument was long and heated, but Innes finally won. Hunter would stay and look after the women.

But no amount of arguing could persuade Carson to let Innes go alone. The two of them would head out at first light.

Innes looked to his son. "Lad, we're leaving ye with a heavy responsibility, looking after the women."

Hunter tore his gaze from Bess and faced his father. "Aye."

"There comes a time in a man's life, if he's lucky," Innes said, flashing a look toward Gussie, then back, "when the most important thing in the world to him is a woman."

He flashed Gussie a second look, and her heart skipped a beat.

"We're leaving you with ours," he finished.

Hunter's shoulders straightened. "I will guard them with my life."

A short time later, Carson reached into the bottom drawer of his bureau and took out his revolver and holster. He had taken them off the first day he'd arrived at the ranch nearly a year and a half ago. He had not worn a side arm since. There was only one purpose for such a gun, the killing of men. He had vowed after the war that he would never kill another man.

And now Crooked Oak had taken Winter Fawn.

He strapped the gun belt around his waist and reached back into the drawer for extra ammunition.

The next morning before dawn, Crooked Oak untied Winter Fawn's feet so he could mount her on the horse he had brought for her. She did not fight him this time, but he was taking no chances. He tied her feet together with a long strip of rawhide that ran beneath the horse's belly. Then he loosened her hands and retied them behind her back.

Using a rope to lead her horse, he and the others started out.

Crooked Oak and his friends had hidden themselves among the rocks atop the bluff behind the ranch house well before dark the day before and waited. They'd seen Red Beard and two other men ride away. The cub, Hunter, had stayed behind.

Crooked Oak dismissed the boy as a threat, and the white man was dead. Red Beard would likely return soon, but Crooked Oak could not guess if the man would follow or not. Winter Fawn was, after all, only a daughter.

He couldn't dismiss Red Beard's tracking or fighting skills, but Crooked Oak was taking care to leave as little sign of their passing as possible. If Red Beard tried to follow, he would not have an easy time of it.

He looked behind him at the woman he had spent so many weeks to locate. She was not so beautiful now. One cheek and eye were swollen where he had hit her.

She had deserved it, he thought again. Deserved that and

more. When he thought of the way she had spread her legs for the white man a violent rage seized him. He had thought that hitting her would appease his anger. He'd been wrong. Not until he drove himself into her and emptied his seed into her would he be able to rid himself of the image of the white man lying between her legs.

He could have taken her last night. Had wanted to. But he would not have it said that he had forced her before they were joined. When they reached the tribe he would make his offer to Two Feathers, who would accept and give Winter Fawn to him for his wife.

If Winter Fawn had known that Crooked Oak was planning her future she would not have cared. She did not care about anything. Without Carson, she had no future. No life.

The sun beat down on her, but she didn't notice the heat. Didn't realize she'd had no food or water since the day before. The first time she became truly aware of her surroundings, she found herself, incredibly, alone.

She was tied to the horse and her hands were still bound behind her back. The horse was tied to the branch of a willow, and just beyond, a stream rushed by. Suddenly she was so thirsty. Terribly thirsty.

She looked around, but no one was in sight. Where had Crooked Oak and the others gone? From all appearances, they had left her, but that made no sense. Why go to all the trouble to track her down, then leave her beside some stream?

Whatever the reason, she did not care. If she could get free she could return to the ranch. Somehow she would find it, even though she had no idea where she was right then.

She realized then what a fool she'd been for not paying attention to what was going on around her all day. Carson might be dead—but surely there was a chance that he wasn't. And there was her father, Hunter, Gussie, and the girls. She still had them, didn't she? But she'd been too cowardly to face the thought of Carson's death to keep her wits about her, and now she had no idea where she was or when—if?—Crooked Oak might return.

She had to get free.

She was struggling against the rawhide around her wrists

when gunshots rang out beyond the bend in the stream. Someone shouted. *In English.* There were white people nearby. Maybe they would help her.

"Here!" she cried. "Help me!"

Then she heard a wild war cry and realized with horror that Crooked Oak, Red Bull, and Spotted Calf were attacking a party of whites. Surely it was a small party, for three warriors to attack.

Unless others had joined them. Had she been so wrapped up in her own misery that she had failed to notice other warriors?

She didn't think so, but she couldn't be sure.

More shouts and shots rang out. She struggled frantically to get free. She had made no progress at all except to rub her wrists raw when a loud splashing in the stream warned someone was coming.

Crooked Oak rode down the middle of the stream from around the bend, his rifle raised high in victory. Behind him rode Red Bull and Spotted Calf.

At the sight of the fresh scalps dangling from their rifle barrels Winter Fawn closed her eyes. There would be no help for her from those poor people.

Crooked Oak rode directly to her side. His eyes glowed with victory, and something else she could not interpret.

"It is true," he said. "with you, I am invincible."

Winter Fawn frowned. "What are you talking about?"

Instead of answering, he tilted back his head and shouted his victory over his enemies.

Finally she noticed battle trophies other than the scalps. New rifles and hand guns. A string of five horses being led by Spotted Calf. A blue coat with brass buttons.

"What have you done?" she cried upon seeing the latter.

"We have killed the enemy."

Eyes wide with horror, she looked at him. "You fool! The army will hunt down Our People like the eagle hunts the rabbit. We will all be slaughtered for this."

"They cannot defeat us," he bragged. "I will lead Our People to a great destiny. You will see."

Winter Fawn spoke not another word. She could not, for the

fear clogging her throat. He was mad. There was no other explanation.

It was late the next day and a line of clouds was building along the mountain ridges to the west when they crested a rise and saw the camp along the Arkansas River where all of the Southern Arapaho had come together for the summer. The sight of those several hundred tepees clutched at Winter Fawn's heart. They looked pitifully few compared to the memories of her childhood when there had been so many more. Was this all there was left of Our People?

Crooked Oak dismounted and sent Red Bull and Spotted Calf on ahead. After they left, he came and stood beside her. "I will untie you now, and you will say nothing of having to be forced to return to your own people."

"If you think I will remain silent—"

"You will, because if you do not, I will reveal that which you do not want known."

"If you are talking about what you saw between me and Carson—"

"That I will not discuss. You are to become my wife."

"You are mad."

"I will not have it said of you that you are a whore. No, that I will not speak of. But I will make you pay."

"My grandfather will never accept your offer without my father's approval."

"You will beg your grandfather to accept, or I will tell him of the rabbit. It will not take much begging. Two Feathers has convinced him to accept my offer."

"Untie me, you stinking coyote. I know nothing of any rab—" The look in his eyes stopped her.

"Ah. I see you remember. You thought no one saw. But I was there in the trees when your father brought the rabbits that day. I saw what happened. I heard him tell you that no one must ever know. But I know." He thumped a fist against his chest for emphasis.

"You don't know what you're talking about."

"The white man has taught you to lie, but he did not teach you well. You will be mine."

Winter Fawn chewed the inside of her jaw. She would say

nothing. Let him think he could force her by threatening to reveal her secret. She did not care if the world knew of her secret. After knowing Carson's touch, she would die—by her own hand if necessary—rather than become Crooked Oak's wife.

She hoped she looked properly subdued, for she wanted her hands and feet free. She would ride into the camp with him and go to her grandmother's lodge. Her father would come for her. If they tried to force her to marry Crooked Oak, she would flee. But she would wait as long as she could, to give her father time to reach her.

She cast her eyes downward in the pose of a shy maiden. "You may untie me now."

Crooked Oak was pleased that he did not have to hit her again. With a grunt, he sliced through her bonds. "You will tell anyone who asks that you fell from your horse and bruised your face. You will tell them the white man held you against your will and that you were overjoyed to see me."

"I will tell them." *I will tell them you are a conceited ass.*

Crooked Oak rode into camp as the conquering hero he knew he was. Red Bull and Spotted Calf had done their work well in announcing his triumphant return. A large crowd was gathered waiting for him. Even Little Raven was there. That was excellent. Crooked Oak would supplant him soon as their leader. Our People would chose him over that old man who constantly counseled peace. Crooked Oak would lead Our People to a glorious victory over the hated white man. Now that he had Winter Fawn, he would become the greatest warrior ever known.

Carson and Innes might have caught up with them the first day out if it hadn't been for the troopers. Two of the five were still alive. The attack had taken place less than two hours earlier. Chafing to ride hard and fast after Winter Fawn, Carson ground his teeth in frustration. Someone had to ride for help, and they couldn't leave the troopers alone, in the unlikely event that Crooked Oak and his men came back. Carson stayed with them while Innes rode the ten miles to Colorado City for help. One of the two survivors would recover; the other probably wouldn't.

As Innes rode for help, his mind and heart were torn in a dozen directions. He wanted to give his horse its head and urge it to speed across the plains toward Winter Fawn, but he could help no one if he ran the beast into the ground. And there were the troopers, poor lads. Barely old enough to shave. Scalped. Butchered.

Damn that Crooked Oak. When Innes got his hands on him— Well, he supposed he might have to stand in line behind Carson if he wanted his hands on Crooked Oak, and he figured, from the grim look in Carson's eyes, there wouldn't be much left of the bloody bastard when the lad finished with him.

Innes was worried, though, about the things Gussie had asked him before they'd left. Things about blood and cuts disappearing before her eyes. What had Winter Fawn been doing?

Then there were Gussie's other words. The ones that left him all shaky inside. The ones that made him say and do crazy things.

"You'll be careful, won't you?" she had asked him with such a tender, worried look on her sweet face.

Ach, when was the last time a woman had worried about him?

"I'll be waiting for you to come home," she'd said softly.

"You do that, Gussie Girl," he'd told her. "When I get back, there'll be changes made atween you and me." Gad, what had made him say such a thing? Yet the words had felt right. He'd been sensing the changes within himself for some time, and they were good.

She had smiled in that way she had that made her eyes twinkle. "We'll see about that."

"Ye're damn right we will. Ye need a man in yer life, lass, and I be the one." If that hadn't been enough to shock everyone to silence, he'd kissed her. Right there in front of everybody.

Aye, Gussie Girl, I'll be comin' back to ye, or die tryin'.

When he made it back to Carson and the troopers with the men from town, they helped load the two into the wagon, then took their leave.

"Did ye hear him?" Innes asked once they were on their way again. "He recognized Crooked Oak."

"You already said you recognized the signs."

"Aye, I'm not concerned with us knowing. 'Tis him we're following, right enough. But now the army will come down on the whole damn Southern Arapaho tribe like a bloody blue and brass plague. It'll be Sand Creek all over again. Damn that glory-hungry bastard."

Carson said nothing. From what little he'd observed of the military's handling of the Indians in the territory, Innes was likely right. And dammit, there'd been enough killing. More than enough. He'd heard the stories about Sand Creek, about the massacre of women and babies and old men.

He hadn't exactly been treated as a guest during his brief stay with the Arapaho, but he'd seen that those who wanted to fight were few in number. He'd seen the children laughing and playing. Mothers with babies at their breasts. Grandparents teaching young ones skills to carry them through life.

He did not want to see them slaughtered.

On the other hand, he would personally kill anyone who kept him from Winter Fawn. The first would be Crooked Oak. The bloodlust rose in him and threatened to strangle him with its strength.

CHAPTER 20

"Crooked Oak stood at his place in the circle around the council fire with fists clenched. "I spit on peace."

Winter Fawn shivered in the evening warmth. As few as there were left of the Southern Arapaho, they would be fewer still. She could see in the faces of many that the tribe would tear itself in two now. Some would follow Little Raven, who preached peace, but many were attracted by the prospect of war.

"What has peace gotten us?" Crooked Oak demanded. "We stand in line at the trading post with our hands out like helpless beggars who can no longer feed ourselves. The white men come and kill off the buffalo and other game, drive us from our hunting grounds, and you speak of peace. They kill our women and children, and you speak of peace. I spit on your peace. It is war for me."

"But we are so few," one man called. "How will we defeat the white man?"

"We are not alone." Two Feathers publicly chose sides with Crooked Oak by standing. "The Cheyenne have long asked us to ride with them. We can also join with our kinsmen in the north, and their allies, the Lakota."

"Yes," cried another. "We have the finest dog soldiers on the plains. Let it be war!"

Little Raven's expression grew more bleak and grim with every word. "And what happens to our women and children while we chase off after white men? Do you not remember Sand Creek? We have been invited to a peace council in the fall. We should go and hear what the whites have to offer. Maybe it will be good this time."

"It is always good—for them," Crooked Oak said heatedly. "We give, and they take. We starve, while they grow fat off our buffalo. While they tear up the grass and plant their crops and leave no place for the deer and the elk. No place for *us.*"

"Do you think I do not see this?" cried Little Raven. "Do you think any of us is blind to what is happening? But what good will war do us but to get us killed? There are too many white men. We can never kill them all."

"Then let us do as they did at Sand Creek. Let us kill their women and children. Such an act turned our warriors into old women. Maybe it will do the same to them."

Murmurs of approval rose from among the younger warriors. Protest from many of the women.

Crooked Oak was not satisfied with only a portion of them agreeing with him. He wanted them all. The whole tribe. "I have had a vision," he claimed loudly.

The crowd quieted.

"We all know the prophecy of the Woman Whose Touch Can Heal."

Nods and murmurs and questions made their way around the fire.

"What has an ancient legend to do with this?" Little Raven asked.

"It has everything to do with this. The prophecy is coming true before you."

The hair on the back of Winter Fawn's neck stood on end. She knew instantly what he was speaking of. She had not thought of the old prophecy in years, and never in connection with herself. She could not be the woman. That woman would be wise in all things, strong enough to choose her own man and keep him beside her. Winter Fawn was none of those things.

"You speak in riddles," said Little Raven.

"I speak the truth," Crooked Oak asserted. "Is not the land consumed by a plague of white locusts, as in the prophecy?"

A murmur of agreement rose.

"Have not our numbers dwindled again and again until we are but a small force of what we once were? Has not the game grown scarce and war filled the land. Are not Our People threatened with extinction, as it says in the prophecy?"

"But where is the woman?" someone called. "For the prophecy to come true we must have Woman Whose Touch Can Heal, and Man Who Walks By Her Side."

"The woman is here, among us."

Everyone followed Crooked Oak's gaze as it centered on Winter Fawn. A hushed silence stretched across the crowd.

With heart pounding, Winter Fawn rose to her feet. This madness must stop. She must put an end to Crooked Oak's plans.

"Crooked Oak is wrong. I am not the woman of the prophecy. Look at me," she cried. "I am half white. I wear the clothes of a white woman, covered in the blood of the white man I chose as my mate. Crooked Oak uses the prophecy as an excuse to kill. We may have no choice but to fight now. Yesterday he and Red Bull and Spotted Calf killed soldiers. The army will fall upon us now as they did at Sand Creek."

"Let them come," Crooked Oak bellowed. "You are Woman Whose Touch Can Heal, and I am Man Who Walks By Her Side. I am invincible!"

"You are a conceited liar, a kidnaper of women, a tormentor of little children. I am not Woman Whose Touch Can Heal."

In a roar of fury, Crooked Oak grabbed her young cousin, Meadowlark. Before anyone knew what he was about he pulled the knife from his belt and cut a slash across her cheek.

The girl screamed. Her father leaped to his feet and pulled his knife.

"Hold!" Winter Fawn cried. Ignoring the smug look of victory on Crooked Oak's face, Winter Fawn reached for the girl. He had won this battle. She could not let the child suffer.

"Hush, Meadowlark," she whispered. When she placed her hand over the girl's cheek, her palm heated, and her own cheek stung viciously. She felt a thin stream of blood trickle down her jaw.

Around her voices rose, cried out. People backed away as if in fear. Meadowlark stared up at Winter Fawn in horrified fascination.

When the pain in Winter Fawn's cheek disappeared, she took her hand from the girl's face and wiped the blood away. "There."

Tentatively, the girl touched her cheek. "It is gone," she whispered. "You *are* her."

"You see?" Crooked Oak called out. "She is Woman Whose Touch Can Heal. A white man stole her from us. I tracked him down and killed him like a dog."

"He did not steal me." Anguish at the reminder of Carson's death—as if she needed a reminder!—colored her voice. "The council had agreed to wait until morning to decide his fate. You gave your word he would be safe."

"Woman, you know not what you say."

"Don't I?" She turned and spoke to the crowd at large. "My brother overheard Crooked Oak telling his friends that he would use an unmarked arrow to kill the white man while everyone slept."

"You lie!"

"The white man was my father's friend. We could not find my father, so I went to set the white man free. Crooked Oak stepped from the shadows and fired an arrow at him. He missed and hit me."

Two Feathers rose again, slowly this time. "I saw the white man carry you from camp. I thought he was kidnaping you. You were bloody and unconscious."

"It was the white man who injured her," Crooked Oak shouted, his eyes wild.

"It was *you,*" she countered hotly. Farther out in camp, dogs barked. Around her, voices rose. "It was you who led your men to chase us into the mountains. It was you who sneaked around in the dark two nights ago and killed him. If I am Woman Whose Touch Can Heal, *he* was Man Who Walks By Her Side."

"*I* am Man Who Walks By Her Side," Crooked Oak claimed. "It is I who will lead Our People to great victory!"

Now the silence was stunned. Pregnant. Ready to erupt into confused disbelief.

"You are *nothing,*" Winter Fawn spat.

Seized by uncontrollable fury, Crooked Oak forgot for a moment that they stood before the whole camp, that she was not yet his woman to punish as he pleased. He raised his fist in the air.

At the sound of a pistol being cocked, followed so quickly by the louder sound of a rifle barrel being snapped closed that the two seemed almost as one noise, Crooked Oak froze.

Innes's voice rang out in the Arapaho language. "Touch her and die."

With a glad cry, Winter Fawn whirled toward her father's voice. But it was the sight of the man next to him that froze her feet to the ground.

Carson! "You're alive!" With blurred vision she flew to his side. She would have flown into his arms, but he held her off and stared at her face. His eyes turned dark with rage.

"Innes, will you translate for me?"

"Aye, lad."

"Ask him if he hit her."

"I don't mean to sound the coward, lad, but it might be the better part of valor if we just hie ourselves out of here while we can."

"Ask him."

With a sigh, Innes turned to Crooked Oak. "He wants to know if you hit her."

"I do not answer questions from white enemies."

"Am I an enemy then? I have lived among Our People for most of your life. You cannot make me an enemy by your words alone. Is he the enemy? Or is he Man Who Walks By Her Side?"

"*I* am the man in the prophecy," Crooked Oak cried. "I have seen it in a vision. I will be known as White Killer and I will lead Our People to great victory. I will fulfill the prophecy."

This time the murmurs were questioning rather than supportive. Crooked Oak's eyes darted around the crowd, desperately seeking support from among the other dog soldiers.

"What if you are wrong?" Little Raven asked. "What if this white man really is Man Who Walks By Her Side?"

"How can he show us the way to survive the Plague of White?" Red Bull asked. "He is part of the plague."

Sentiment throughout the crowd again swayed toward war.

Innes was translating all of this for Carson. "Little Raven wants to accept the government's invitation to a peace council at Medicine Lodge Creek this fall. Crooked Oak and his followers are trying to convince the others to join them and go to war."

"War?" Carson fought back a shudder. "Don't they understand that there's no way to win against the whites?"

"Nae, lad, they dinna. Ye'll have to be tellin' them."

"Me?"

"They—some of them—think ye're part of a prophecy. They will listen to you."

Somehow Carson found himself among the inner circle around the fire. He stood until Crooked Oak lowered himself to his own blanket, then Carson finally sat. He looked around at the faces staring at him. On some he could see the hatred. On others, wariness, doubt, hope.

"You are brave fighters," Carson began, with Innes translating. "But you are not enough to win a war against the army."

"We will join with the Cheyenne," one man said. "And the Lakota, and our kin in the north."

Carson shook his head. "If every tribe in the land joined together, you would still not be enough."

"You say that so we will think we are weak."

"I do not believe you are weak. Only too few. The army you want to fight is too many, their weapons too strong."

"Bah."

"Listen to me," Carson urged. "I have fought against this army."

"You?" Little Raven asked, stunned. "A white man has fought the bluecoats?"

"For four years," he said. "There was a war in the east."

"We heard of this," another man said.

"The graycoats," another muttered.

"Yes. I wore gray and fought the bluecoats. Our gray army was larger than any you can imagine, yet the bluecoats were more. We killed them in such numbers . . . you cannot imagine how many tens of thousands of bluecoats we killed. Yet still they kept coming, more and more of them, until we were finally defeated. Our guns were far better than yours, yet theirs were better than ours. You *cannot* win. Peace is your only chance to survive."

"Another treaty that the white man will break?" someone said with disgust.

"They probably will break it," Carson admitted. "White men have a way of forgetting their promises to suit themselves. But another treaty might buy you time, time for your children to grow up, time to find a place for yourselves where you can live as you want."

Little Raven nodded. "His words are strong and good. We should go to this council at Medicine Lodge Creek and hear what the white fathers have to say."

"Yes," said Deer Stalker, Winter Fawn's grandfather. "We should give this peace another try."

"We can always fight later if we change our minds," another offered.

"We are agreed, then?" Little Raven asked around. "We go to the peace council in the fall."

"Yes," said first one, then another. "Yes. Peace is good."

Seeing his destiny slip from his grasp, Crooked Oak felt the rage erupt within him. "No!" He would kill the white man, but it was Little Raven now that must die. The old man was a traitor to their people, selling them into slavery in exchange for trinkets and broken promises. "No!" he roared again.

From beneath his blanket he pulled one of the pistols he'd taken yesterday from the bluecoats he'd killed. Jumping to his feet, he aimed at Little Raven and pulled back the hammer.

Directly across the fire, Carson saw what was happening. Around him sat unarmed men, except for Innes. Without thought, Carson drew his revolver and fired, hitting Crooked Oak in the shoulder.

The impact staggered him, but he kept his feet and swung the gun around to aim at Carson.

Carson fired again, hitting him in the chest this time.

Crooked Oak's finger squeezed the trigger, but his aim had been knocked off. Instead of hitting Carson, the bullet struck Innes.

Winter Fawn stared in shock as blood blossomed across the front of her father's shirt. When he fell backward, she screamed.

"Da! Oh, Da, hold on, I'll help you." She started tearing at his shirt to get to the wound.

Innes looked down at the hole in his gut and stayed her hands. "Nae, lass, 'tis too much."

Carson knelt on Innes's other side. "How bad is it?"

"Bad enough," Innes managed. "I'm kilt."

"Nae," Winter Fawn cried, wrenching her hands from his hold. "I can make it better."

"Dinna let her," Innes begged Carson. " Everyone will see. 'Tis too . . . much. It could . . . kill her."

"Everyone has already seen," she said, pulling the tail of his shirt free of his pants. "You missed Crooked Oak's demonstration. He cut Meadlowlark."

A ghost of a smile touched Innes's lips. "And ye healed it."

"I couldna let her suffer, just as I canna let you suffer."

"Ye canna heal this one, lass. Do not try."

"I must," she cried. "I canna sit here and watch ye die. Ye've never accepted this part of me." She shot a look at Carson, wondering if he had accepted what he'd seen her do the other night. "This is who I am, *what* I am. If ye wish to turn away from me after, so be it, but I willna sit here and do nothing."

"Carson," Innes said with a groan. "Stop her. If ye love her, stop her. This could kill her."

For the space of two heartbeats, Winter Fawn's gaze met Carson's. In her eyes he read a plea for help, for understanding and acceptance. And the determination to help her father no matter the risk to herself.

Fear sliced through him. He'd seen the cut on his own arm disappear as it appeared on hers, had seen her bleed while healing his wound. The hole in Innes's gut looked small, but Carson had caught a glimpse of the man's back before he fell. The bullet had gone all the way through and torn a chunk of flesh with it on its way out. This was far, far worse than a thin cut on the arm. He didn't see how she could survive.

"Winter Fawn . . ."

She closed her eyes briefly and dipped her head. "If you won't help me, at least do not hinder me. I willna let my father die without trying to save him."

"Can you save him?"

She swallowed. "I dinna know."

"Ye canna, lass. Believe me, I know."

Carson took a deep breath. If he let her do this, he could lose her. She might die. If he carried her away and let her father die, he would lose her just as surely, and he would lose a part of himself. They could lose Innes either way.

"Damn. How can I help?"

Winter Fawn nearly sagged in relief. "I need to know if the bullet came out."

"It did."

"Then that hole will be larger. I should start there."

Start? Carson swallowed. He helped her turn Innes onto his side. When she saw the size of the hole in his back, she paled. Her hands shook as she reached out to place them over the wound.

Almost at once she moaned, then cried out in pain. Deep lines etched themselves across her face. Her skin turned as white as milk. This was killing her.

He wanted to tear her hands from Innes and pull her away from the pain. But he could not. She had made her decision, and he respected her too much to take that away from her.

Even if it kills her?

He refused to dwell on that. He motioned for the old man next to him to keep Innes propped on his side and moved around until he knelt behind Winter Fawn. Blood seeped through the back of her dress at the same spot where the bullet had left Innes.

Carson wrapped his arms around her and pressed himself against her back. "You're all right," he whispered. "You're doing fine, honey, just take your time. Find your way through the pain and you'll be fine.'' *Please, God, let her be fine.*

Eyes closed, Winter Fawn heard Carson's voice as if from a great distance. The pain was greater than any she'd ever imagined. Her father's pain.

But she was not alone with it. There was a warmth surrounding her almost equal to the healing warmth in her hands. It steadied her, eased her, helped her concentrate through the pain.

But there was so much pain. She could not stifle the groan that came from her throat and seemed to go on and on forever. Or was that her father's groan? Their pain was so entwined that she couldn't tell his from hers.

''Carson,'' she managed.

''I'm here.''

Yes. She could feel him all around her. ''If . . . when I pass out . . .''

Carson moaned in protest and tightened his arms around her.

Her head began to swim. ''Hold my hands to the wound after I pass out.''

''Shh. You'll be fine.''

She felt herself fading, fading. *Not yet! There's too much more to heal. I must concentrate.* ''Promise me.''

''Yes,'' he told her, his voice cracking. ''I promise.''

Her concentration waned as the pain continued and mounted. The dizziness increased. She opened her eyes and saw only more blackness. Black pain surrounding her, filling her.

And then there was nothing.

Carson felt her go limp in his arms. With his heart tearing itself apart, he held her, not knowing if she was alive or dead. ''God, please.'' There were tears on his face when he buried it in her hair and kept his promise. He held her hands against her father's wound.

CHAPTER 21

Once again Carson kept a vigil at Winter Fawn's bedside. But this time it was harder, because this time she did not toss and turn while fighting for her life. This time she lay so still that he had to check every few minutes to assure himself that she still breathed. For four days she had lain without moving.

Her grandmother sat across from him, on Winter Fawn's other side. The tribal medicine man knelt at Winter Fawn's head, chanting and burning foul-smelling weeds, waving them in the close air of the tepee.

They had tried to make Carson leave. Language had been no barrier to their quick understanding that he would kill the next person who tried.

He closed his eyes again and offered up another prayer. He'd prayed a lot in the past few days.

She had asked for acceptance of who and what she was. Judging by his own reaction, and what he'd seen on the faces of the Arapaho after Innes was shot, he thought he understood why her father had wanted her gift kept a secret.

He hadn't believed her. Even when he'd cut himself and she had healed him, he hadn't believed. Not really.

By the way she'd said it that night when she'd asked for his acceptance, and the way she'd said it again four days ago to him and her father, Carson had come to understand that it was she who needed to accept the gift she'd been given. She who needed to learn to accept herself. She was a healing woman. But first, she was a woman, one with a big heart and more courage than any ten men combined. She had no idea how special she was, because no one had ever told her.

If he got the chance, Carson vowed to spend the rest of his days telling her. Telling her how special she was, how beautiful, how much he loved her.

Please, God, just give me the chance. Bring her back to me.

At first he didn't notice the movement, it was so slight, but there it was again, a faint twitch of her fingers entwined with his. "Winter Fawn?"

Her chest heaved, then her eyelids fluttered open. "Carson?"

Her voice was so weak it was barely audible, but it was the most beautiful sound he'd ever heard. He squeezed her hand. "Welcome back."

He looked terrible, she thought. His eyes were red, his hair mussed, and he hadn't shaved in days. Just like . . . oh, no, had another snake bitten her? She glanced around, wondering what she was doing in her grandmother's lodge, and why the medicine man was looming above her head.

Then she remembered. Crooked Oak. The council. The gunshot. "Da!"

"Shh, easy, honey, he's fine."

"He . . . is?"

"Well, he's just now getting up and around, but you saved his life. And I hope you never have to do anything like that again," he said with feeling. "I don't think I could survive watching you nearly kill yourself that way."

She lowered her gaze and swallowed, her heart breaking. "I'm sorry if you canna accept what I am."

"Winter Fawn, look at me."

She didn't want to. She was afraid of what she might see in his eyes. But this might be the last time she saw his face, so she did as he asked.

"What you are," he said slowly, "is the woman I love. A beautiful, very special woman with a very special gift. There isn't any part of you, inside or out, that I don't love. You should know that as soon as you're recovered, I plan to offer your father twenty head of cattle for you. I happen to think he'll accept. Will you be my wife, Winter Fawn MacDougall?"

Tears clogged her throat and streamed from her eyes. She would have thrown her arms around him, but she was too weak to move. "Carson Dulaney," she whispered, "I would be honored." Then she smiled. "But twenty cattle are too many. You only have to give him one."

EPILOG

Snow held off until late November that year, and Carson was grateful. He'd had plenty of time to get the herd to market and help Innes build his own house upriver on his own homestead. Unless Carson missed his guess, the man wouldn't be living there alone for long, not if Innes himself had anything to say about it.

But Carson figured Innes was going to have to wait, because there would be no blasting Gussie from her place in Carson's home until after the baby was born.

He felt it move now beneath his hand as he stroked Winter Fawn's abdomen.

"What are you smiling about?" she asked him.

It was a lazy Sunday morning. The sun was full up and they were still in bed. "I was just thinking about the baby, and he kicked me."

"Beggin' yer pardon," she said, laying the burr on thick, "but 'twas me he kicked."

Carson smoothed his hand over the mound that was their child. "When's the last time I told you I loved you?"

"Hours," she said with a dramatic sigh. "A lifetime. I think you don't care anymore, now that I'm fat."

"I told you not to swallow those melon seeds."

Winter Fawn laughed and swatted his shoulder. "But they were such good melons, were they not?"

"Aye," he said, imitating her accent. "You're quite the farmer."

"Gardener," she corrected. "But I think you were right, we should put in a few acres of corn next year."

From out in the main room, they heard Megan giggle. "Bess is sweet on Hunter, Bess is sweet on Hunter," she sang.

"Oh, you, shush!" came Bess's cross reply.

"She is, you know," Winter Fawn said.

"Sweet on Hunter?" Carson kissed his wife's jaw. "I've noticed. But she's not as far gone as he is. Yesterday I caught him grinning like an idiot when she went sashaying past the corral."

"He does grin a lot around her," Winter Fawn allowed. "But he grins as much at Megan, and Gussie, too."

"Yeah, but this time there was a horse standing on his foot, and he didn't even notice."

They were quiet for a few minutes, Carson enjoying the luxury of lying in bed in the daylight with his wife. A pensive look crossed her face. "What are you thinking?"

She smiled sadly. "I was wishing that my grandmother could be here when the baby comes."

The Southern Arapaho had gone to Medicine Lodge Creek. At Carson's urging they had taken their own interpreter—Innes—and they had insisted, through Innes, on being dealt with as their own tribe, separate from the other tribes there. They had tried hard to get a reservation in Colorado, but the government would not give in. They had finally settled for land in Kansas, between the Arkansas and the Cimarron rivers.

"Maybe your father can go visit, and sneak her off the reservation."

Winter Fawn's eyes lit. "Do you think so?"

He kissed her nose. "We'll work on it."

It wasn't likely to happen, Winter Fawn thought, but it was nice to think of it. She didn't often dwell on sad things. It was impossible to be sad for more than a moment since becoming Carson's wife. He had completely accepted who and what she was without reservation. He was even helping her accept it, in her mind, and in her heart.

"When's the last time I told you I loved you?" she asked with a warm smile.

"Hours." He leaned up on one arm and brushed his lips over hers. "A lifetime."

"I love you, Carson Dulaney."

He kissed her then, fully, and with all the love in his heart. Carson Dulaney had found his peace, and it was in the woman who had healed his soul with her touch.

ABOUT THE AUTHOR

Janis Reams Hudson's romance novels have earned numerous awards, including the coveted National Readers' Choice Award, two Colorado Romance Writers Awards of Excellence, and *Romantic Times* Reviewers' Choice Awards. She is also a three-time RITA finalist and has more than two million copies of her books in print. She lives in Choctaw, OK, where she is currently working on her next Zebra historical romance. For a copy of her latest newsletter, send a #10 self-addressed stamped envelope to her c/o Zebra Books. You can also E-mail Janis from her Web site at <http://www.JanisReamsHudson.com>.